For Janna, whose love, patience, and
support has no vertical limit.

Ibrahim

To Chris and Allison, who cleared a space
and pulled me back in from the storm.

Christopher

HIGH

CHRISTOPHER SEBELA
Script, Lettering
& Design

SHAWN ALDRIDGE
Lettering Assists

HASSAN OTSMANE-ELHAOU
Revised Lettering

Production Artist • Erika Schnatz

IMAGE COMICS, INC. • Robert Kirkman: Chief Operating Officer • Erik Larsen: Chief Financial Officer • Todd McFarlane: President • Marc Silvestri: Chief Executive Officer • Jim Valentino: Vice President • Eric Stephenson: Publisher / Chief Creative Officer • Corey Hart: Director of Sales • Jeff Boison: Director of Publishing Planning & Book Trade Sales • Chris Ross: Director of Digital Sales • Jeff Stang: Director of Specialty Sales • Kat Salazar: Director of PR & Marketing • Drew Gill: Art Director • Heather Doornink: Production Director • Nicole Lapalme: Controller • IMAGECOMICS.COM

CRIMES

IBRAHIM MOUSTAFA
Line Art, Colors
& Covers

LESLEY ATLANSKY
Color Assists

High Crimes created by Sebela & Moustafa

IGH CRIMES. First printing. February 2019. Published by Image Comics, Inc. Office of publication: 2701 NW Vaughn St., Suite 780, Portland, OR 97210. Copyright © 2019 Christopher Sebela & Ibrahim Moustafa. All rights reserved. Contains material originally published in single magazine form as HIGH CRIMES #1-12. "High Crimes," its logos, and he likenesses of all characters herein are trademarks of Christopher Sebela & Ibrahim Moustafa, unless otherwise noted. "Image" and the Image Comics logos are registered rademarks of Image Comics, Inc. No part of this publication may be reproduced or transmitted, in any form or by any means (except for short excerpts for journalistic or review purposes), without the express written permission of Christopher Sebela & Ibrahim Moustafa, or Image Comics, Inc. All names, characters, events, and locales n this publication are entirely fictional. Any resemblance to actual persons (living or dead), events, or places, without satirical intent, is coincidental. Printed in the USA. For nformation regarding the CPSIA on this printed material call: 203-595-3636. For international rights, contact: foreignlicensing@imagecomics.com. ISBN: 978-1-5343-1047-6

28,894 feet above sea level

MOUNT EVEREST.
SOUTHEAST RIDGE.

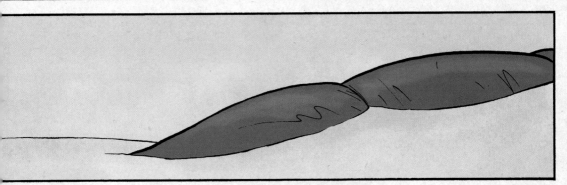

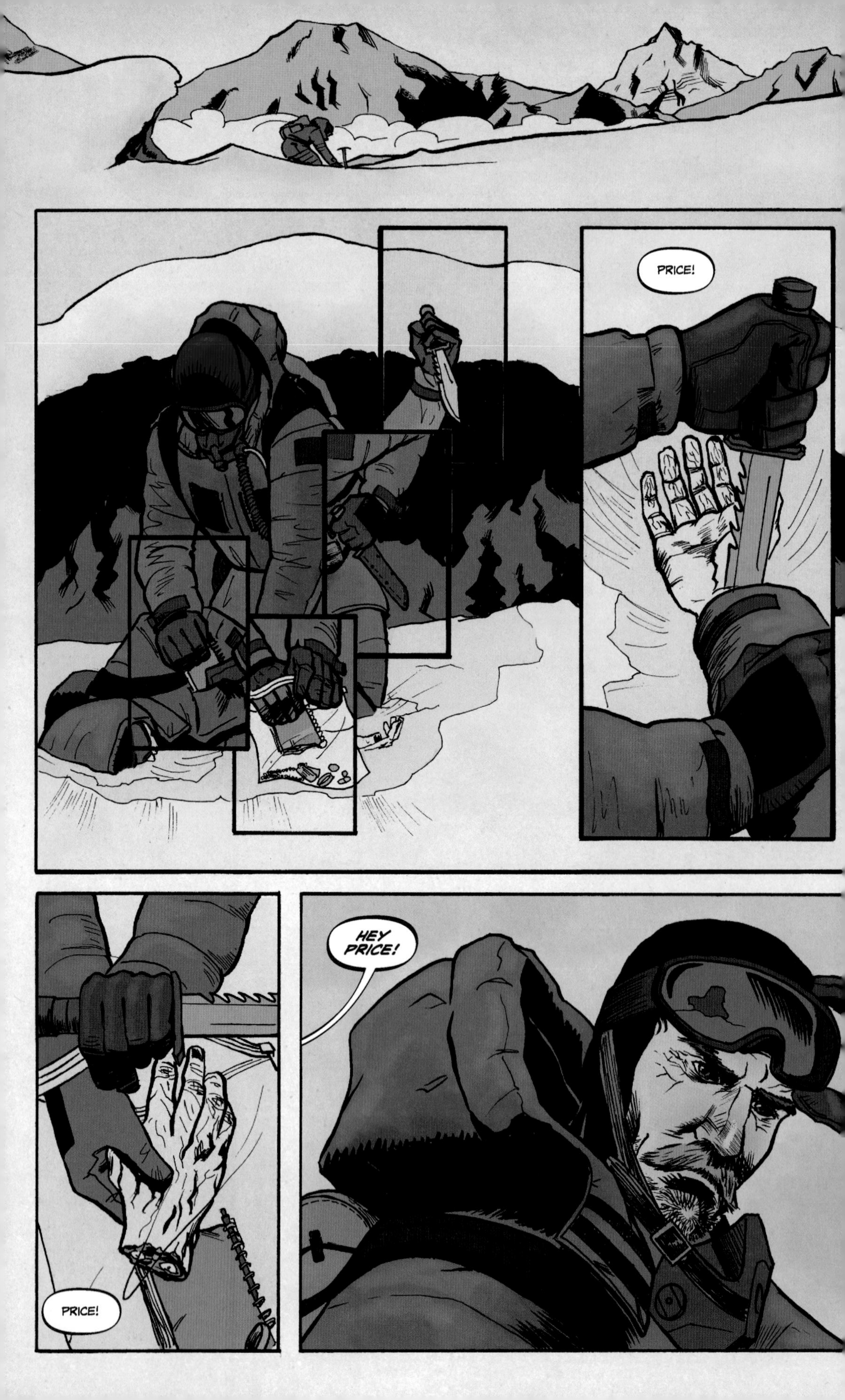
PRICE!
PRICE!
HEY PRICE!

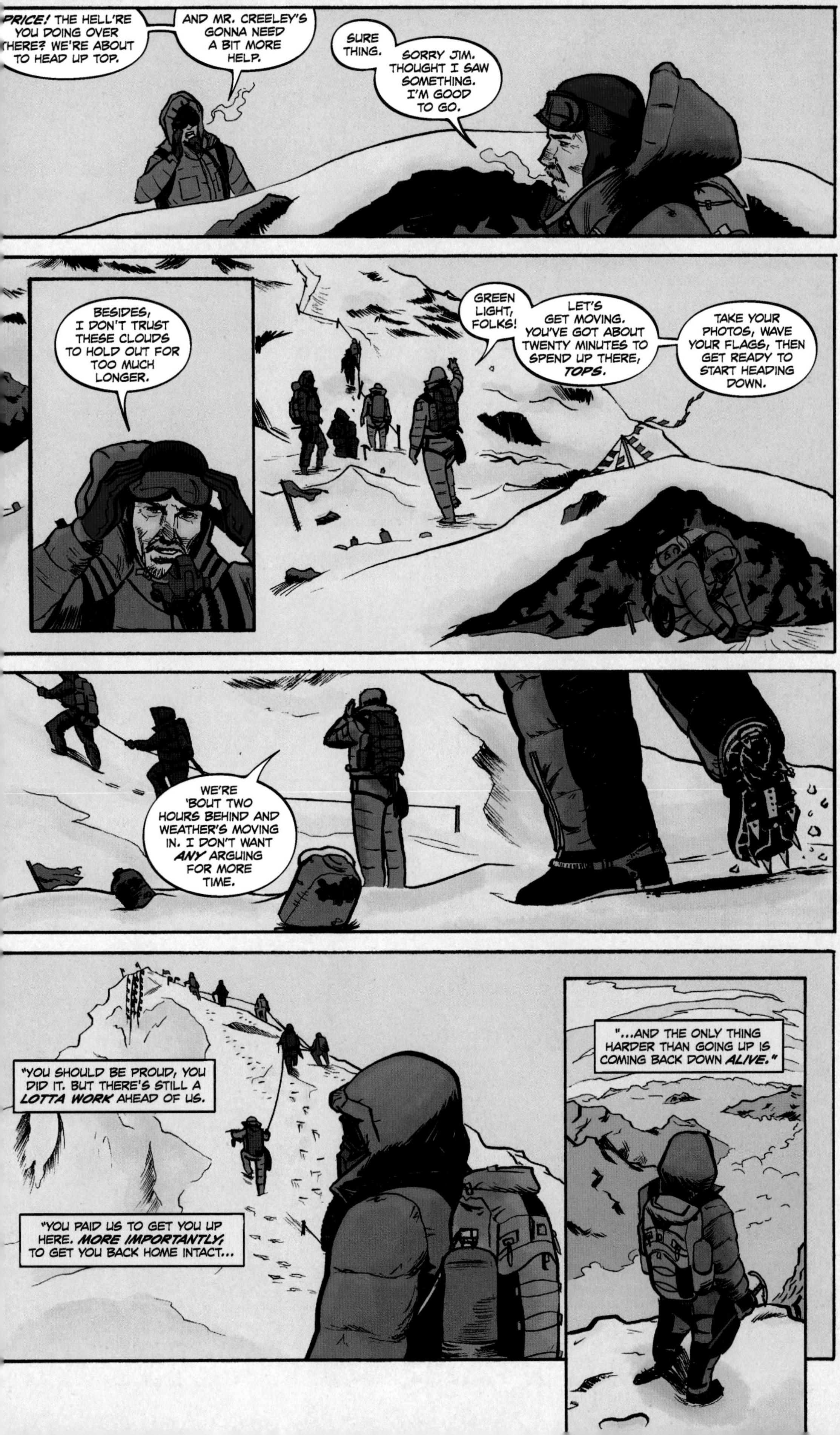
PRICE! THE HELL'RE YOU DOING OVER THERE? WE'RE ABOUT TO HEAD UP TOP.
AND MR. CREELEY'S GONNA NEED A BIT MORE HELP.
SURE THING.
SORRY JIM. THOUGHT I SAW SOMETHING. I'M GOOD TO GO.
BESIDES, I DON'T TRUST THESE CLOUDS TO HOLD OUT FOR TOO MUCH LONGER.
GREEN LIGHT, FOLKS!
LET'S GET MOVING. YOU'VE GOT ABOUT TWENTY MINUTES TO SPEND UP THERE, TOPS.
TAKE YOUR PHOTOS, WAVE YOUR FLAGS, THEN GET READY TO START HEADING DOWN.
WE'RE 'BOUT TWO HOURS BEHIND AND WEATHER'S MOVING IN. I DON'T WANT ANY ARGUING FOR MORE TIME.
"YOU SHOULD BE PROUD, YOU DID IT. BUT THERE'S STILL A LOTTA WORK AHEAD OF US.
"YOU PAID US TO GET YOU UP HERE. MORE IMPORTANTLY, TO GET YOU BACK HOME INTACT...
"...AND THE ONLY THING HARDER THAN GOING UP IS COMING BACK DOWN ALIVE."

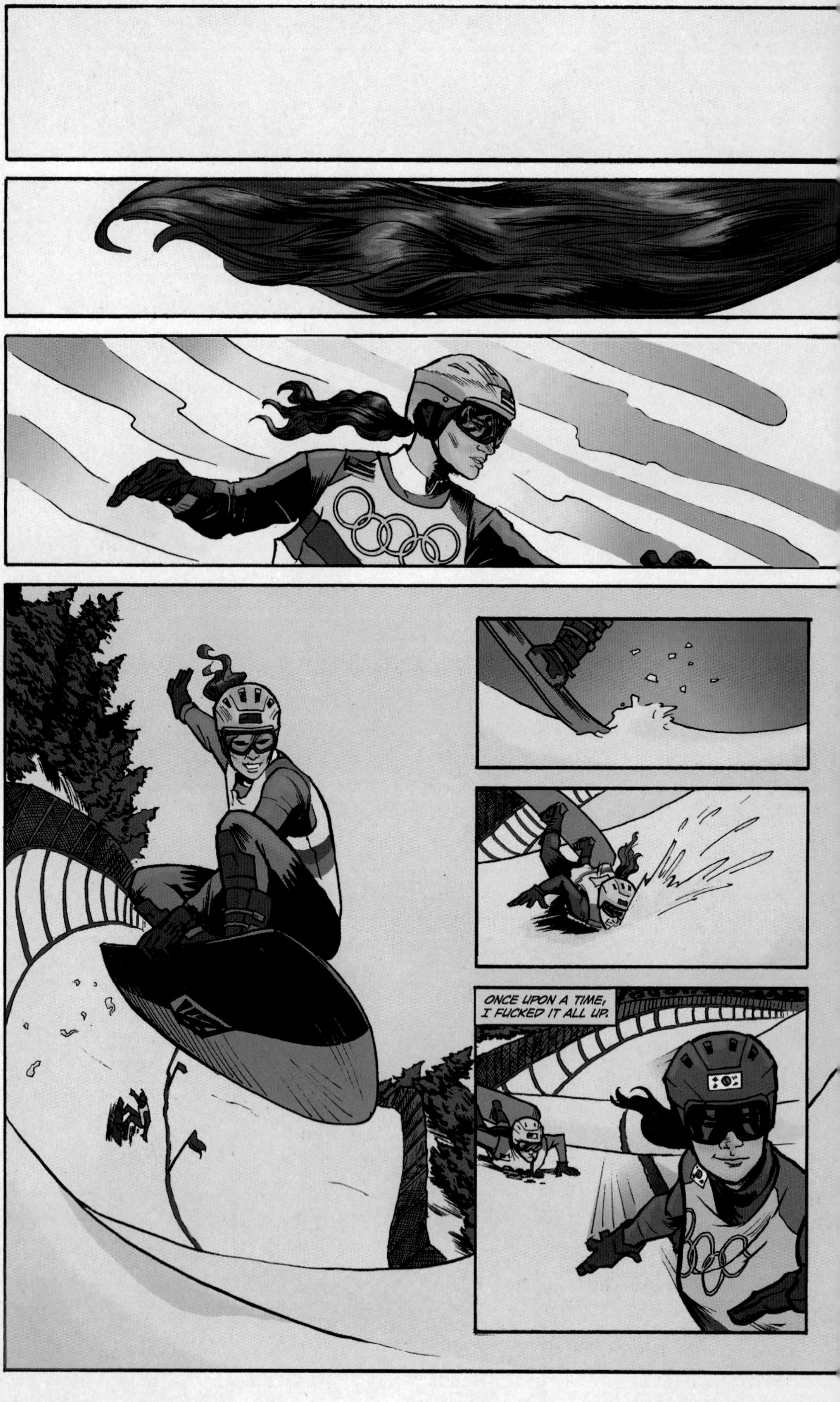
ONCE UPON A TIME,
I FUCKED IT ALL UP.

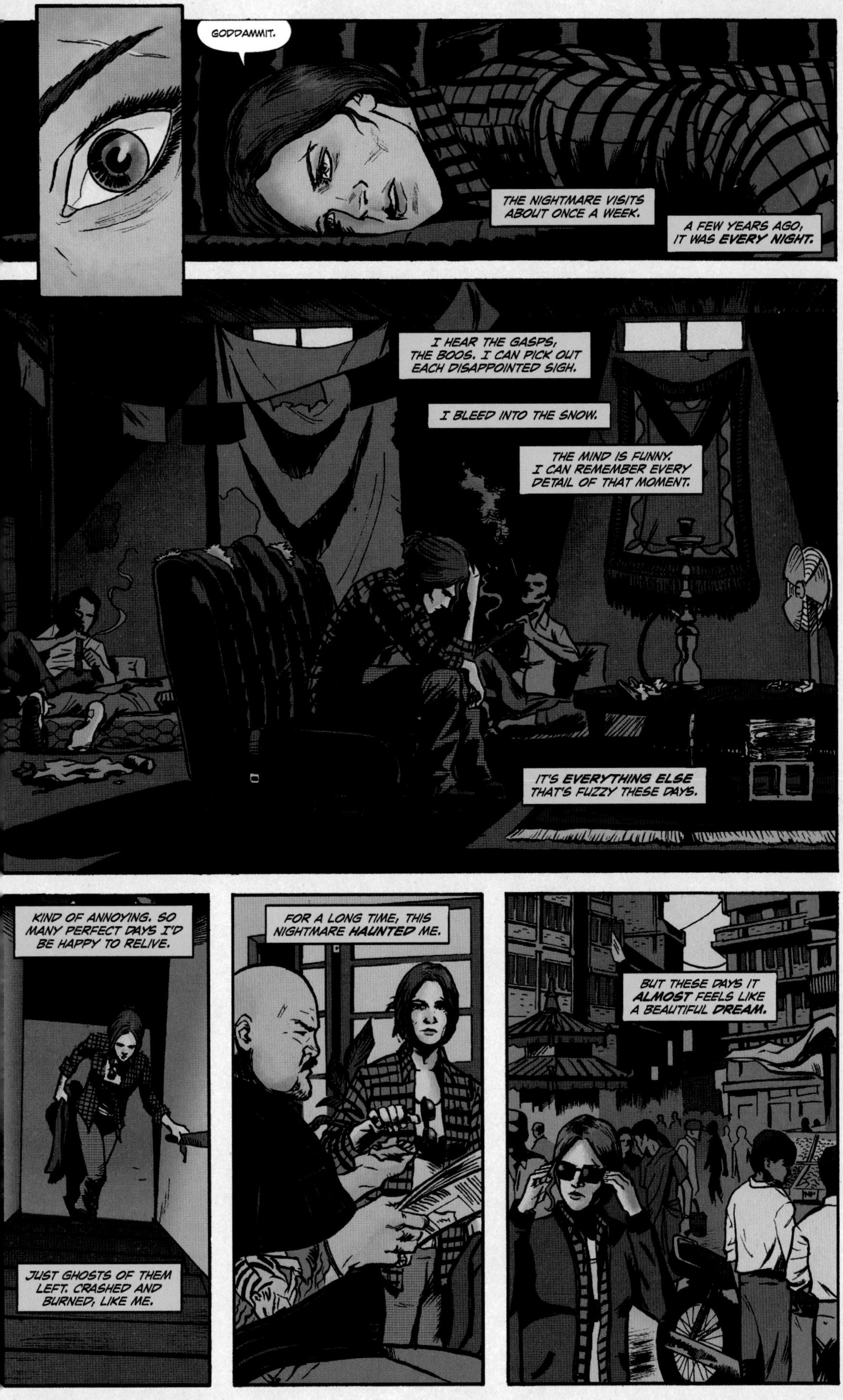
GODDAMMIT.
THE NIGHTMARE VISITS ABOUT ONCE A WEEK.
A FEW YEARS AGO, IT WAS EVERY NIGHT.
I HEAR THE GASPS, THE BOOS. I CAN PICK OUT EACH DISAPPOINTED SIGH.
I BLEED INTO THE SNOW.
THE MIND IS FUNNY. I CAN REMEMBER EVERY DETAIL OF THAT MOMENT.
IT'S EVERYTHING ELSE THAT'S FUZZY THESE DAYS.
KIND OF ANNOYING. SO MANY PERFECT DAYS I'D BE HAPPY TO RELIVE.
JUST GHOSTS OF THEM LEFT. CRASHED AND BURNED, LIKE ME.
FOR A LONG TIME, THIS NIGHTMARE HAUNTED ME.
BUT THESE DAYS IT ALMOST FEELS LIKE A BEAUTIFUL DREAM.

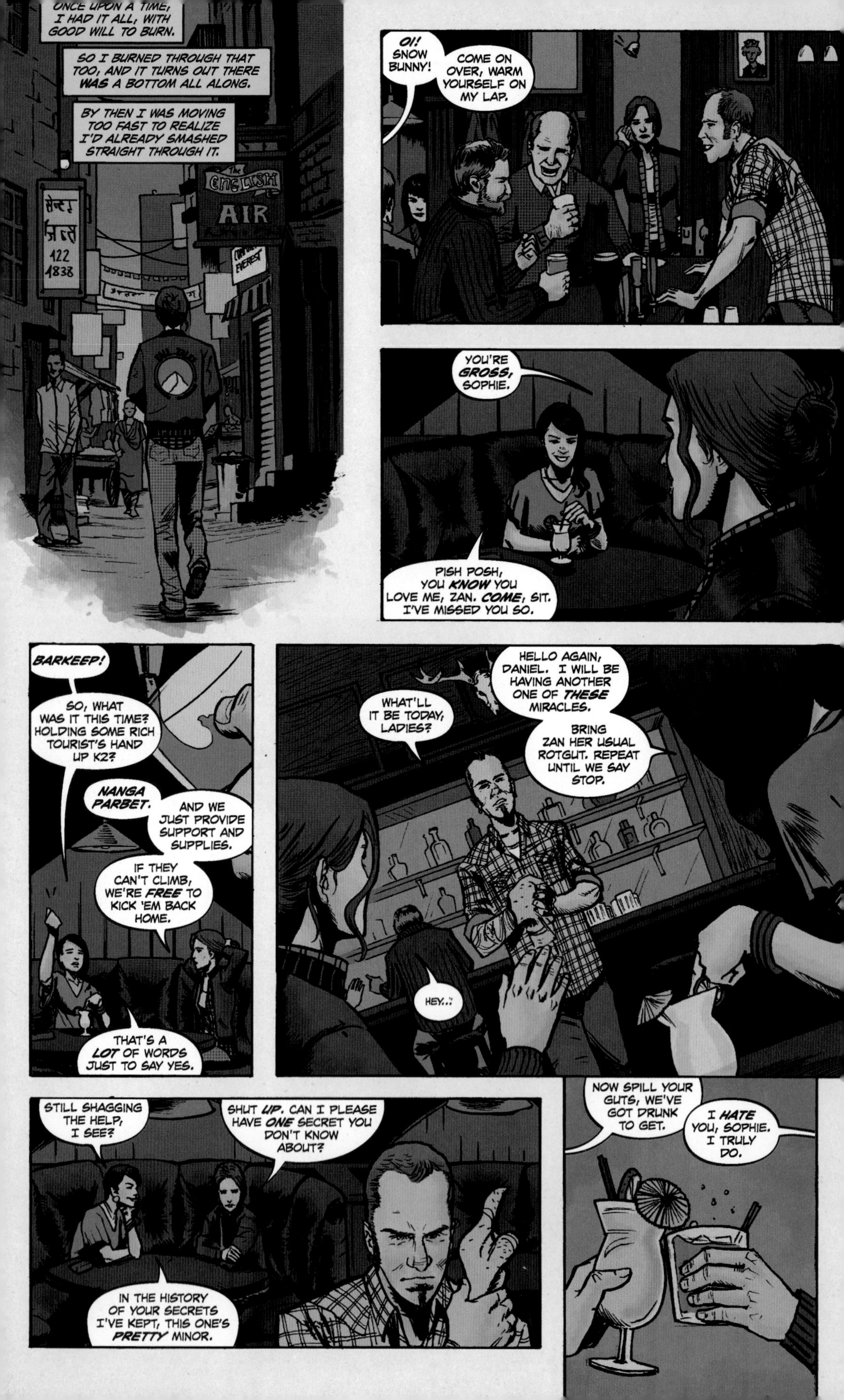

ONCE UPON A TIME, I HAD IT ALL, WITH GOOD WILL TO BURN.
SO I BURNED THROUGH THAT TOO, AND IT TURNS OUT THERE WAS A BOTTOM ALL ALONG.
BY THEN I WAS MOVING TOO FAST TO REALIZE I'D ALREADY SMASHED STRAIGHT THROUGH IT.
The ENGLISH AIR
122 1838
EVEREST
OI! SNOW BUNNY!
COME ON OVER, WARM YOURSELF ON MY LAP.
YOU'RE GROSS, SOPHIE.
PISH POSH, YOU KNOW YOU LOVE ME, ZAN. COME, SIT. I'VE MISSED YOU SO.
BARKEEP!
SO, WHAT WAS IT THIS TIME? HOLDING SOME RICH TOURIST'S HAND UP K2?
NANGA PARBET.
AND WE JUST PROVIDE SUPPORT AND SUPPLIES.
IF THEY CAN'T CLIMB, WE'RE FREE TO KICK 'EM BACK HOME.
THAT'S A LOT OF WORDS JUST TO SAY YES.
WHAT'LL IT BE TODAY, LADIES?
HELLO AGAIN, DANIEL. I WILL BE HAVING ANOTHER ONE OF THESE MIRACLES.
BRING ZAN HER USUAL ROTGUT. REPEAT UNTIL WE SAY STOP.
HEY...?
STILL SHAGGING THE HELP, I SEE?
SHUT UP. CAN I PLEASE HAVE ONE SECRET YOU DON'T KNOW ABOUT?
IN THE HISTORY OF YOUR SECRETS I'VE KEPT, THIS ONE'S PRETTY MINOR.
NOW SPILL YOUR GUTS, WE'VE GOT DRUNK TO GET.
I HATE YOU, SOPHIE. I TRULY DO.

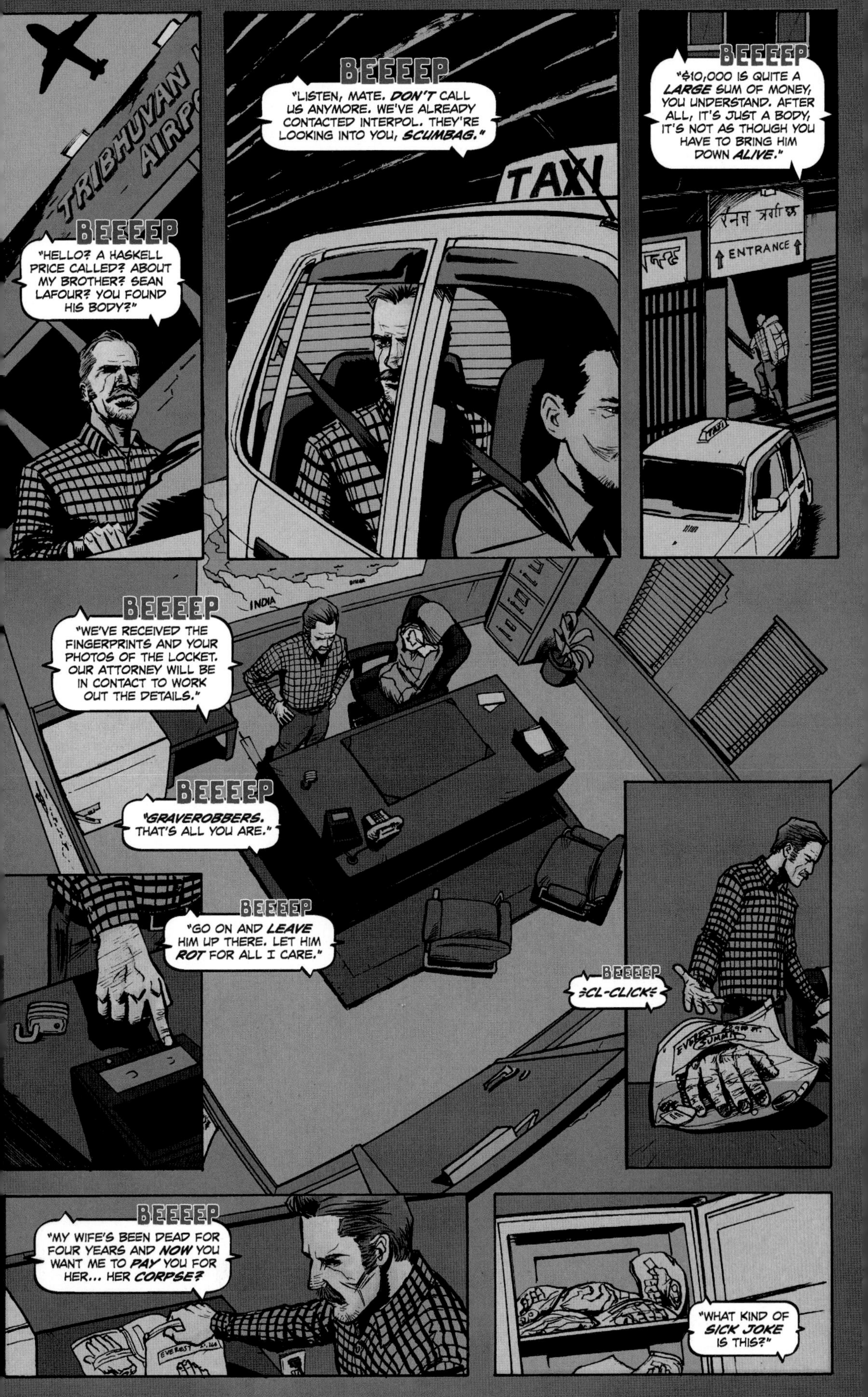
TRIBHUVAN
AIRP
BEEEEP
"HELLO? A HASKELL PRICE CALLED? ABOUT MY BROTHER? SEAN LAFOUR? YOU FOUND HIS BODY?"
BEEEEP
"LISTEN, MATE. DON'T CALL US ANYMORE. WE'VE ALREADY CONTACTED INTERPOL. THEY'RE LOOKING INTO YOU, SCUMBAG."
TAXI
BEEEEP
"$10,000 IS QUITE A LARGE SUM OF MONEY, YOU UNDERSTAND. AFTER ALL, IT'S JUST A BODY, IT'S NOT AS THOUGH YOU HAVE TO BRING HIM DOWN ALIVE."
ENTRANCE
INDIA
BEEEEP
"WE'VE RECEIVED THE FINGERPRINTS AND YOUR PHOTOS OF THE LOCKET. OUR ATTORNEY WILL BE IN CONTACT TO WORK OUT THE DETAILS."
BEEEEP
"GRAVEROBBERS. THAT'S ALL YOU ARE."
BEEEEP
"GO ON AND LEAVE HIM UP THERE. LET HIM ROT FOR ALL I CARE."
BEEEEP
≈CL-CLICK≈
BEEEEP
"MY WIFE'S BEEN DEAD FOR FOUR YEARS AND NOW YOU WANT ME TO PAY YOU FOR HER... HER CORPSE?"
EVEREST
"WHAT KIND OF SICK JOKE IS THIS?"

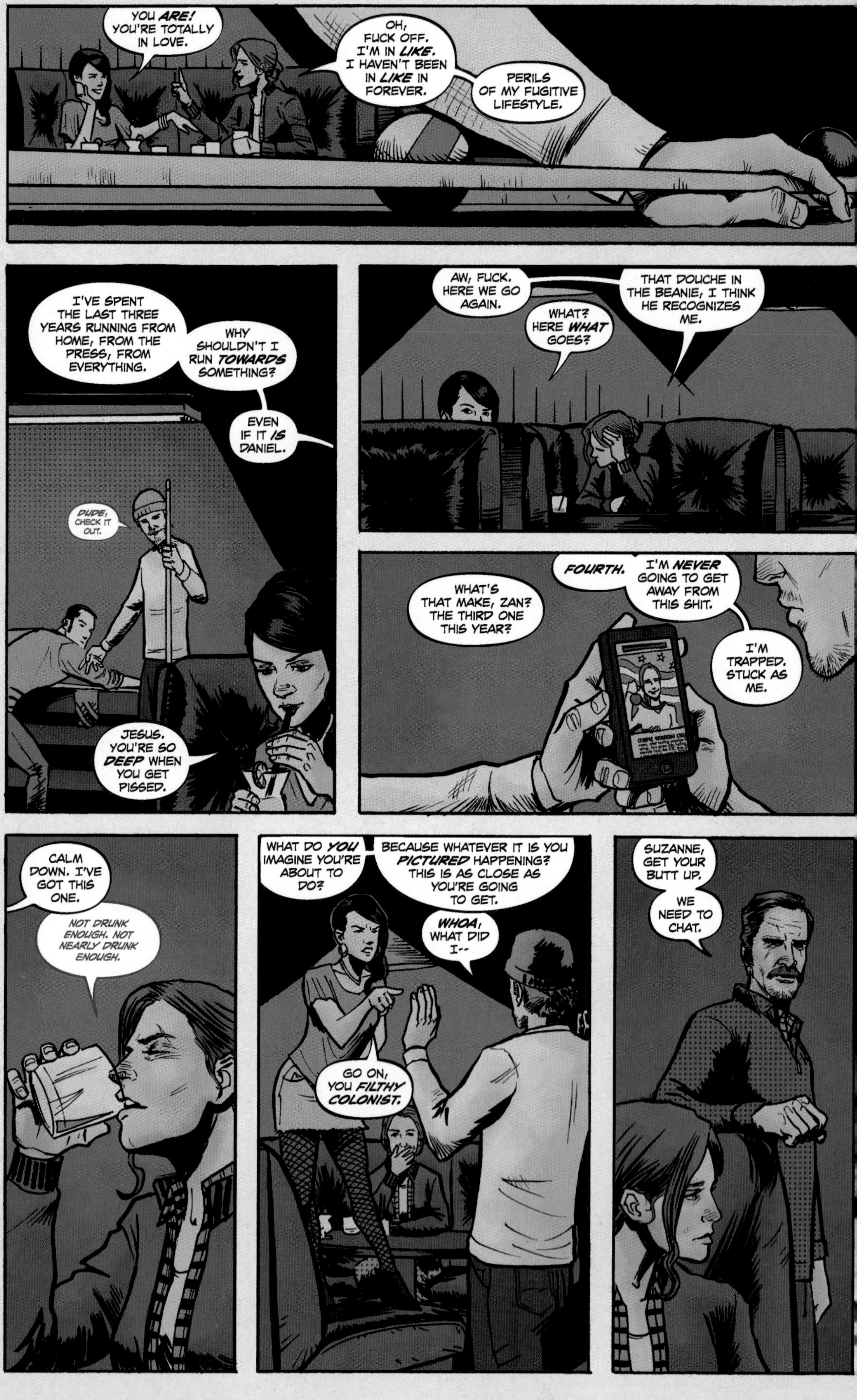
YOU ARE! YOU'RE TOTALLY IN LOVE.
OH, FUCK OFF. I'M IN LIKE. I HAVEN'T BEEN IN LIKE IN FOREVER.
PERILS OF MY FUGITIVE LIFESTYLE.
I'VE SPENT THE LAST THREE YEARS RUNNING FROM HOME; FROM THE PRESS; FROM EVERYTHING.
WHY SHOULDN'T I RUN TOWARDS SOMETHING?
EVEN IF IT IS DANIEL.
DUDE, CHECK IT OUT.
JESUS. YOU'RE SO DEEP WHEN YOU GET PISSED.
AW, FUCK. HERE WE GO AGAIN.
WHAT? HERE WHAT GOES?
THAT DOUCHE IN THE BEANIE, I THINK HE RECOGNIZES ME.
WHAT'S THAT MAKE, ZAN? THE THIRD ONE THIS YEAR?
FOURTH.
I'M NEVER GOING TO GET AWAY FROM THIS SHIT.
I'M TRAPPED. STUCK AS ME.
CALM DOWN. I'VE GOT THIS ONE.
NOT DRUNK ENOUGH. NOT NEARLY DRUNK ENOUGH.
WHAT DO YOU IMAGINE YOU'RE ABOUT TO DO?
BECAUSE WHATEVER IT IS YOU PICTURED HAPPENING? THIS IS AS CLOSE AS YOU'RE GOING TO GET.
WHOA, WHAT DID I--
GO ON, YOU FILTHY COLONIST.
SUZANNE, GET YOUR BUTT UP.
WE NEED TO CHAT.

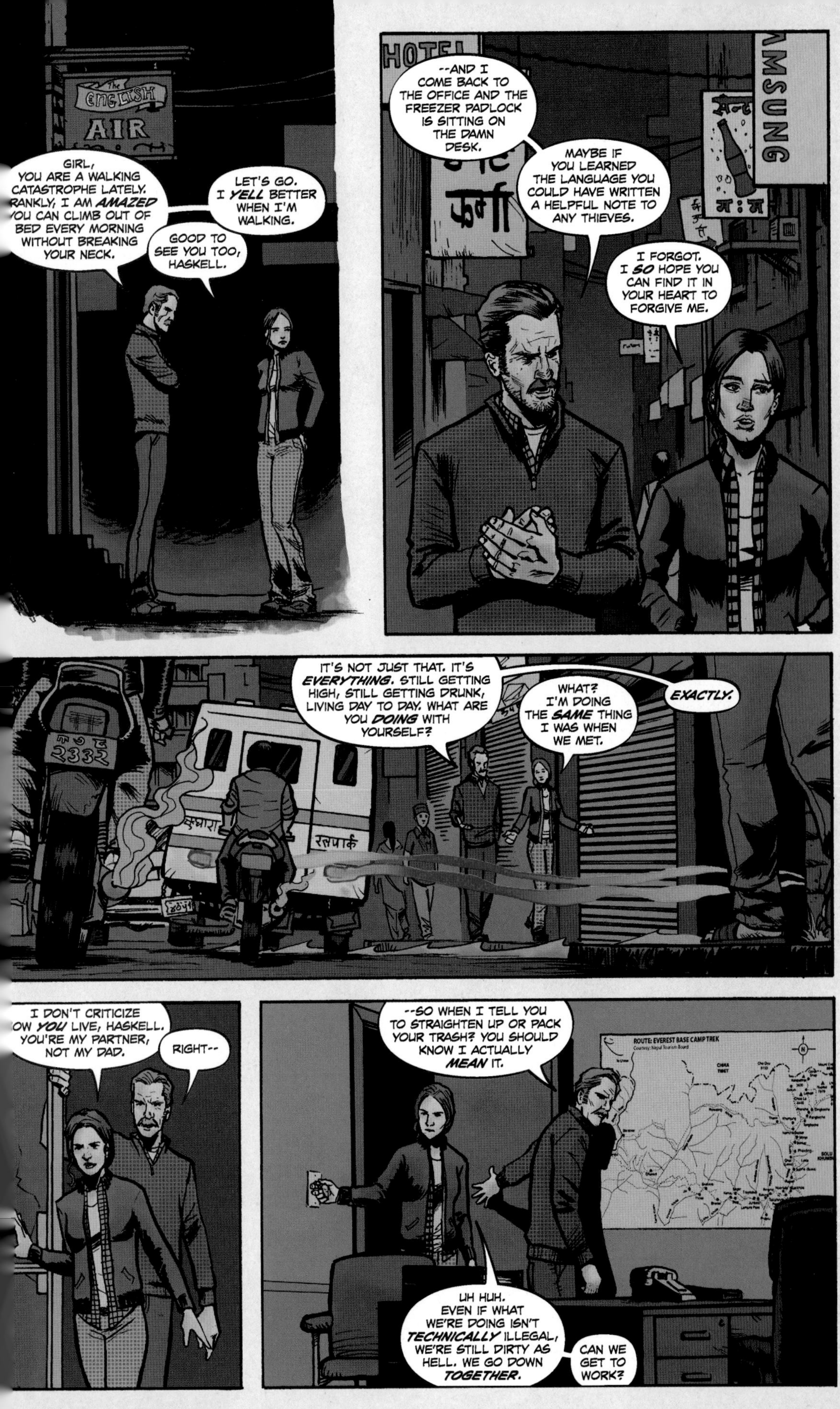
The ENGLISH AIR
GIRL, YOU ARE A WALKING CATASTROPHE LATELY. FRANKLY, I AM AMAZED YOU CAN CLIMB OUT OF BED EVERY MORNING WITHOUT BREAKING YOUR NECK.
LET'S GO. I YELL BETTER WHEN I'M WALKING.
GOOD TO SEE YOU TOO, HASKELL.
HOTEL
AMSUNG
--AND I COME BACK TO THE OFFICE AND THE FREEZER PADLOCK IS SITTING ON THE DAMN DESK.
MAYBE IF YOU LEARNED THE LANGUAGE YOU COULD HAVE WRITTEN A HELPFUL NOTE TO ANY THIEVES.
I FORGOT. I SO HOPE YOU CAN FIND IT IN YOUR HEART TO FORGIVE ME.
IT'S NOT JUST THAT. IT'S EVERYTHING. STILL GETTING HIGH, STILL GETTING DRUNK, LIVING DAY TO DAY. WHAT ARE YOU DOING WITH YOURSELF?
WHAT? I'M DOING THE SAME THING I WAS WHEN WE MET.
EXACTLY.
2332
I DON'T CRITICIZE HOW YOU LIVE, HASKELL. YOU'RE MY PARTNER, NOT MY DAD.
RIGHT--
--SO WHEN I TELL YOU TO STRAIGHTEN UP OR PACK YOUR TRASH? YOU SHOULD KNOW I ACTUALLY MEAN IT.
ROUTE: EVEREST BASE CAMP TREK
UH HUH. EVEN IF WHAT WE'RE DOING ISN'T TECHNICALLY ILLEGAL, WE'RE STILL DIRTY AS HELL. WE GO DOWN TOGETHER.
CAN WE GET TO WORK?

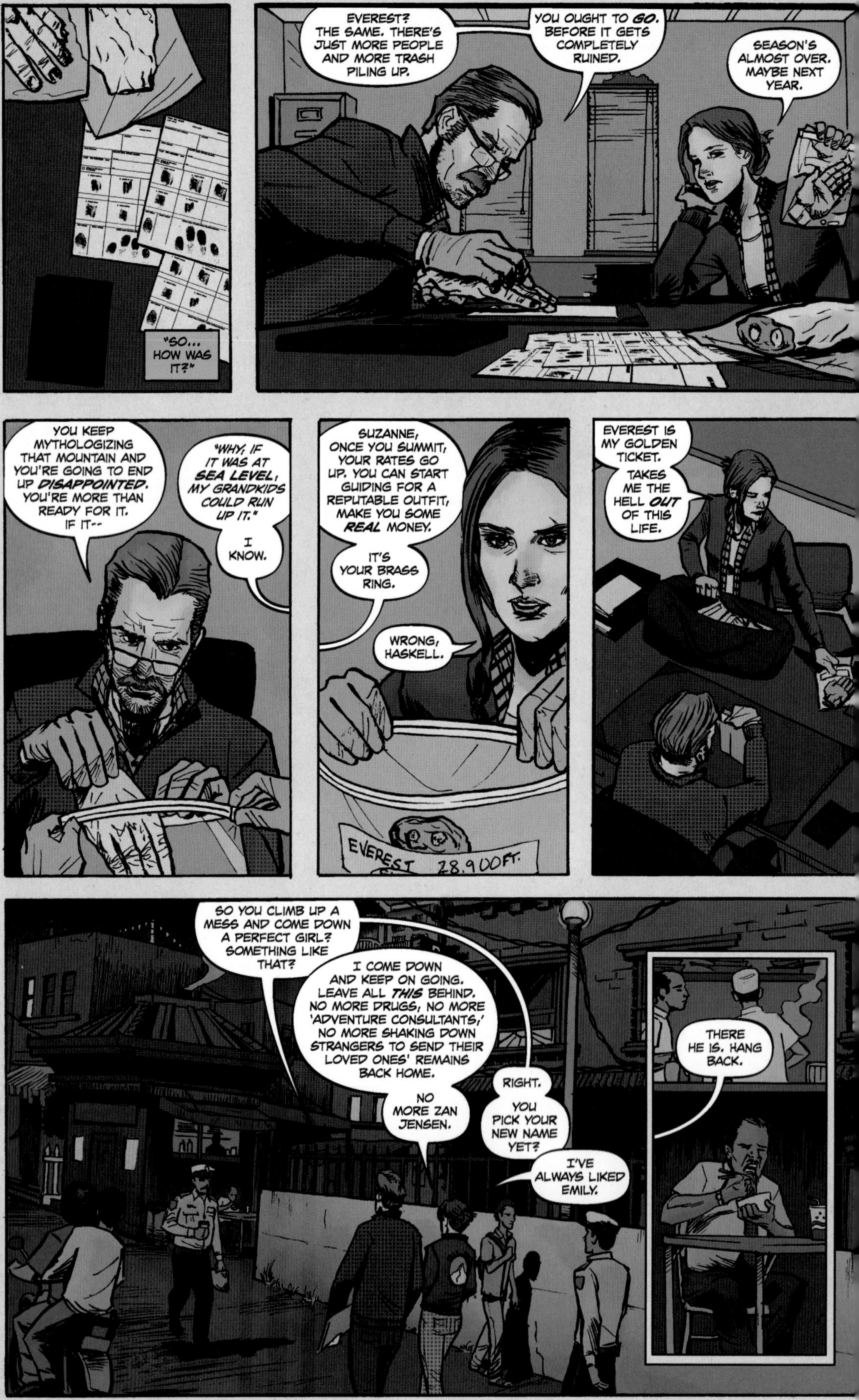

"SO... HOW WAS IT?"
EVEREST? THE SAME. THERE'S JUST MORE PEOPLE AND MORE TRASH PILING UP.
YOU OUGHT TO GO. BEFORE IT GETS COMPLETELY RUINED.
SEASON'S ALMOST OVER. MAYBE NEXT YEAR.
YOU KEEP MYTHOLOGIZING THAT MOUNTAIN AND YOU'RE GOING TO END UP DISAPPOINTED. YOU'RE MORE THAN READY FOR IT. IF IT--
"WHY, IF IT WAS AT SEA LEVEL, MY GRANDKIDS COULD RUN UP IT."
I KNOW.
SUZANNE, ONCE YOU SUMMIT, YOUR RATES GO UP. YOU CAN START GUIDING FOR A REPUTABLE OUTFIT, MAKE YOU SOME REAL MONEY.
IT'S YOUR BRASS RING.
WRONG, HASKELL.
EVEREST 28,900FT.
EVEREST IS MY GOLDEN TICKET.
TAKES ME THE HELL OUT OF THIS LIFE.
SO YOU CLIMB UP A MESS AND COME DOWN A PERFECT GIRL? SOMETHING LIKE THAT?
I COME DOWN AND KEEP ON GOING. LEAVE ALL THIS BEHIND. NO MORE DRUGS, NO MORE 'ADVENTURE CONSULTANTS,' NO MORE SHAKING DOWN STRANGERS TO SEND THEIR LOVED ONES' REMAINS BACK HOME.
NO MORE ZAN JENSEN.
RIGHT.
YOU PICK YOUR NEW NAME YET?
I'VE ALWAYS LIKED EMILY.
THERE HE IS. HANG BACK.

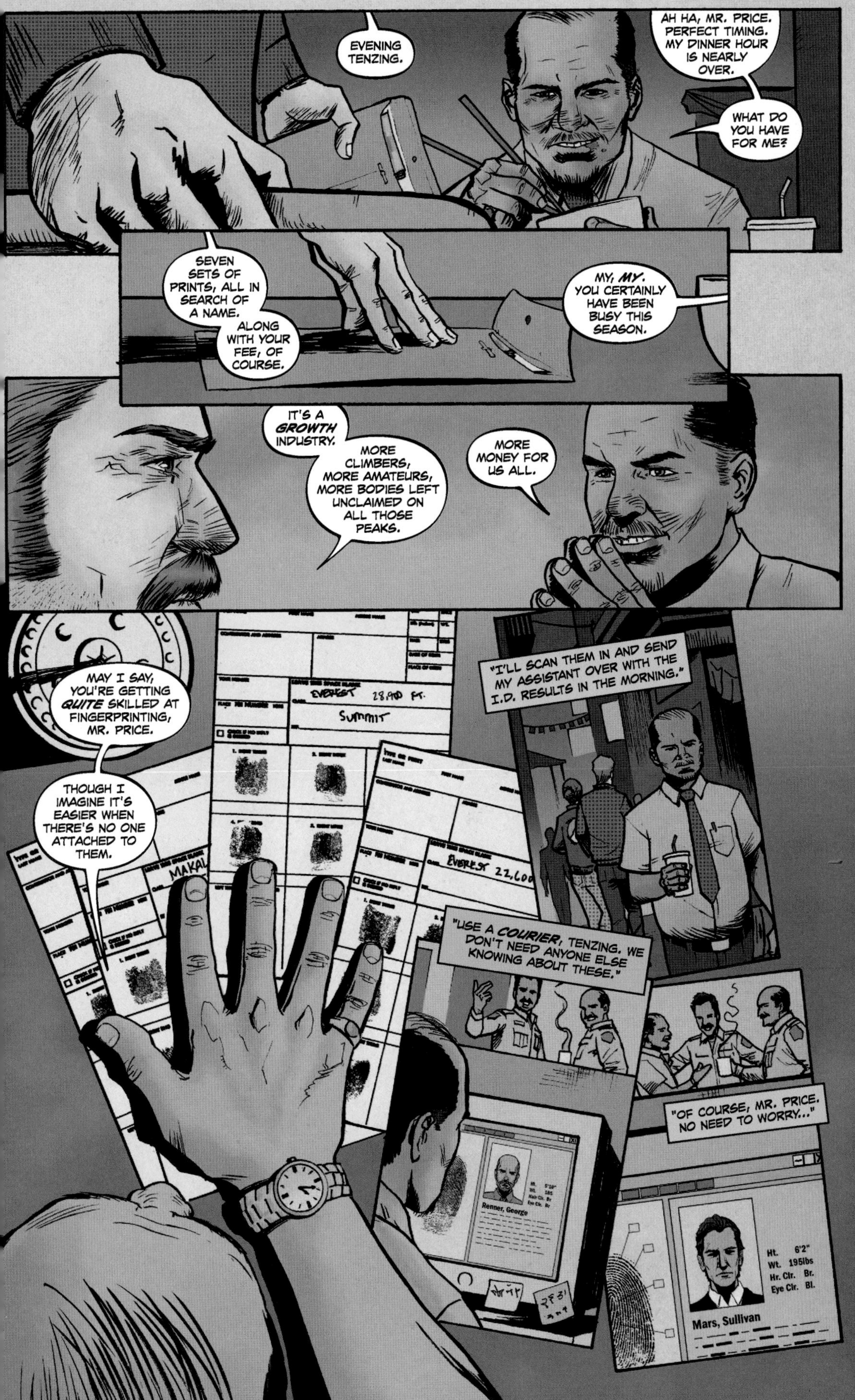
EVENING TENZING.
AH HA, MR. PRICE. PERFECT TIMING. MY DINNER HOUR IS NEARLY OVER.
WHAT DO YOU HAVE FOR ME?
SEVEN SETS OF PRINTS, ALL IN SEARCH OF A NAME.
ALONG WITH YOUR FEE, OF COURSE.
MY, MY. YOU CERTAINLY HAVE BEEN BUSY THIS SEASON.
IT'S A GROWTH INDUSTRY.
MORE CLIMBERS, MORE AMATEURS, MORE BODIES LEFT UNCLAIMED ON ALL THOSE PEAKS.
MORE MONEY FOR US ALL.
MAY I SAY, YOU'RE GETTING QUITE SKILLED AT FINGERPRINTING, MR. PRICE.
THOUGH I IMAGINE IT'S EASIER WHEN THERE'S NO ONE ATTACHED TO THEM.
EVEREST 28,900 FT.
SUMMIT
MAKAL
EVEREST 22,600
"I'LL SCAN THEM IN AND SEND MY ASSISTANT OVER WITH THE I.D. RESULTS IN THE MORNING."
"USE A COURIER, TENZING. WE DON'T NEED ANYONE ELSE KNOWING ABOUT THESE."
"OF COURSE, MR. PRICE. NO NEED TO WORRY..."
Renner, George
Ht. 6'2"
Wt. 195lbs
Hr. Clr. Br.
Eye Clr. Bl.
Mars, Sullivan

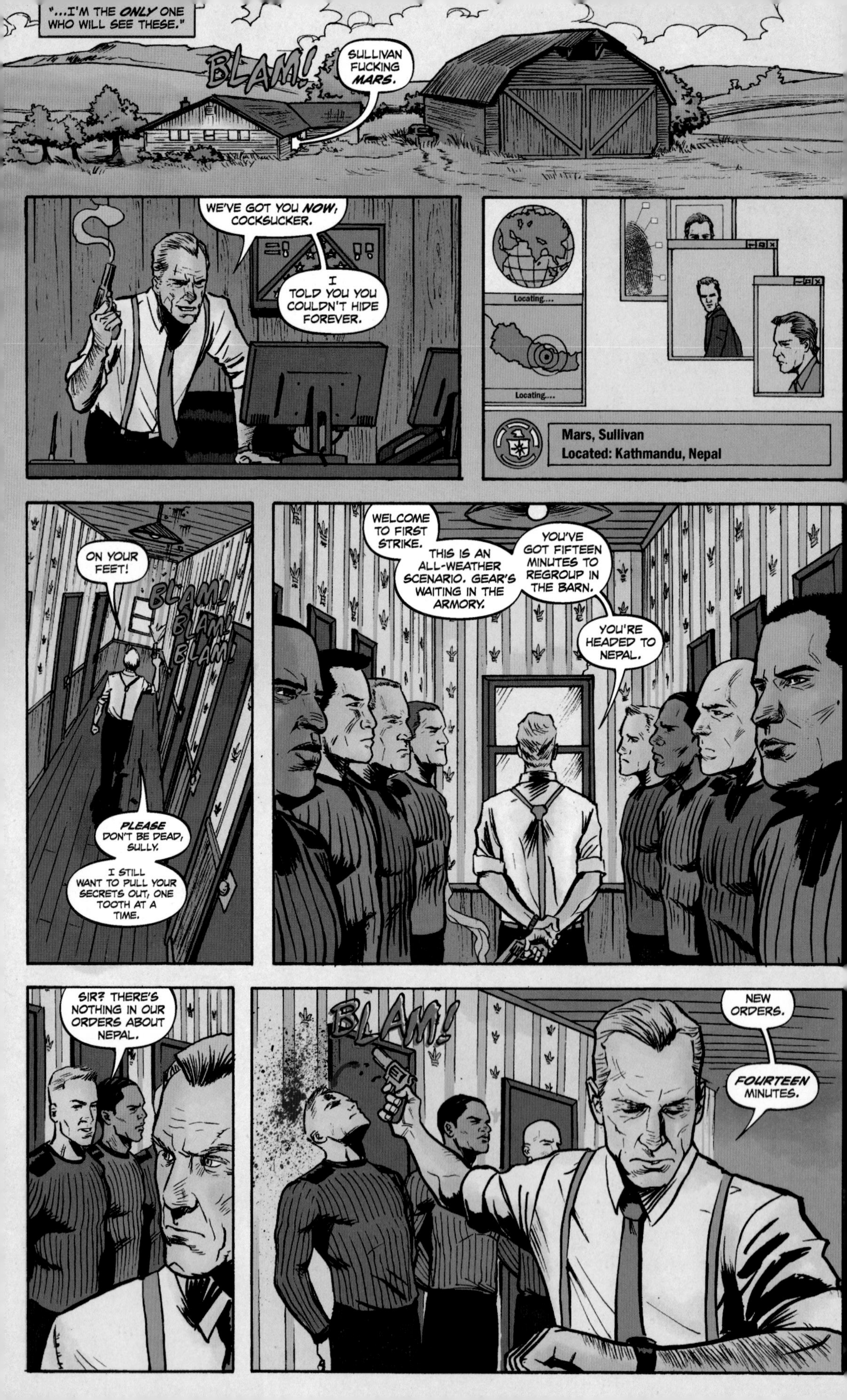
"...I'M THE ONLY ONE WHO WILL SEE THESE."
BLAM!
SULLIVAN FUCKING MARS.
WE'VE GOT YOU NOW, COCKSUCKER.
I TOLD YOU YOU COULDN'T HIDE FOREVER.
Locating....
Locating....
Mars, Sullivan
Located: Kathmandu, Nepal
ON YOUR FEET!
BLAM! BLAM! BLAM!
PLEASE DON'T BE DEAD, SULLY.
I STILL WANT TO PULL YOUR SECRETS OUT, ONE TOOTH AT A TIME.
WELCOME TO FIRST STRIKE.
THIS IS AN ALL-WEATHER SCENARIO. GEAR'S WAITING IN THE ARMORY.
YOU'VE GOT FIFTEEN MINUTES TO REGROUP IN THE BARN.
YOU'RE HEADED TO NEPAL.
SIR? THERE'S NOTHING IN OUR ORDERS ABOUT NEPAL.
BLAM!
NEW ORDERS.
FOURTEEN MINUTES.

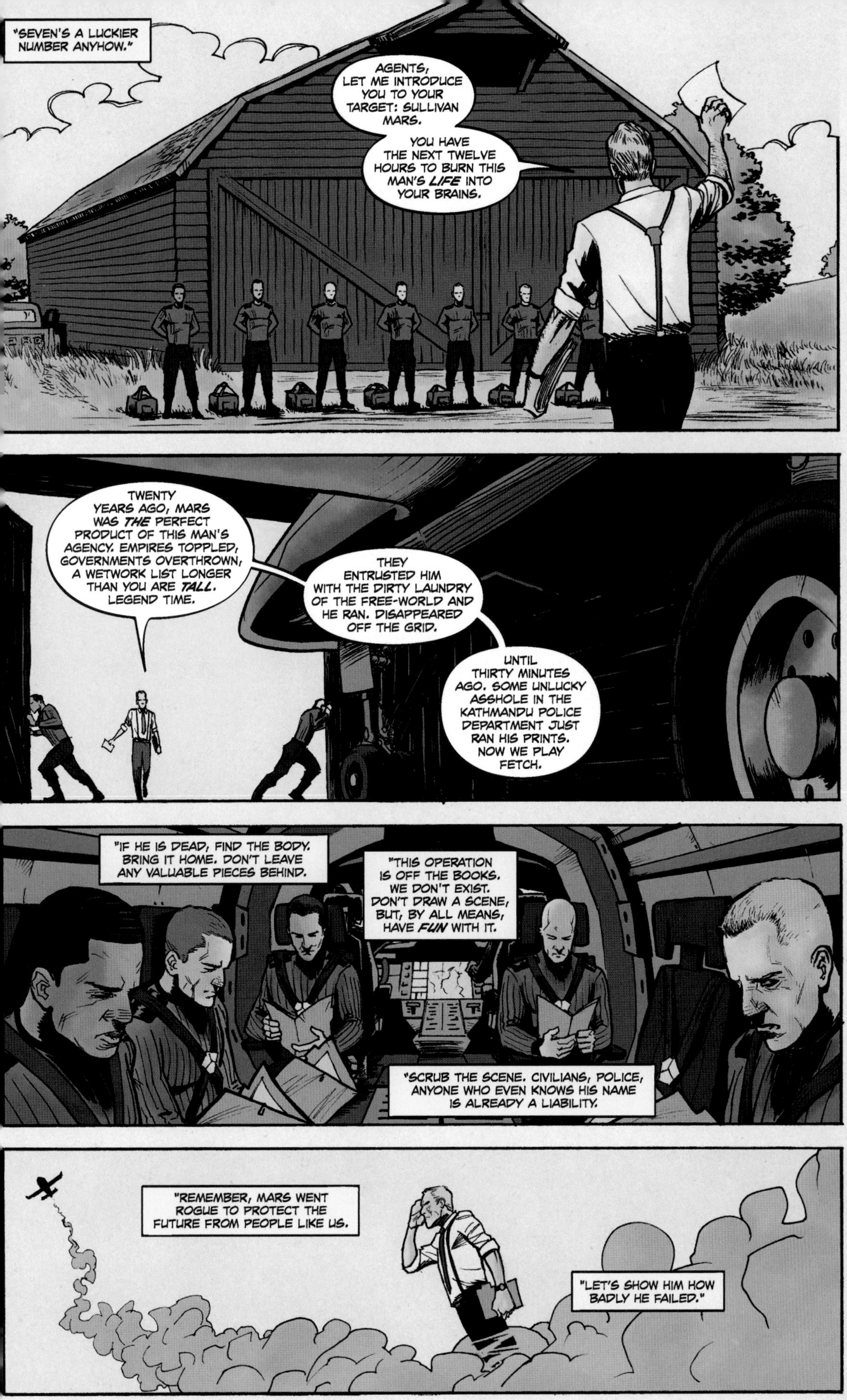
"SEVEN'S A LUCKIER NUMBER ANYHOW."
AGENTS, LET ME INTRODUCE YOU TO YOUR TARGET: SULLIVAN MARS.
YOU HAVE THE NEXT TWELVE HOURS TO BURN THIS MAN'S *LIFE* INTO YOUR BRAINS.
TWENTY YEARS AGO, MARS WAS *THE* PERFECT PRODUCT OF THIS MAN'S AGENCY. EMPIRES TOPPLED, GOVERNMENTS OVERTHROWN, A WETWORK LIST LONGER THAN YOU ARE *TALL*. LEGEND TIME.
THEY ENTRUSTED HIM WITH THE DIRTY LAUNDRY OF THE FREE-WORLD AND HE RAN. DISAPPEARED OFF THE GRID.
UNTIL THIRTY MINUTES AGO. SOME UNLUCKY ASSHOLE IN THE KATHMANDU POLICE DEPARTMENT JUST RAN HIS PRINTS. NOW WE PLAY FETCH.
"IF HE IS DEAD, FIND THE BODY. BRING IT HOME. DON'T LEAVE ANY VALUABLE PIECES BEHIND.
"THIS OPERATION IS OFF THE BOOKS. WE DON'T EXIST. DON'T DRAW A SCENE, BUT, BY ALL MEANS, HAVE *FUN* WITH IT.
"SCRUB THE SCENE. CIVILIANS, POLICE, ANYONE WHO EVEN KNOWS HIS NAME IS ALREADY A LIABILITY.
"REMEMBER, MARS WENT ROGUE TO PROTECT THE FUTURE FROM PEOPLE LIKE US.
"LET'S SHOW HIM HOW BADLY HE FAILED."

I FIGURE *FORTY* GRAND APIECE BY THE END OF THE YEAR.

IF TENZING PULLS UP THEIR RECORDS, *IF* THE FAMILIES CONSENT, IF WE CAN GET THE BODIES DOWN.

I'M NOT EXACTLY SPENDING IT YET, HASKELL.

HAVE SOME FAITH IN HUMANITY, SUZANNE.

SOMEONE WILL *ALWAYS* PAY. PEOPLE GET FUNNY ABOUT THEIR DEAD.

PLEASE DON'T TELL ME YOU'RE PLAYING WITH THE HANDS.

NOT PLAYING. *LOOKING.*

THIS ONE'S *ANCIENT.*

THE *SUMMIT* ONE?

IT'S NOT *THAT* OLD. MAYBE TWENTY YEARS. YOUNG BY EVEREST'S YARDSTICK.

A LONG SHOT THAT ANYONE'S STILL WORRIED ABOUT HIM, BUT HELL, I WAS ALREADY UP THERE.

TIK

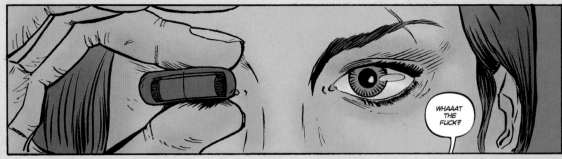

WHAAAT THE FUCK?

HERE, EAT. MAYBE IT'LL SOAK UP THE BOOZE.

AND WE'RE NOT EATING WITH *THOSE* ON THE TABLE.

PUT 'EM IN THE *BANK.* BEFORE THEY GO BAD.

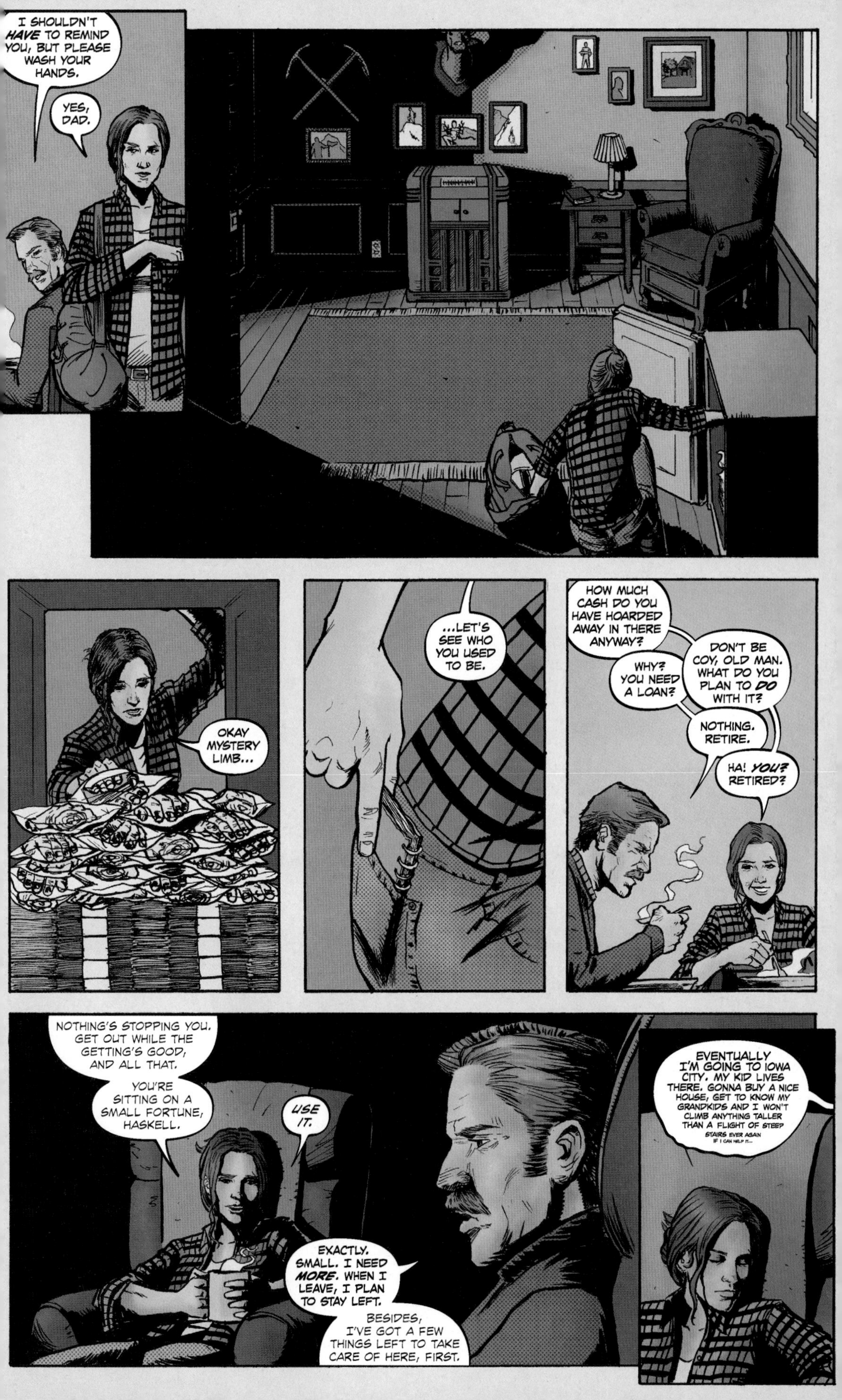
I SHOULDN'T *HAVE* TO REMIND YOU, BUT PLEASE WASH YOUR HANDS.
YES, DAD.
OKAY MYSTERY LIMB...
...LET'S SEE WHO YOU USED TO BE.
HOW MUCH CASH DO YOU HAVE HOARDED AWAY IN THERE ANYWAY?
WHY? YOU NEED A LOAN?
DON'T BE COY, OLD MAN. WHAT DO YOU PLAN TO *DO* WITH IT?
NOTHING. RETIRE.
HA! *YOU?* RETIRED?
NOTHING'S STOPPING YOU. GET OUT WHILE THE GETTING'S GOOD, AND ALL THAT.
YOU'RE SITTING ON A SMALL FORTUNE, HASKELL.
USE IT.
EXACTLY. SMALL. I NEED *MORE.* WHEN I LEAVE, I PLAN TO STAY LEFT.
BESIDES, I'VE GOT A FEW THINGS LEFT TO TAKE CARE OF HERE, FIRST.
EVENTUALLY I'M GOING TO IOWA CITY. MY KID LIVES THERE. GONNA BUY A NICE HOUSE, GET TO KNOW MY GRANDKIDS AND I WON'T CLIMB ANYTHING TALLER THAN A FLIGHT OF STEEP STAIRS EVER AGAIN IF I CAN HELP IT...

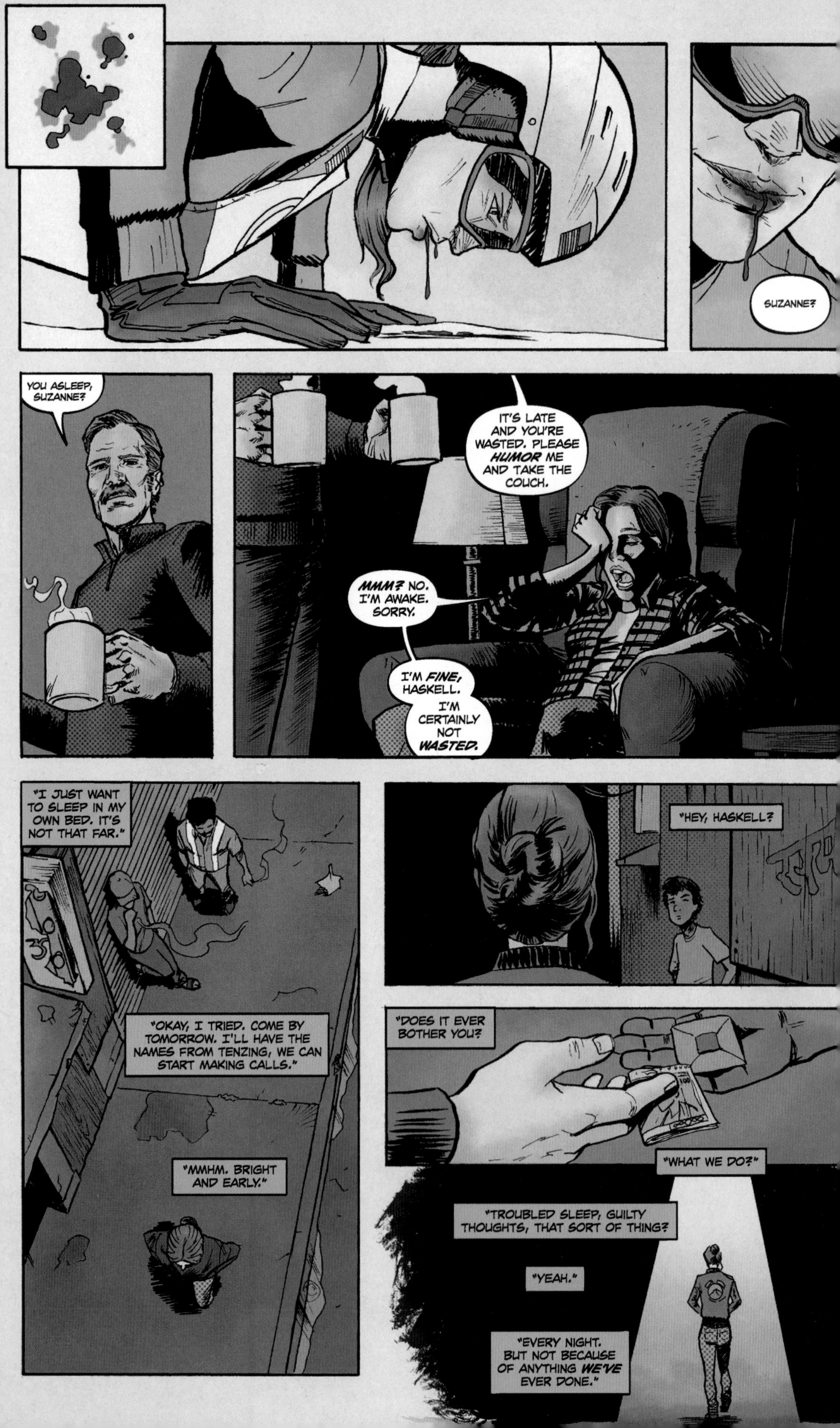
SUZANNE?
YOU ASLEEP, SUZANNE?
IT'S LATE AND YOU'RE WASTED. PLEASE HUMOR ME AND TAKE THE COUCH.
MMM? NO. I'M AWAKE. SORRY.
I'M FINE, HASKELL.
I'M CERTAINLY NOT WASTED.
"I JUST WANT TO SLEEP IN MY OWN BED. IT'S NOT THAT FAR."
"OKAY, I TRIED. COME BY TOMORROW. I'LL HAVE THE NAMES FROM TENZING, WE CAN START MAKING CALLS."
"MMHM. BRIGHT AND EARLY."
"HEY, HASKELL?
"DOES IT EVER BOTHER YOU?
"WHAT WE DO?"
"TROUBLED SLEEP, GUILTY THOUGHTS, THAT SORT OF THING?
"YEAH."
"EVERY NIGHT. BUT NOT BECAUSE OF ANYTHING WE'VE EVER DONE."

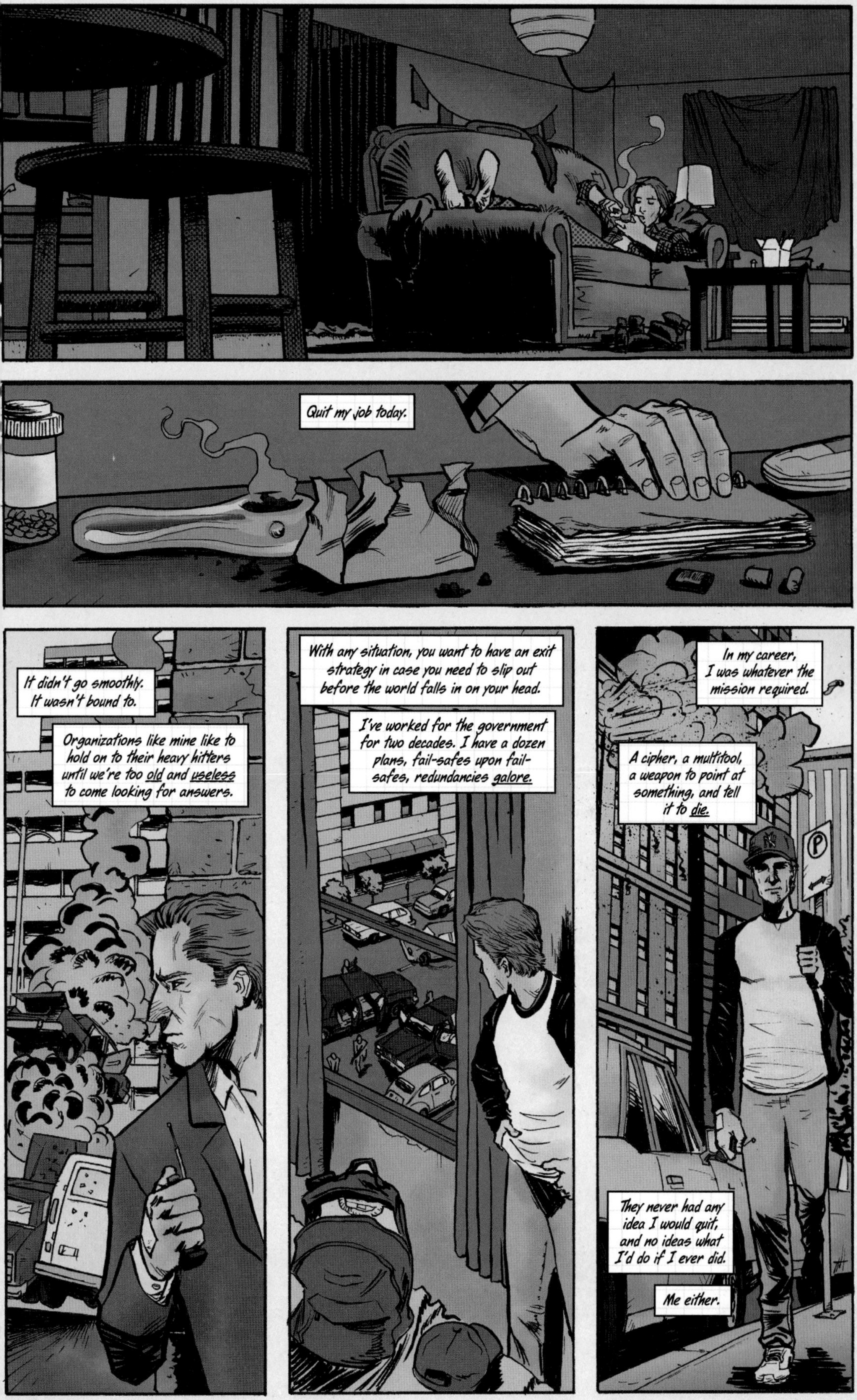
Quit my job today.
It didn't go smoothly. It wasn't bound to.
Organizations like mine like to hold on to their heavy hitters until we're too old and useless to come looking for answers.
With any situation, you want to have an exit strategy in case you need to slip out before the world falls in on your head.
I've worked for the government for two decades. I have a dozen plans, fail-safes upon fail-safes, redundancies galore.
In my career, I was whatever the mission required.
A cipher, a multitool, a weapon to point at something, and tell it to die.
They never had any idea I would quit, and no ideas what I'd do if I ever did.
Me either.

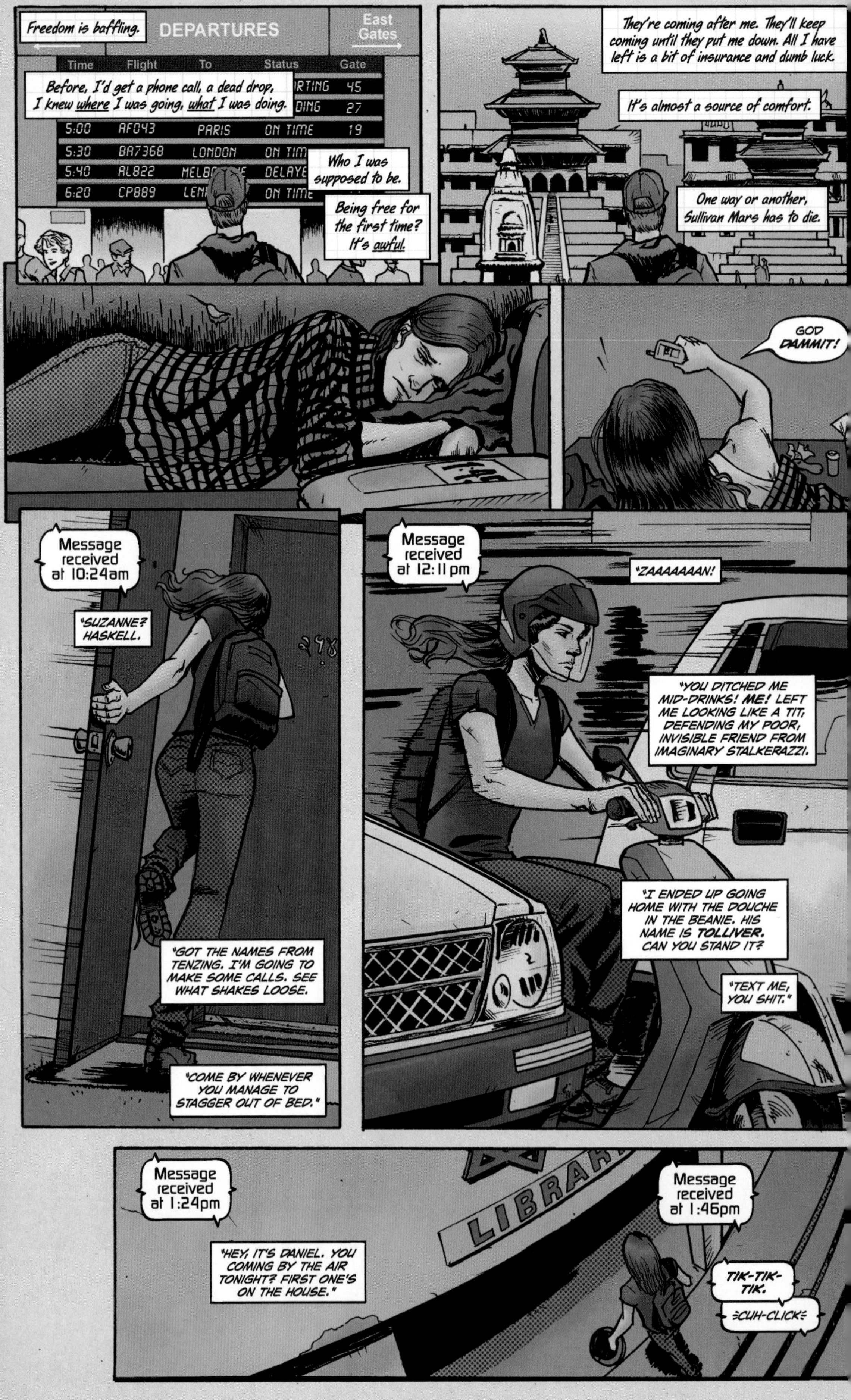

Freedom is baffling.
DEPARTURES
East Gates
Time Flight To Status Gate
Before, I'd get a phone call, a dead drop, I knew where I was going, what I was doing.
5:00 AF043 PARIS ON TIME 19
5:30 BA7368 LONDON
5:40 AL822 DELAYE
6:20 CP889 ON TIME
Who I was supposed to be.
Being free for the first time? It's awful.
They're coming after me. They'll keep coming until they put me down. All I have left is a bit of insurance and dumb luck.
It's almost a source of comfort.
One way or another, Sullivan Mars has to die.
GOD DAMMIT!
Message received at 10:24am
"SUZANNE? HASKELL.
"GOT THE NAMES FROM TENZING. I'M GOING TO MAKE SOME CALLS. SEE WHAT SHAKES LOOSE.
"COME BY WHENEVER YOU MANAGE TO STAGGER OUT OF BED."
Message received at 12:11pm
"ZAAAAAAAN!
"YOU DITCHED ME MID-DRINKS! ME! LEFT ME LOOKING LIKE A TIT, DEFENDING MY POOR, INVISIBLE FRIEND FROM IMAGINARY STALKERAZZI.
"I ENDED UP GOING HOME WITH THE DOUCHE IN THE BEANIE. HIS NAME IS TOLLIVER. CAN YOU STAND IT?
"TEXT ME, YOU SHIT."
Message received at 1:24pm
"HEY, IT'S DANIEL. YOU COMING BY THE AIR TONIGHT? FIRST ONE'S ON THE HOUSE."
LIBRAR
Message received at 1:46pm
TIK-TIK-TIK.
CUH-CLICK

NOW, IT'S *FUSSY,* BUT IT STILL WORKS.
THOUGH OUR MICROFILM LIBRARY IS OF FAIRLY *LIMITED* INTEREST.
THAT'S OKAY, I BROUGHT MY OWN.
ZOOM 13x -27x
THIS BETTER NOT BE YOUR VACATION PHOTOS, MARS.
SECRET
EYES ONLY
DEALEY PLAZA
THE SECRETARY OF DEFENSE
WASHINGTON D C 20301
CONFIDENTIAL
MEMORANDUM FOR COMMANDER IN CHIEF
SUBJECT: Guyana Support Operations
HOLY CATS.
THE ATTACHED DOCUMENT CONTAINS
SECRET
INFORMATION
AND AS SUCH IT MUST BE
CLASSIFIED
REEL 3 OF 7

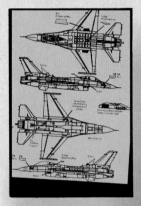

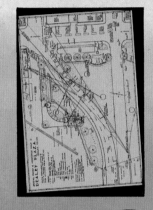

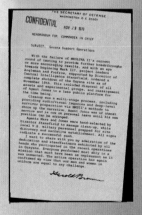

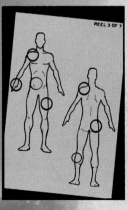

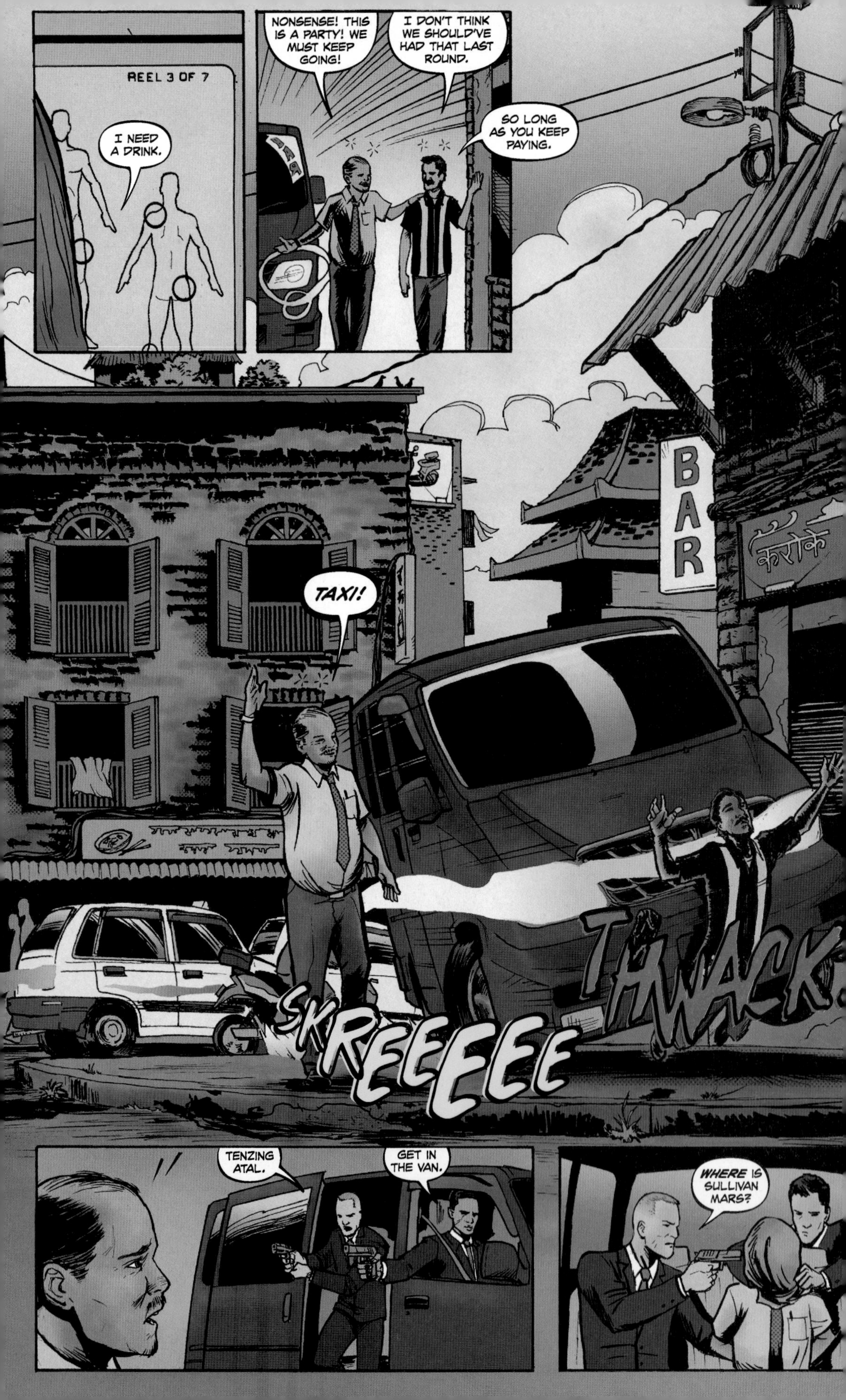
REEL 3 OF 7
I NEED A DRINK.
NONSENSE! THIS IS A PARTY! WE MUST KEEP GOING!
I DON'T THINK WE SHOULD'VE HAD THAT LAST ROUND.
SO LONG AS YOU KEEP PAYING.
BAR
करोके
TAXI!
SKREEEEEE
THWACK.
TENZING ATAL.
GET IN THE VAN.
WHERE IS SULLIVAN MARS?

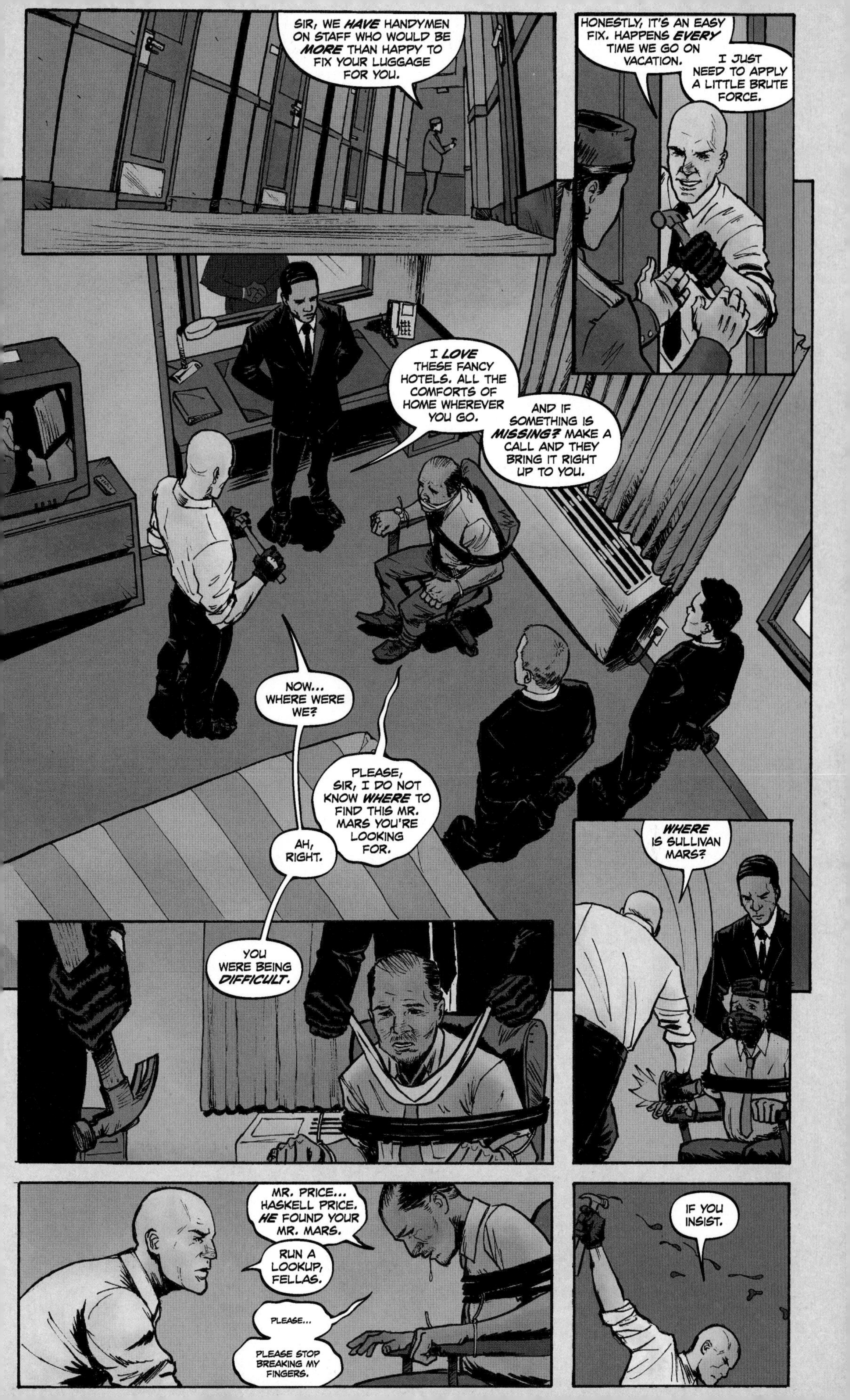
SIR, WE HAVE HANDYMEN ON STAFF WHO WOULD BE MORE THAN HAPPY TO FIX YOUR LUGGAGE FOR YOU.
HONESTLY, IT'S AN EASY FIX. HAPPENS EVERY TIME WE GO ON VACATION.
I JUST NEED TO APPLY A LITTLE BRUTE FORCE.
I LOVE THESE FANCY HOTELS. ALL THE COMFORTS OF HOME WHEREVER YOU GO.
AND IF SOMETHING IS MISSING? MAKE A CALL AND THEY BRING IT RIGHT UP TO YOU.
NOW... WHERE WERE WE?
PLEASE, SIR, I DO NOT KNOW WHERE TO FIND THIS MR. MARS YOU'RE LOOKING FOR.
AH, RIGHT.
YOU WERE BEING DIFFICULT.
WHERE IS SULLIVAN MARS?
MR. PRICE... HASKELL PRICE. HE FOUND YOUR MR. MARS.
RUN A LOOKUP, FELLAS.
PLEASE...
PLEASE STOP BREAKING MY FINGERS.
IF YOU INSIST.

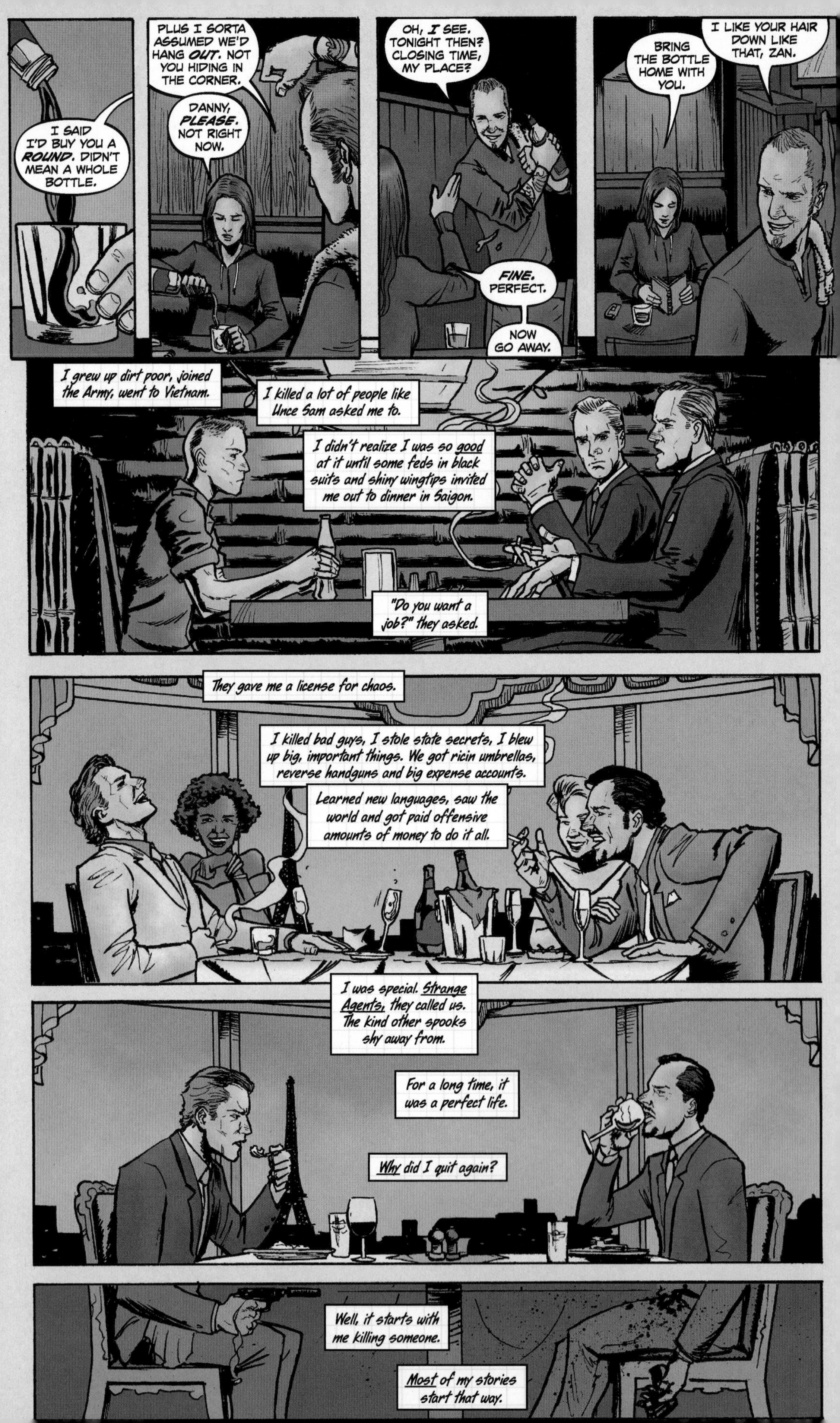

I SAID I'D BUY YOU A ROUND. DIDN'T MEAN A WHOLE BOTTLE.
PLUS I SORTA ASSUMED WE'D HANG OUT. NOT YOU HIDING IN THE CORNER.
DANNY, PLEASE. NOT RIGHT NOW.
OH, I SEE. TONIGHT THEN? CLOSING TIME, MY PLACE?
FINE. PERFECT.
NOW GO AWAY.
BRING THE BOTTLE HOME WITH YOU.
I LIKE YOUR HAIR DOWN LIKE THAT, ZAN.
I grew up dirt poor, joined the Army, went to Vietnam.
I killed a lot of people like Unce Sam asked me to.
I didn't realize I was so good at it until some feds in black suits and shiny wingtips invited me out to dinner in Saigon.
"Do you want a job?" they asked.
They gave me a license for chaos.
I killed bad guys, I stole state secrets, I blew up big, important things. We got ricin umbrellas, reverse handguns and big expense accounts.
Learned new languages, saw the world and got paid offensive amounts of money to do it all.
I was special. Strange Agents, they called us. The kind other spooks shy away from.
For a long time, it was a perfect life.
Why did I quit again?
Well, it starts with me killing someone.
Most of my stories start that way.

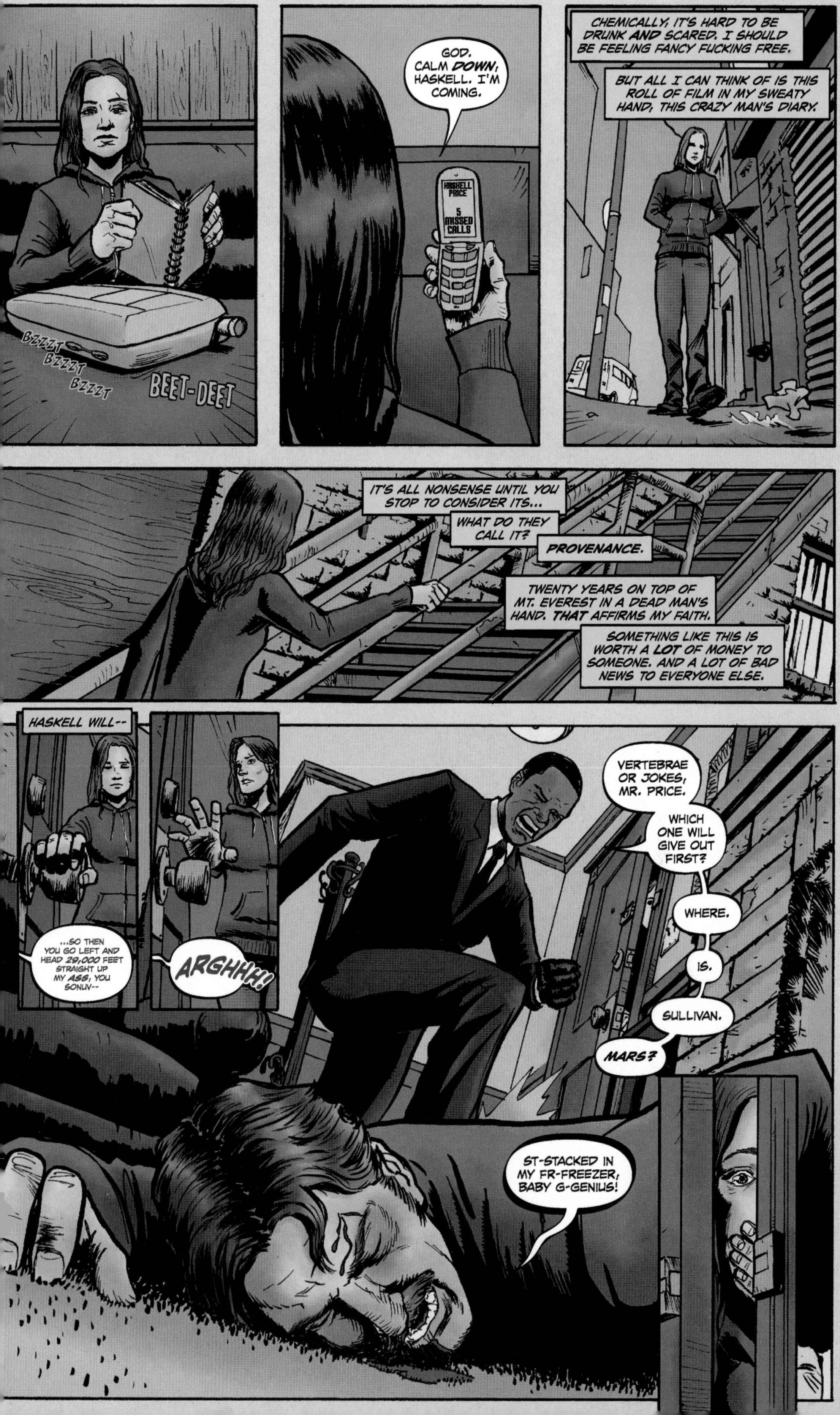
BZZZT
BZZZT
BZZZT
BEET-DEET
GOD. CALM DOWN, HASKELL. I'M COMING.
HASKELL PRICE 5 MISSED CALLS
CHEMICALLY, IT'S HARD TO BE DRUNK AND SCARED. I SHOULD BE FEELING FANCY FUCKING FREE.
BUT ALL I CAN THINK OF IS THIS ROLL OF FILM IN MY SWEATY HAND, THIS CRAZY MAN'S DIARY.
IT'S ALL NONSENSE UNTIL YOU STOP TO CONSIDER ITS...
WHAT DO THEY CALL IT?
PROVENANCE.
TWENTY YEARS ON TOP OF MT. EVEREST IN A DEAD MAN'S HAND. THAT AFFIRMS MY FAITH.
SOMETHING LIKE THIS IS WORTH A LOT OF MONEY TO SOMEONE. AND A LOT OF BAD NEWS TO EVERYONE ELSE.
HASKELL WILL--
...SO THEN YOU GO LEFT AND HEAD 29,000 FEET STRAIGHT UP MY ASS, YOU SONUV--
ARGHHH!
VERTEBRAE OR JOKES, MR. PRICE.
WHICH ONE WILL GIVE OUT FIRST?
WHERE.
IS.
SULLIVAN.
MARS?
ST-STACKED IN MY FR-FREEZER, BABY G-GENIUS!

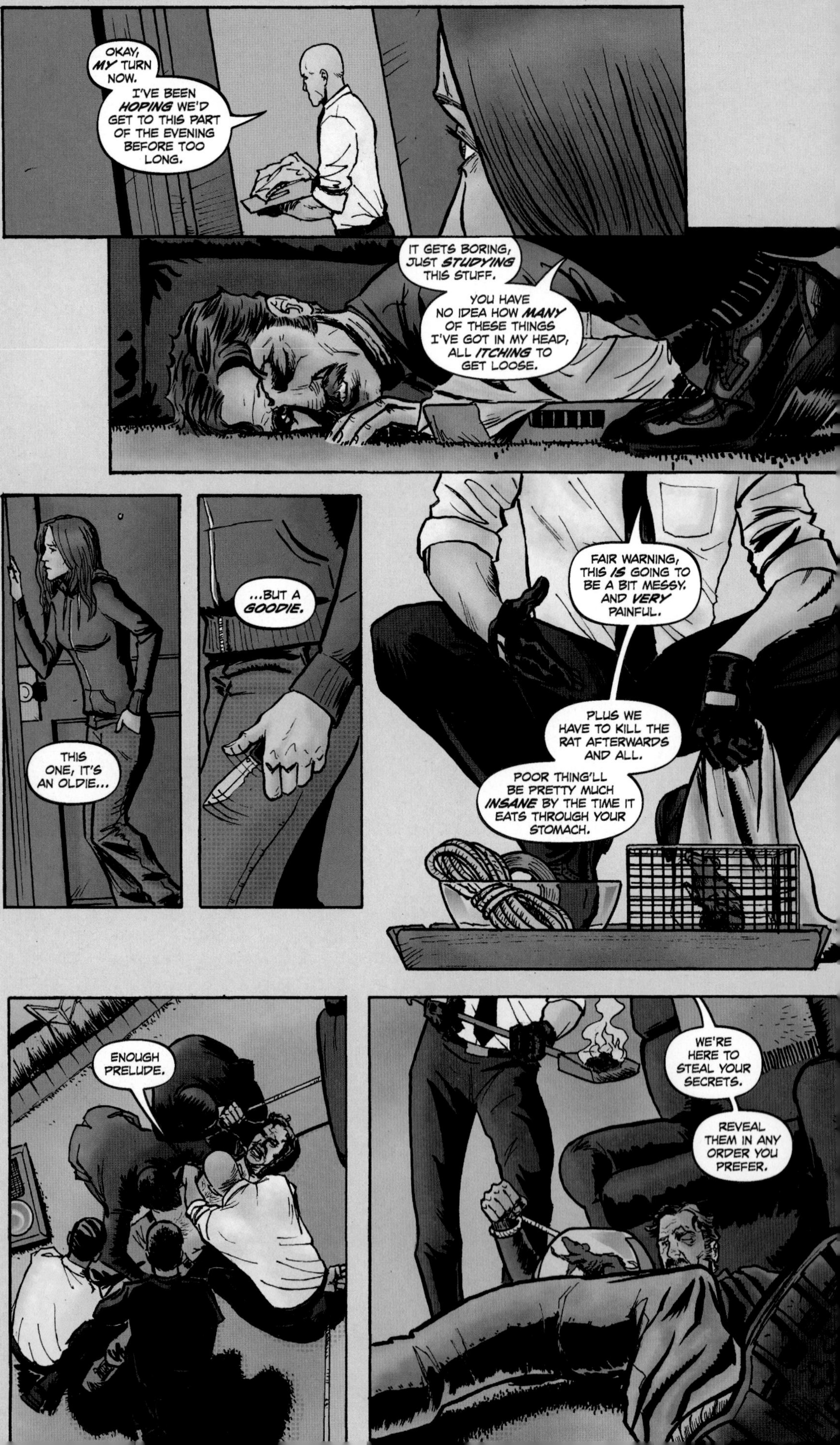
OKAY, MY TURN NOW.
I'VE BEEN HOPING WE'D GET TO THIS PART OF THE EVENING BEFORE TOO LONG.
IT GETS BORING, JUST STUDYING THIS STUFF.
YOU HAVE NO IDEA HOW MANY OF THESE THINGS I'VE GOT IN MY HEAD, ALL ITCHING TO GET LOOSE.
THIS ONE, IT'S AN OLDIE...
...BUT A GOODIE.
FAIR WARNING, THIS IS GOING TO BE A BIT MESSY. AND VERY PAINFUL.
PLUS WE HAVE TO KILL THE RAT AFTERWARDS AND ALL.
POOR THING'LL BE PRETTY MUCH INSANE BY THE TIME IT EATS THROUGH YOUR STOMACH.
ENOUGH PRELUDE.
WE'RE HERE TO STEAL YOUR SECRETS.
REVEAL THEM IN ANY ORDER YOU PREFER.

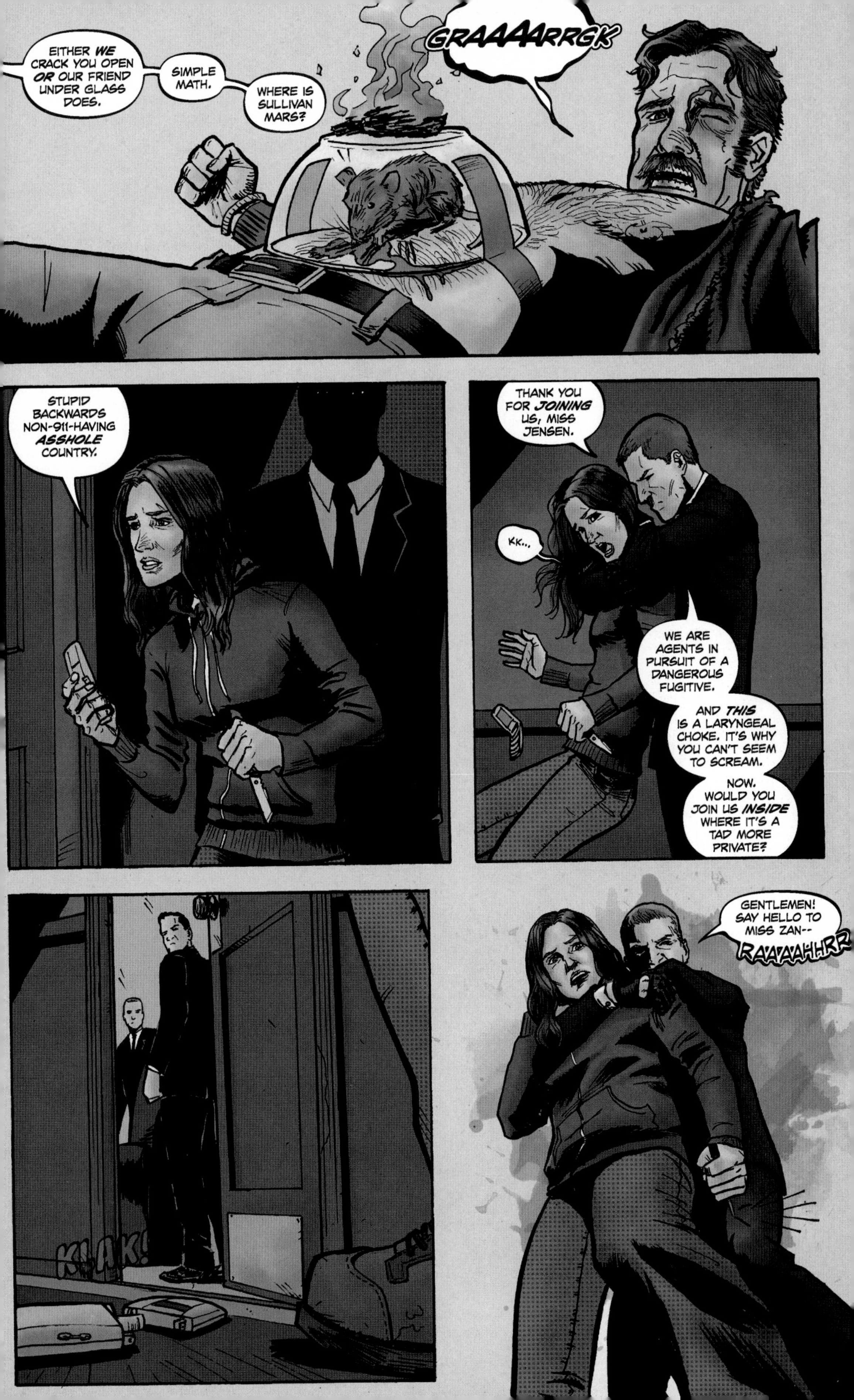
EITHER WE CRACK YOU OPEN OR OUR FRIEND UNDER GLASS DOES.
SIMPLE MATH.
WHERE IS SULLIVAN MARS?
GRAAAArrRGK
STUPID BACKWARDS NON-911-HAVING ASSHOLE COUNTRY.
THANK YOU FOR JOINING US, MISS JENSEN.
KK...
WE ARE AGENTS IN PURSUIT OF A DANGEROUS FUGITIVE.
AND THIS IS A LARYNGEAL CHOKE. IT'S WHY YOU CAN'T SEEM TO SCREAM.
NOW. WOULD YOU JOIN US INSIDE WHERE IT'S A TAD MORE PRIVATE?
KLAK!
GENTLEMEN! SAY HELLO TO MISS ZAN--
RAAAAHHRR

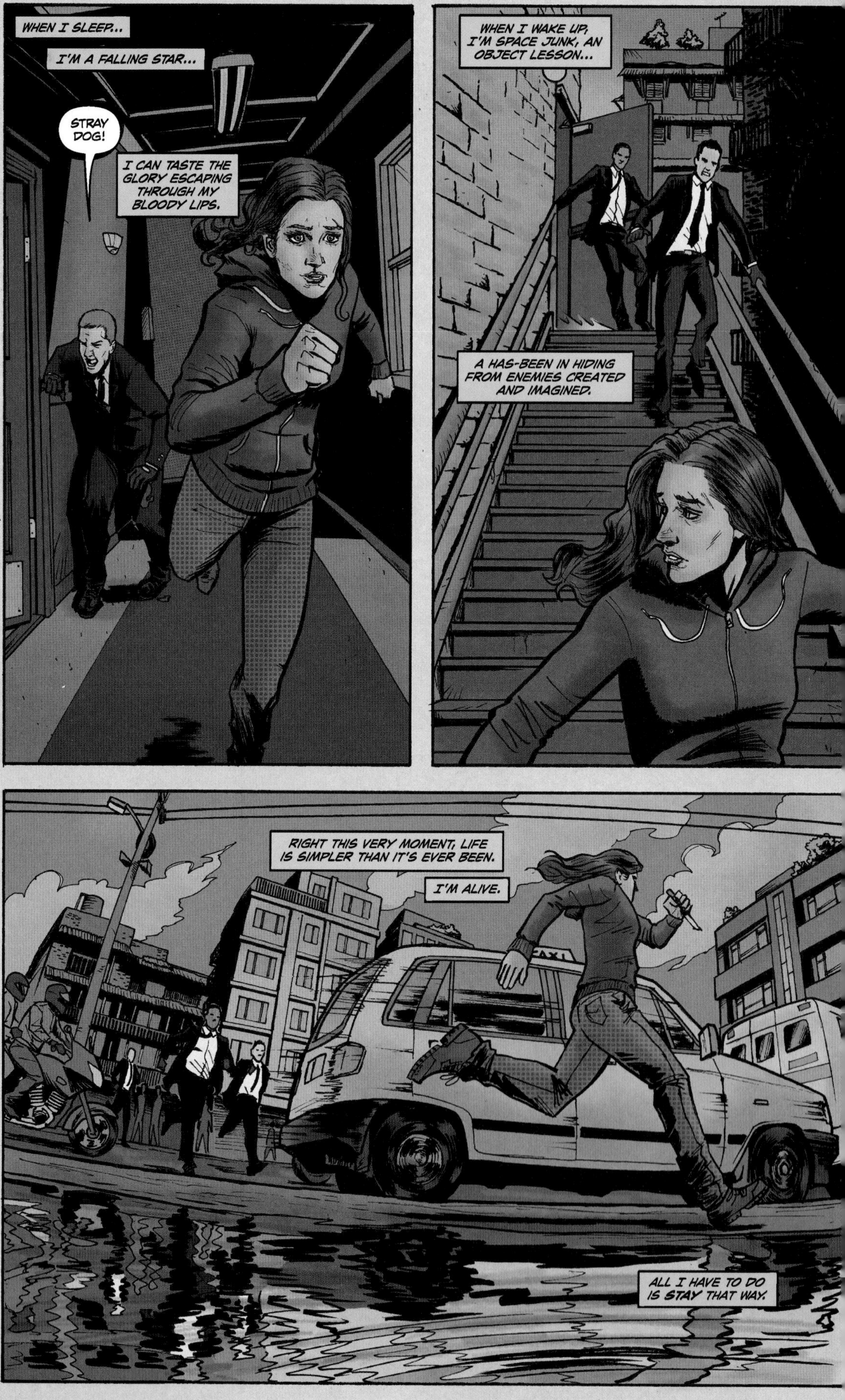
WHEN I SLEEP...
I'M A FALLING STAR...
STRAY DOG!
I CAN TASTE THE GLORY ESCAPING THROUGH MY BLOODY LIPS.
WHEN I WAKE UP, I'M SPACE JUNK, AN OBJECT LESSON...
A HAS-BEEN IN HIDING FROM ENEMIES CREATED AND IMAGINED.
RIGHT THIS VERY MOMENT, LIFE IS SIMPLER THAN IT'S EVER BEEN.
I'M ALIVE.
TAXI
ALL I HAVE TO DO IS STAY THAT WAY.

SOME HELPFUL HINTS WHEN BEING PURSUED:

BREATHE.

GET YOUR HEAD TOGETHER.

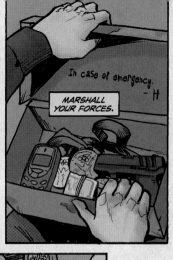

In case of emergency. —H

MARSHALL YOUR FORCES.

STAY CALM.

STAY HIGH.

THE PAST IS LUGGAGE.

PICK YOUR ESCAPE ROUTE.

AND WHEN THINGS GO SIDEWAYS...

...AND THEY ALWAYS WILL...

...BE READY TO RUN.

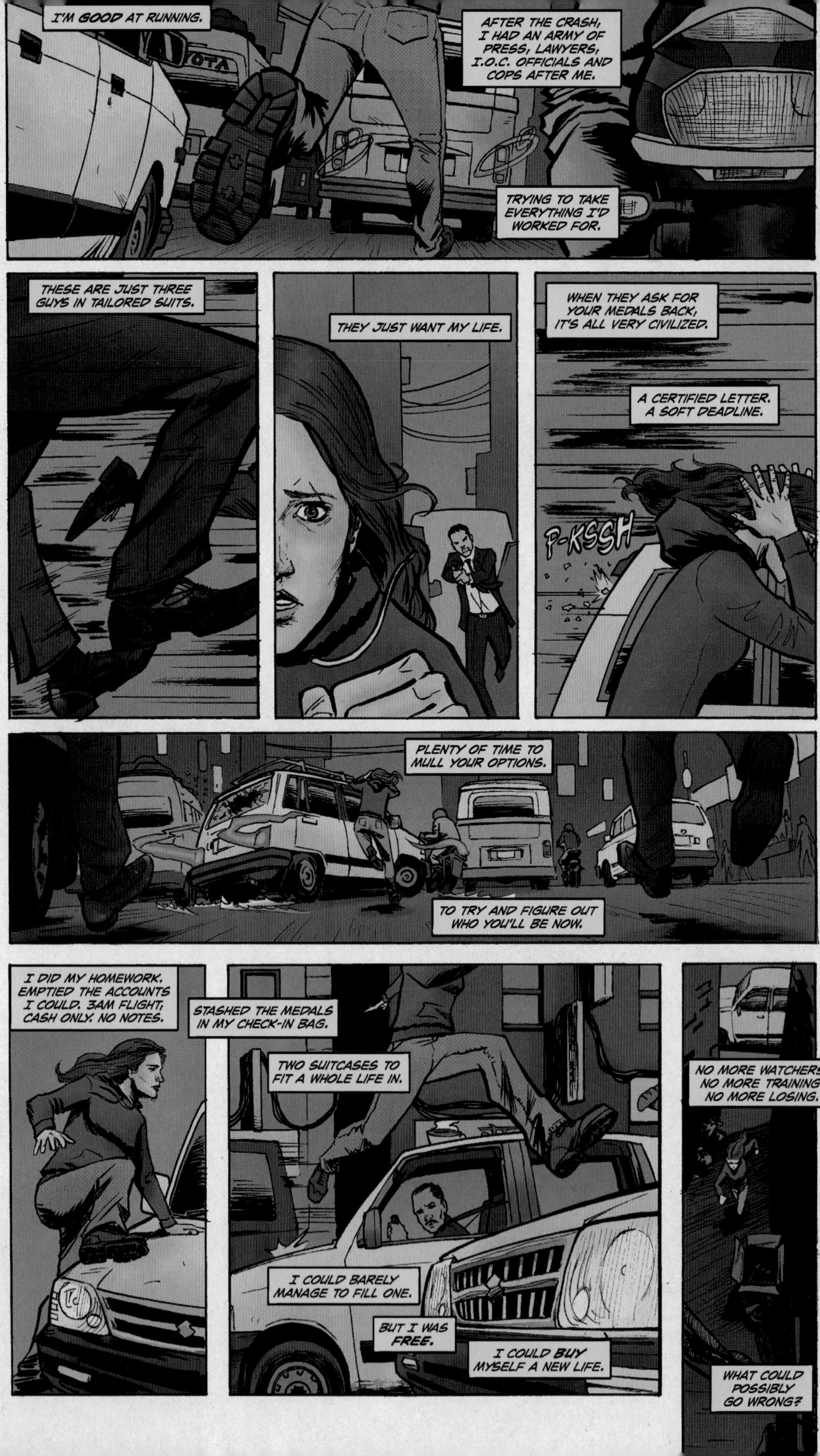
I'M GOOD AT RUNNING.
AFTER THE CRASH, I HAD AN ARMY OF PRESS, LAWYERS, I.O.C. OFFICIALS AND COPS AFTER ME.
TRYING TO TAKE EVERYTHING I'D WORKED FOR.
THESE ARE JUST THREE GUYS IN TAILORED SUITS.
THEY JUST WANT MY LIFE.
WHEN THEY ASK FOR YOUR MEDALS BACK, IT'S ALL VERY CIVILIZED.
A CERTIFIED LETTER. A SOFT DEADLINE.
P-KSSH
PLENTY OF TIME TO MULL YOUR OPTIONS.
TO TRY AND FIGURE OUT WHO YOU'LL BE NOW.
I DID MY HOMEWORK. EMPTIED THE ACCOUNTS I COULD. 3AM FLIGHT, CASH ONLY. NO NOTES.
STASHED THE MEDALS IN MY CHECK-IN BAG.
TWO SUITCASES TO FIT A WHOLE LIFE IN.
I COULD BARELY MANAGE TO FILL ONE.
BUT I WAS FREE.
I COULD BUY MYSELF A NEW LIFE.
NO MORE WATCHERS. NO MORE TRAINING. NO MORE LOSING.
WHAT COULD POSSIBLY GO WRONG?

FIRST I BURNED MY WAY THROUGH EUROPE.

LIVING OUT ALL THOSE TEENAGE FANTASIES LOST TO A RIGOROUSLY SCHEDULED LIFE.

THINK. *THINK.* FUCK.

IT GETS A BIT SORDID. THE BITS I REMEMBER.

THEN CAME ASIA, RECOVERY.

WHERE ENLIGHTENMENT OVERTOOK HEDONISM.

IN DIRECT RELATION TO MY DWINDLING BANK BALANCE.

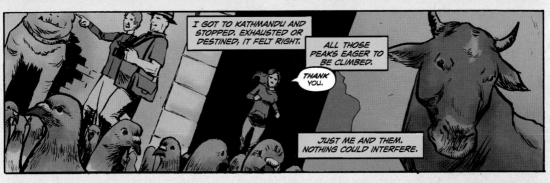

I GOT TO KATHMANDU AND STOPPED. EXHAUSTED OR DESTINED; IT FELT RIGHT.

ALL THOSE PEAKS EAGER TO BE CLIMBED.

THANK YOU.

JUST ME AND THEM. NOTHING COULD INTERFERE.

HOME AT LAST.

NO MORE RUNNING, I TOLD MYSELF.

I'M SUCH A FUCKING IDIOT SOMETIMES.

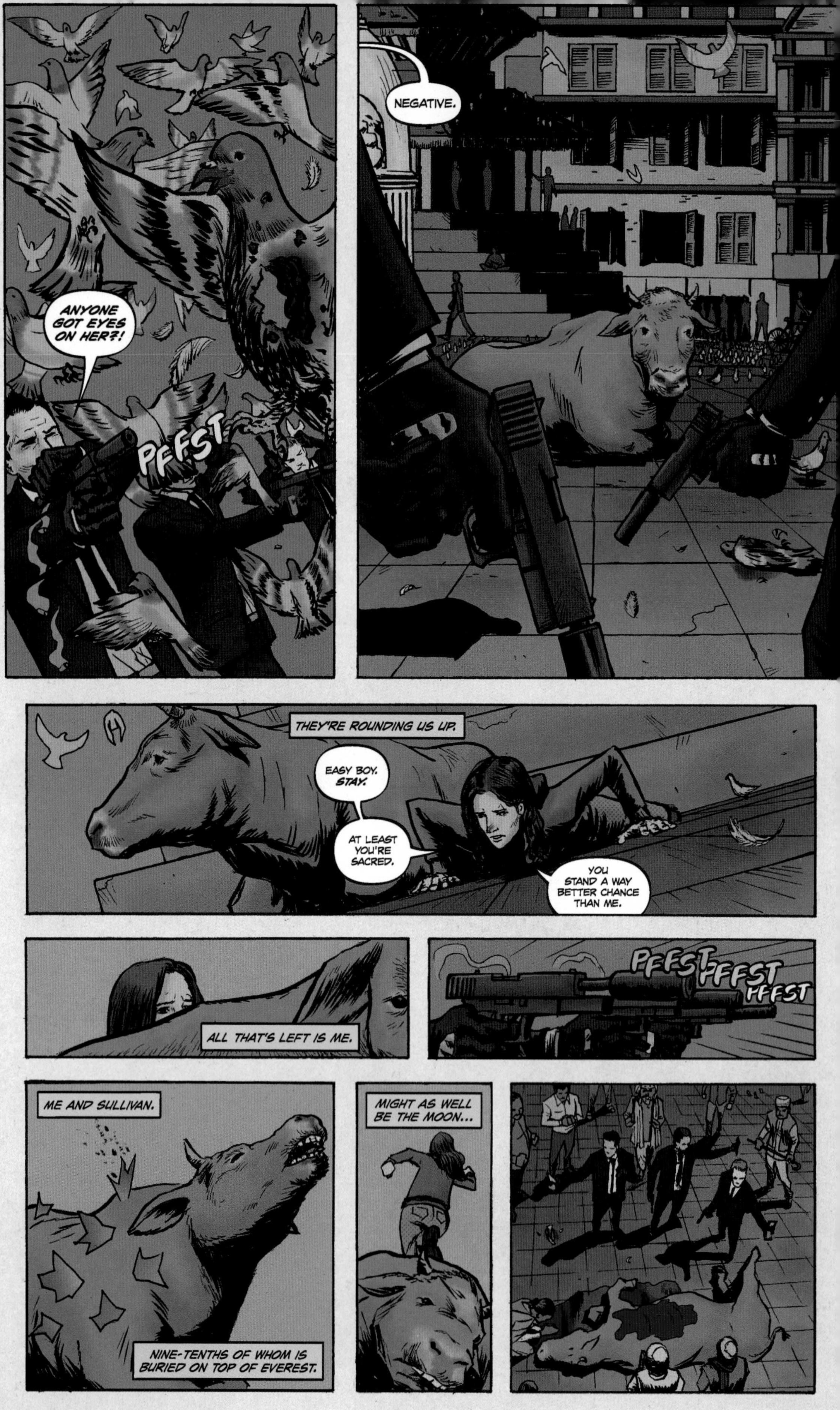
ANYONE GOT EYES ON HER?!
PFFST
NEGATIVE.
THEY'RE ROUNDING US UP.
EASY BOY. STAY.
AT LEAST YOU'RE SACRED.
YOU STAND A WAY BETTER CHANCE THAN ME.
ALL THAT'S LEFT IS ME.
PFFST PFFST PFFST
ME AND SULLIVAN.
NINE-TENTHS OF WHOM IS BURIED ON TOP OF EVEREST.
MIGHT AS WELL BE THE MOON...

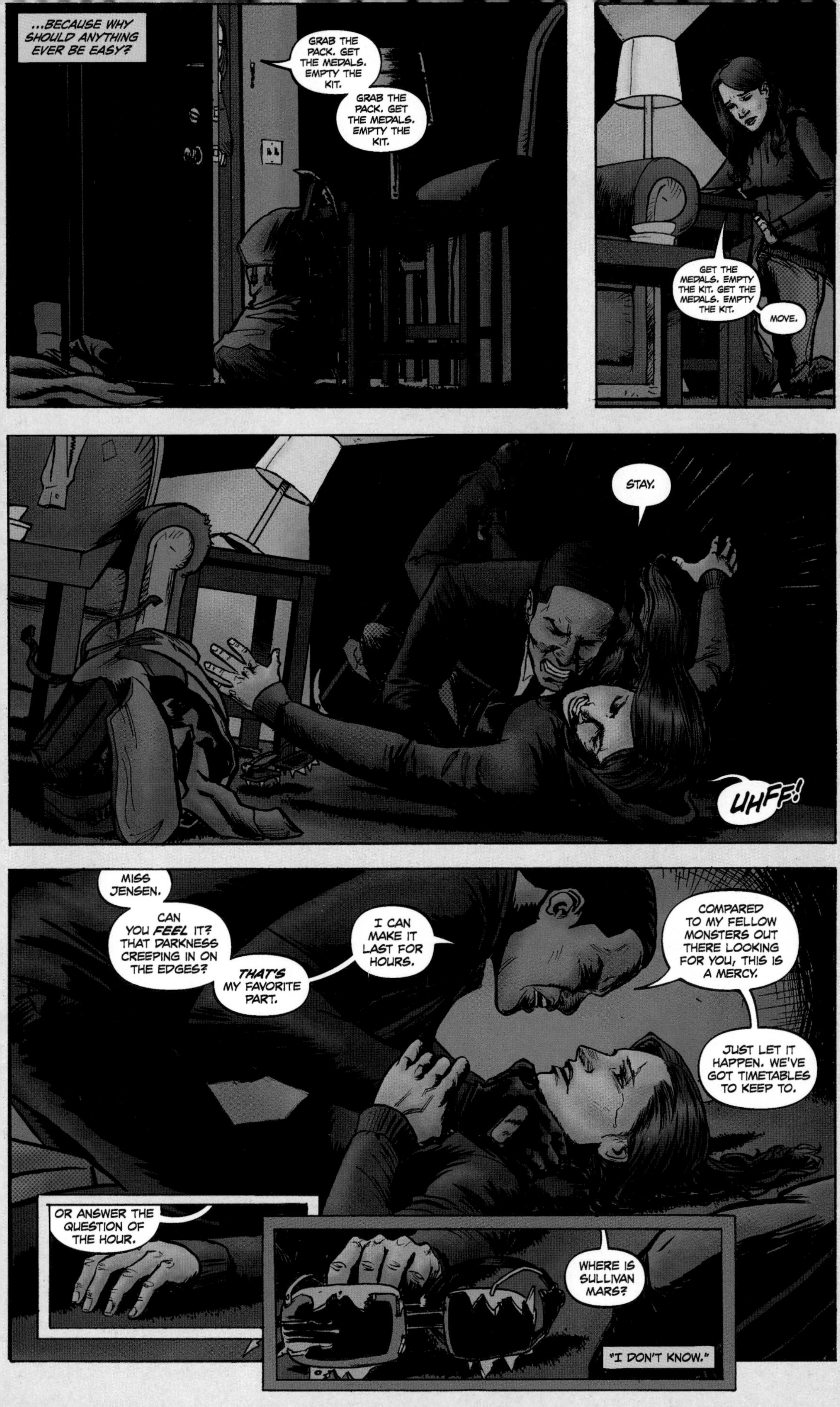
...BECAUSE WHY SHOULD ANYTHING EVER BE EASY?
GRAB THE PACK. GET THE MEDALS. EMPTY THE KIT.
GRAB THE PACK. GET THE MEDALS. EMPTY THE KIT.
GET THE MEDALS. EMPTY THE KIT. GET THE MEDALS. EMPTY THE KIT.
MOVE.
STAY.
UHFF!
MISS JENSEN.
CAN YOU FEEL IT? THAT DARKNESS CREEPING IN ON THE EDGES?
THAT'S MY FAVORITE PART.
I CAN MAKE IT LAST FOR HOURS.
COMPARED TO MY FELLOW MONSTERS OUT THERE LOOKING FOR YOU, THIS IS A MERCY.
JUST LET IT HAPPEN. WE'VE GOT TIMETABLES TO KEEP TO.
OR ANSWER THE QUESTION OF THE HOUR.
WHERE IS SULLIVAN MARS?
"I DON'T KNOW."

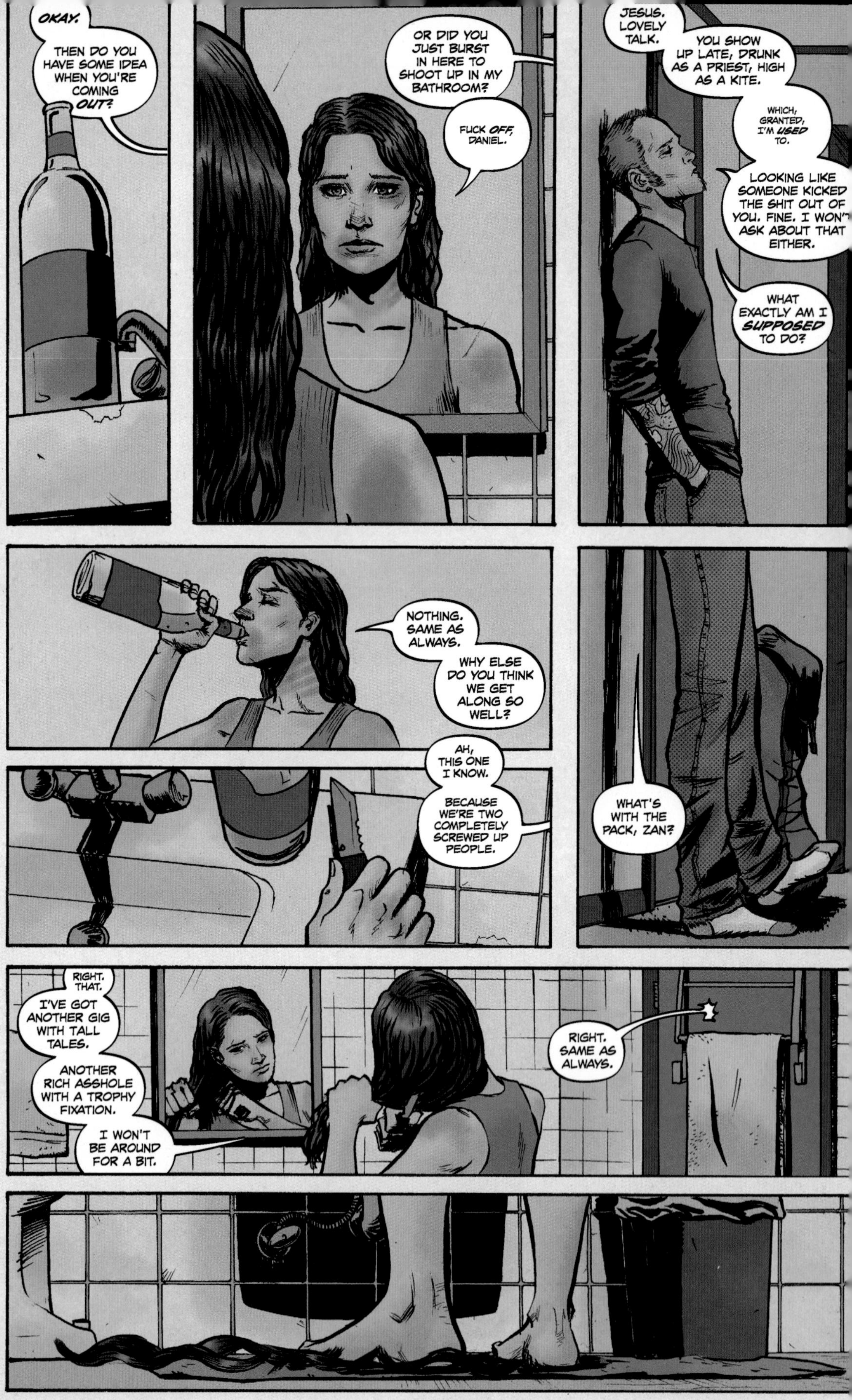
OKAY.
THEN DO YOU HAVE SOME IDEA WHEN YOU'RE COMING OUT?
OR DID YOU JUST BURST IN HERE TO SHOOT UP IN MY BATHROOM?
FUCK OFF, DANIEL.
JESUS. LOVELY TALK.
YOU SHOW UP LATE, DRUNK AS A PRIEST, HIGH AS A KITE.
WHICH, GRANTED, I'M USED TO.
LOOKING LIKE SOMEONE KICKED THE SHIT OUT OF YOU. FINE. I WON'T ASK ABOUT THAT EITHER.
WHAT EXACTLY AM I SUPPOSED TO DO?
NOTHING. SAME AS ALWAYS.
WHY ELSE DO YOU THINK WE GET ALONG SO WELL?
AH, THIS ONE I KNOW.
BECAUSE WE'RE TWO COMPLETELY SCREWED UP PEOPLE.
WHAT'S WITH THE PACK, ZAN?
RIGHT. THAT.
I'VE GOT ANOTHER GIG WITH TALL TALES.
ANOTHER RICH ASSHOLE WITH A TROPHY FIXATION.
I WON'T BE AROUND FOR A BIT.
RIGHT. SAME AS ALWAYS.

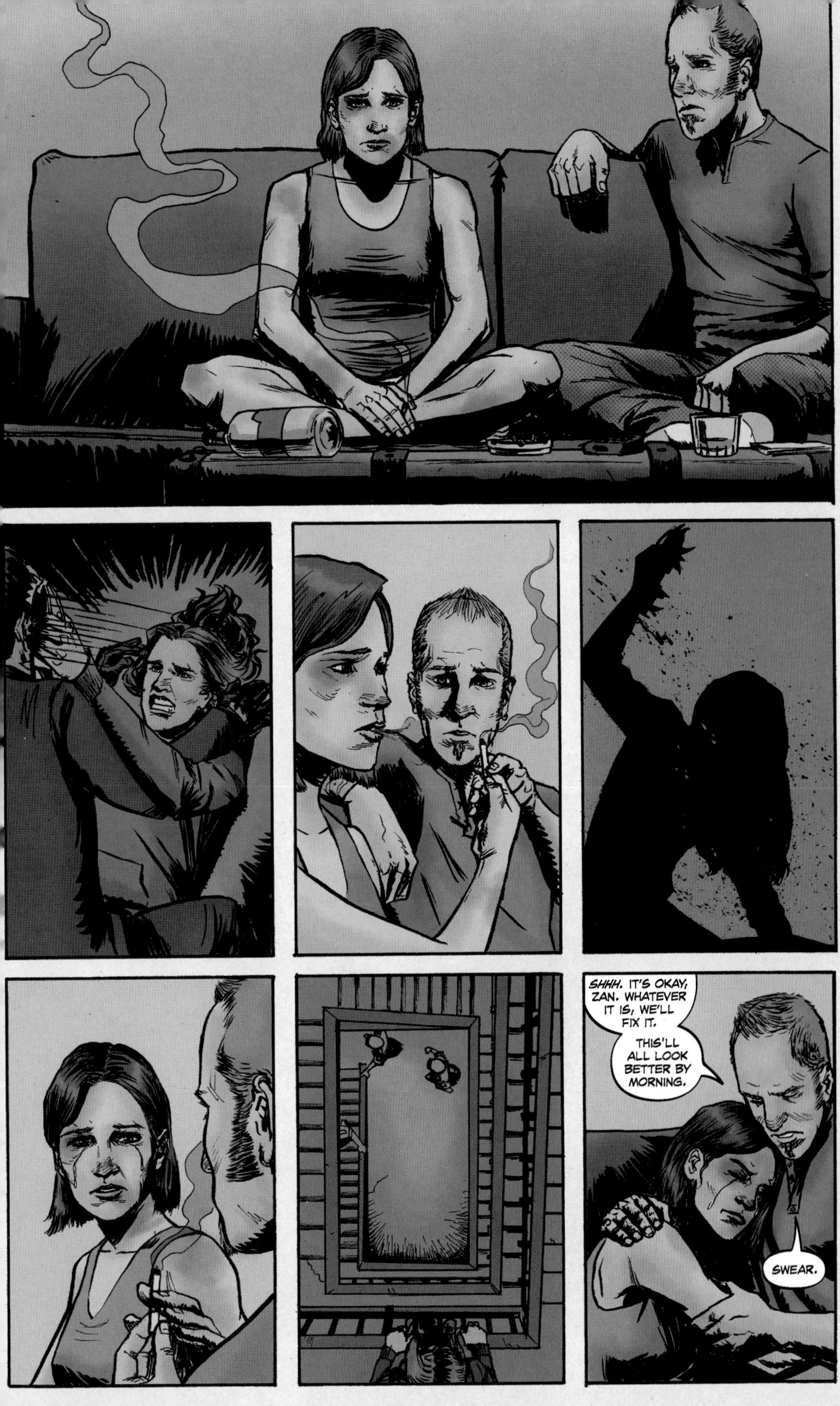
SHHH. IT'S OKAY, ZAN. WHATEVER IT IS, WE'LL FIX IT.
THIS'LL ALL LOOK BETTER BY MORNING.
SWEAR.

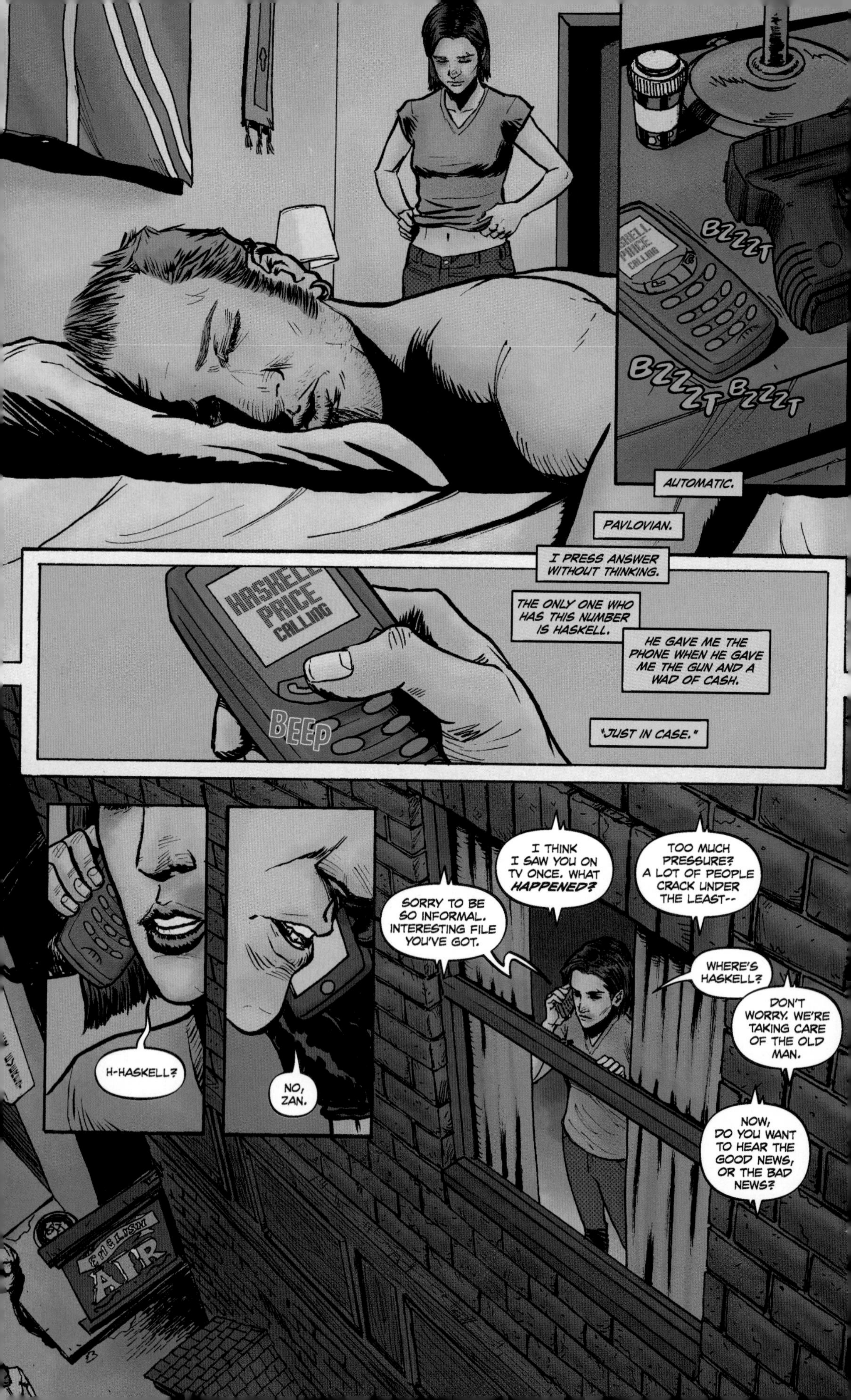
SHELL
PRICE
CALLING
BZZZT
BZZZT BZZZT
AUTOMATIC.
PAVLOVIAN.
I PRESS ANSWER WITHOUT THINKING.
HASKELL PRICE CALLING
THE ONLY ONE WHO HAS THIS NUMBER IS HASKELL.
HE GAVE ME THE PHONE WHEN HE GAVE ME THE GUN AND A WAD OF CASH.
BEEP
"JUST IN CASE."
H-HASKELL?
NO, ZAN.
SORRY TO BE SO INFORMAL. INTERESTING FILE YOU'VE GOT.
I THINK I SAW YOU ON TV ONCE. WHAT *HAPPENED?*
TOO MUCH PRESSURE? A LOT OF PEOPLE CRACK UNDER THE LEAST--
WHERE'S HASKELL?
DON'T WORRY. WE'RE TAKING CARE OF THE OLD MAN.
NOW, DO YOU WANT TO HEAR THE GOOD NEWS, OR THE BAD NEWS?
ENGLISH AIR

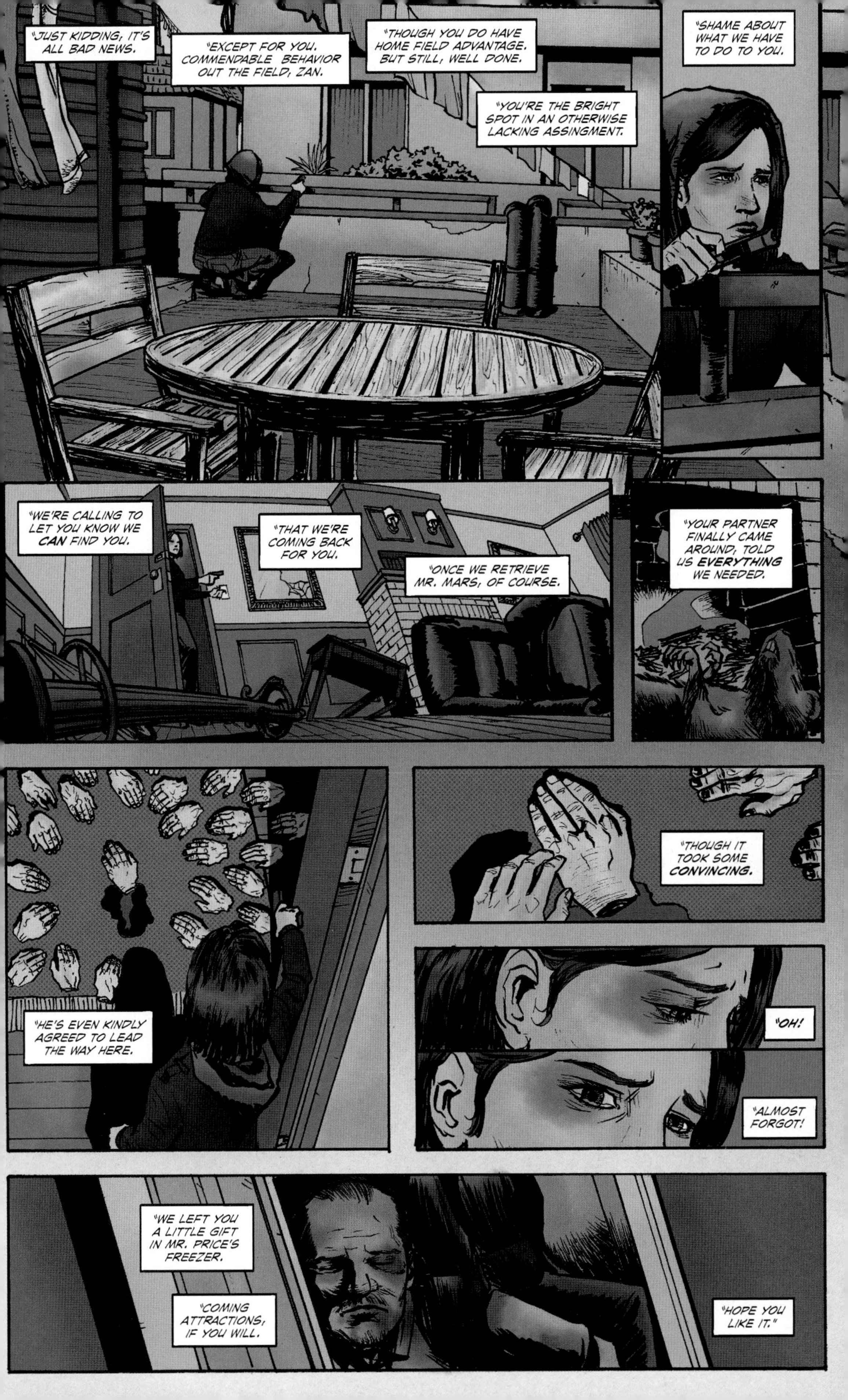
"JUST KIDDING, IT'S ALL BAD NEWS.
"EXCEPT FOR YOU. COMMENDABLE BEHAVIOR OUT THE FIELD, ZAN.
"THOUGH YOU DO HAVE HOME FIELD ADVANTAGE. BUT STILL, WELL DONE.
"YOU'RE THE BRIGHT SPOT IN AN OTHERWISE LACKING ASSINGMENT.
"SHAME ABOUT WHAT WE HAVE TO DO TO YOU.
"WE'RE CALLING TO LET YOU KNOW WE **CAN** FIND YOU.
"THAT WE'RE COMING BACK FOR YOU.
"ONCE WE RETRIEVE MR. MARS, OF COURSE.
"YOUR PARTNER FINALLY CAME AROUND, TOLD US **EVERYTHING** WE NEEDED.
"HE'S EVEN KINDLY AGREED TO LEAD THE WAY HERE.
"THOUGH IT TOOK SOME **CONVINCING.**
"OH!
"ALMOST FORGOT!
"WE LEFT YOU A LITTLE GIFT IN MR. PRICE'S FREEZER.
"COMING ATTRACTIONS, IF YOU WILL.
"HOPE YOU LIKE IT."

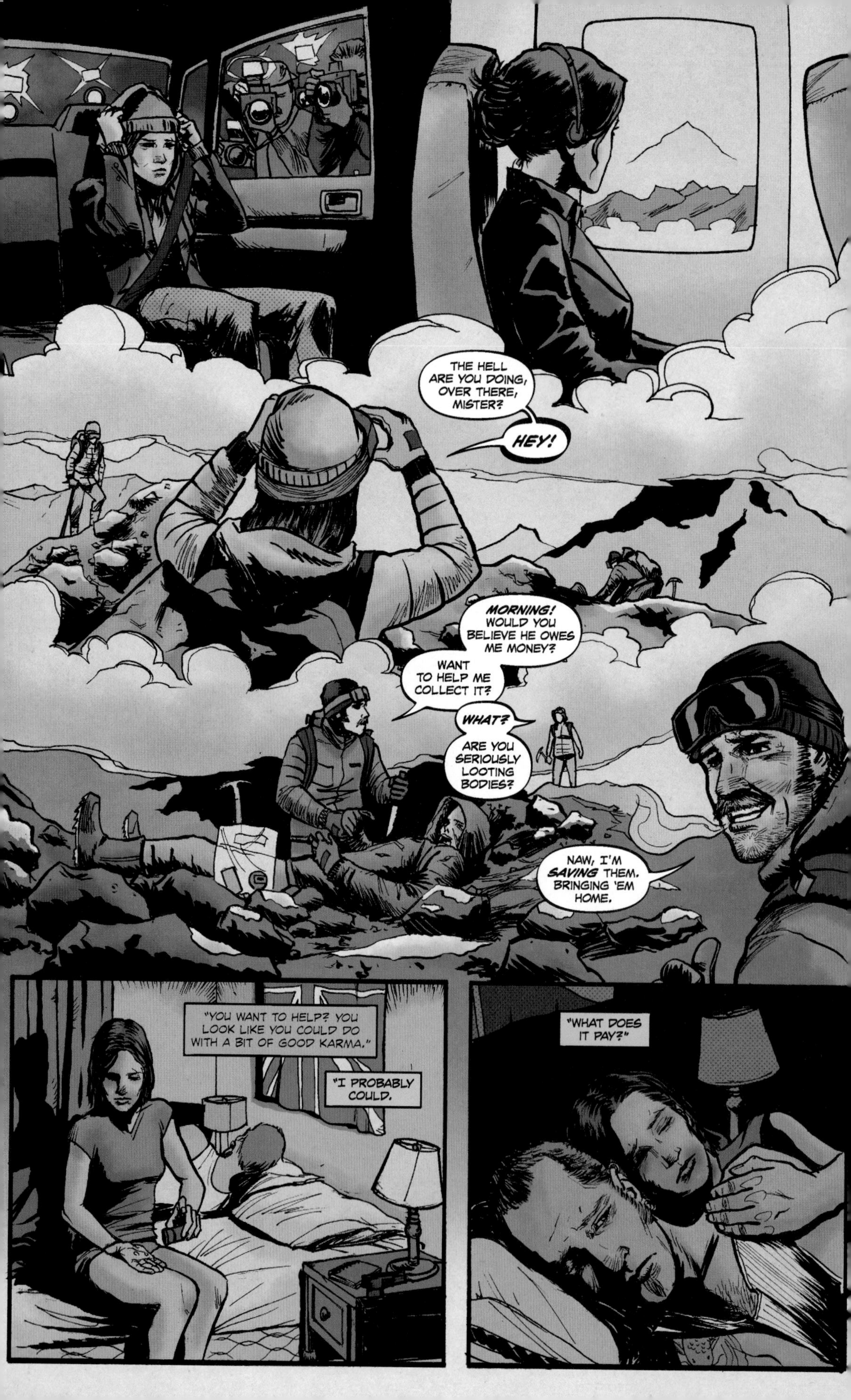
THE HELL ARE YOU DOING, OVER THERE, MISTER?
HEY!
MORNING! WOULD YOU BELIEVE HE OWES ME MONEY?
WANT TO HELP ME COLLECT IT?
WHAT?
ARE YOU SERIOUSLY LOOTING BODIES?
NAW, I'M SAVING THEM. BRINGING 'EM HOME.
"YOU WANT TO HELP? YOU LOOK LIKE YOU COULD DO WITH A BIT OF GOOD KARMA."
"I PROBABLY COULD.
"WHAT DOES IT PAY?"

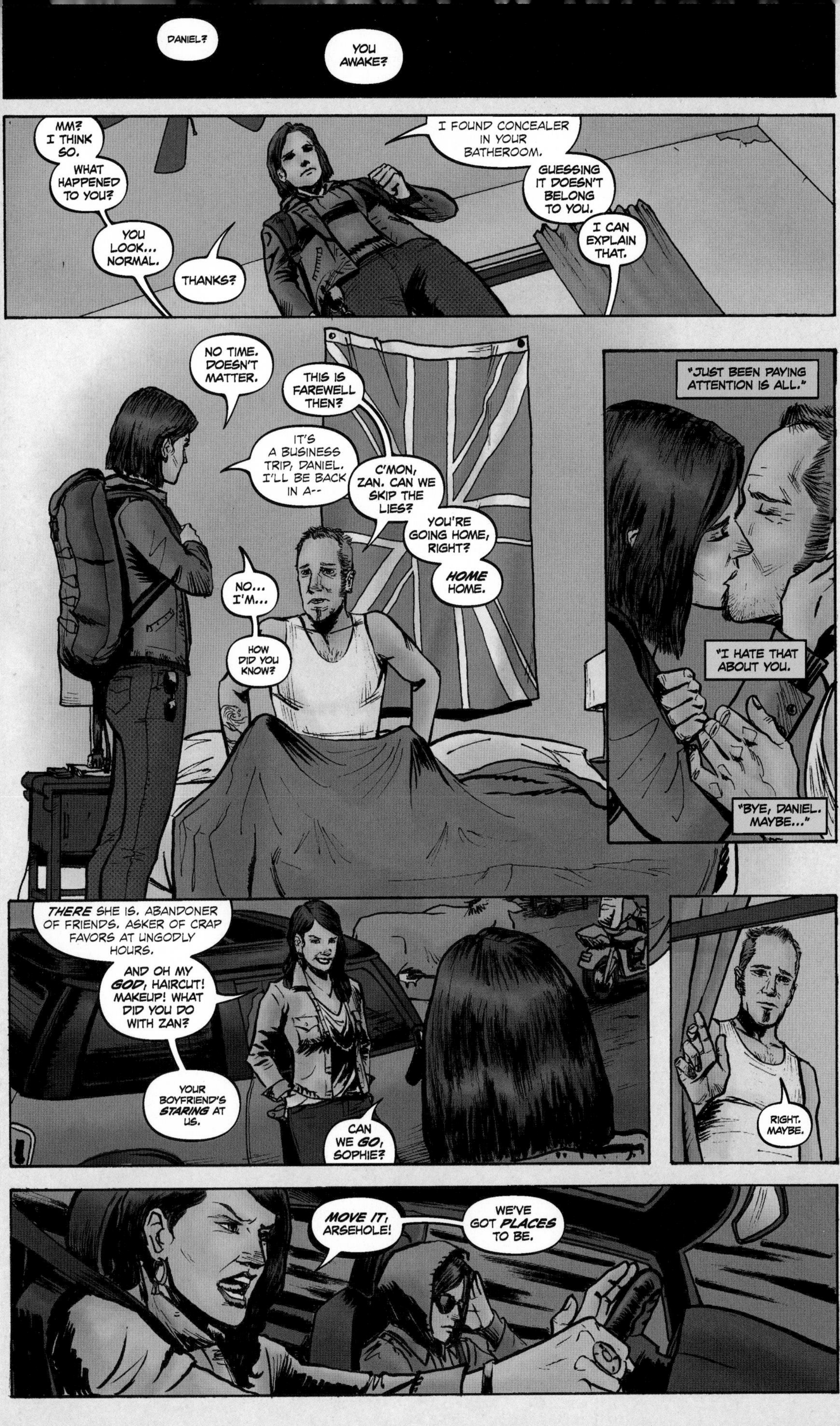

DANIEL?
YOU AWAKE?
MM? I THINK SO.
WHAT HAPPENED TO YOU?
YOU LOOK... NORMAL.
THANKS?
I FOUND CONCEALER IN YOUR BATHEROOM.
GUESSING IT DOESN'T BELONG TO YOU.
I CAN EXPLAIN THAT.
NO TIME. DOESN'T MATTER.
THIS IS FAREWELL THEN?
IT'S A BUSINESS TRIP, DANIEL. I'LL BE BACK IN A--
C'MON, ZAN. CAN WE SKIP THE LIES?
YOU'RE GOING HOME, RIGHT?
HOME HOME.
NO... I'M...
HOW DID YOU KNOW?
"JUST BEEN PAYING ATTENTION IS ALL."
"I HATE THAT ABOUT YOU.
"BYE, DANIEL. MAYBE..."
THERE SHE IS. ABANDONER OF FRIENDS. ASKER OF CRAP FAVORS AT UNGODLY HOURS.
AND OH MY *GOD*, HAIRCUT! MAKEUP! WHAT DID YOU DO WITH ZAN?
YOUR BOYFRIEND'S *STARING* AT US.
CAN WE *GO*, SOPHIE?
RIGHT. MAYBE.
MOVE IT, ARSEHOLE!
WE'VE GOT *PLACES* TO BE.

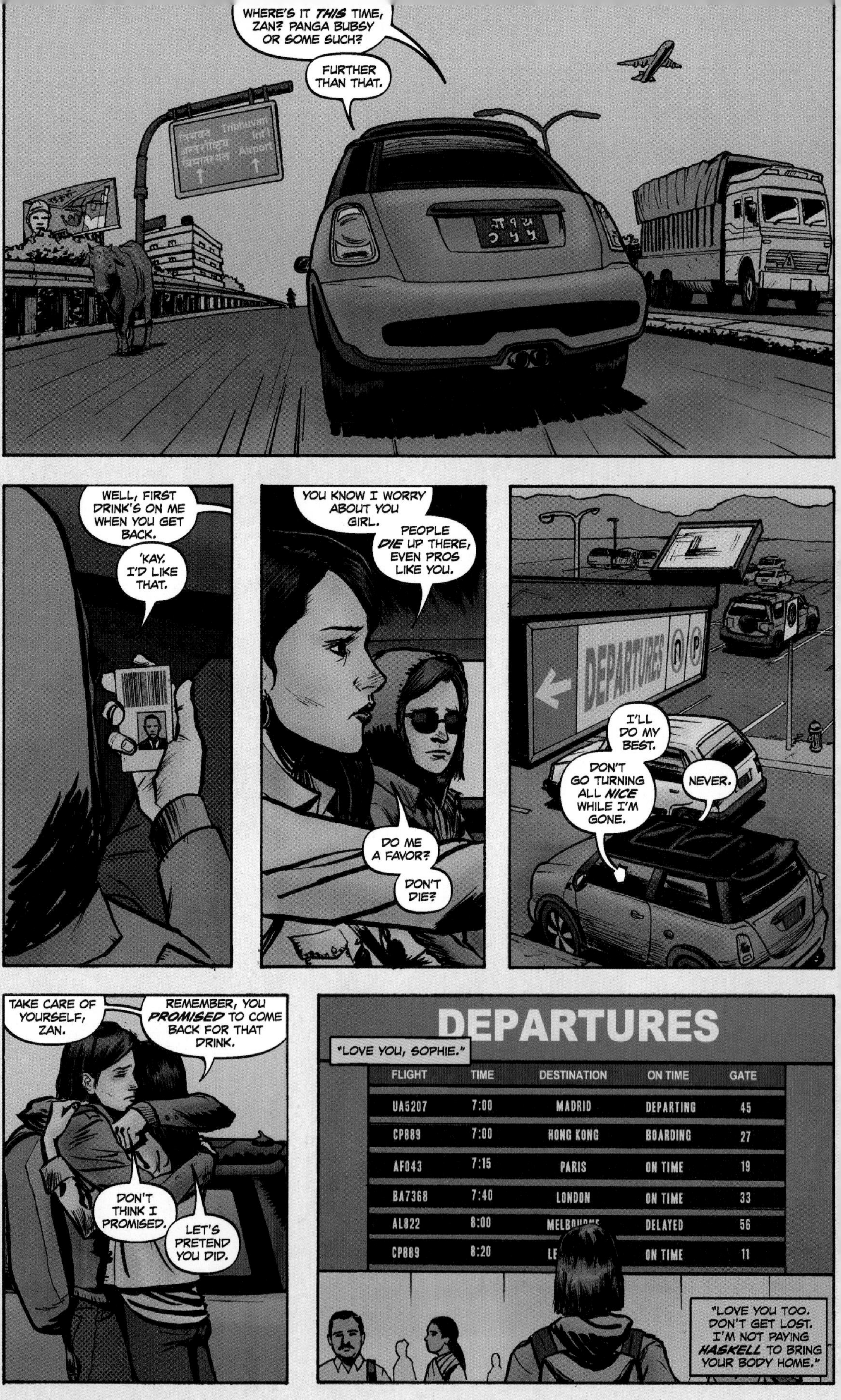
WHERE'S IT THIS TIME, ZAN? PANGA BUBSY OR SOME SUCH?
FURTHER THAN THAT.
Tribhuvan Int'l Airport
WELL, FIRST DRINK'S ON ME WHEN YOU GET BACK.
'KAY. I'D LIKE THAT.
YOU KNOW I WORRY ABOUT YOU GIRL.
PEOPLE DIE UP THERE, EVEN PROS LIKE YOU.
DO ME A FAVOR?
DON'T DIE?
DEPARTURES
I'LL DO MY BEST.
DON'T GO TURNING ALL NICE WHILE I'M GONE.
NEVER.
TAKE CARE OF YOURSELF, ZAN.
REMEMBER, YOU PROMISED TO COME BACK FOR THAT DRINK.
DON'T THINK I PROMISED.
LET'S PRETEND YOU DID.
DEPARTURES
"LOVE YOU, SOPHIE."
FLIGHT TIME DESTINATION ON TIME GATE
UA5207 7:00 MADRID DEPARTING 45
CP889 7:00 HONG KONG BOARDING 27
AF043 7:15 PARIS ON TIME 19
BA7368 7:40 LONDON ON TIME 33
AL822 8:00 DELAYED 56
CP889 8:20 ON TIME 11
"LOVE YOU TOO. DON'T GET LOST. I'M NOT PAYING HASKELL TO BRING YOUR BODY HOME."

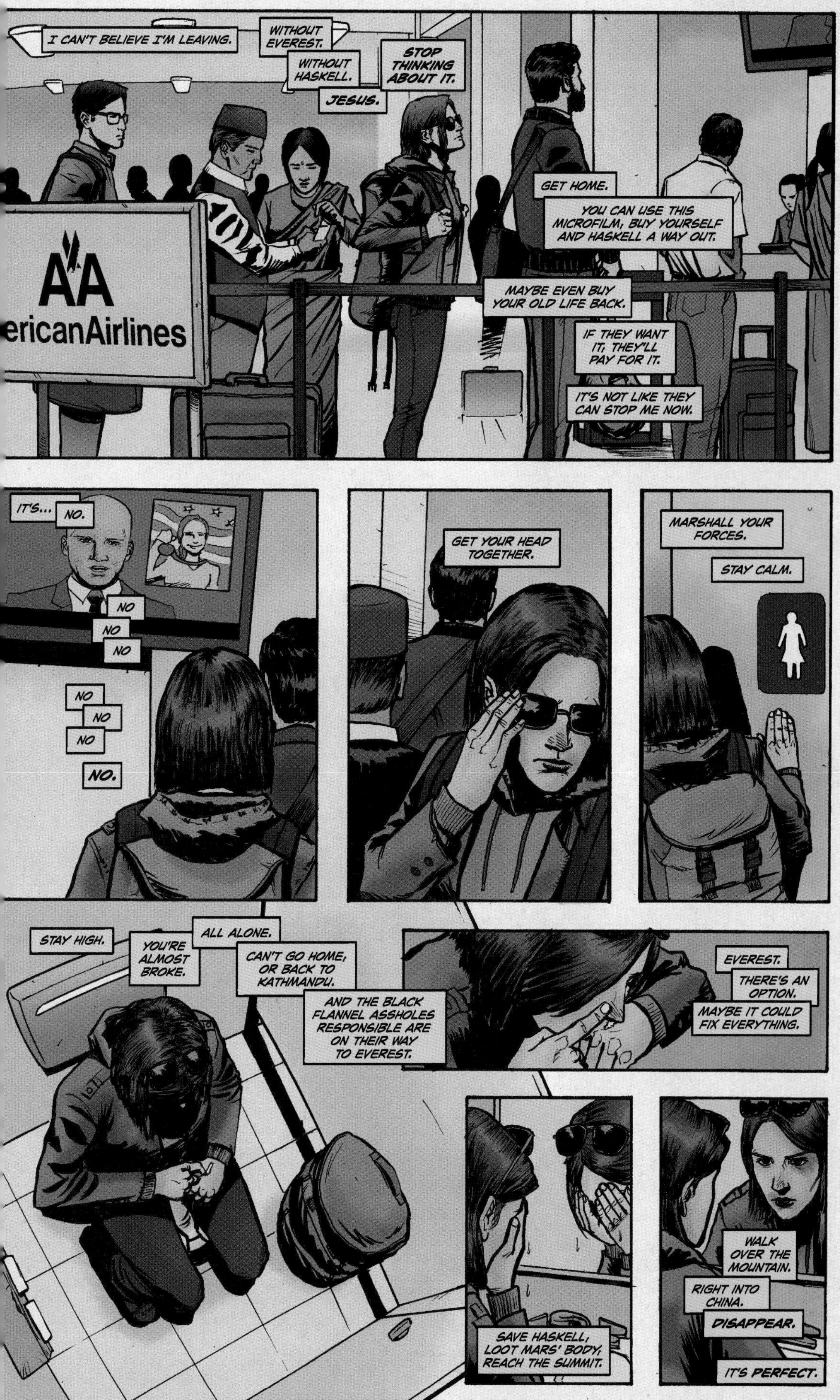

I CAN'T BELIEVE I'M LEAVING.
WITHOUT EVEREST.
WITHOUT HASKELL.
JESUS.
STOP THINKING ABOUT IT.
AA
ericanAirlines
GET HOME.
YOU CAN USE THIS MICROFILM, BUY YOURSELF AND HASKELL A WAY OUT.
MAYBE EVEN BUY YOUR OLD LIFE BACK.
IF THEY WANT IT, THEY'LL PAY FOR IT.
IT'S NOT LIKE THEY CAN STOP ME NOW.
IT'S...
NO.
NO
NO
NO
NO
NO
NO
NO.
GET YOUR HEAD TOGETHER.
MARSHALL YOUR FORCES.
STAY CALM.
STAY HIGH.
YOU'RE ALMOST BROKE.
ALL ALONE.
CAN'T GO HOME, OR BACK TO KATHMANDU.
AND THE BLACK FLANNEL ASSHOLES RESPONSIBLE ARE ON THEIR WAY TO EVEREST.
EVEREST.
THERE'S AN OPTION.
MAYBE IT COULD FIX EVERYTHING.
SAVE HASKELL, LOOT MARS' BODY, REACH THE SUMMIT.
WALK OVER THE MOUNTAIN.
RIGHT INTO CHINA.
DISAPPEAR.
IT'S PERFECT.

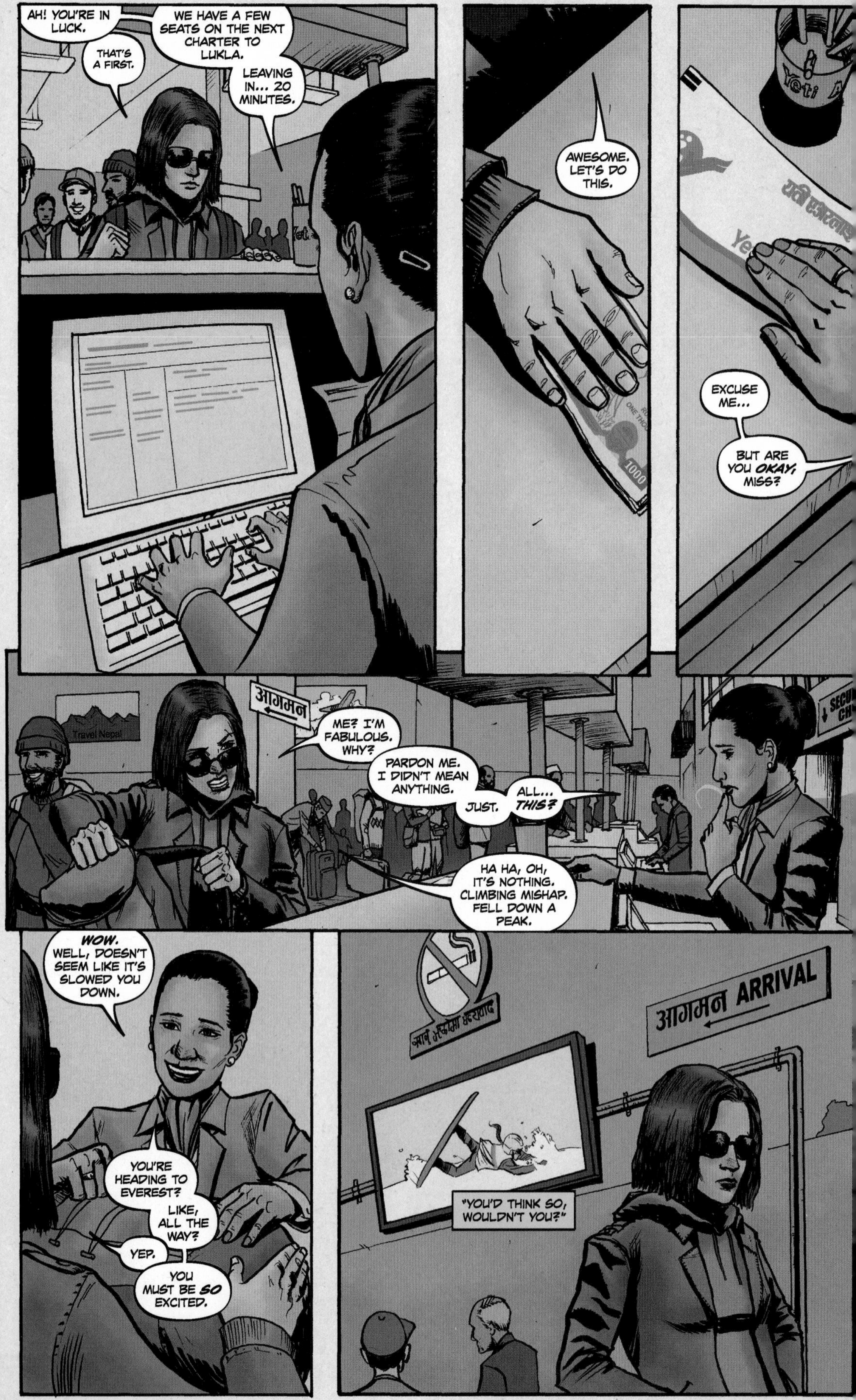

AH! YOU'RE IN LUCK.
THAT'S A FIRST.
WE HAVE A FEW SEATS ON THE NEXT CHARTER TO LUKLA.
LEAVING IN... 20 MINUTES.
AWESOME. LET'S DO THIS.
EXCUSE ME...
BUT ARE YOU *OKAY*, MISS?
आगमन
Travel Nepal
ME? I'M FABULOUS. WHY?
PARDON ME. I DIDN'T MEAN ANYTHING.
JUST.
ALL... *THIS?*
HA HA, OH, IT'S NOTHING. CLIMBING MISHAP. FELL DOWN A PEAK.
WOW. WELL, DOESN'T SEEM LIKE IT'S SLOWED YOU DOWN.
YOU'RE HEADING TO EVEREST?
LIKE, ALL THE WAY?
YEP.
YOU MUST BE *SO* EXCITED.
आगमन ARRIVAL
"YOU'D THINK SO, WOULDN'T YOU?"

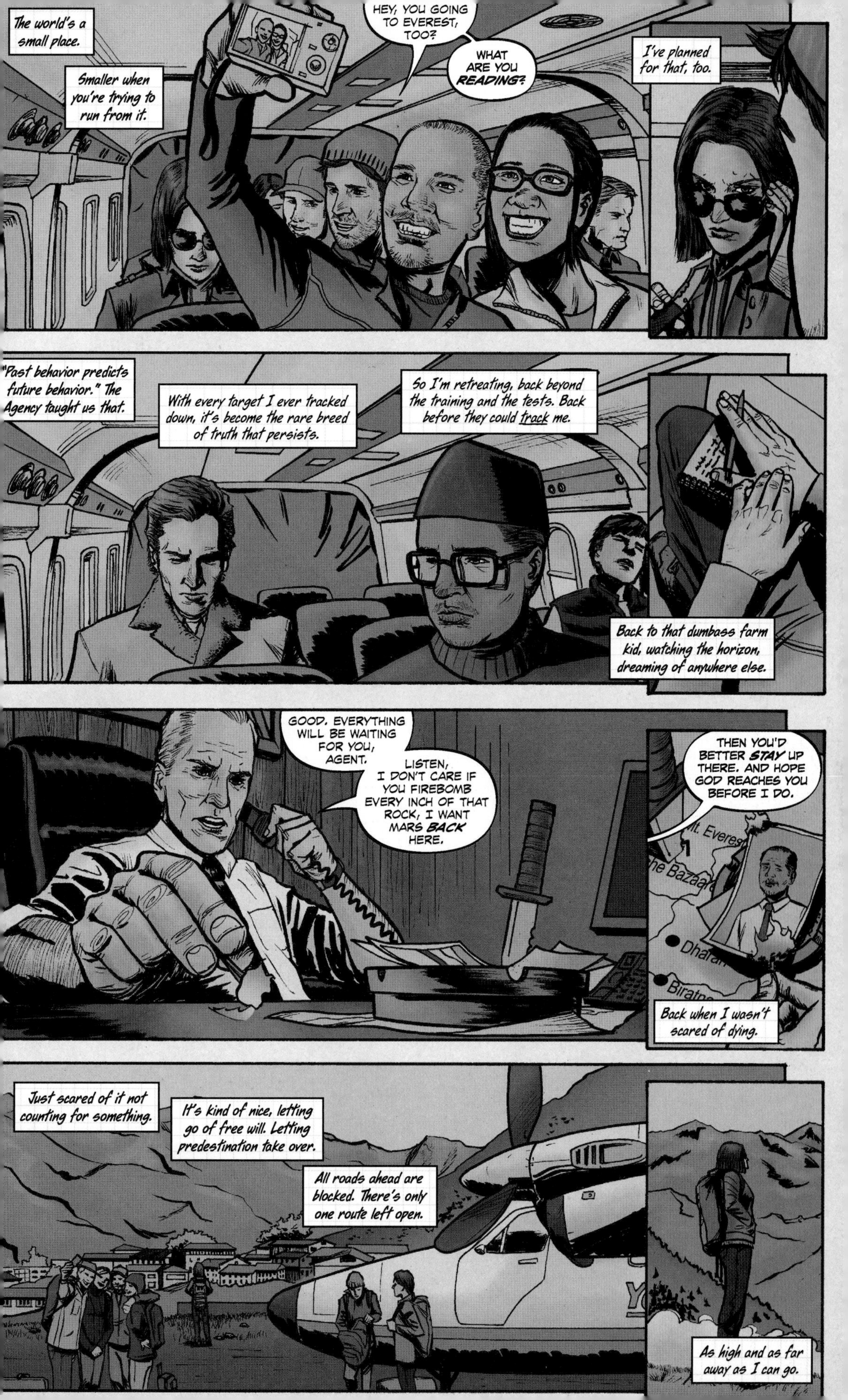
The world's a small place.
Smaller when you're trying to run from it.
HEY, YOU GOING TO EVEREST, TOO?
WHAT ARE YOU **READING?**
I've planned for that, too.
"Past behavior predicts future behavior." The Agency taught us that.
With every target I ever tracked down, it's become the rare breed of truth that persists.
So I'm retreating, back beyond the training and the tests. Back before they could track me.
Back to that dumbass farm kid, watching the horizon, dreaming of anywhere else.
GOOD. EVERYTHING WILL BE WAITING FOR YOU, AGENT.
LISTEN, I DON'T CARE IF YOU FIREBOMB EVERY INCH OF THAT ROCK, I WANT MARS **BACK** HERE.
THEN YOU'D BETTER **STAY** UP THERE. AND HOPE GOD REACHES YOU BEFORE I DO.
Back when I wasn't scared of dying.
Just scared of it not counting for something.
It's kind of nice, letting go of free will. Letting predestination take over.
All roads ahead are blocked. There's only one route left open.
As high and as far away as I can go.

Let me show you how to

CLIMB EVEREST

as a PRACTICAL PROFESSION

Train in . . . JUST 12 WEEKS!

AVERAGE PROFIT per CLIMB USUALLY $1700

EXPLORE THE ROOF OF THE WORLD

Demand far exceeds supply — Work is steady in good times or bad — Offers opportunities for travel, fine social contacts, luxurious living. Win respect and honor in this humane profession!

The slopes of Mount Everest have grown more crowded, creating a demand for adventure guides – who can be trained in 12 weeks of very exciting study in and around the Himalayas – that shows no signs of stopping!

No months or years of apprenticeship are needed. You don't start as a beginner at low pay. You don't need to be a sherpa to graduate from our training program. Turn your love of climbing from a passion into a payday in your spare time – without giving up your present job. Within 3 short months, you can be ready to enjoy the security and good income; the social advantages! luxurious living in four star hotels or on the flanks of majestic peaks most dare not dream of; and opportunities for travel that make Professional Guiding such a wonderful profession for men and women of all ages.

Shortage of Climbing Guides Increases on Mount Everest

Kathmandu — Local climbing expedition outfits say the present shortage of climbing guides is almost a national emergency. There will not be enough guides to meet the demand until at

You can easily find out all about Professional Guiding without investing any money. Simply fill out and mail the coupon below, or a postcard, for a free copy of our fascinating 16-page book, "Careers in Climbing." Read about all the things you will learn – how easily you will absorb the training. See the wonderful opportunities open to you. Contrast the life of a climbing guide with that of any other profession that combines adventure and accomplishment all in one. Then see how this can be yours for a low enrollment fee.

Hundreds of hobby climbers, amateur alpinists and thrill seekers have given up their "blind alley" drudgery to embrace the world-respected profession of Professional Guide, some earning as much as $1700 per climb.

Thus they have gained increased pay, steady work, fascinating co-workers from all cultures and opportunities for contacts with interesting clients – people of wealth and position – on a level of equality and respect. You can certainly do the same!

Send your name today. There is no charge, now or ever, for this interesting book. It is your free, and postage prepaid. No salesman will call to bother you. Read it in the quiet of your own home. Then decide whether the romance of guiding people to their dreams atop the cloudy summits appeals more to you than the drudgery of ordinary work. Mail the coupon today. This one little step may be the most important you've ever taken.

FREE BOOKLET

CAREERS IN CLIMBING
TALL TALES
ADVENTURE CONSULTANTS

READ WHAT GRADUATES SAY . . .

"After graduation, with all my lessons, I got hired by Tall Tales, now I'm making a living doing what I love!"
Ms. Z. Jensen, Kathmandu

"The graduates of Tall Tales are the finest guides available. The next best thing to having your own sherpa next to you."
Sherpa D. Baral, Namche Bazaar

TALL TALES SCHOOL OF CLIMBING GUIDES
DEPT 402, GPO 5313, THAMEL KATHMANDU, NEPAL

JUST MAIL THIS COUPON
(OR SEND A POSTCARD)

TALL TALES ADVENTURE CONSULTANTS, DEPT. 402
GPO 5313, THAMEL - KATHMANDU, NEPAL

Send me, without obligation, your FREE 16-page book "Careers in Climbing"

NAME ______________________
(Please Print)

ADDRESS ______________________

____

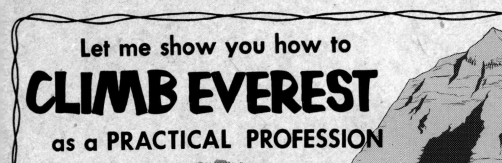

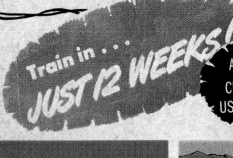

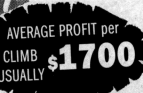

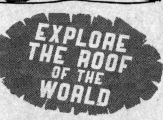

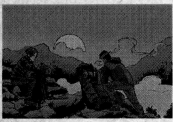

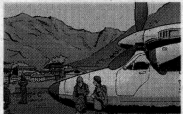

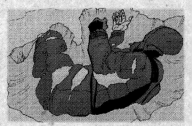

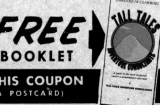

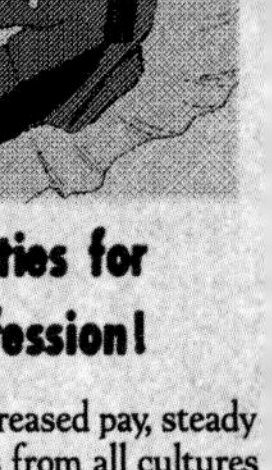

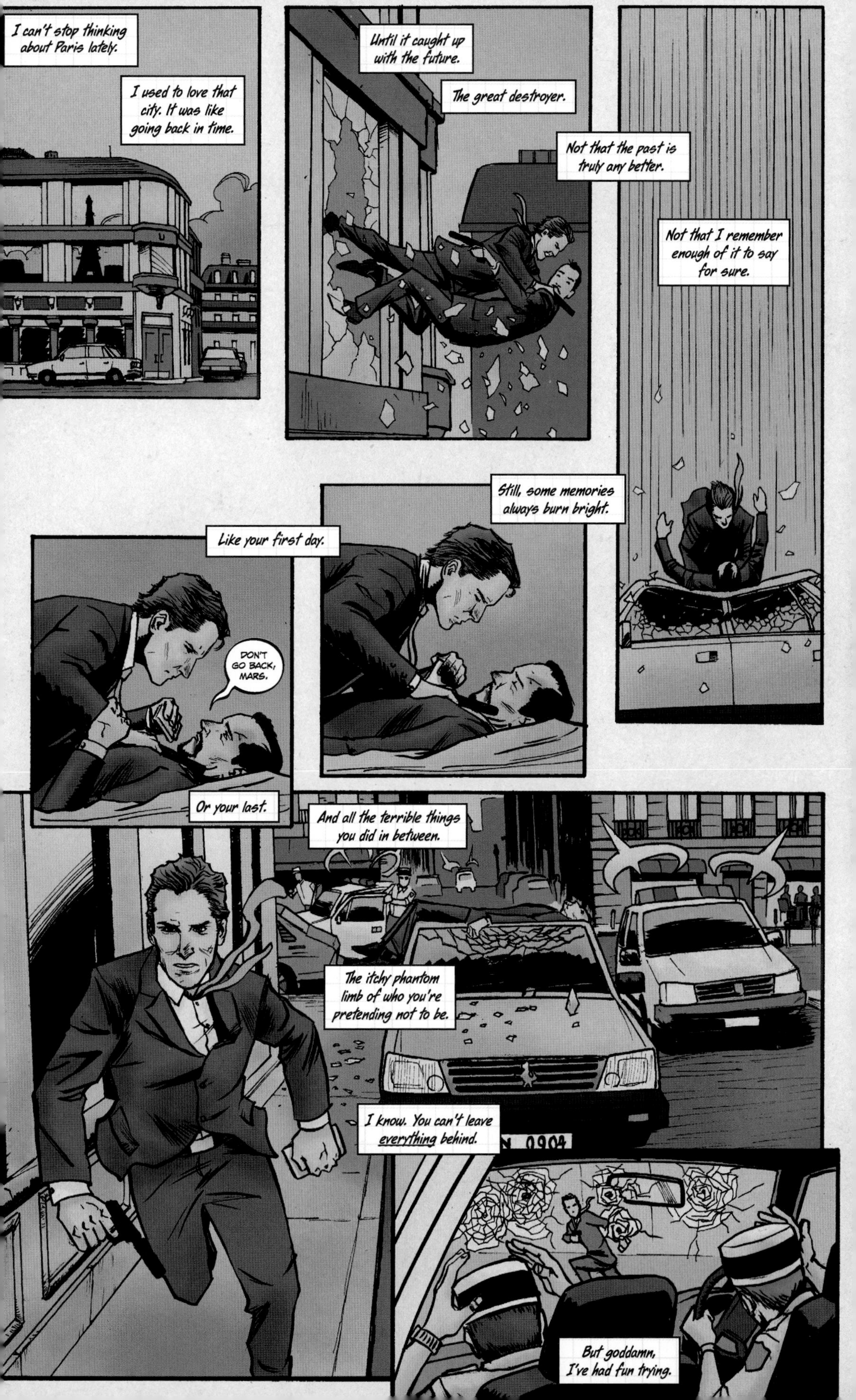
I can't stop thinking about Paris lately.
I used to love that city. It was like going back in time.
Until it caught up with the future.
The great destroyer.
Not that the past is truly any better.
Not that I remember enough of it to say for sure.
Still, some memories always burn bright.
Like your first day.
DON'T GO BACK, MARS.
Or your last.
And all the terrible things you did in between.
The itchy phantom limb of who you're pretending not to be.
I know. You can't leave everything behind.
But goddamn, I've had fun trying.

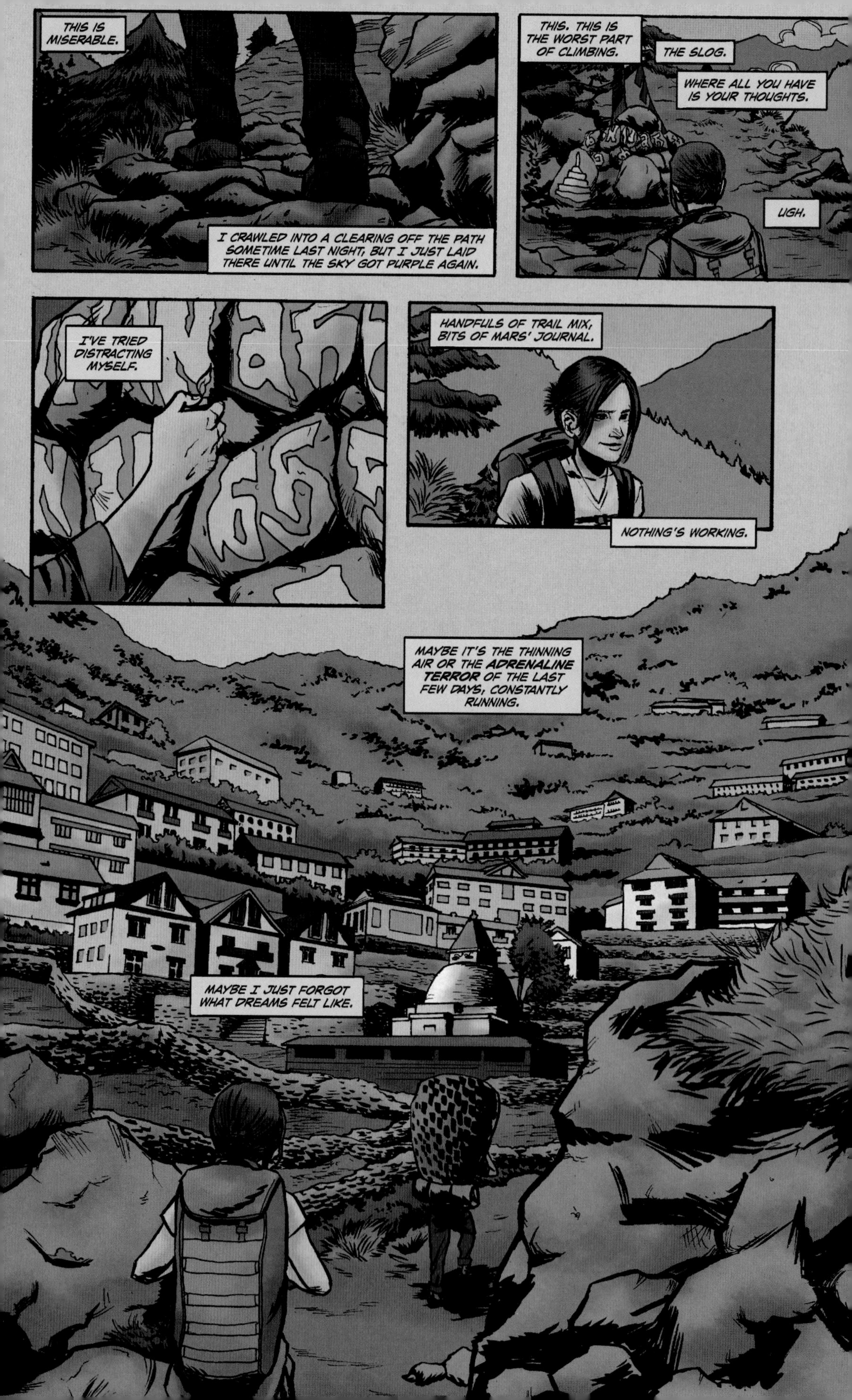
THIS IS MISERABLE.
I CRAWLED INTO A CLEARING OFF THE PATH SOMETIME LAST NIGHT, BUT I JUST LAID THERE UNTIL THE SKY GOT PURPLE AGAIN.
THIS. THIS IS THE WORST PART OF CLIMBING.
THE SLOG.
WHERE ALL YOU HAVE IS YOUR THOUGHTS.
UGH.
I'VE TRIED DISTRACTING MYSELF.
HANDFULS OF TRAIL MIX, BITS OF MARS' JOURNAL.
NOTHING'S WORKING.
MAYBE IT'S THE THINNING AIR OR THE ADRENALINE TERROR OF THE LAST FEW DAYS, CONSTANTLY RUNNING.
MAYBE I JUST FORGOT WHAT DREAMS FELT LIKE.

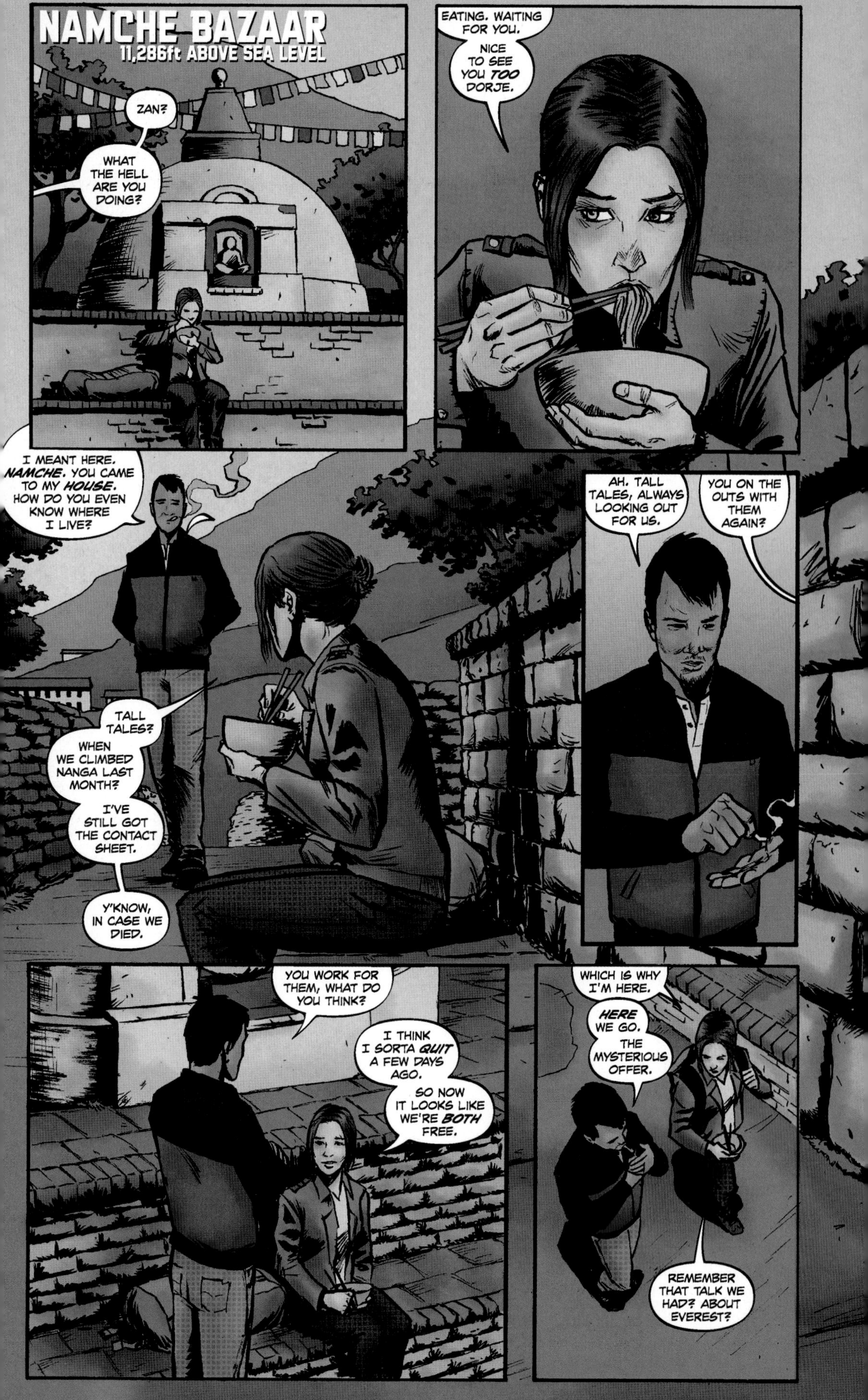
NAMCHE BAZAAR
11,286ft ABOVE SEA LEVEL
ZAN?
WHAT THE HELL ARE YOU DOING?
EATING. WAITING FOR YOU.
NICE TO SEE YOU *TOO* DORJE.
I MEANT HERE. *NAMCHE.* YOU CAME TO MY *HOUSE.* HOW DO YOU EVEN KNOW WHERE I LIVE?
TALL TALES?
WHEN WE CLIMBED NANGA LAST MONTH?
I'VE STILL GOT THE CONTACT SHEET.
Y'KNOW, IN CASE WE DIED.
AH. TALL TALES, ALWAYS LOOKING OUT FOR US.
YOU ON THE OUTS WITH THEM AGAIN?
YOU WORK FOR THEM, WHAT DO YOU THINK?
I THINK I SORTA *QUIT* A FEW DAYS AGO.
SO NOW IT LOOKS LIKE WE'RE *BOTH* FREE.
WHICH IS WHY I'M HERE.
HERE WE GO.
THE MYSTERIOUS OFFER.
REMEMBER THAT TALK WE HAD? ABOUT EVEREST?

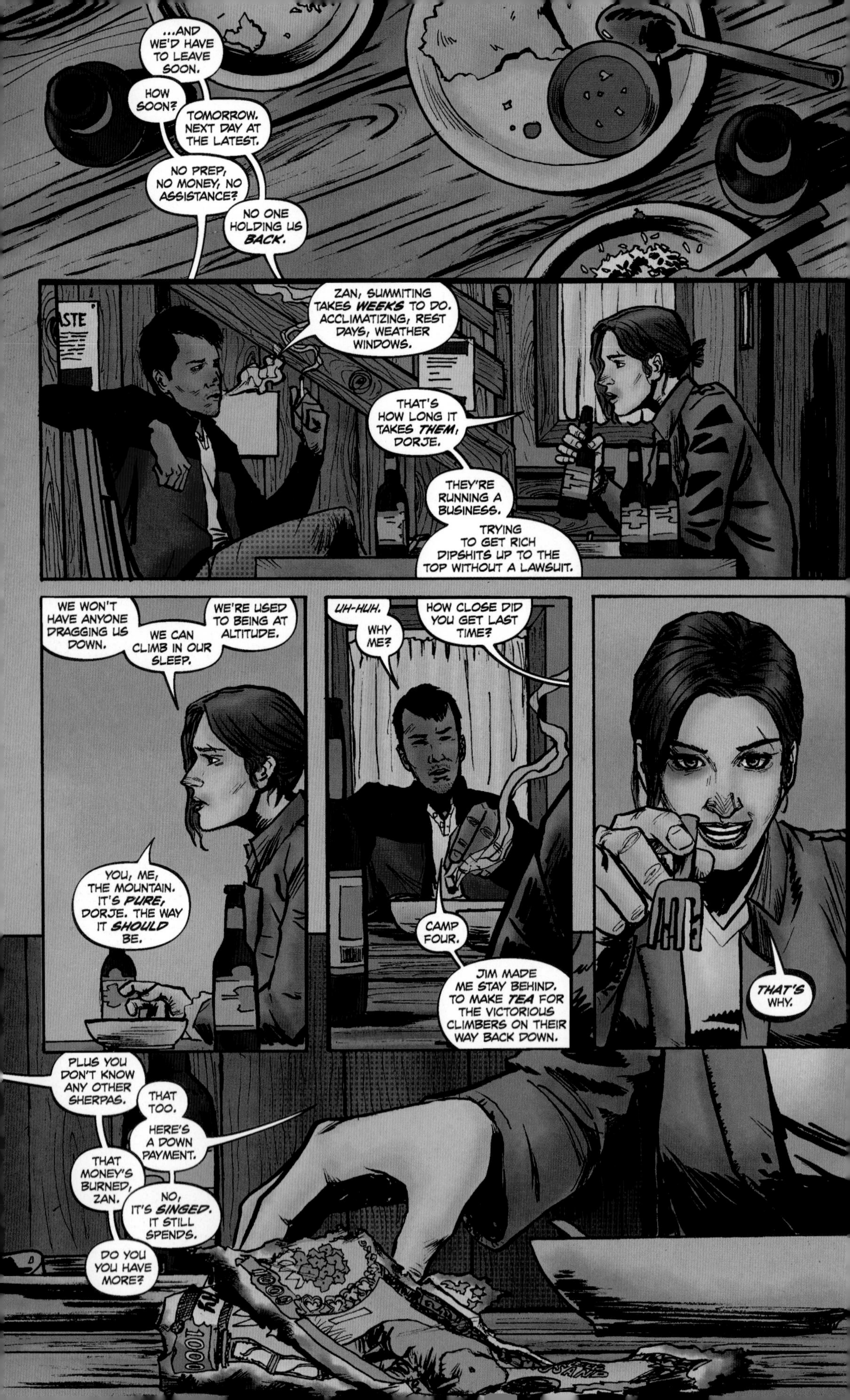
...AND WE'D HAVE TO LEAVE SOON.
HOW SOON?
TOMORROW. NEXT DAY AT THE LATEST.
NO PREP, NO MONEY, NO ASSISTANCE?
NO ONE HOLDING US BACK.
ASTE
ZAN, SUMMITING TAKES WEEKS TO DO. ACCLIMATIZING, REST DAYS, WEATHER WINDOWS.
THAT'S HOW LONG IT TAKES THEM, DORJE.
THEY'RE RUNNING A BUSINESS.
TRYING TO GET RICH DIPSHITS UP TO THE TOP WITHOUT A LAWSUIT.
WE WON'T HAVE ANYONE DRAGGING US DOWN.
WE CAN CLIMB IN OUR SLEEP.
WE'RE USED TO BEING AT ALTITUDE.
YOU, ME, THE MOUNTAIN. IT'S PURE, DORJE. THE WAY IT SHOULD BE.
UH-HUH.
WHY ME?
HOW CLOSE DID YOU GET LAST TIME?
CAMP FOUR.
JIM MADE ME STAY BEHIND. TO MAKE TEA FOR THE VICTORIOUS CLIMBERS ON THEIR WAY BACK DOWN.
THAT'S WHY.
PLUS YOU DON'T KNOW ANY OTHER SHERPAS.
THAT TOO.
HERE'S A DOWN PAYMENT.
THAT MONEY'S BURNED, ZAN.
NO, IT'S SINGED. IT STILL SPENDS.
DO YOU YOU HAVE MORE?

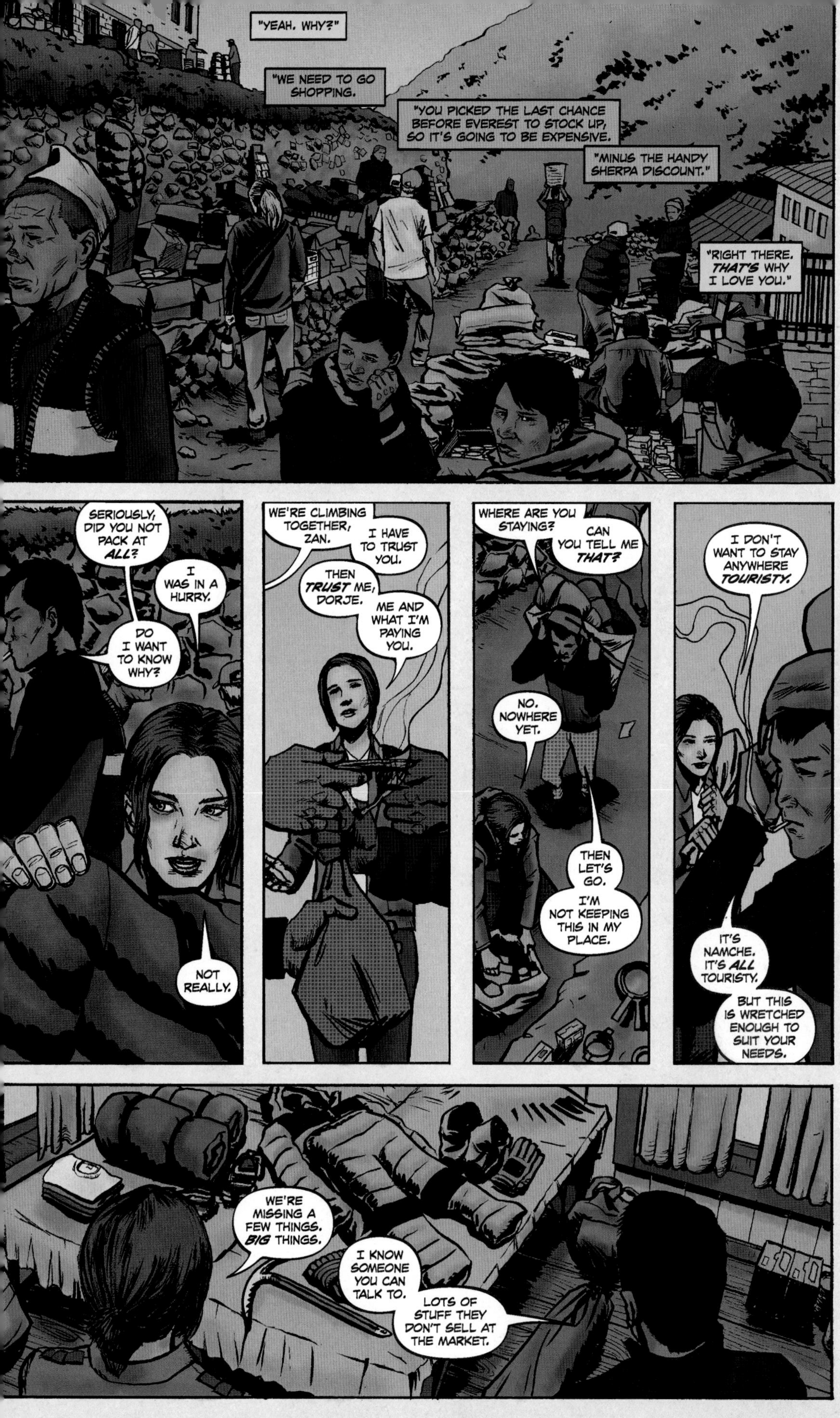
"YEAH. WHY?"
"WE NEED TO GO SHOPPING.
"YOU PICKED THE LAST CHANCE BEFORE EVEREST TO STOCK UP, SO IT'S GOING TO BE EXPENSIVE.
"MINUS THE HANDY SHERPA DISCOUNT."
"RIGHT THERE. THAT'S WHY I LOVE YOU."
SERIOUSLY, DID YOU NOT PACK AT ALL?
I WAS IN A HURRY.
DO I WANT TO KNOW WHY?
NOT REALLY.
WE'RE CLIMBING TOGETHER, ZAN.
I HAVE TO TRUST YOU.
THEN TRUST ME, DORJE.
ME AND WHAT I'M PAYING YOU.
WHERE ARE YOU STAYING?
CAN YOU TELL ME THAT?
NO. NOWHERE YET.
THEN LET'S GO.
I'M NOT KEEPING THIS IN MY PLACE.
I DON'T WANT TO STAY ANYWHERE TOURISTY.
IT'S NAMCHE. IT'S ALL TOURISTY.
BUT THIS IS WRETCHED ENOUGH TO SUIT YOUR NEEDS.
WE'RE MISSING A FEW THINGS. BIG THINGS.
I KNOW SOMEONE YOU CAN TALK TO.
LOTS OF STUFF THEY DON'T SELL AT THE MARKET.

"I'LL BE BY EARLY. GET SOME SLEEP."

NOT FUCKING LIKELY.

Protocol says to clear the scene within an hour. Every hour beyond that, you put yourself at risk.

But I'd just killed a good friend. Maybe the last one I had left.

I deserved a party.

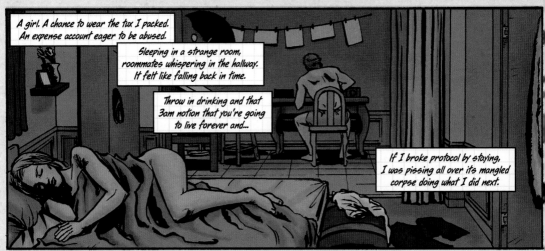

A girl. A chance to wear the tux I packed. An expense account eager to be abused.

Sleeping in a strange room, roommates whispering in the hallway. It felt like falling back in time.

Throw in drinking and that 3am notion that you're going to live forever and...

If I broke protocol by staying, I was pissing all over its mangled corpse doing what I did next.

Call me an unsatisfied employee.

A traitor to the cause.

I was just curious.

Wanted to see if anything could surprise me anymore.

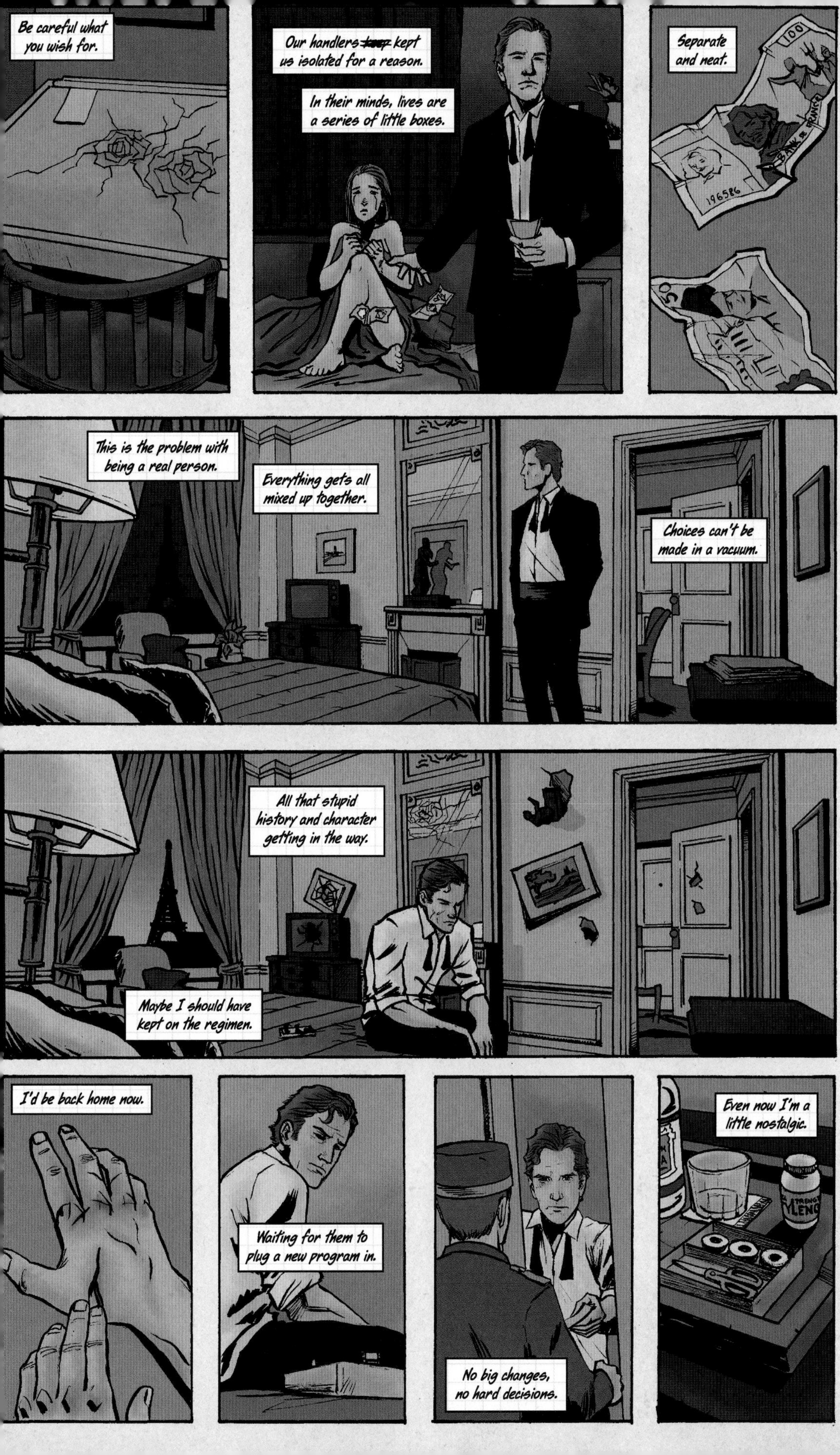
Be careful what you wish for.
Our handlers ~~keep~~ kept us isolated for a reason.
In their minds, lives are a series of little boxes.
Separate and neat.
This is the problem with being a real person.
Everything gets all mixed up together.
Choices can't be made in a vacuum.
All that stupid history and character getting in the way.
Maybe I should have kept on the regimen.
I'd be back home now.
Waiting for them to plug a new program in.
No big changes, no hard decisions.
Even now I'm a little nostalgic.

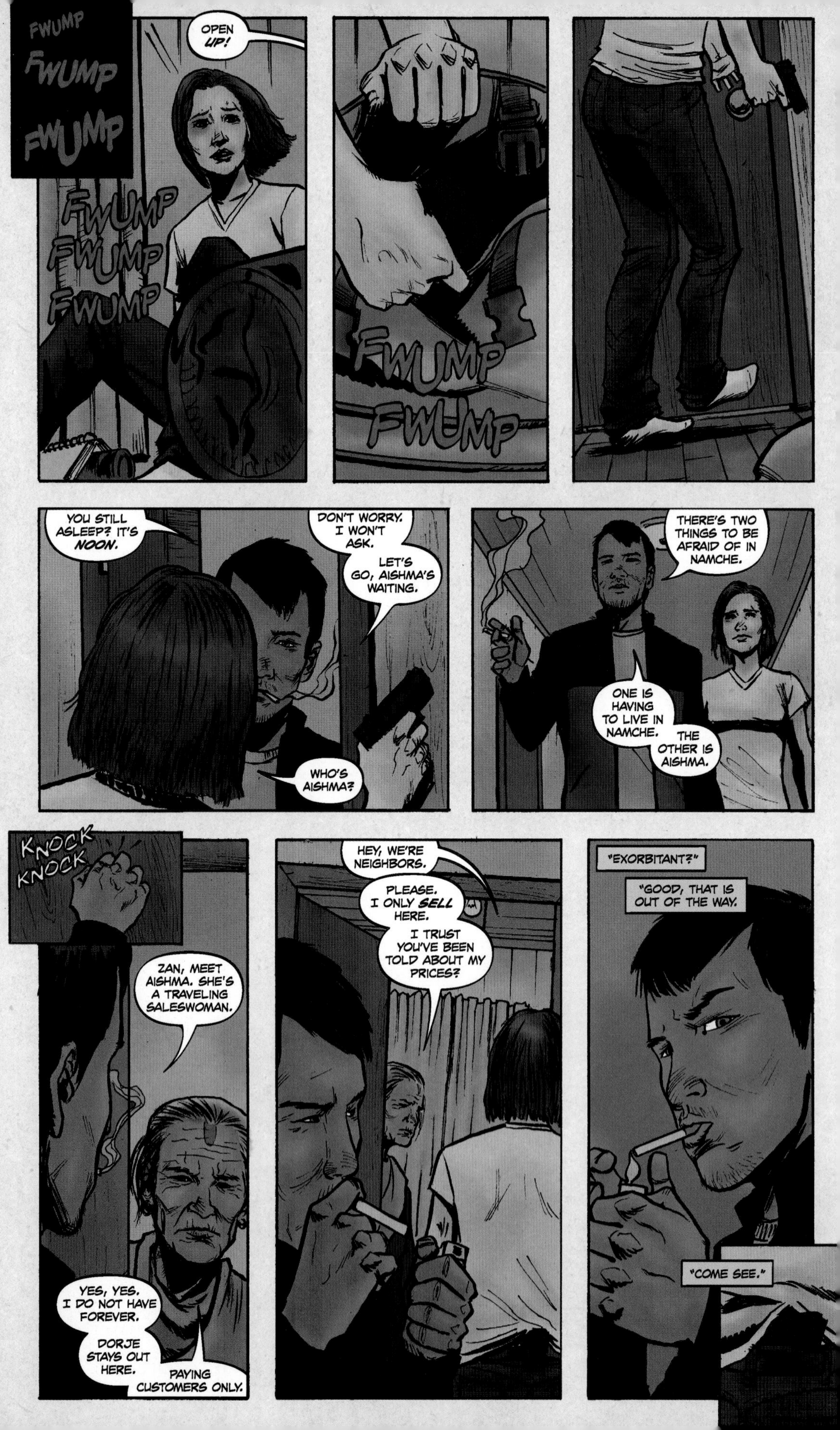
FWUMP
FWUMP
FWUMP
OPEN UP!
FWUMP
FWUMP
FWUMP
FWUMP
FWUMP
YOU STILL ASLEEP? IT'S NOON.
DON'T WORRY. I WON'T ASK.
LET'S GO, AISHMA'S WAITING.
WHO'S AISHMA?
THERE'S TWO THINGS TO BE AFRAID OF IN NAMCHE.
ONE IS HAVING TO LIVE IN NAMCHE.
THE OTHER IS AISHMA.
KNOCK KNOCK
ZAN, MEET AISHMA. SHE'S A TRAVELING SALESWOMAN.
YES, YES. I DO NOT HAVE FOREVER.
DORJE STAYS OUT HERE.
PAYING CUSTOMERS ONLY.
HEY, WE'RE NEIGHBORS.
PLEASE. I ONLY SELL HERE.
I TRUST YOU'VE BEEN TOLD ABOUT MY PRICES?
"EXORBITANT?"
"GOOD, THAT IS OUT OF THE WAY.
"COME SEE."

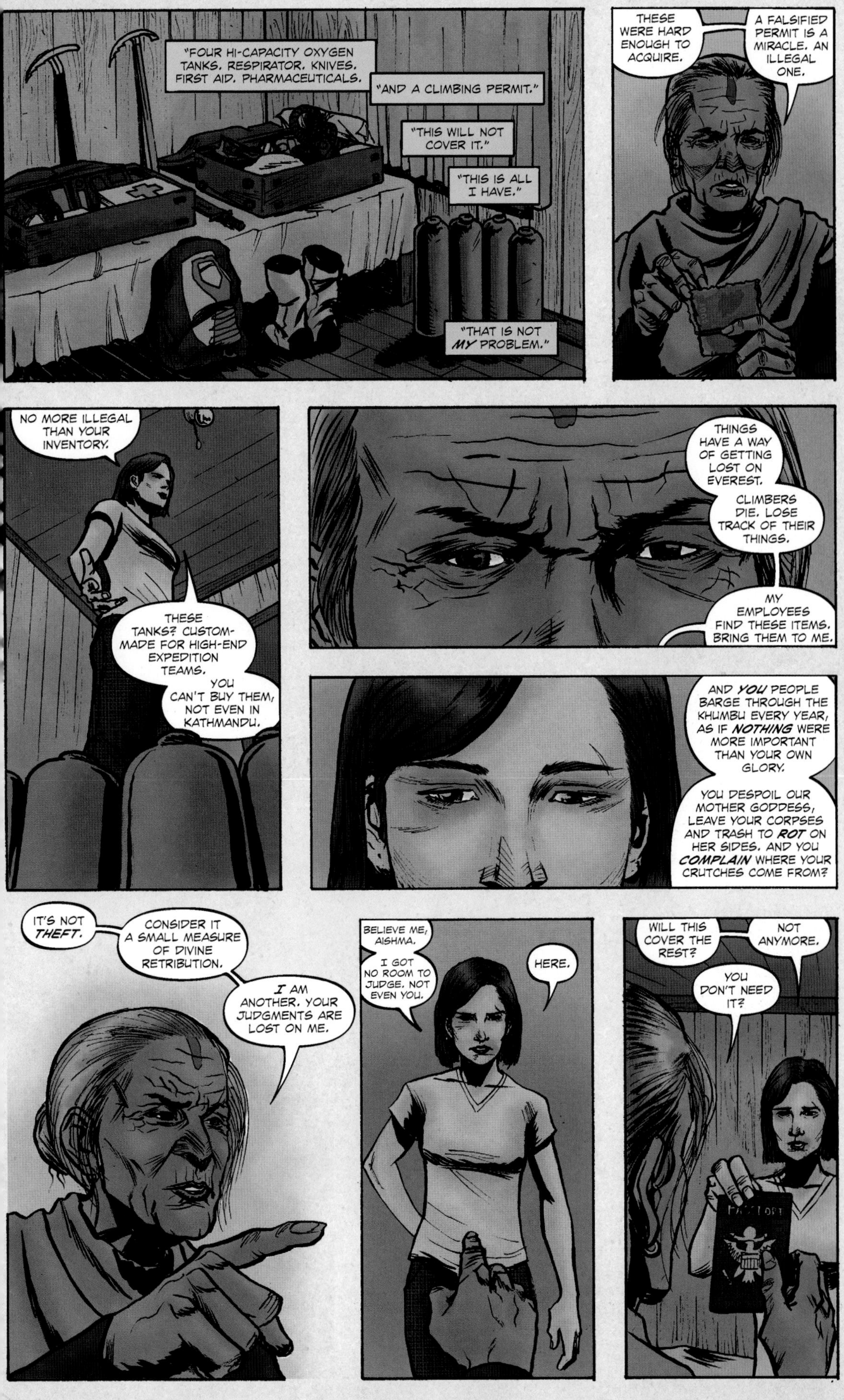

"FOUR HI-CAPACITY OXYGEN TANKS. RESPIRATOR. KNIVES. FIRST AID. PHARMACEUTICALS.
"AND A CLIMBING PERMIT."
"THIS WILL NOT COVER IT."
"THIS IS ALL I HAVE."
"THAT IS NOT *MY* PROBLEM."
THESE WERE HARD ENOUGH TO ACQUIRE.
A FALSIFIED PERMIT IS A MIRACLE. AN ILLEGAL ONE.
NO MORE ILLEGAL THAN YOUR INVENTORY.
THESE TANKS? CUSTOM-MADE FOR HIGH-END EXPEDITION TEAMS.
YOU CAN'T BUY THEM, NOT EVEN IN KATHMANDU.
THINGS HAVE A WAY OF GETTING LOST ON EVEREST.
CLIMBERS DIE. LOSE TRACK OF THEIR THINGS.
MY EMPLOYEES FIND THESE ITEMS. BRING THEM TO ME.
AND *YOU* PEOPLE BARGE THROUGH THE KHUMBU EVERY YEAR, AS IF *NOTHING* WERE MORE IMPORTANT THAN YOUR OWN GLORY.
YOU DESPOIL OUR MOTHER GODDESS, LEAVE YOUR CORPSES AND TRASH TO *ROT* ON HER SIDES. AND YOU *COMPLAIN* WHERE YOUR CRUTCHES COME FROM?
IT'S NOT *THEFT*.
CONSIDER IT A SMALL MEASURE OF DIVINE RETRIBUTION.
I AM ANOTHER. YOUR JUDGMENTS ARE LOST ON ME.
BELIEVE ME, AISHMA.
I GOT NO ROOM TO JUDGE. NOT EVEN YOU.
HERE.
WILL THIS COVER THE REST?
NOT ANYMORE.
YOU DON'T NEED IT?

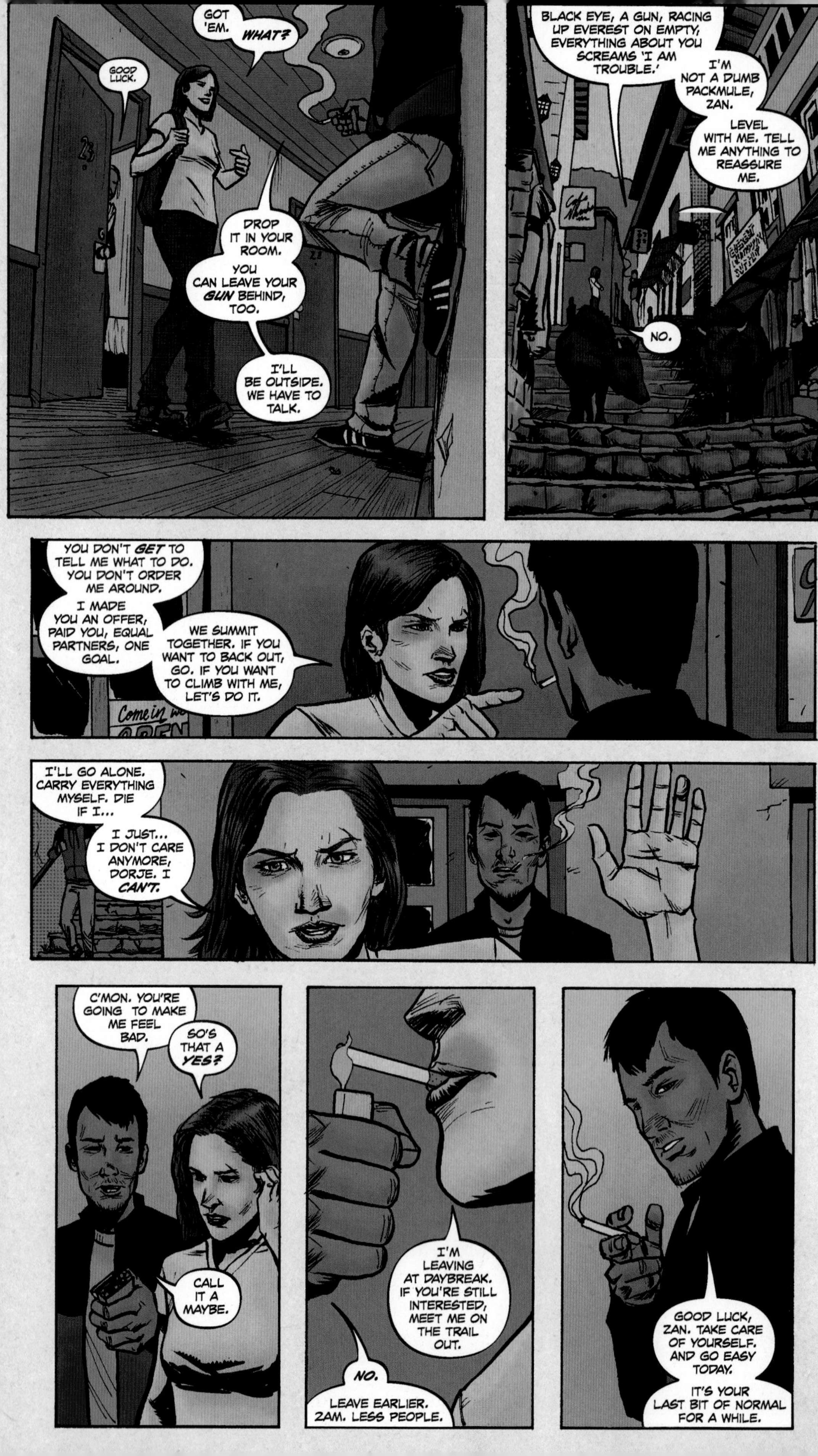
GOOD LUCK.
GOT 'EM. WHAT?
DROP IT IN YOUR ROOM.
YOU CAN LEAVE YOUR GUN BEHIND, TOO.
I'LL BE OUTSIDE. WE HAVE TO TALK.
BLACK EYE, A GUN, RACING UP EVEREST ON EMPTY, EVERYTHING ABOUT YOU SCREAMS 'I AM TROUBLE.'
I'M NOT A DUMB PACKMULE, ZAN.
LEVEL WITH ME. TELL ME ANYTHING TO REASSURE ME.
NO.
YOU DON'T GET TO TELL ME WHAT TO DO. YOU DON'T ORDER ME AROUND.
I MADE YOU AN OFFER, PAID YOU, EQUAL PARTNERS, ONE GOAL.
WE SUMMIT TOGETHER. IF YOU WANT TO BACK OUT, GO. IF YOU WANT TO CLIMB WITH ME, LET'S DO IT.
I'LL GO ALONE. CARRY EVERYTHING MYSELF. DIE IF I...
I JUST... I DON'T CARE ANYMORE, DORJE. I CAN'T.
C'MON. YOU'RE GOING TO MAKE ME FEEL BAD.
SO'S THAT A YES?
CALL IT A MAYBE.
I'M LEAVING AT DAYBREAK. IF YOU'RE STILL INTERESTED, MEET ME ON THE TRAIL OUT.
NO.
LEAVE EARLIER. 2AM. LESS PEOPLE.
GOOD LUCK, ZAN. TAKE CARE OF YOURSELF. AND GO EASY TODAY.
IT'S YOUR LAST BIT OF NORMAL FOR A WHILE.

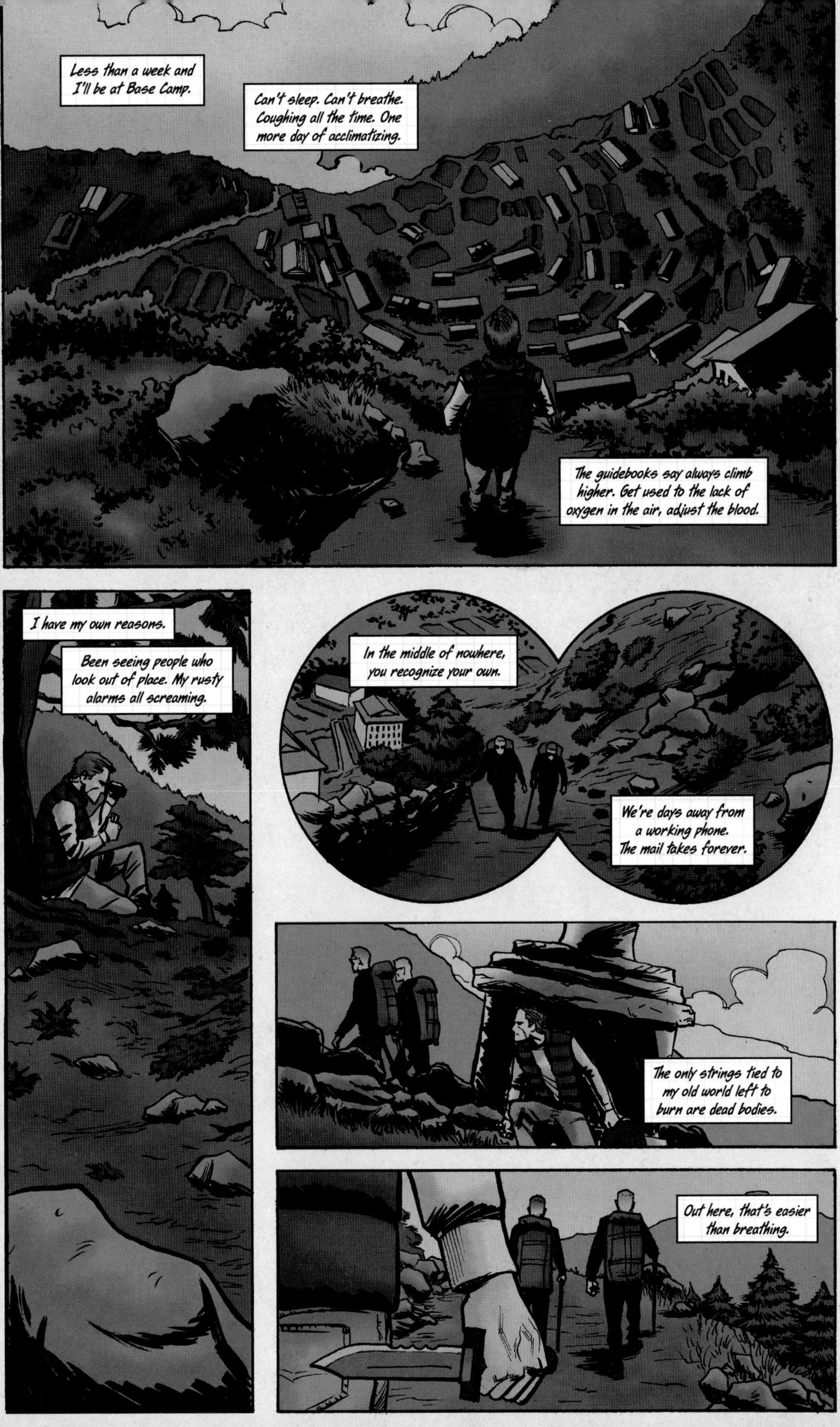
Less than a week and I'll be at Base Camp.
Can't sleep. Can't breathe. Coughing all the time. One more day of acclimatizing.
The guidebooks say always climb higher. Get used to the lack of oxygen in the air, adjust the blood.
I have my own reasons.
Been seeing people who look out of place. My rusty alarms all screaming.
In the middle of nowhere, you recognize your own.
We're days away from a working phone. The mail takes forever.
The only strings tied to my old world left to burn are dead bodies.
Out here, that's easier than breathing.

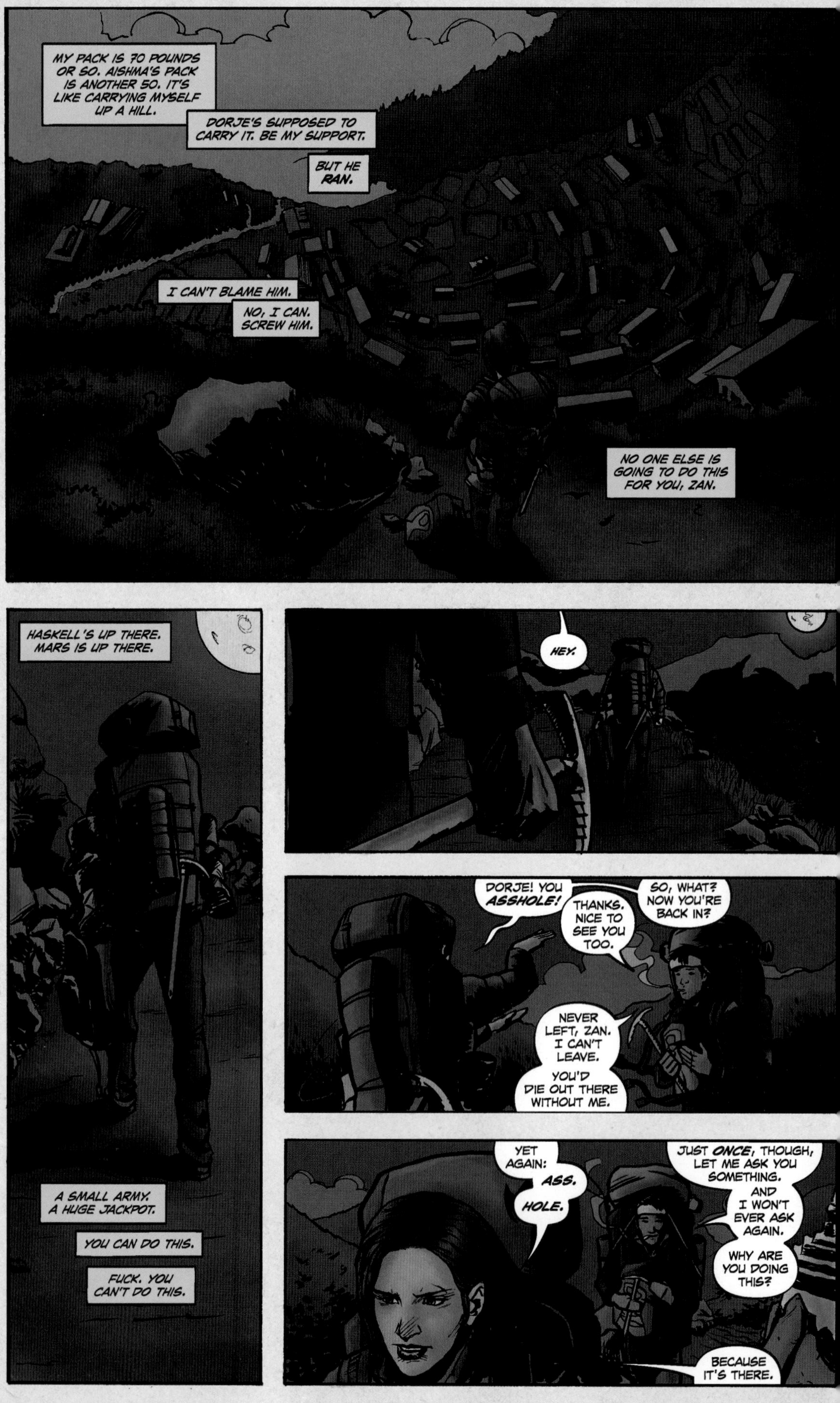
MY PACK IS 70 POUNDS OR SO. AISHMA'S PACK IS ANOTHER 50. IT'S LIKE CARRYING MYSELF UP A HILL.
DORJE'S SUPPOSED TO CARRY IT. BE MY SUPPORT.
BUT HE RAN.
I CAN'T BLAME HIM.
NO, I CAN. SCREW HIM.
NO ONE ELSE IS GOING TO DO THIS FOR YOU, ZAN.
HASKELL'S UP THERE. MARS IS UP THERE.
A SMALL ARMY. A HUGE JACKPOT.
YOU CAN DO THIS.
FUCK. YOU CAN'T DO THIS.
HEY.
DORJE! YOU ASSHOLE!
THANKS. NICE TO SEE YOU TOO.
SO, WHAT? NOW YOU'RE BACK IN?
NEVER LEFT, ZAN. I CAN'T LEAVE.
YOU'D DIE OUT THERE WITHOUT ME.
YET AGAIN: ASS.
HOLE.
JUST ONCE, THOUGH, LET ME ASK YOU SOMETHING.
AND I WON'T EVER ASK AGAIN.
WHY ARE YOU DOING THIS?
BECAUSE IT'S THERE.

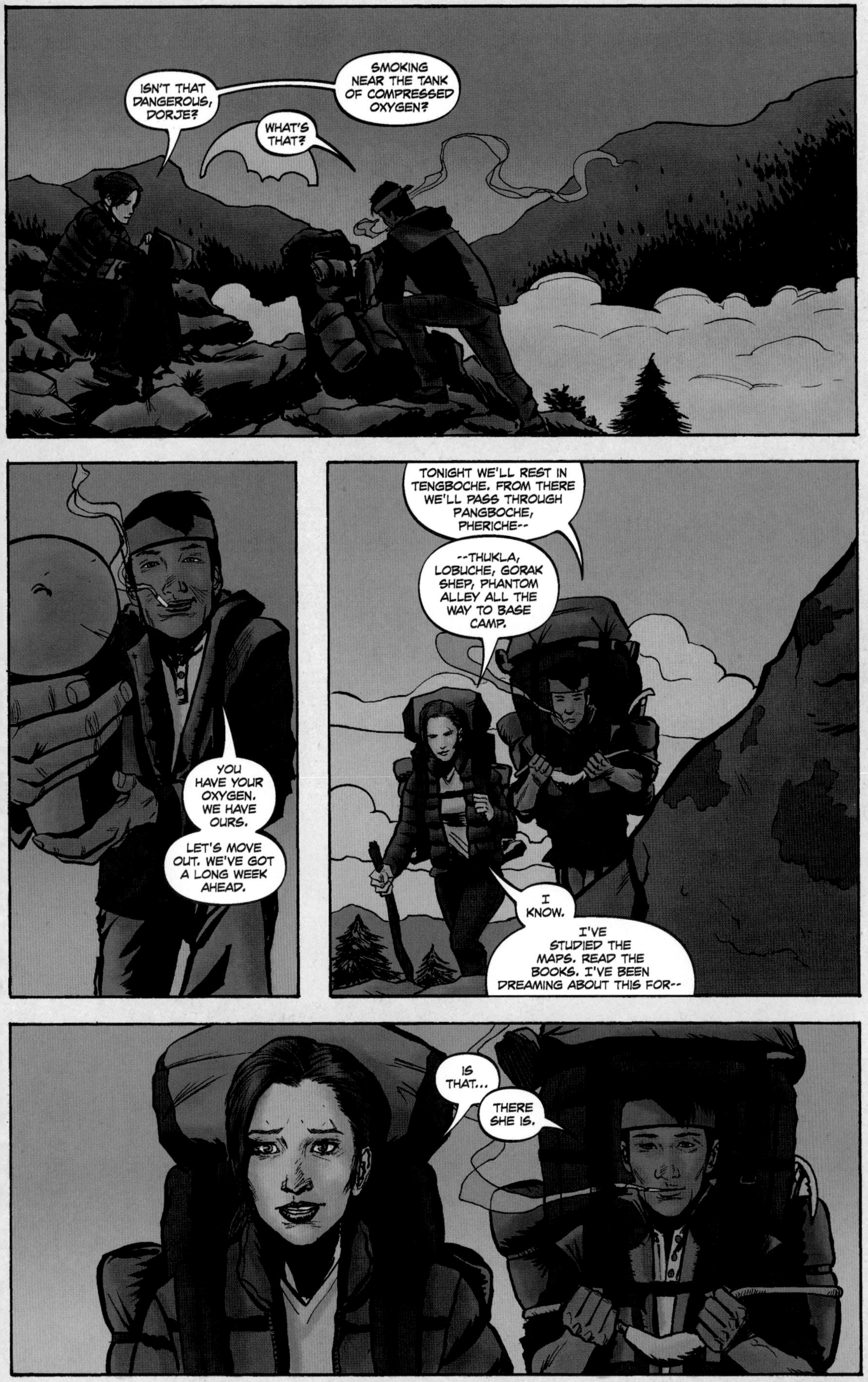
ISN'T THAT DANGEROUS, DORJE?
SMOKING NEAR THE TANK OF COMPRESSED OXYGEN?
WHAT'S THAT?
YOU HAVE YOUR OXYGEN. WE HAVE OURS.
LET'S MOVE OUT. WE'VE GOT A LONG WEEK AHEAD.
TONIGHT WE'LL REST IN TENGBOCHE. FROM THERE WE'LL PASS THROUGH PANGBOCHE, PHERICHE--
--THUKLA, LOBUCHE, GORAK SHEP, PHANTOM ALLEY ALL THE WAY TO BASE CAMP.
I KNOW.
I'VE STUDIED THE MAPS. READ THE BOOKS. I'VE BEEN DREAMING ABOUT THIS FOR--
IS THAT...
THERE SHE IS.

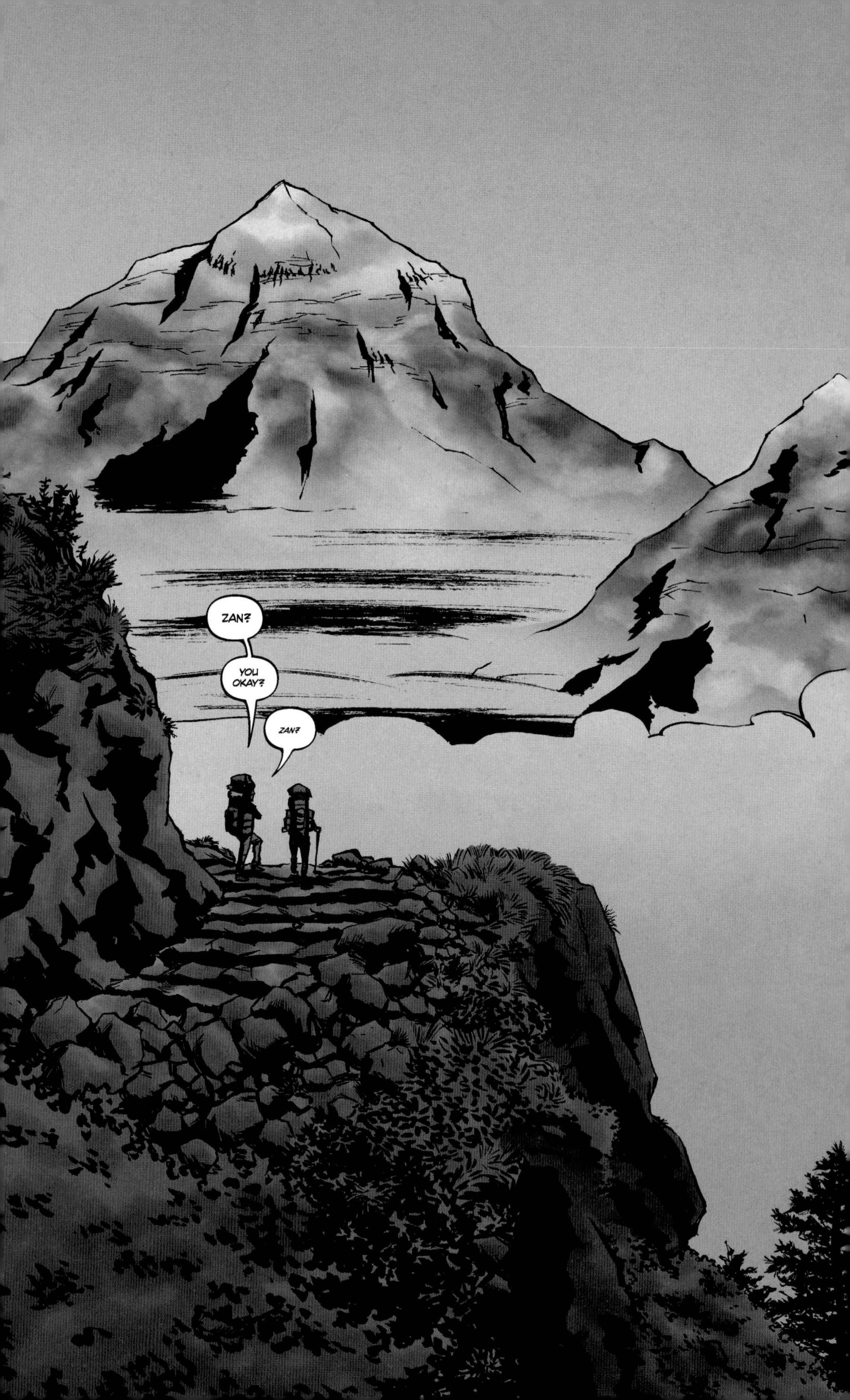
ZAN?
YOU OKAY?
ZAN?

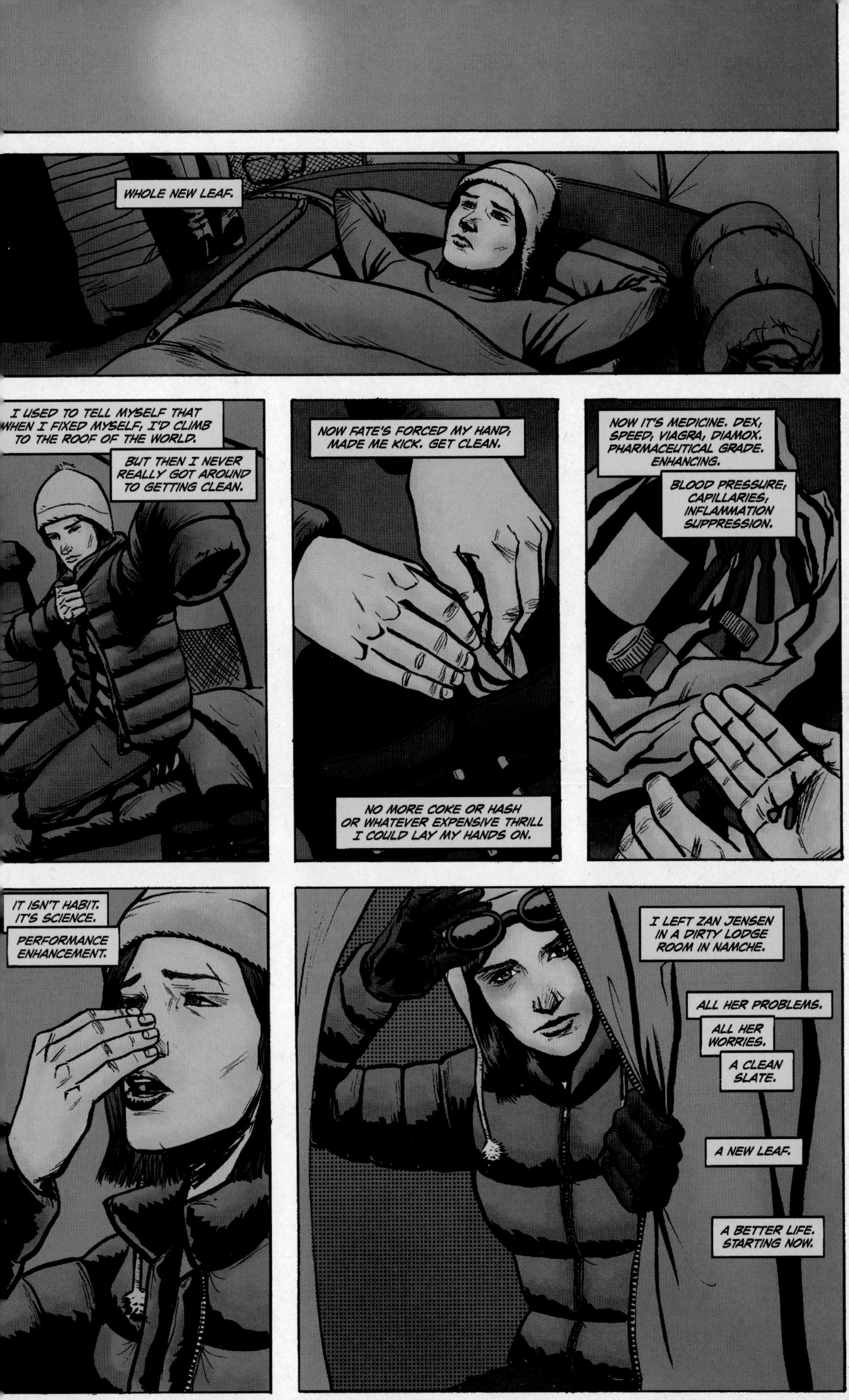
WHOLE NEW LEAF.
I USED TO TELL MYSELF THAT WHEN I FIXED MYSELF, I'D CLIMB TO THE ROOF OF THE WORLD.
BUT THEN I NEVER REALLY GOT AROUND TO GETTING CLEAN.
NOW FATE'S FORCED MY HAND, MADE ME KICK. GET CLEAN.
NO MORE COKE OR HASH OR WHATEVER EXPENSIVE THRILL I COULD LAY MY HANDS ON.
NOW IT'S MEDICINE. DEX, SPEED, VIAGRA, DIAMOX. PHARMACEUTICAL GRADE. ENHANCING.
BLOOD PRESSURE, CAPILLARIES, INFLAMMATION SUPPRESSION.
IT ISN'T HABIT. IT'S SCIENCE.
PERFORMANCE ENHANCEMENT.
I LEFT ZAN JENSEN IN A DIRTY LODGE ROOM IN NAMCHE.
ALL HER PROBLEMS.
ALL HER WORRIES.
A CLEAN SLATE.
A NEW LEAF.
A BETTER LIFE. STARTING NOW.

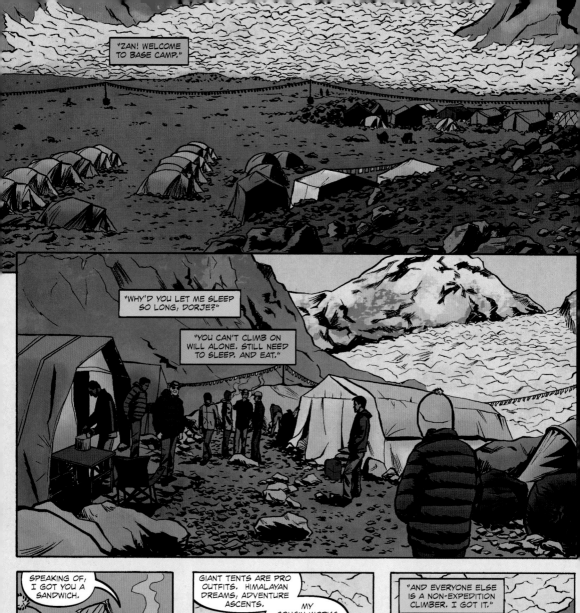

"ZAN! WELCOME TO BASE CAMP."

"WHY'D YOU LET ME SLEEP SO LONG, DORJE?"

"YOU CAN'T CLIMB ON WILL ALONE. STILL NEED TO SLEEP. AND EAT."

SPEAKING OF, I GOT YOU A SANDWICH.

NOT HUNGRY.

YOU EAT, I'LL SHOW YOU THE SIGHTS. DEAL?

GIANT TENTS ARE PRO OUTFITS. HIMALAYAN DREAMS, ADVENTURE ASCENTS.

MY COUSIN WORKS FOR THEM, I GOT US A DINNER INVITATION.

I TOLD YOU DORJE, I DON'T WANT TO SOCIALIZE.

MM. THOSE BIG TENTS ARE CHINESE, AMERICAN. THAT'S QATAR, I THINK?

"AND EVERYONE ELSE IS A NON-EXPEDITION CLIMBER. I GOT IT."

"NOW *THEM*; THEY'RE THE TALK OF CAMP. SHERPAS SAY THEY KEEP TO THEMSELVES, HAVE A LOT OF MONEY BEHIND THEM.

"NO ONE HAS A CLUE WHO THEY ARE."

"I DO."

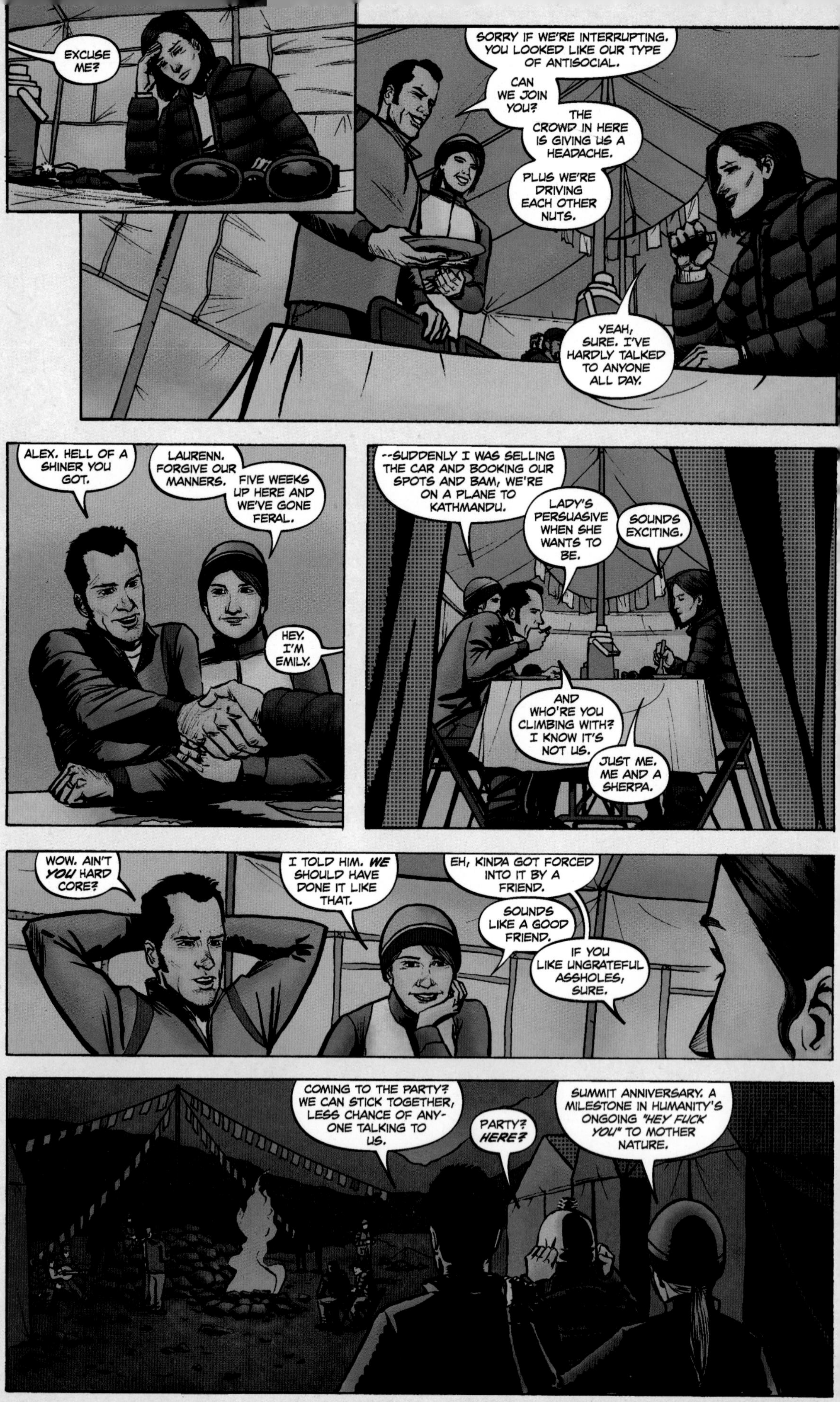
EXCUSE ME?
SORRY IF WE'RE INTERRUPTING. YOU LOOKED LIKE OUR TYPE OF ANTISOCIAL.
CAN WE JOIN YOU?
THE CROWD IN HERE IS GIVING US A HEADACHE.
PLUS WE'RE DRIVING EACH OTHER NUTS.
YEAH, SURE. I'VE HARDLY TALKED TO ANYONE ALL DAY.
ALEX. HELL OF A SHINER YOU GOT.
LAURENN. FORGIVE OUR MANNERS.
FIVE WEEKS UP HERE AND WE'VE GONE FERAL.
HEY. I'M EMILY.
--SUDDENLY I WAS SELLING THE CAR AND BOOKING OUR SPOTS AND BAM, WE'RE ON A PLANE TO KATHMANDU.
LADY'S PERSUASIVE WHEN SHE WANTS TO BE.
SOUNDS EXCITING.
AND WHO'RE YOU CLIMBING WITH? I KNOW IT'S NOT US.
JUST ME. ME AND A SHERPA.
WOW. AIN'T *YOU* HARD CORE?
I TOLD HIM. *WE* SHOULD HAVE DONE IT LIKE THAT.
EH, KINDA GOT FORCED INTO IT BY A FRIEND.
SOUNDS LIKE A GOOD FRIEND.
IF YOU LIKE UNGRATEFUL ASSHOLES, SURE.
COMING TO THE PARTY? WE CAN STICK TOGETHER, LESS CHANCE OF ANY-ONE TALKING TO US.
PARTY? *HERE?*
SUMMIT ANNIVERSARY. A MILESTONE IN HUMANITY'S ONGOING *"HEY FUCK YOU"* TO MOTHER NATURE.

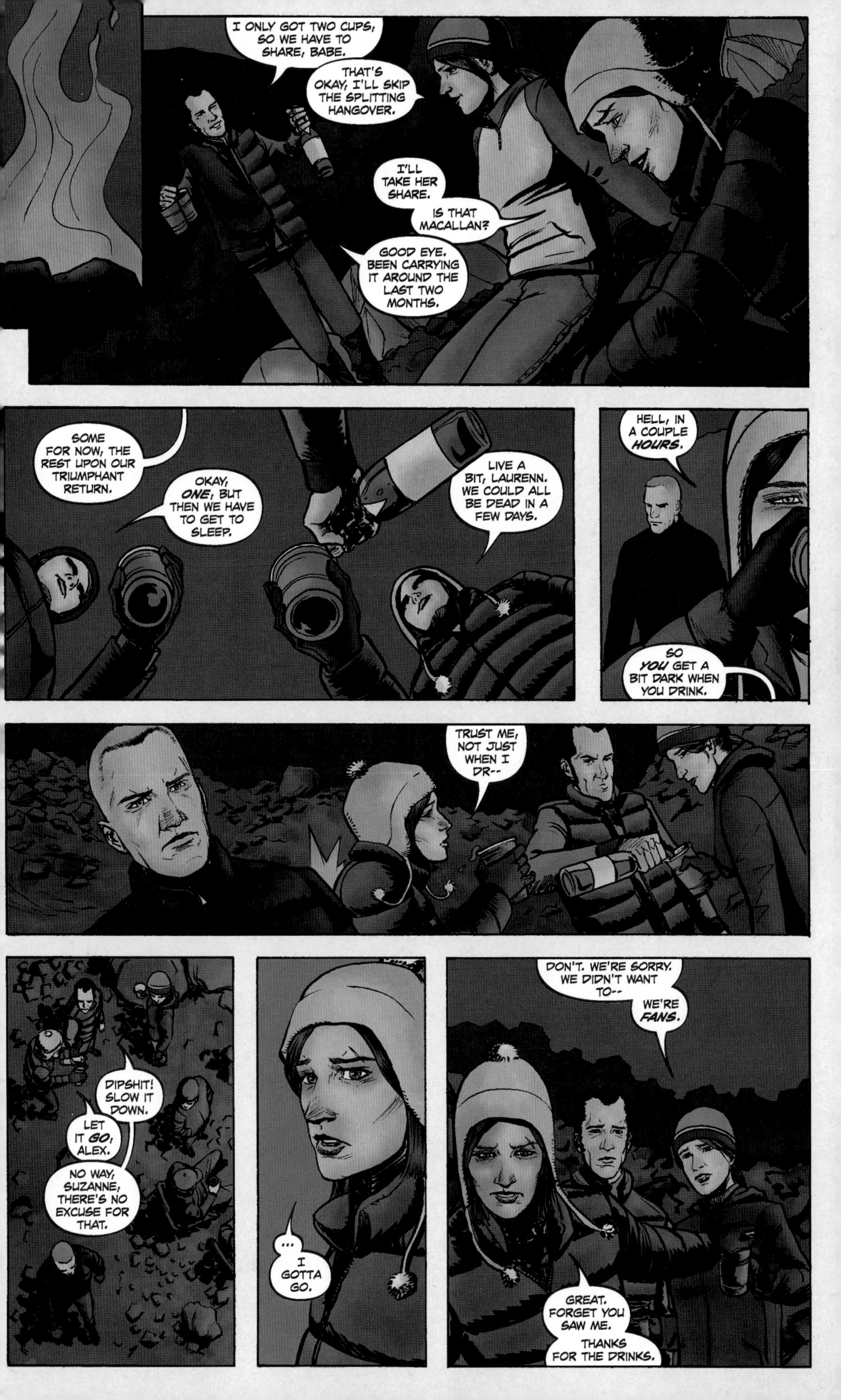
I ONLY GOT TWO CUPS, SO WE HAVE TO SHARE, BABE.
THAT'S OKAY, I'LL SKIP THE SPLITTING HANGOVER.
I'LL TAKE HER SHARE.
IS THAT MACALLAN?
GOOD EYE. BEEN CARRYING IT AROUND THE LAST TWO MONTHS.
SOME FOR NOW, THE REST UPON OUR TRIUMPHANT RETURN.
OKAY, ONE, BUT THEN WE HAVE TO GET TO SLEEP.
LIVE A BIT, LAURENN. WE COULD ALL BE DEAD IN A FEW DAYS.
HELL, IN A COUPLE HOURS.
SO YOU GET A BIT DARK WHEN YOU DRINK.
TRUST ME, NOT JUST WHEN I DR--
DIPSHIT! SLOW IT DOWN.
LET IT GO, ALEX.
NO WAY, SUZANNE, THERE'S NO EXCUSE FOR THAT.
... I GOTTA GO.
DON'T. WE'RE SORRY. WE DIDN'T WANT TO--
WE'RE FANS.
GREAT. FORGET YOU SAW ME.
THANKS FOR THE DRINKS.

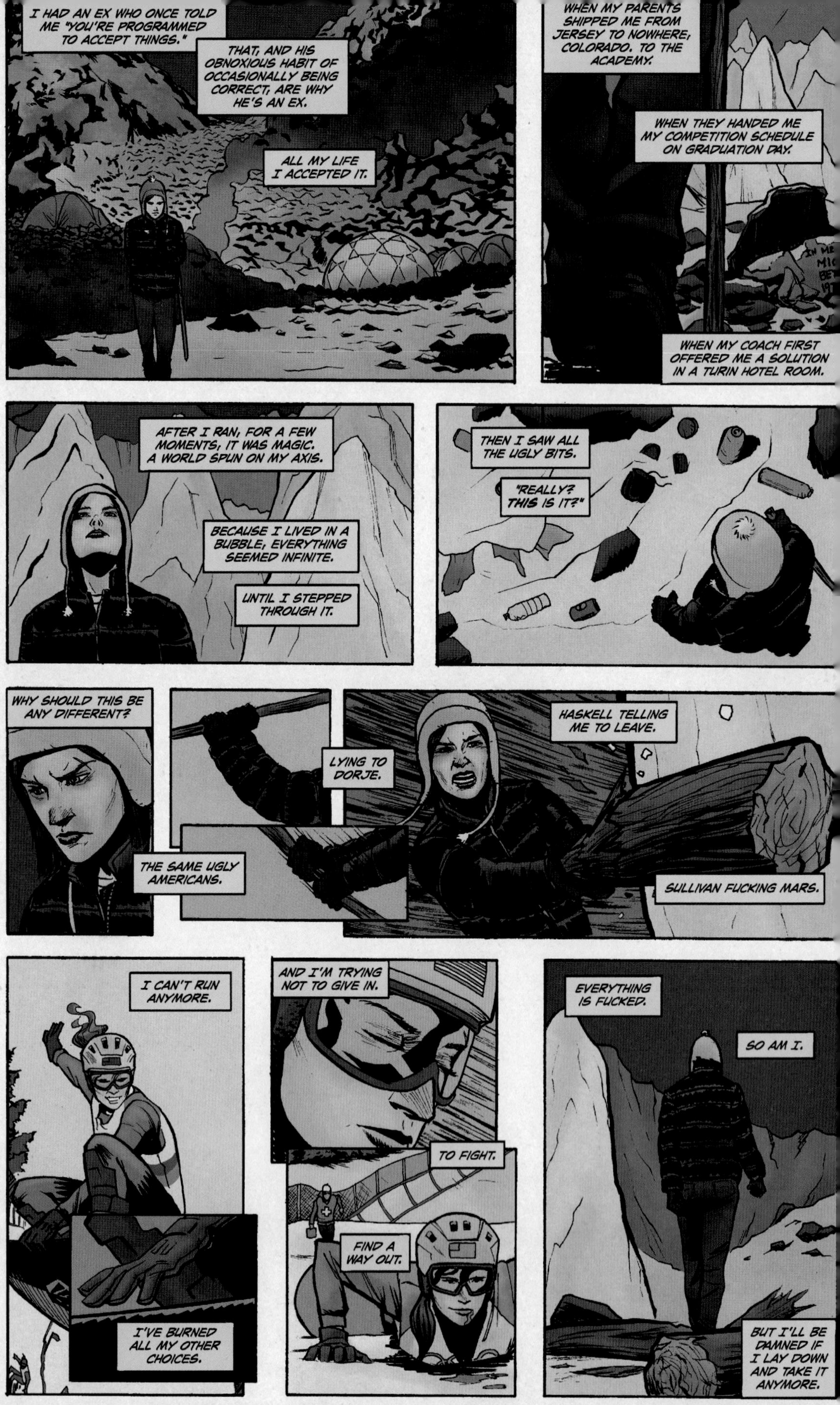
I HAD AN EX WHO ONCE TOLD ME "YOU'RE PROGRAMMED TO ACCEPT THINGS."
THAT, AND HIS OBNOXIOUS HABIT OF OCCASIONALLY BEING CORRECT, ARE WHY HE'S AN EX.
ALL MY LIFE I ACCEPTED IT.
WHEN MY PARENTS SHIPPED ME FROM JERSEY TO NOWHERE, COLORADO. TO THE ACADEMY.
WHEN THEY HANDED ME MY COMPETITION SCHEDULE ON GRADUATION DAY.
WHEN MY COACH FIRST OFFERED ME A SOLUTION IN A TURIN HOTEL ROOM.
AFTER I RAN, FOR A FEW MOMENTS, IT WAS MAGIC. A WORLD SPUN ON MY AXIS.
BECAUSE I LIVED IN A BUBBLE, EVERYTHING SEEMED INFINITE.
UNTIL I STEPPED THROUGH IT.
THEN I SAW ALL THE UGLY BITS.
"REALLY? THIS IS IT?"
WHY SHOULD THIS BE ANY DIFFERENT?
THE SAME UGLY AMERICANS.
LYING TO DORJE.
HASKELL TELLING ME TO LEAVE.
SULLIVAN FUCKING MARS.
I CAN'T RUN ANYMORE.
I'VE BURNED ALL MY OTHER CHOICES.
AND I'M TRYING NOT TO GIVE IN.
TO FIGHT.
FIND A WAY OUT.
EVERYTHING IS FUCKED.
SO AM I.
BUT I'LL BE DAMNED IF I LAY DOWN AND TAKE IT ANYMORE.

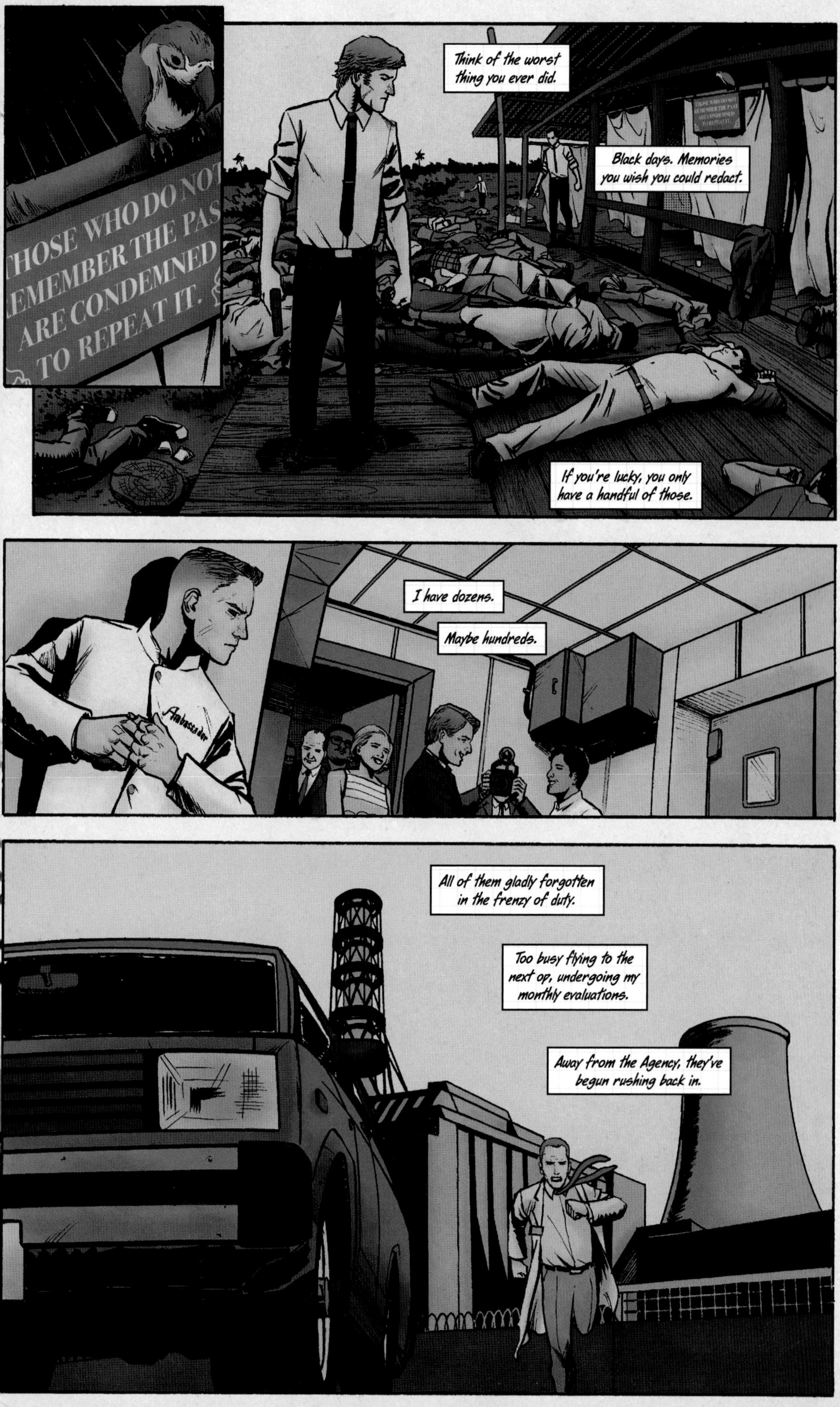
THOSE WHO DO NOT
REMEMBER THE PAS
ARE CONDEMNED
TO REPEAT IT.
Think of the worst thing you ever did.
Black days. Memories you wish you could redact.
If you're lucky, you only have a handful of those.
I have dozens.
Maybe hundreds.
All of them gladly forgotten in the frenzy of duty.
Too busy flying to the next op, undergoing my monthly evaluations.
Away from the Agency, they've begun rushing back in.

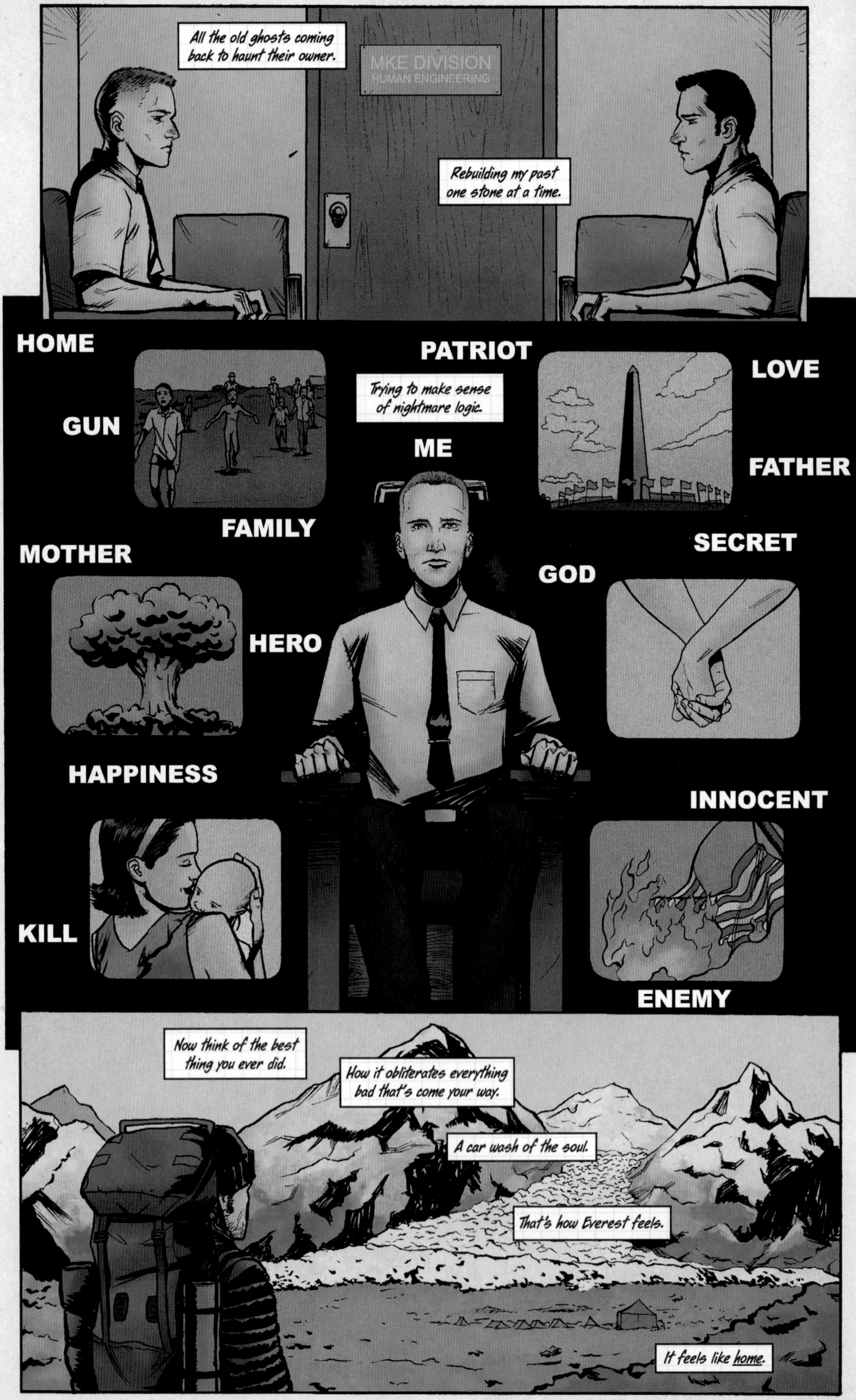
All the old ghosts coming back to haunt their owner.
MKE DIVISION
HUMAN ENGINEERING
Rebuilding my past one stone at a time.
HOME
GUN
PATRIOT
Trying to make sense of nightmare logic.
ME
LOVE
FATHER
FAMILY
MOTHER
SECRET
GOD
HERO
HAPPINESS
INNOCENT
KILL
ENEMY
Now think of the best thing you ever did.
How it obliterates everything bad that's come your way.
A car wash of the soul.
That's how Everest feels.
It feels like home.

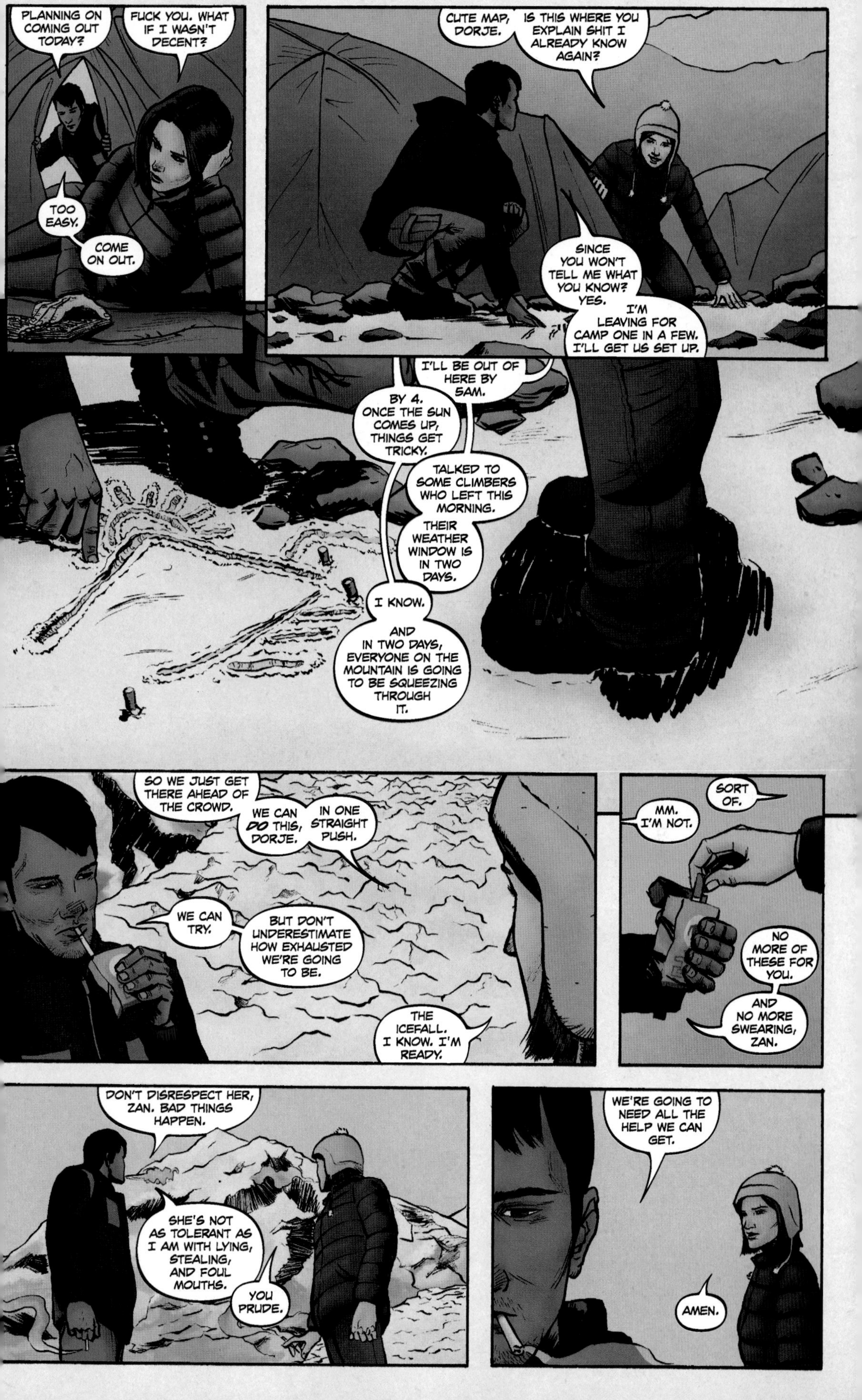
PLANNING ON COMING OUT TODAY?
FUCK YOU. WHAT IF I WASN'T DECENT?
TOO EASY.
COME ON OUT.
CUTE MAP, DORJE.
IS THIS WHERE YOU EXPLAIN SHIT I ALREADY KNOW AGAIN?
SINCE YOU WON'T TELL ME WHAT YOU KNOW? YES.
I'M LEAVING FOR CAMP ONE IN A FEW. I'LL GET US SET UP.
I'LL BE OUT OF HERE BY 3AM.
BY 4. ONCE THE SUN COMES UP, THINGS GET TRICKY.
TALKED TO SOME CLIMBERS WHO LEFT THIS MORNING.
THEIR WEATHER WINDOW IS IN TWO DAYS.
I KNOW.
AND IN TWO DAYS, EVERYONE ON THE MOUNTAIN IS GOING TO BE SQUEEZING THROUGH IT.
SO WE JUST GET THERE AHEAD OF THE CROWD.
WE CAN *DO* THIS, DORJE.
IN ONE STRAIGHT PUSH.
WE CAN TRY.
BUT DON'T UNDERESTIMATE HOW EXHAUSTED WE'RE GOING TO BE.
THE ICEFALL. I KNOW. I'M READY.
SORT OF.
MM. I'M NOT.
NO MORE OF THESE FOR YOU.
AND NO MORE SWEARING, ZAN.
DON'T DISRESPECT HER, ZAN. BAD THINGS HAPPEN.
SHE'S NOT AS TOLERANT AS I AM WITH LYING, STEALING, AND FOUL MOUTHS.
YOU PRUDE.
WE'RE GOING TO NEED ALL THE HELP WE CAN GET.
AMEN.

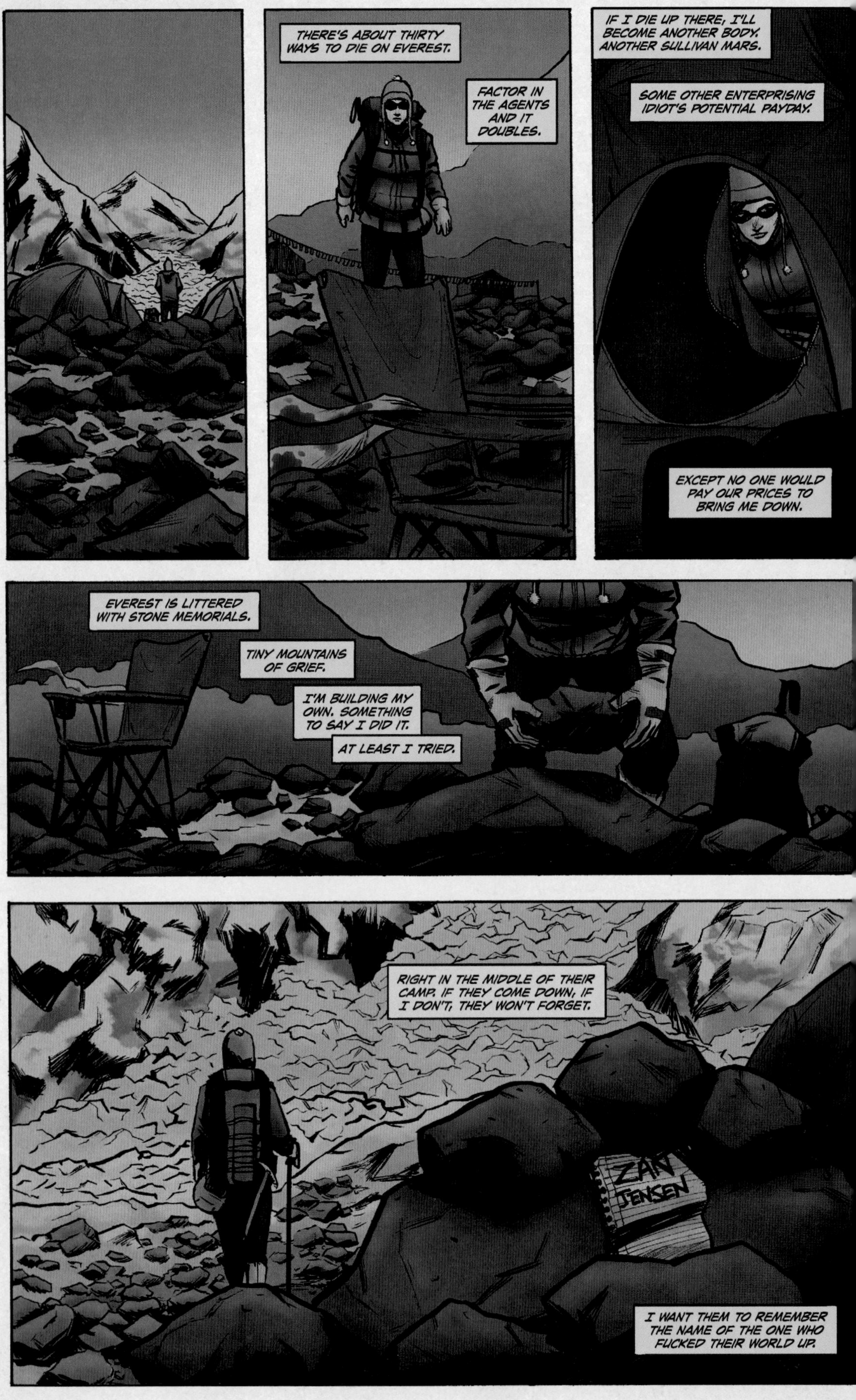

THERE'S ABOUT THIRTY WAYS TO DIE ON EVEREST.
FACTOR IN THE AGENTS AND IT DOUBLES.
IF I DIE UP THERE, I'LL BECOME ANOTHER BODY. ANOTHER SULLIVAN MARS.
SOME OTHER ENTERPRISING IDIOT'S POTENTIAL PAYDAY.
EXCEPT NO ONE WOULD PAY OUR PRICES TO BRING ME DOWN.
EVEREST IS LITTERED WITH STONE MEMORIALS.
TINY MOUNTAINS OF GRIEF.
I'M BUILDING MY OWN. SOMETHING TO SAY I DID IT.
AT LEAST I TRIED.
RIGHT IN THE MIDDLE OF THEIR CAMP. IF THEY COME DOWN, IF I DON'T, THEY WON'T FORGET.
ZAN JENSEN
I WANT THEM TO REMEMBER THE NAME OF THE ONE WHO FUCKED THEIR WORLD UP.

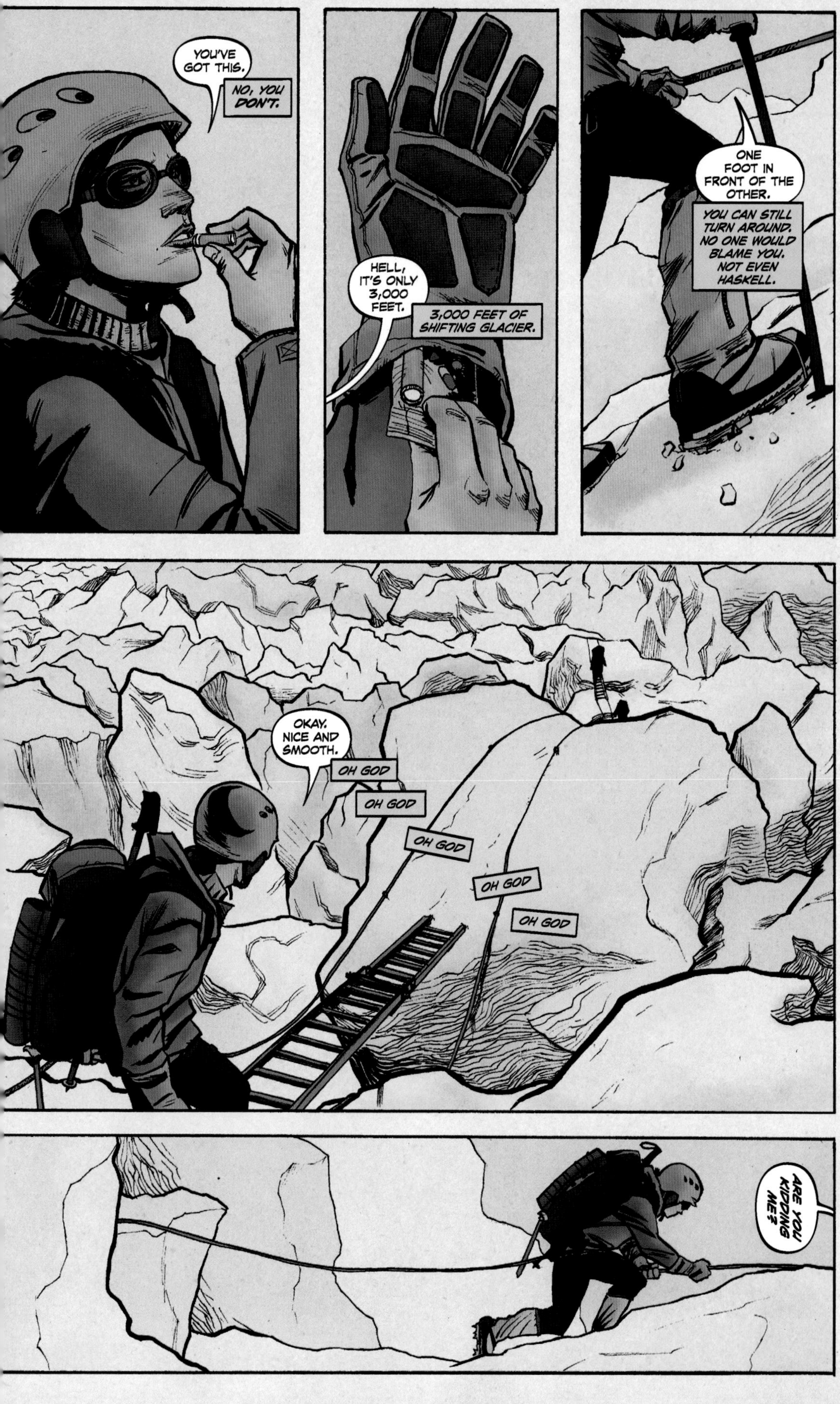

YOU'VE GOT THIS.
NO, YOU DON'T.
HELL, IT'S ONLY 3,000 FEET.
3,000 FEET OF SHIFTING GLACIER.
ONE FOOT IN FRONT OF THE OTHER.
YOU CAN STILL TURN AROUND. NO ONE WOULD BLAME YOU. NOT EVEN HASKELL.
OKAY. NICE AND SMOOTH.
OH GOD
OH GOD
OH GOD
OH GOD
OH GOD
ARE YOU KIDDING ME?

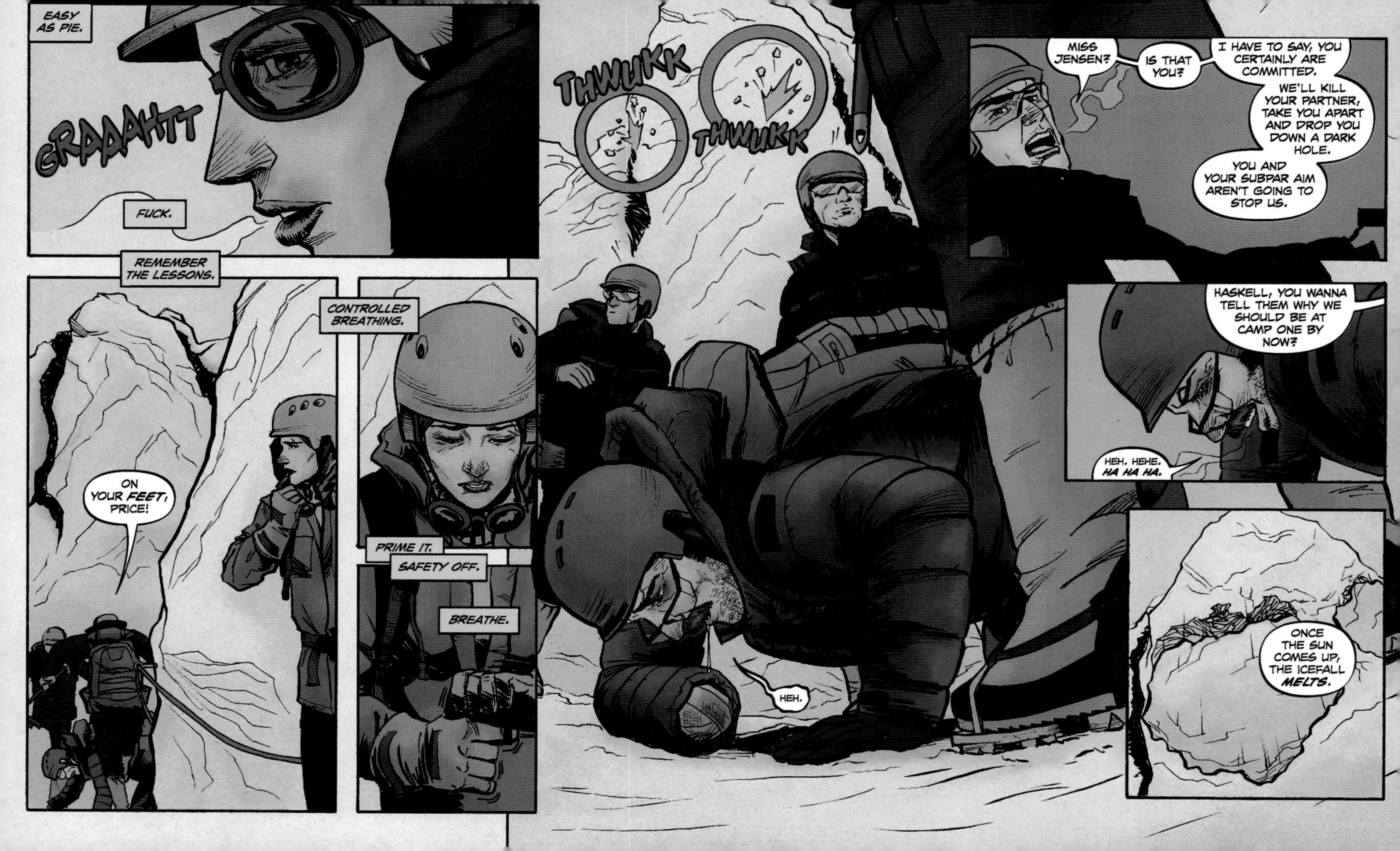
EASY AS PIE.
GRAAAHTT
FUCK.
REMEMBER THE LESSONS.
ON YOUR FEET, PRICE!
CONTROLLED BREATHING.
PRIME IT.
SAFETY OFF.
BREATHE.
THWUKK
THWUKK
HEH.
MISS JENSEN?
IS THAT YOU?
I HAVE TO SAY, YOU CERTAINLY ARE COMMITTED.
WE'LL KILL YOUR PARTNER, TAKE YOU APART AND DROP YOU DOWN A DARK HOLE.
YOU AND YOUR SUBPAR AIM AREN'T GOING TO STOP US.
HASKELL, YOU WANNA TELL THEM WHY WE SHOULD BE AT CAMP ONE BY NOW?
HEH. HEHE. HA HA HA.
ONCE THE SUN COMES UP, THE ICEFALL MELTS.

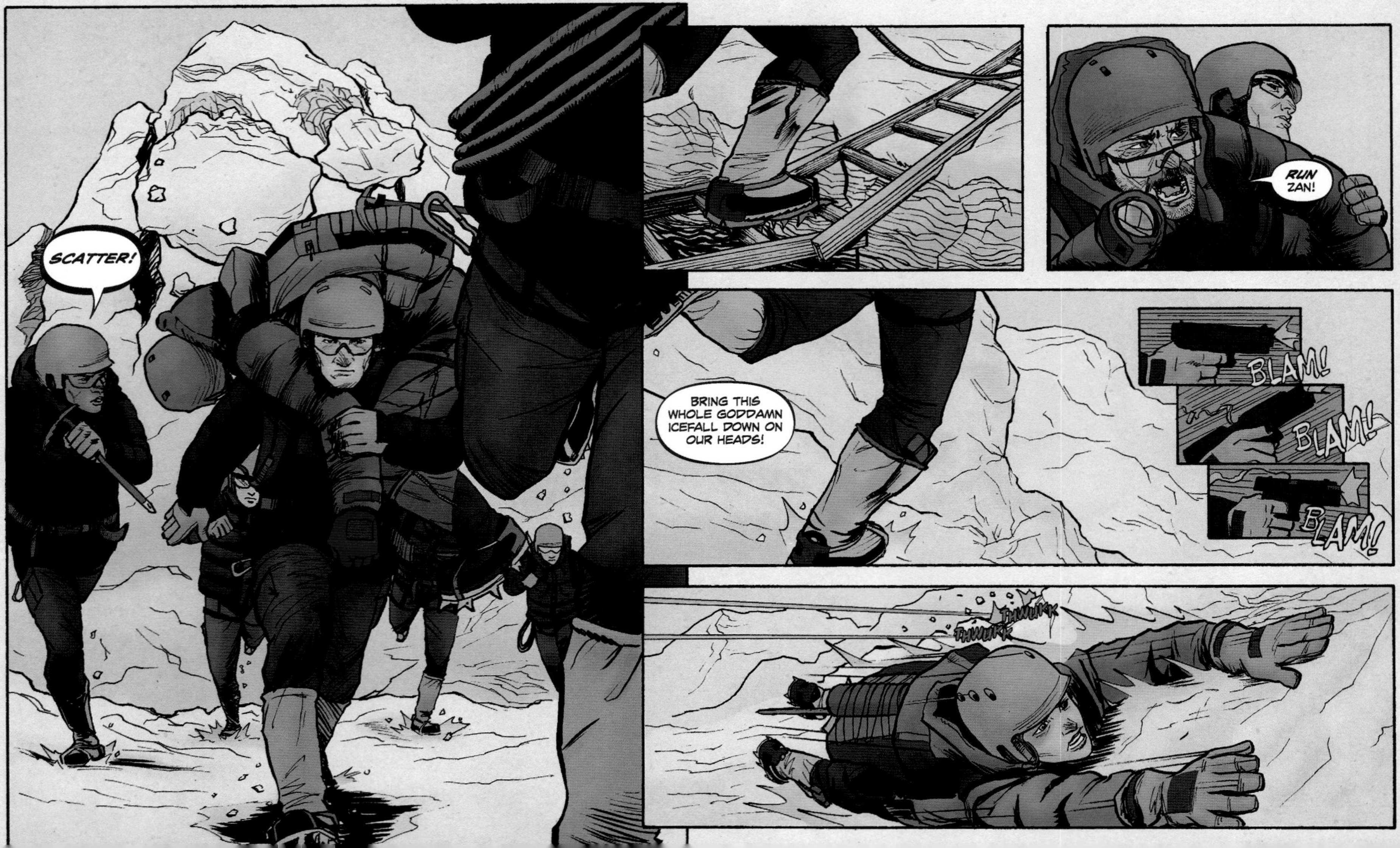
SCATTER!
RUN ZAN!
BRING THIS WHOLE GODDAMN ICEFALL DOWN ON OUR HEADS!
BLAM!
BLAM!
BLAM!
THWUKK
THWUKK

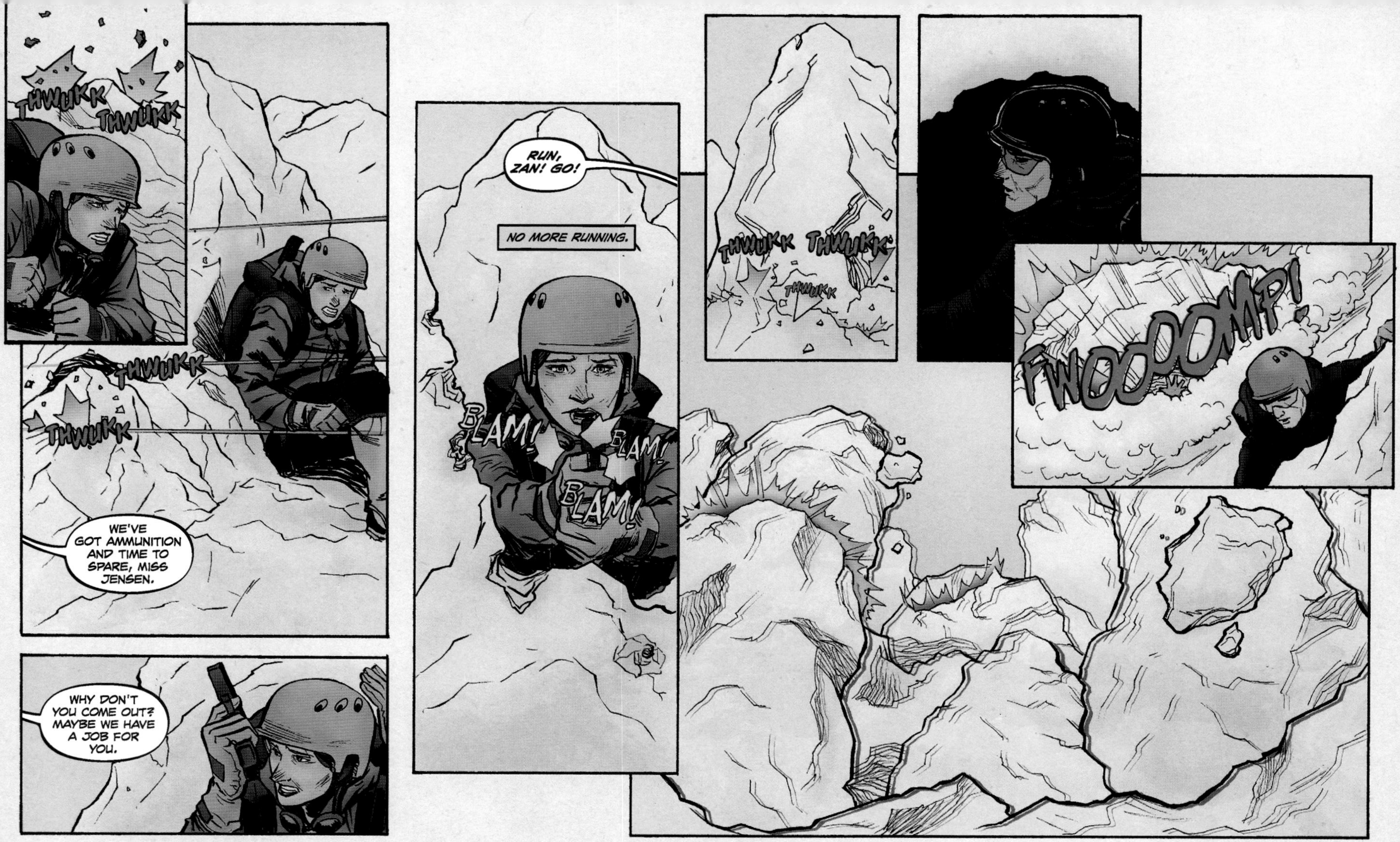
THWUKK
THWUKK
THWUKK
THWUKK
WE'VE GOT AMMUNITION AND TIME TO SPARE, MISS JENSEN.
WHY DON'T YOU COME OUT? MAYBE WE HAVE A JOB FOR YOU.
RUN, ZAN! GO!
NO MORE RUNNING.
BLAM!
BLAM!
BLAM!
THWUKK
THWUKK
THWUKK
FWOOOOMP!

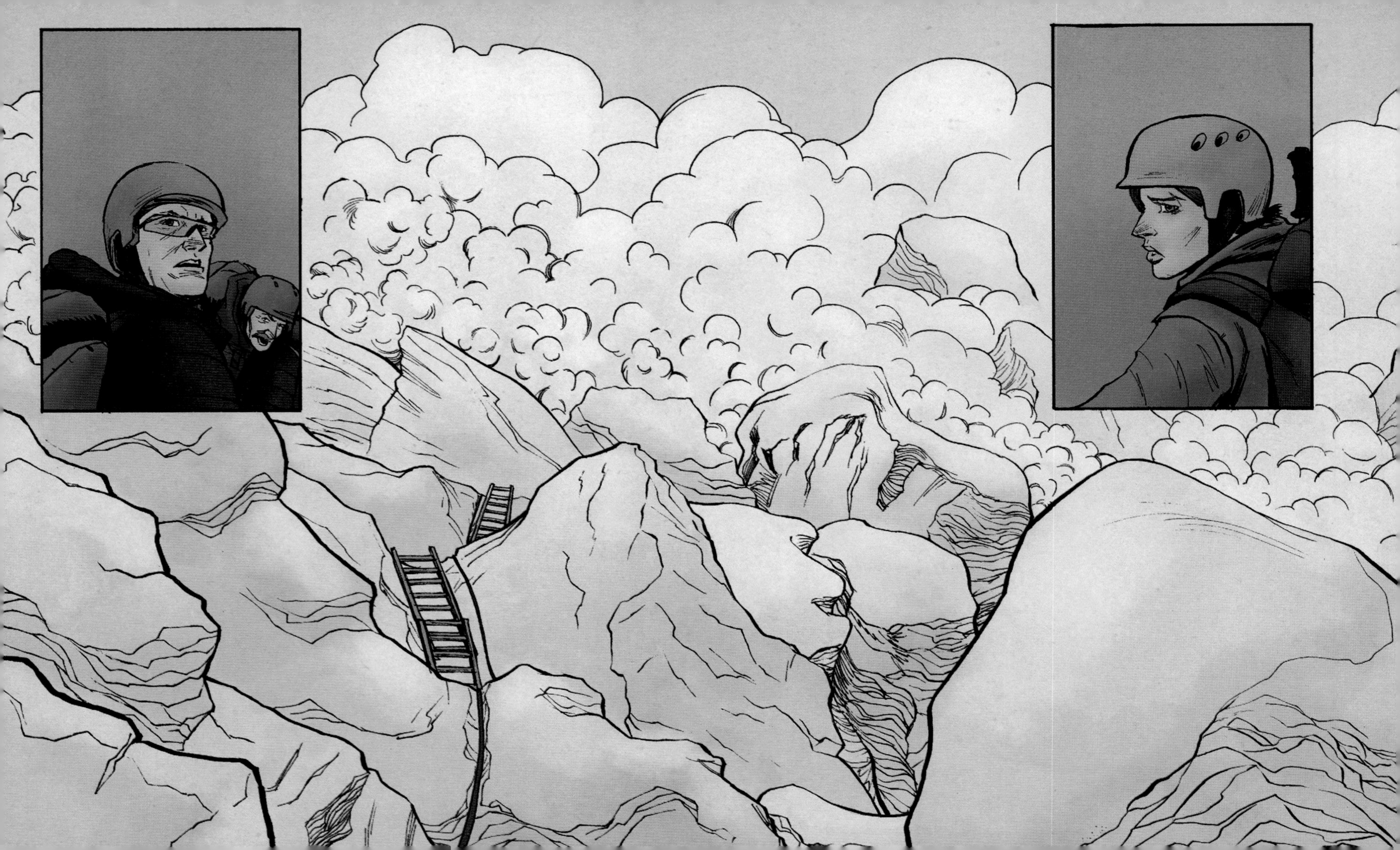

YOU SPEND ENOUGH TIME ON A
MOUNTAIN, PEOPLE WILL TALK
YOUR EAR OFF ABOUT AVALANCHES.

THE BIG BAD NIGHTMARES
OF WINTER SPORTS.

HOW TO WATCH
FOR THEM.

HOW TO GET OUT
OF THEIR WAY.

HOW TO SURVIVE
IF YOU GET HIT.

IT'S LIKE FLIGHT ATTENDANTS
EXPLAINING EMERGENCY
LANDING PROCEDURE.

THE FIRST TIME, YOU LISTEN.
THE FIFTH TIME YOU SKIM.
EVENTUALLY YOU TUNE IT OUT.

AND EVERY TIME, YOU THINK
TO YOURSELF "NOT ME."

"NOT IT."

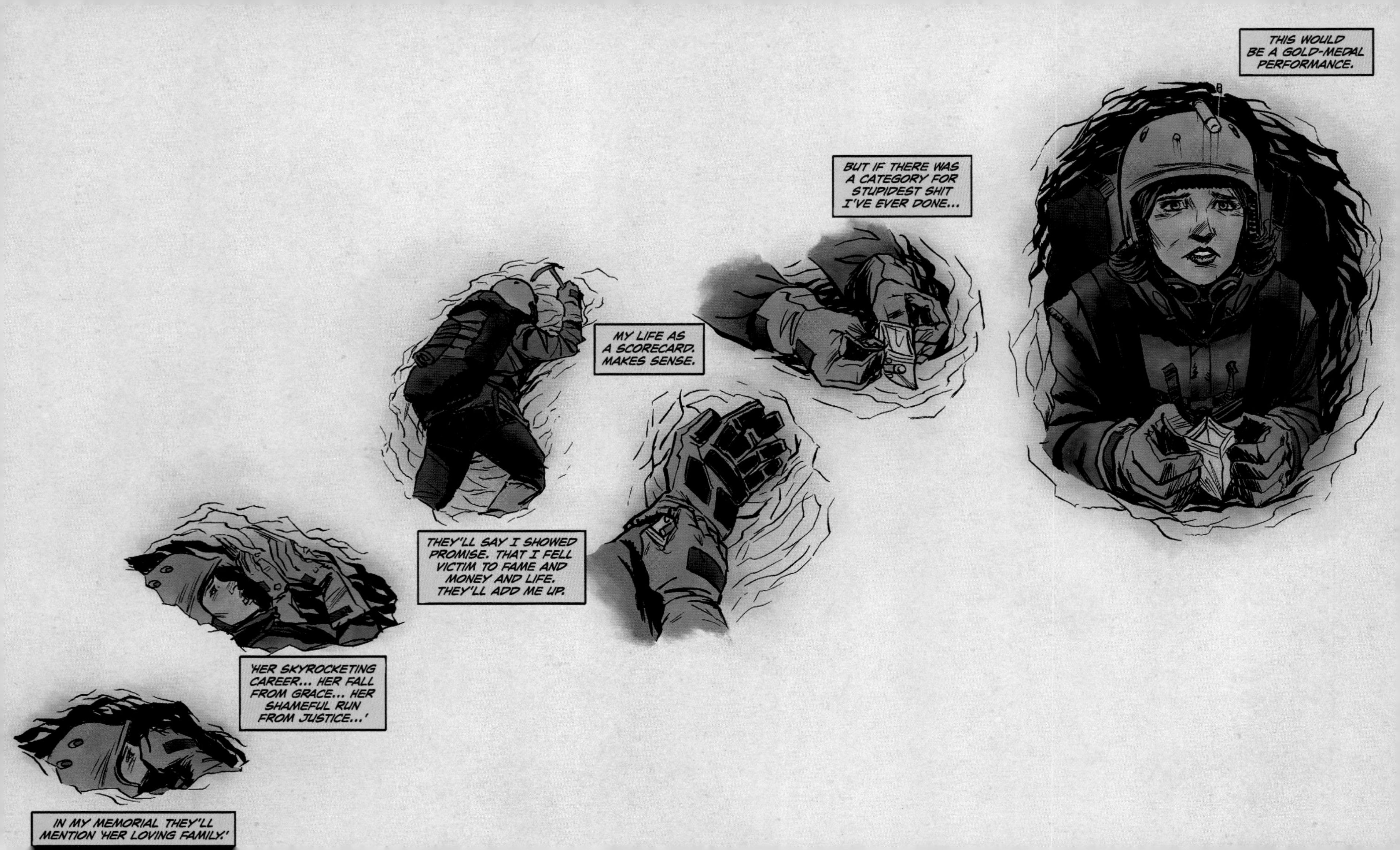
THIS WOULD BE A GOLD-MEDAL PERFORMANCE.
BUT IF THERE WAS A CATEGORY FOR STUPIDEST SHIT I'VE EVER DONE...
MY LIFE AS A SCORECARD. MAKES SENSE.
THEY'LL SAY I SHOWED PROMISE. THAT I FELL VICTIM TO FAME AND MONEY AND LIFE. THEY'LL ADD ME UP.
'HER SKYROCKETING CAREER... HER FALL FROM GRACE... HER SHAMEFUL RUN FROM JUSTICE...'
IN MY MEMORIAL THEY'LL MENTION 'HER LOVING FAMILY.'

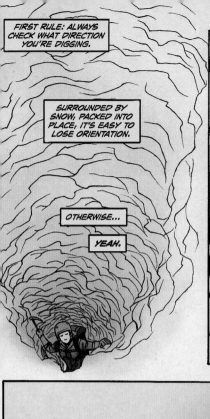

FIRST RULE: ALWAYS CHECK WHAT DIRECTION YOU'RE DIGGING.

SURROUNDED BY SNOW, PACKED INTO PLACE, IT'S EASY TO LOSE ORIENTATION.

OTHERWISE...

YEAH.

SECOND RULE: DITCH YOUR PACK, ANYTHING THAT'S WEIGHING YOU DOWN.

I'VE DONE TOO MUCH OF THAT.

SURE, IT'S FULL OF THINGS THAT COULD SAVE MY LIFE.

BUT ALL I CAN THINK OF ARE THE MEDALS.

CAN FEEL THEM THROUGH THE BOTTOM OF THE BAG.

I WORKED TOO HARD TO EARN THEM, FOUGHT TOO HARD TO KEEP THEM.

TOO HARD TO LEAVE THEM TO VANISH IN A GLACIER.

TOO HARD TO SAVE MYSELF INSTEAD OF THEM.

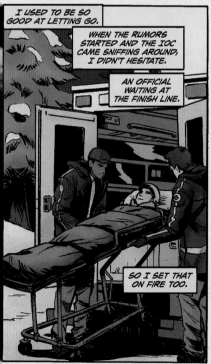

I USED TO BE SO GOOD AT LETTING GO.

WHEN THE RUMORS STARTED AND THE IOC CAME SNIFFING AROUND, I DIDN'T HESITATE.

AN OFFICIAL WAITING AT THE FINISH LINE.

SO I SET THAT ON FIRE TOO.

DAD LOVED TO TALK SHOP AT DINNER. STORIES OF D.U.I. DRUNKS IN HIS AMBULANCE, FAKING INJURIES TO ESCAPE A BREATHALYZER.

"THE KEY IS TO COMMIT, NO MATTER HOW DUMB OR DOOMED IT SEEMS," HE ONCE SAID.

"LIFE LESSONS," HE'D TELL MY HORRIFIED MOM.

I CAN'T REMEMBER WHAT HE SOUNDS LIKE, BUT I REMEMBER THAT.

IT'S SO WARM IN HERE. HOT EVEN.

SHOULD REST.

TAKE A BREAK.

TAKE...

TAKE IT...

TAKE...

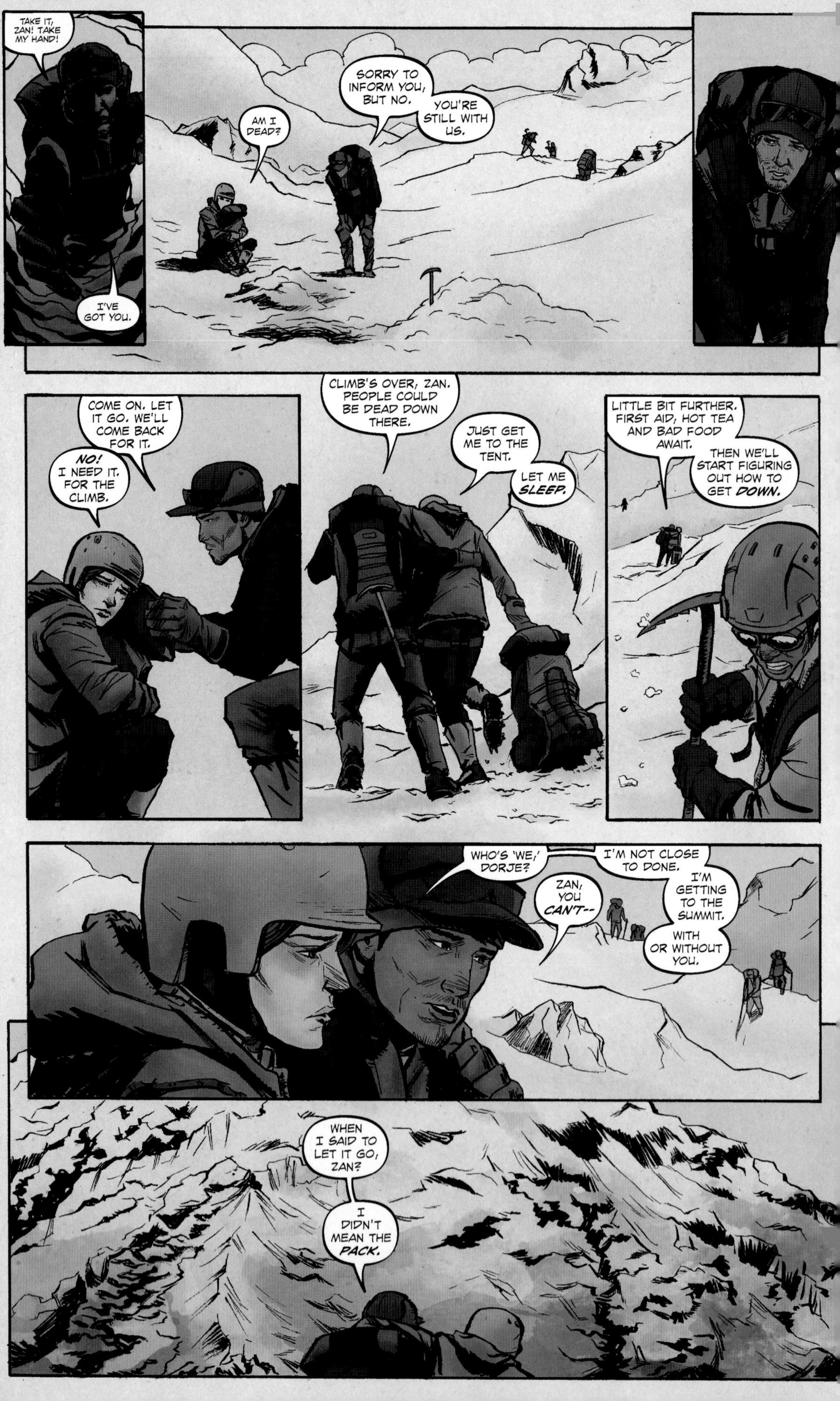
TAKE IT, ZAN! TAKE MY HAND!
I'VE GOT YOU.
AM I DEAD?
SORRY TO INFORM YOU, BUT NO.
YOU'RE STILL WITH US.
COME ON. LET IT GO. WE'LL COME BACK FOR IT.
NO! I NEED IT. FOR THE CLIMB.
CLIMB'S OVER, ZAN. PEOPLE COULD BE DEAD DOWN THERE.
JUST GET ME TO THE TENT.
LET ME SLEEP.
LITTLE BIT FURTHER. FIRST AID, HOT TEA AND BAD FOOD AWAIT.
THEN WE'LL START FIGURING OUT HOW TO GET DOWN.
WHO'S 'WE,' DORJE?
ZAN, YOU CAN'T--
I'M NOT CLOSE TO DONE.
I'M GETTING TO THE SUMMIT.
WITH OR WITHOUT YOU.
WHEN I SAID TO LET IT GO, ZAN?
I DIDN'T MEAN THE PACK.

GODDAM--

SAVE YOUR VOICE, ZAN. BREATHE. AND PLEASE STOP SWEARING.

WE'RE STUCK FOR THE NIGHT. WAITING FOR A TEAM FROM BASE CAMP TO COME CLEAR A PATH.

I DON'T *NEED* OXYGEN.

YOU'VE BEEN ASLEEP FOR A DAY. YOU'RE A WALKING BRUISE. YOU NEED TO HEAL.

WE'RE WASTING IT. I'M GONNA SHUT THIS OFF.

FINE. STOP. I'LL DO IT. DO YOU SEE HOW OUT OF IT YOU ARE?

LOOK AT YOUR HANDS.

A SPECK OF THIS LIP BALM ALL OVER THEM MEETS THE VALVE? YOU TRYING TO BLOW US ALL UP?

TOO LATE. ALREADY DID THAT.

TAKE SMALL SIPS. THEN IT'S BACK ON OXYGEN, BACK TO SLEEP FOR YOU.

WE CAN TALK LATER.

NOTHING TO TALK ABOUT. UNLESS YOU WANT TO GIVE ME ONE OF THOSE SMOKES?

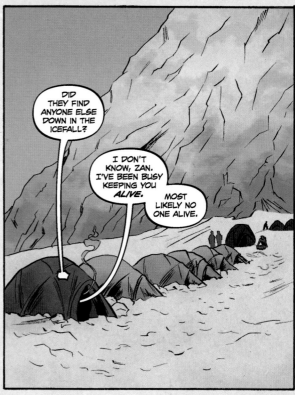

DID THEY FIND ANYONE ELSE DOWN IN THE ICEFALL?

I DON'T KNOW, ZAN. I'VE BEEN BUSY KEEPING YOU *ALIVE.*

MOST LIKELY NO ONE ALIVE.

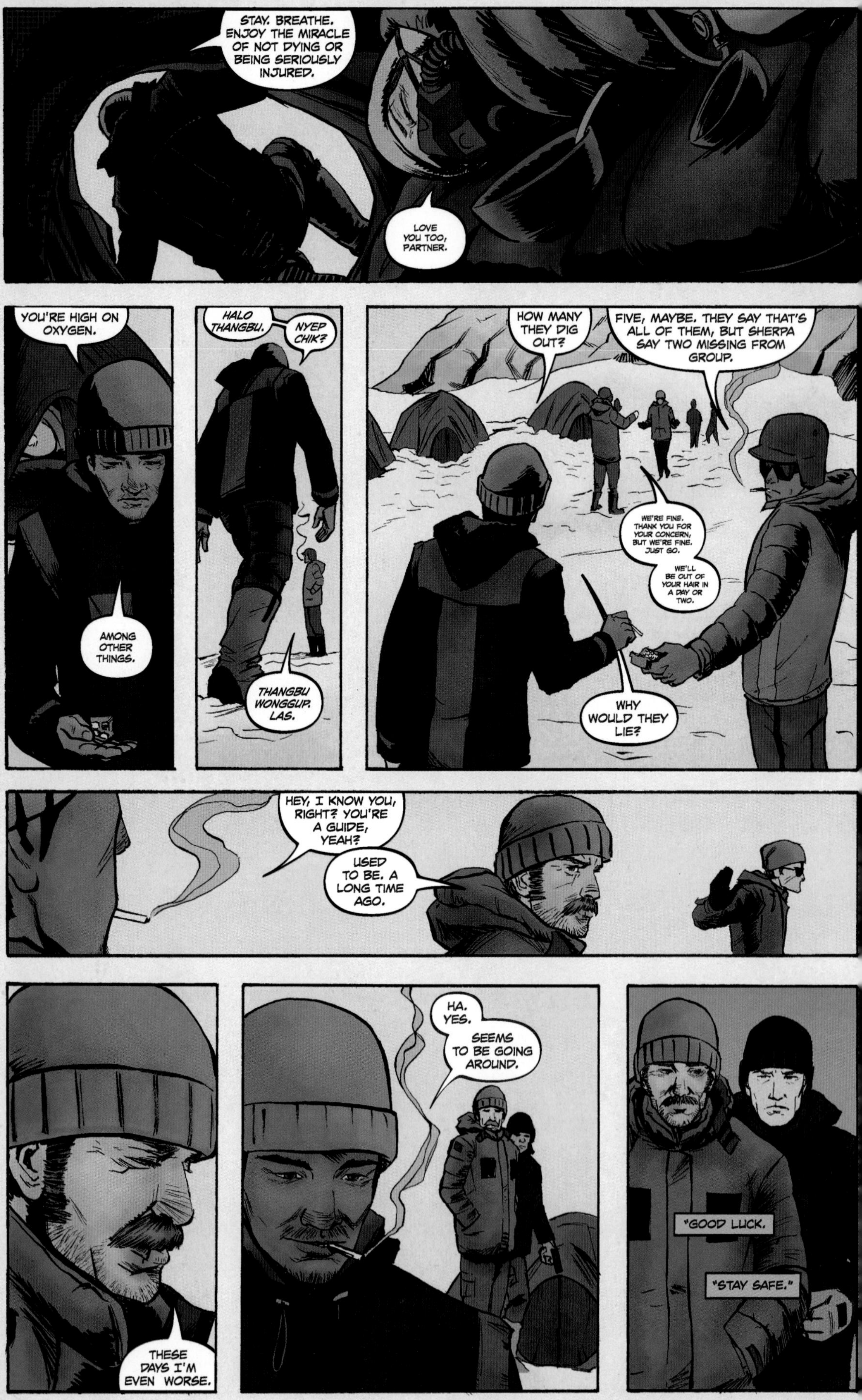
STAY. BREATHE. ENJOY THE MIRACLE OF NOT DYING OR BEING SERIOUSLY INJURED.
LOVE YOU TOO, PARTNER.
YOU'RE HIGH ON OXYGEN.
AMONG OTHER THINGS.
HALO THANGBU.
NYEP CHIK?
THANGBU WONGGUP. LAS.
HOW MANY THEY DIG OUT?
FIVE, MAYBE. THEY SAY THAT'S ALL OF THEM, BUT SHERPA SAY TWO MISSING FROM GROUP.
WE'RE FINE. THANK YOU FOR YOUR CONCERN, BUT WE'RE FINE. JUST GO.
WE'LL BE OUT OF YOUR HAIR IN A DAY OR TWO.
WHY WOULD THEY LIE?
HEY, I KNOW YOU, RIGHT? YOU'RE A GUIDE, YEAH?
USED TO BE. A LONG TIME AGO.
THESE DAYS I'M EVEN WORSE.
HA. YES.
SEEMS TO BE GOING AROUND.
"GOOD LUCK.
"STAY SAFE."

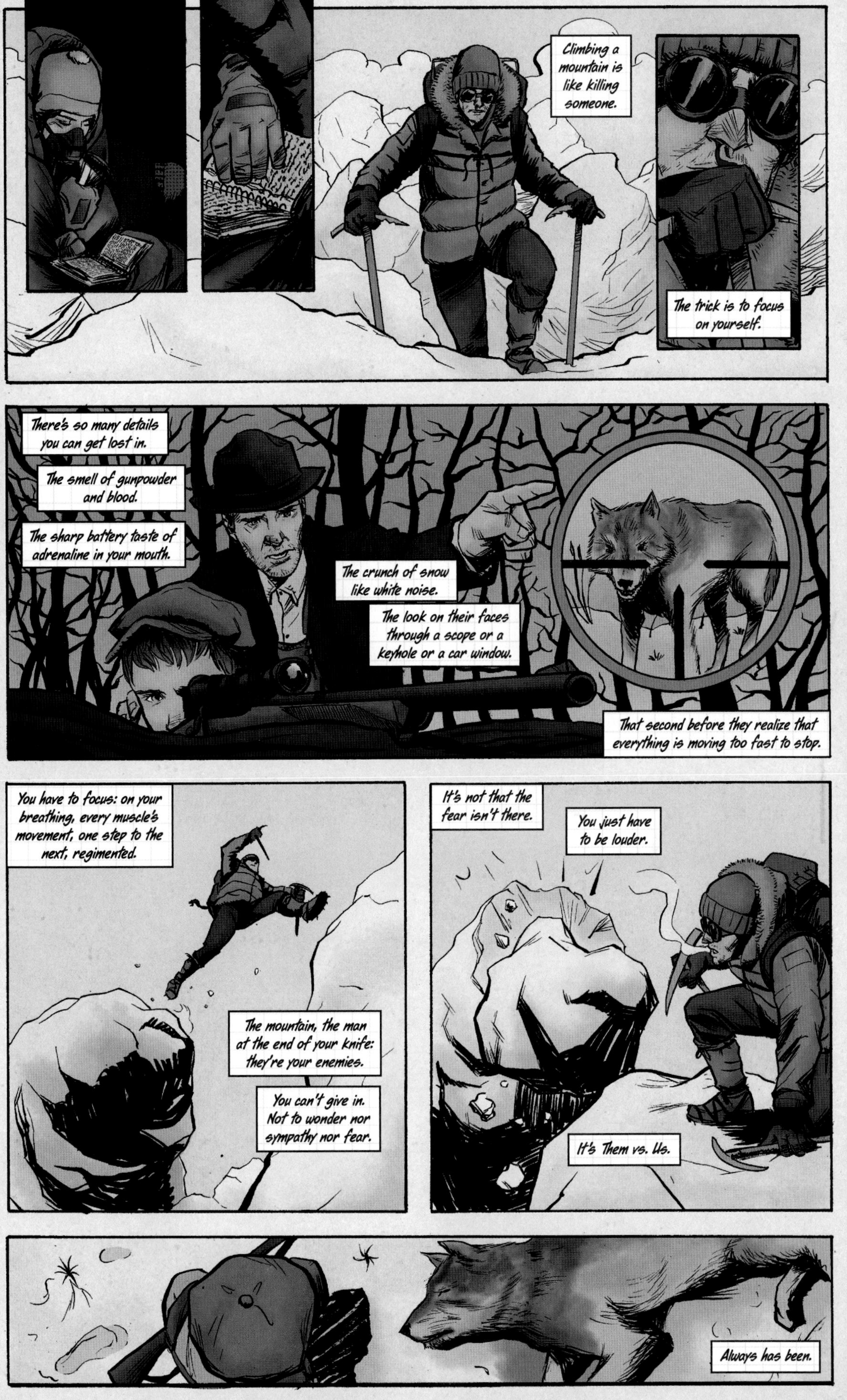
Climbing a mountain is like killing someone.
The trick is to focus on yourself.
There's so many details you can get lost in.
The smell of gunpowder and blood.
The sharp battery taste of adrenaline in your mouth.
The crunch of snow like white noise.
The look on their faces through a scope or a keyhole or a car window.
That second before they realize that everything is moving too fast to stop.
You have to focus: on your breathing, every muscle's movement, one step to the next, regimented.
The mountain, the man at the end of your knife: they're your enemies.
You can't give in. Not to wonder nor sympathy nor fear.
It's not that the fear isn't there.
You just have to be louder.
It's Them vs. Us.
Always has been.

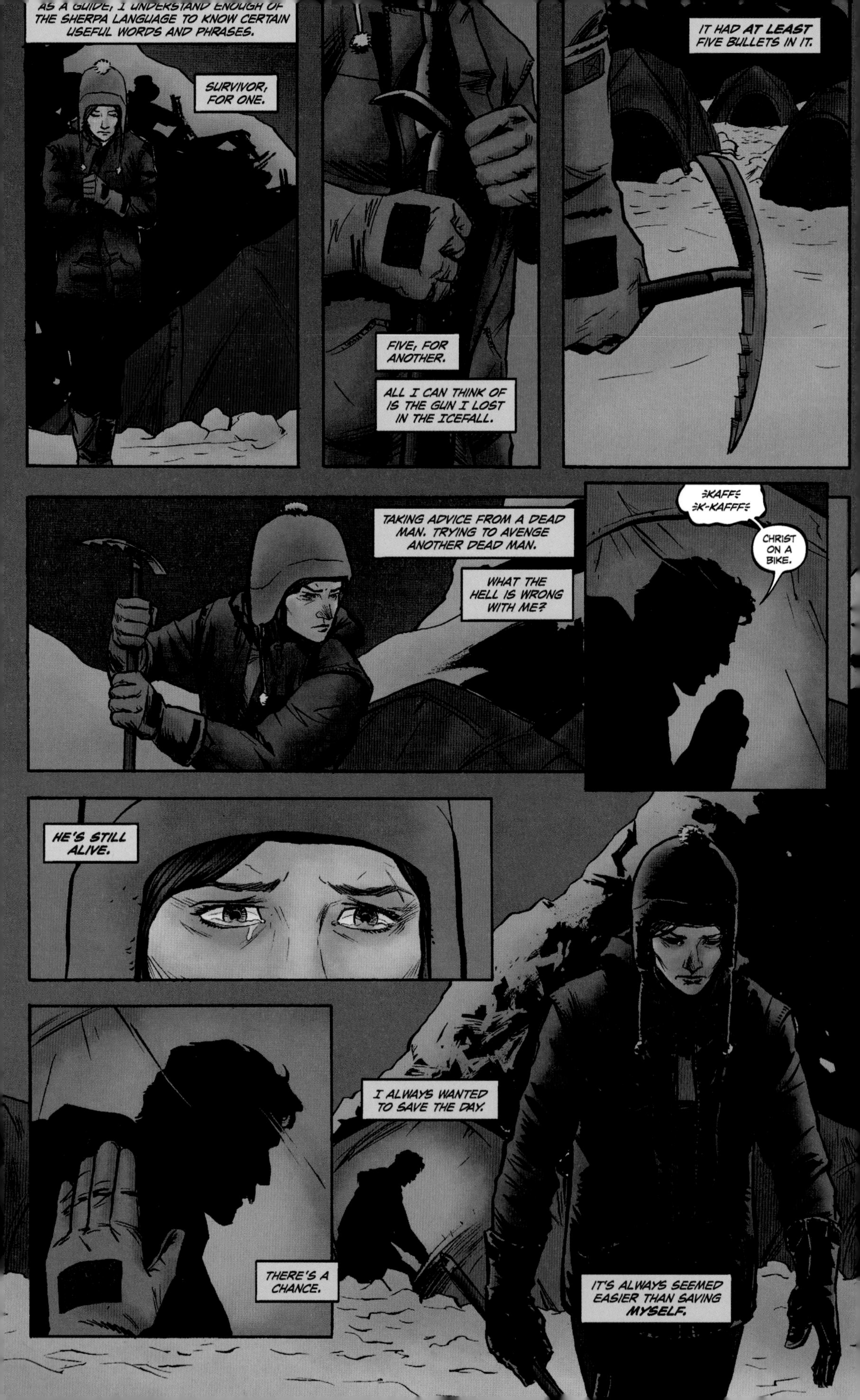
AS A GUIDE, I UNDERSTAND ENOUGH OF THE SHERPA LANGUAGE TO KNOW CERTAIN USEFUL WORDS AND PHRASES.
SURVIVOR, FOR ONE.
FIVE, FOR ANOTHER.
ALL I CAN THINK OF IS THE GUN I LOST IN THE ICEFALL.
IT HAD AT LEAST FIVE BULLETS IN IT.
TAKING ADVICE FROM A DEAD MAN. TRYING TO AVENGE ANOTHER DEAD MAN.
WHAT THE HELL IS WRONG WITH ME?
KAFF
K-KAFFF
CHRIST ON A BIKE.
HE'S STILL ALIVE.
THERE'S A CHANCE.
I ALWAYS WANTED TO SAVE THE DAY.
IT'S ALWAYS SEEMED EASIER THAN SAVING MYSELF.

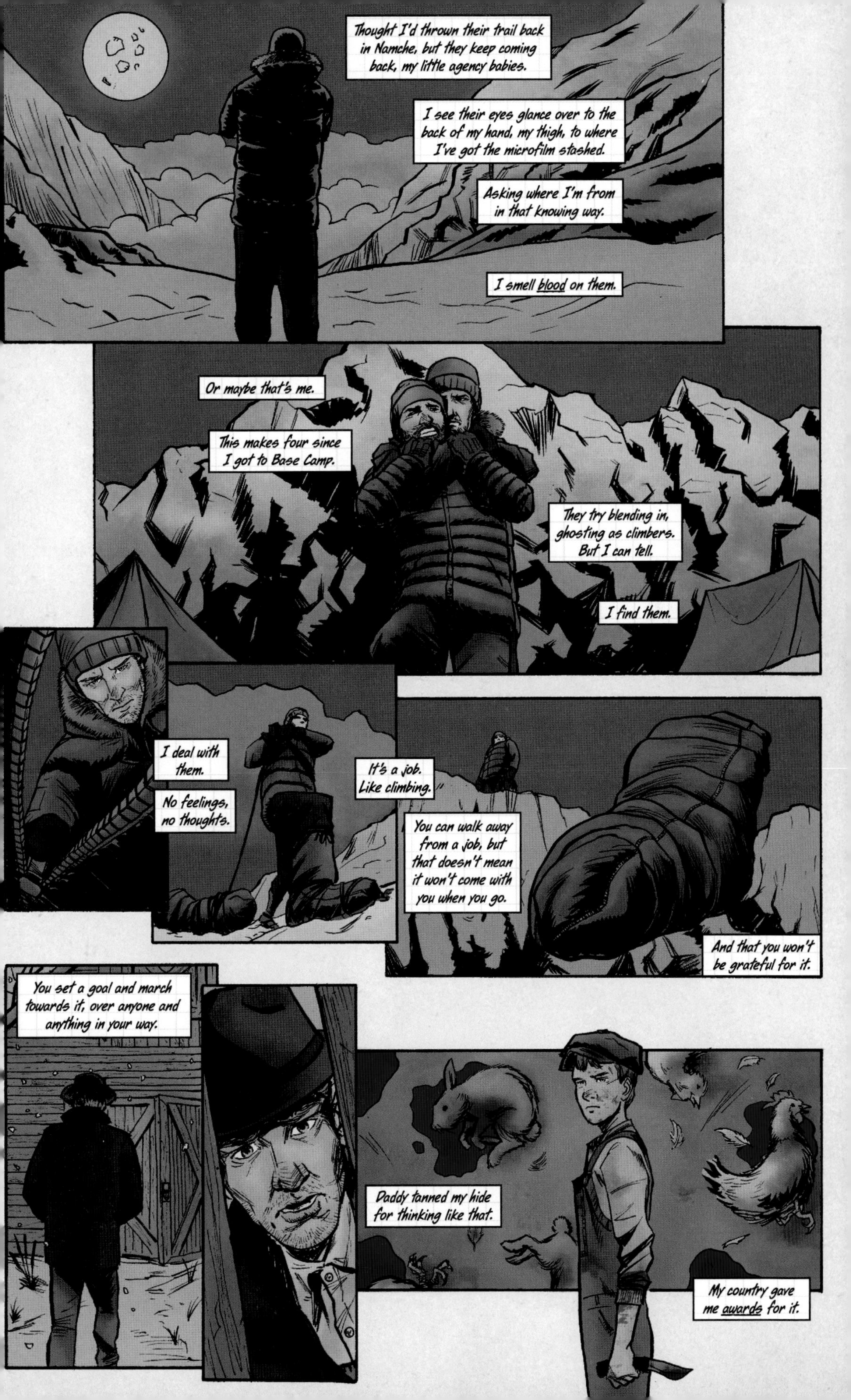
Thought I'd thrown their trail back in Namche, but they keep coming back, my little agency babies.
I see their eyes glance over to the back of my hand, my thigh, to where I've got the microfilm stashed.
Asking where I'm from in that knowing way.
I smell blood on them.
Or maybe that's me.
This makes four since I got to Base Camp.
They try blending in, ghosting as climbers. But I can tell.
I find them.
I deal with them.
No feelings, no thoughts.
It's a job. Like climbing.
You can walk away from a job, but that doesn't mean it won't come with you when you go.
And that you won't be grateful for it.
You set a goal and march towards it, over anyone and anything in your way.
Daddy tanned my hide for thinking like that.
My country gave me awards for it.

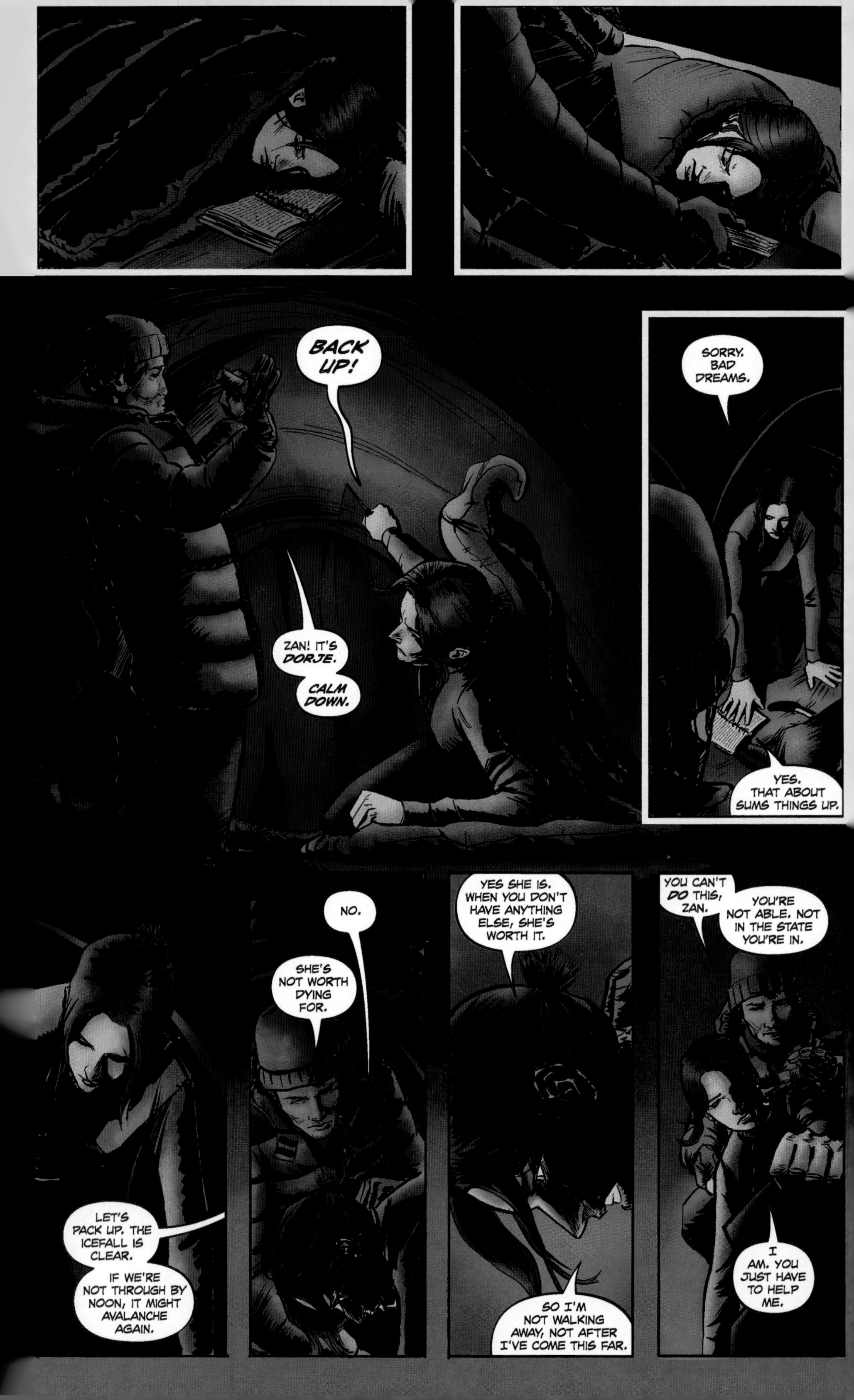
BACK UP!
ZAN! IT'S DORJE.
CALM DOWN.
SORRY. BAD DREAMS.
YES. THAT ABOUT SUMS THINGS UP.
LET'S PACK UP. THE ICEFALL IS CLEAR.
IF WE'RE NOT THROUGH BY NOON, IT MIGHT AVALANCHE AGAIN.
SHE'S NOT WORTH DYING FOR.
NO.
YES SHE IS. WHEN YOU DON'T HAVE ANYTHING ELSE, SHE'S WORTH IT.
SO I'M NOT WALKING AWAY, NOT AFTER I'VE COME THIS FAR.
YOU CAN'T DO THIS, ZAN.
YOU'RE NOT ABLE. NOT IN THE STATE YOU'RE IN.
I AM. YOU JUST HAVE TO HELP ME.

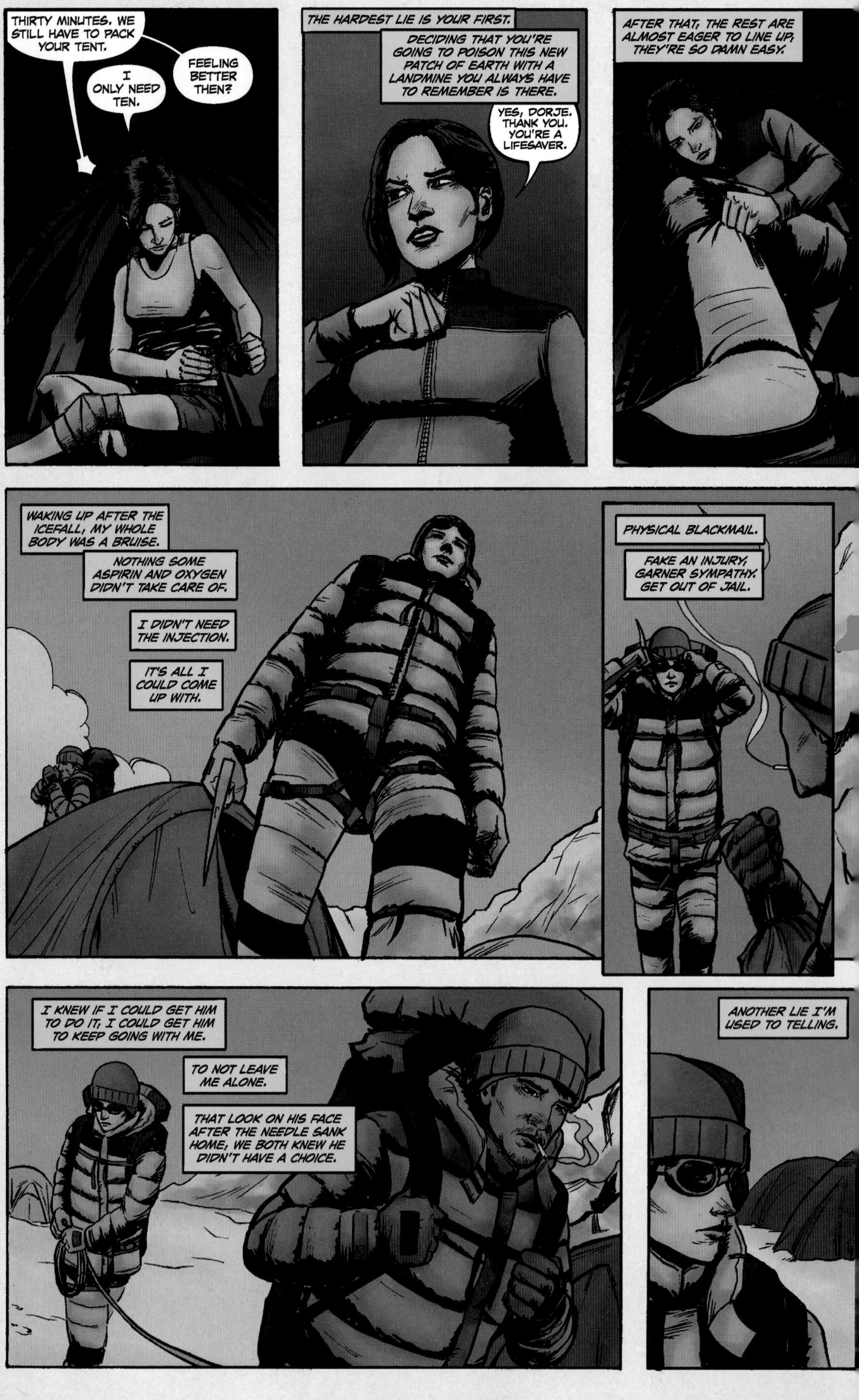
THIRTY MINUTES. WE STILL HAVE TO PACK YOUR TENT.
I ONLY NEED TEN.
FEELING BETTER THEN?
THE HARDEST LIE IS YOUR FIRST.
DECIDING THAT YOU'RE GOING TO POISON THIS NEW PATCH OF EARTH WITH A LANDMINE YOU ALWAYS HAVE TO REMEMBER IS THERE.
YES, DORJE. THANK YOU. YOU'RE A LIFESAVER.
AFTER THAT, THE REST ARE ALMOST EAGER TO LINE UP, THEY'RE SO DAMN EASY.
WAKING UP AFTER THE ICEFALL, MY WHOLE BODY WAS A BRUISE.
NOTHING SOME ASPIRIN AND OXYGEN DIDN'T TAKE CARE OF.
I DIDN'T NEED THE INJECTION.
IT'S ALL I COULD COME UP WITH.
PHYSICAL BLACKMAIL.
FAKE AN INJURY, GARNER SYMPATHY. GET OUT OF JAIL.
I KNEW IF I COULD GET HIM TO DO IT, I COULD GET HIM TO KEEP GOING WITH ME.
TO NOT LEAVE ME ALONE.
THAT LOOK ON HIS FACE AFTER THE NEEDLE SANK HOME; WE BOTH KNEW HE DIDN'T HAVE A CHOICE.
ANOTHER LIE I'M USED TO TELLING.

HATE TO BREAK IT TO YOU.

WE'VE GOT A TRAFFIC JAM AHEAD OF US.

"ZAN, PLEASE. PAY ATTENTION."

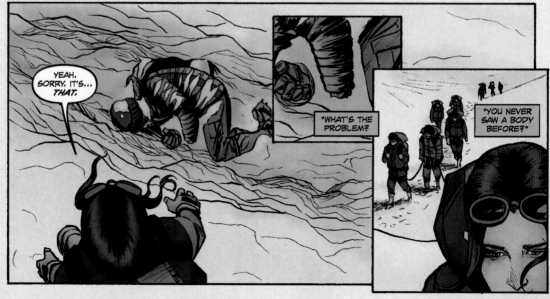

YEAH. SORRY. IT'S... THAT.

"WHAT'S THE PROBLEM?

"YOU NEVER SAW A BODY BEFORE?"

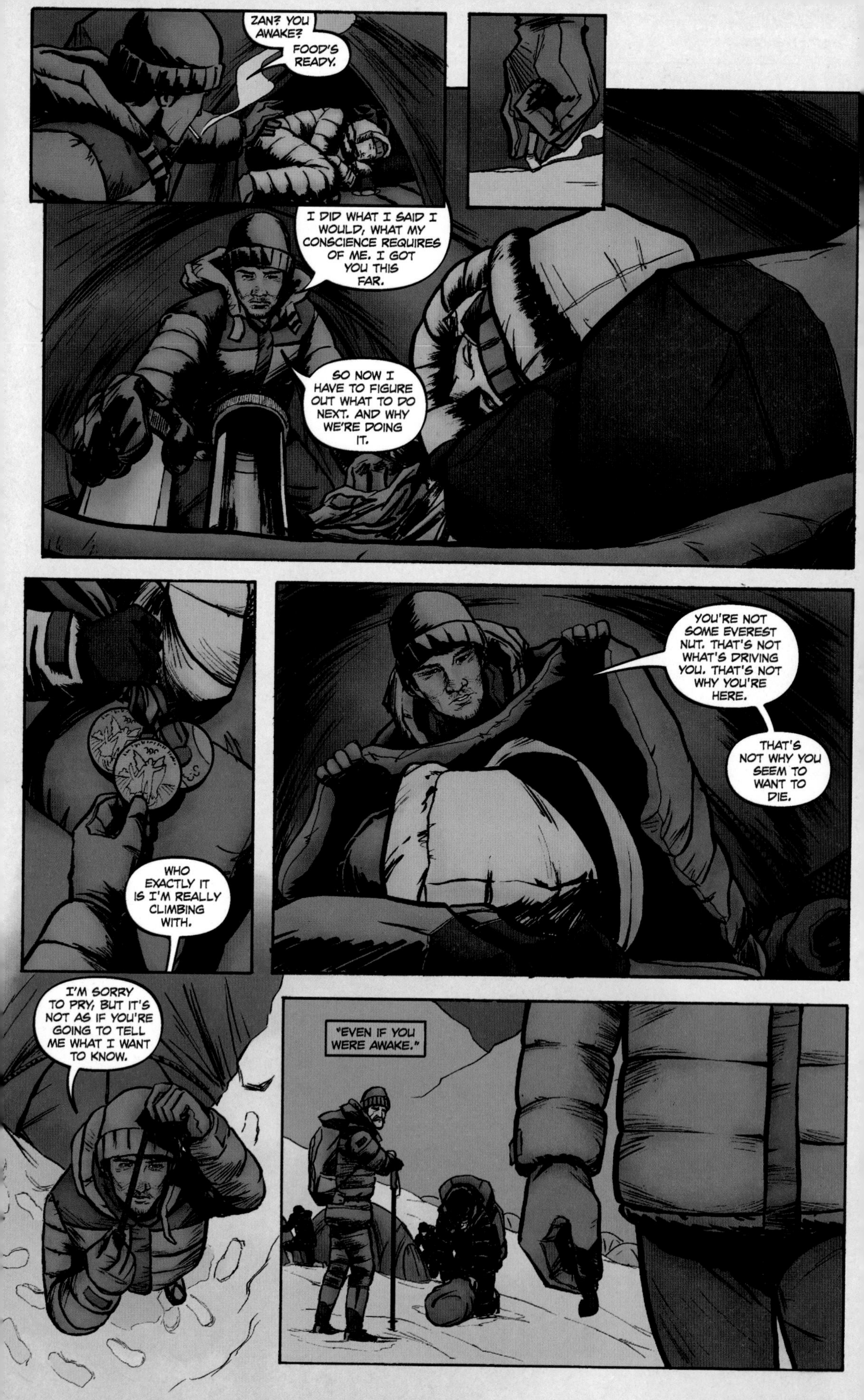

ZAN? YOU AWAKE?
FOOD'S READY.
I DID WHAT I SAID I WOULD, WHAT MY CONSCIENCE REQUIRES OF ME. I GOT YOU THIS FAR.
SO NOW I HAVE TO FIGURE OUT WHAT TO DO NEXT. AND WHY WE'RE DOING IT.
WHO EXACTLY IT IS I'M REALLY CLIMBING WITH.
YOU'RE NOT SOME EVEREST NUT. THAT'S NOT WHAT'S DRIVING YOU. THAT'S NOT WHY YOU'RE HERE.
THAT'S NOT WHY YOU SEEM TO WANT TO DIE.
I'M SORRY TO PRY, BUT IT'S NOT AS IF YOU'RE GOING TO TELL ME WHAT I WANT TO KNOW.
"EVEN IF YOU WERE AWAKE."

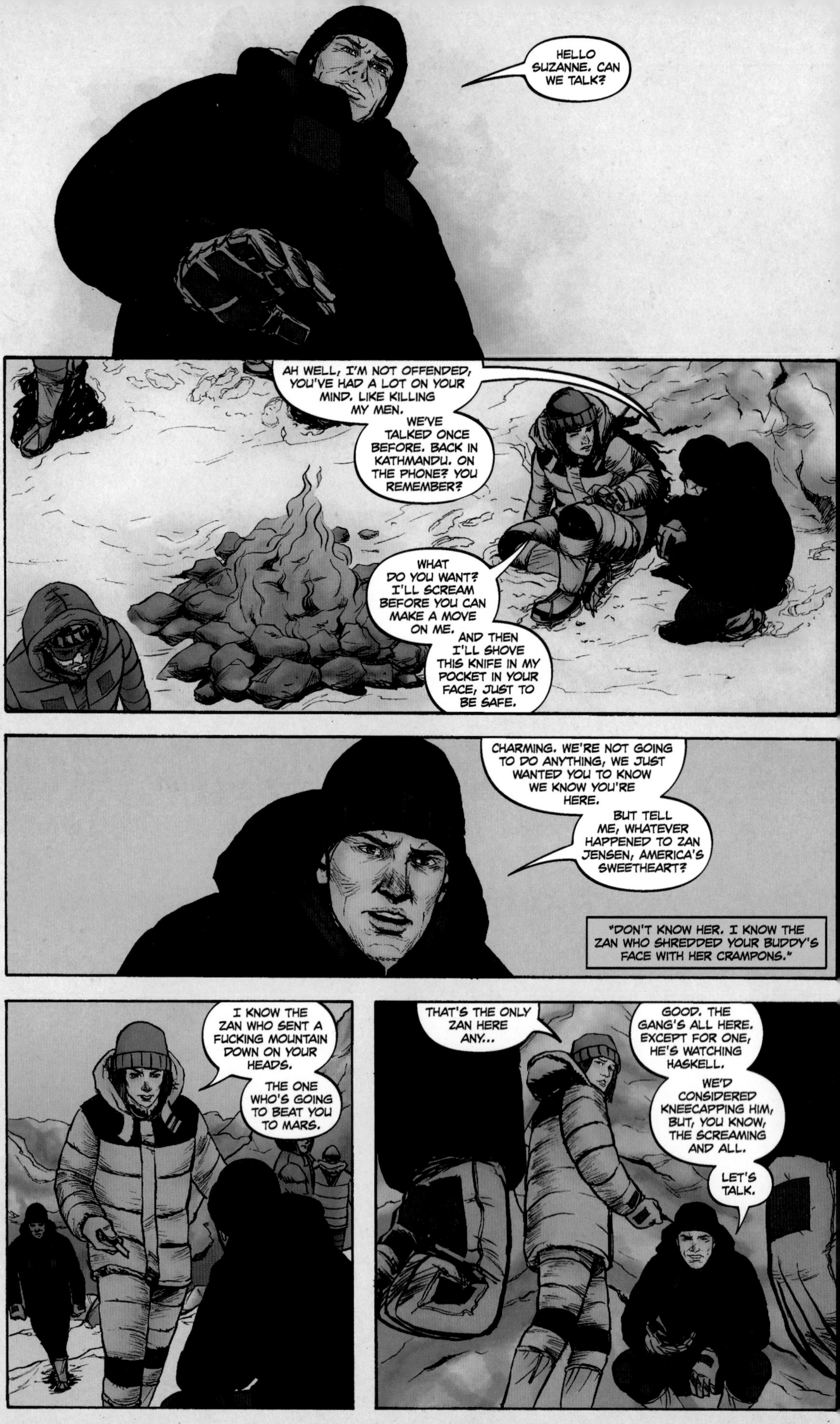
HELLO SUZANNE. CAN WE TALK?
AH WELL, I'M NOT OFFENDED, YOU'VE HAD A LOT ON YOUR MIND. LIKE KILLING MY MEN.
WE'VE TALKED ONCE BEFORE. BACK IN KATHMANDU. ON THE PHONE? YOU REMEMBER?
WHAT DO YOU WANT? I'LL SCREAM BEFORE YOU CAN MAKE A MOVE ON ME.
AND THEN I'LL SHOVE THIS KNIFE IN MY POCKET IN YOUR FACE, JUST TO BE SAFE.
CHARMING. WE'RE NOT GOING TO DO ANYTHING, WE JUST WANTED YOU TO KNOW WE KNOW YOU'RE HERE.
BUT TELL ME, WHATEVER HAPPENED TO ZAN JENSEN, AMERICA'S SWEETHEART?
"DON'T KNOW HER. I KNOW THE ZAN WHO SHREDDED YOUR BUDDY'S FACE WITH HER CRAMPONS."
I KNOW THE ZAN WHO SENT A FUCKING MOUNTAIN DOWN ON YOUR HEADS.
THE ONE WHO'S GOING TO BEAT YOU TO MARS.
THAT'S THE ONLY ZAN HERE ANY...
GOOD. THE GANG'S ALL HERE. EXCEPT FOR ONE, HE'S WATCHING HASKELL.
WE'D CONSIDERED KNEECAPPING HIM, BUT, YOU KNOW, THE SCREAMING AND ALL.
LET'S TALK.

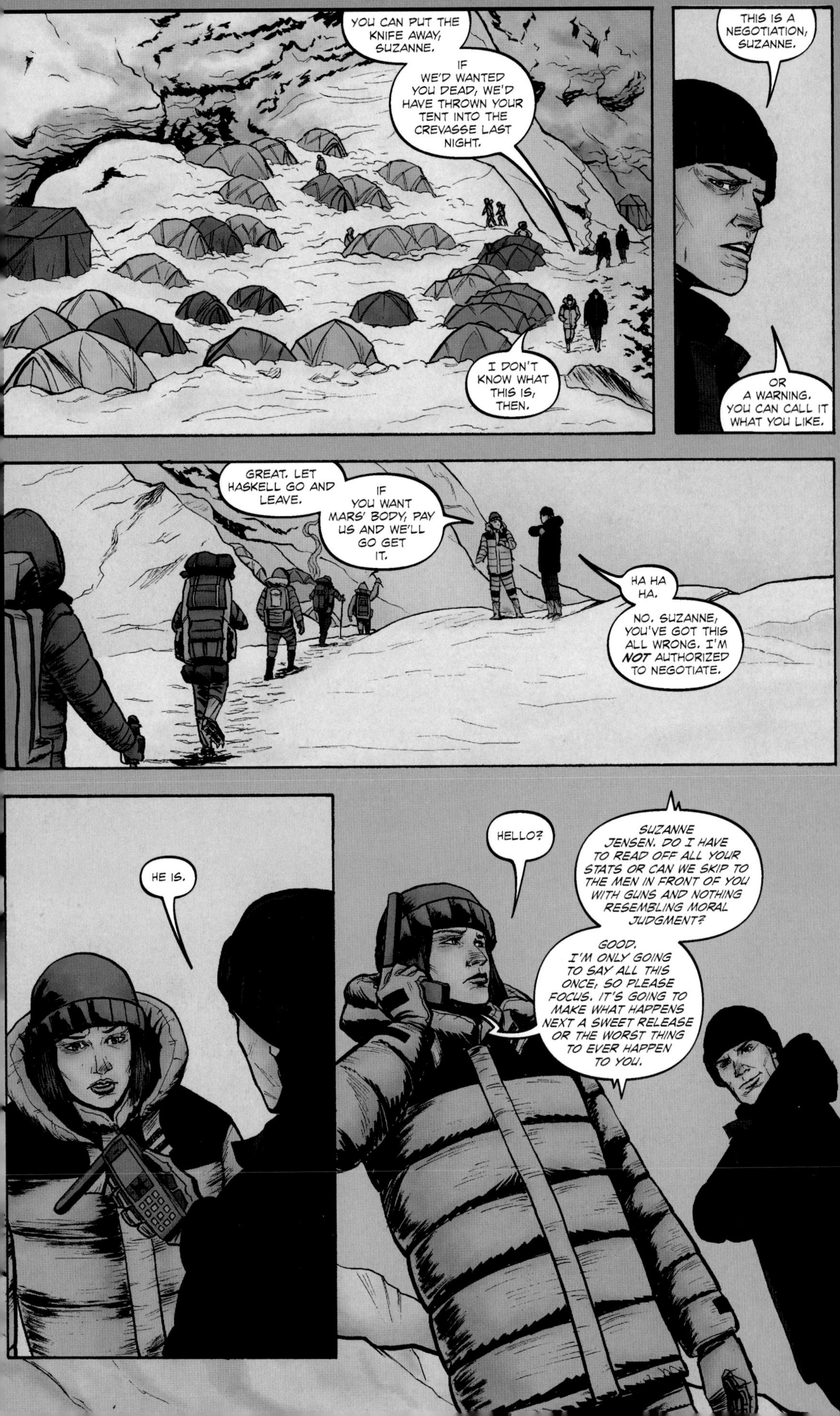
YOU CAN PUT THE KNIFE AWAY, SUZANNE.
IF WE'D WANTED YOU DEAD, WE'D HAVE THROWN YOUR TENT INTO THE CREVASSE LAST NIGHT.
I DON'T KNOW WHAT THIS IS, THEN.
THIS IS A NEGOTIATION, SUZANNE.
OR A WARNING. YOU CAN CALL IT WHAT YOU LIKE.
GREAT. LET HASKELL GO AND LEAVE.
IF YOU WANT MARS' BODY, PAY US AND WE'LL GO GET IT.
HA HA HA.
NO. SUZANNE, YOU'VE GOT THIS ALL WRONG. I'M NOT AUTHORIZED TO NEGOTIATE.
HE IS.
HELLO?
SUZANNE JENSEN. DO I HAVE TO READ OFF ALL YOUR STATS OR CAN WE SKIP TO THE MEN IN FRONT OF YOU WITH GUNS AND NOTHING RESEMBLING MORAL JUDGMENT?
GOOD. I'M ONLY GOING TO SAY ALL THIS ONCE, SO PLEASE FOCUS. IT'S GOING TO MAKE WHAT HAPPENS NEXT A SWEET RELEASE OR THE WORST THING TO EVER HAPPEN TO YOU.

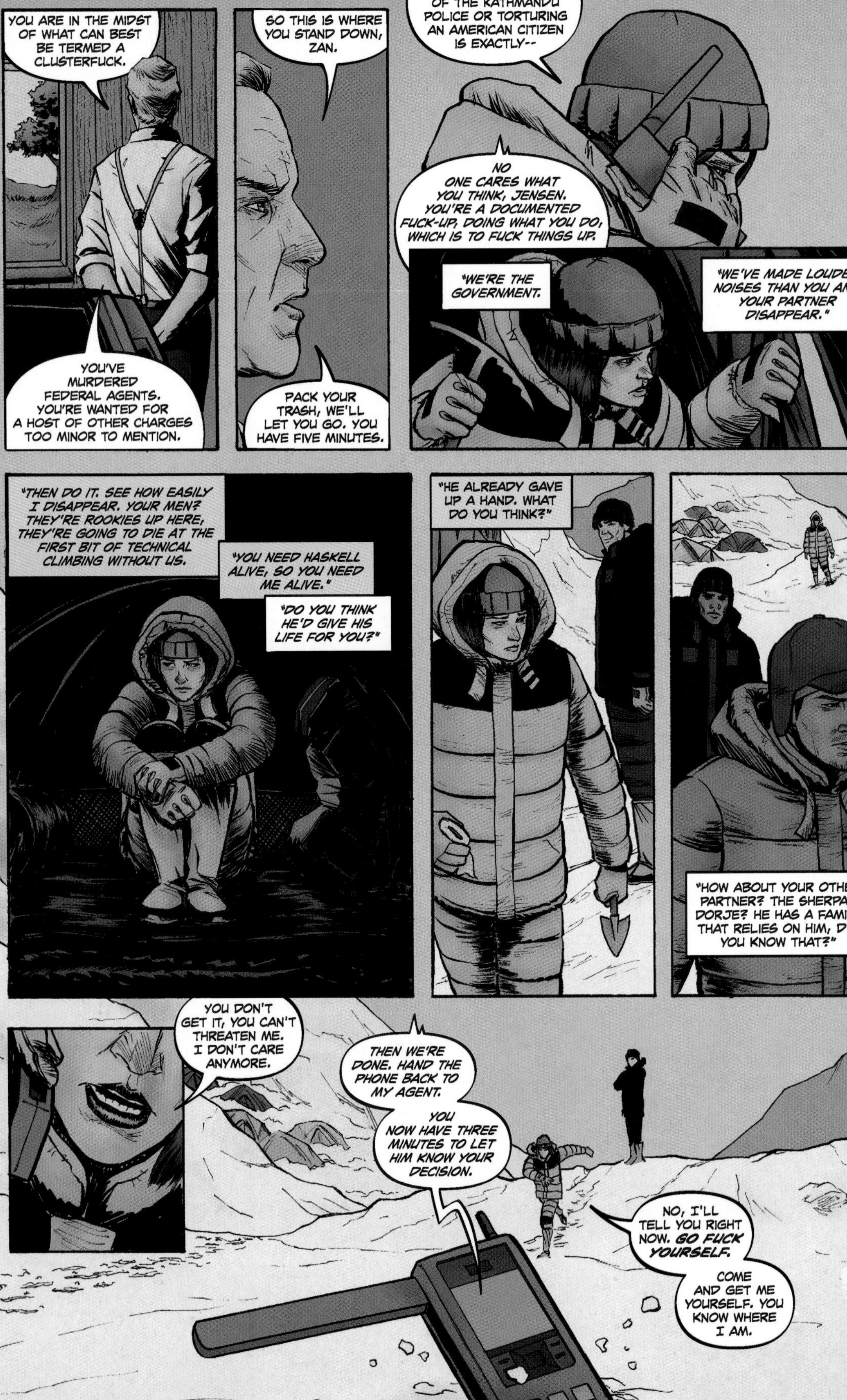
YOU ARE IN THE MIDST OF WHAT CAN BEST BE TERMED A CLUSTERFUCK.
YOU'VE MURDERED FEDERAL AGENTS. YOU'RE WANTED FOR A HOST OF OTHER CHARGES TOO MINOR TO MENTION.
SO THIS IS WHERE YOU STAND DOWN, ZAN.
PACK YOUR TRASH, WE'LL LET YOU GO. YOU HAVE FIVE MINUTES.
I DON'T THINK FEDERAL AGENTS MURDERING A MEMBER OF THE KATHMANDU POLICE OR TORTURING AN AMERICAN CITIZEN IS EXACTLY--
NO ONE CARES WHAT YOU THINK, JENSEN. YOU'RE A DOCUMENTED FUCK-UP, DOING WHAT YOU DO, WHICH IS TO FUCK THINGS UP.
"WE'RE THE GOVERNMENT.
"WE'VE MADE LOUDER NOISES THAN YOU AND YOUR PARTNER DISAPPEAR."
"THEN DO IT. SEE HOW EASILY I DISAPPEAR. YOUR MEN? THEY'RE ROOKIES UP HERE; THEY'RE GOING TO DIE AT THE FIRST BIT OF TECHNICAL CLIMBING WITHOUT US.
"YOU NEED HASKELL ALIVE, SO YOU NEED ME ALIVE."
"DO YOU THINK HE'D GIVE HIS LIFE FOR YOU?"
"HE ALREADY GAVE UP A HAND. WHAT DO YOU THINK?"
"HOW ABOUT YOUR OTHER PARTNER? THE SHERPA? DORJE? HE HAS A FAMILY THAT RELIES ON HIM, DID YOU KNOW THAT?"
YOU DON'T GET IT, YOU CAN'T THREATEN ME. I DON'T CARE ANYMORE.
THEN WE'RE DONE. HAND THE PHONE BACK TO MY AGENT.
YOU NOW HAVE THREE MINUTES TO LET HIM KNOW YOUR DECISION.
NO, I'LL TELL YOU RIGHT NOW. GO FUCK YOURSELF.
COME AND GET ME YOURSELF. YOU KNOW WHERE I AM.

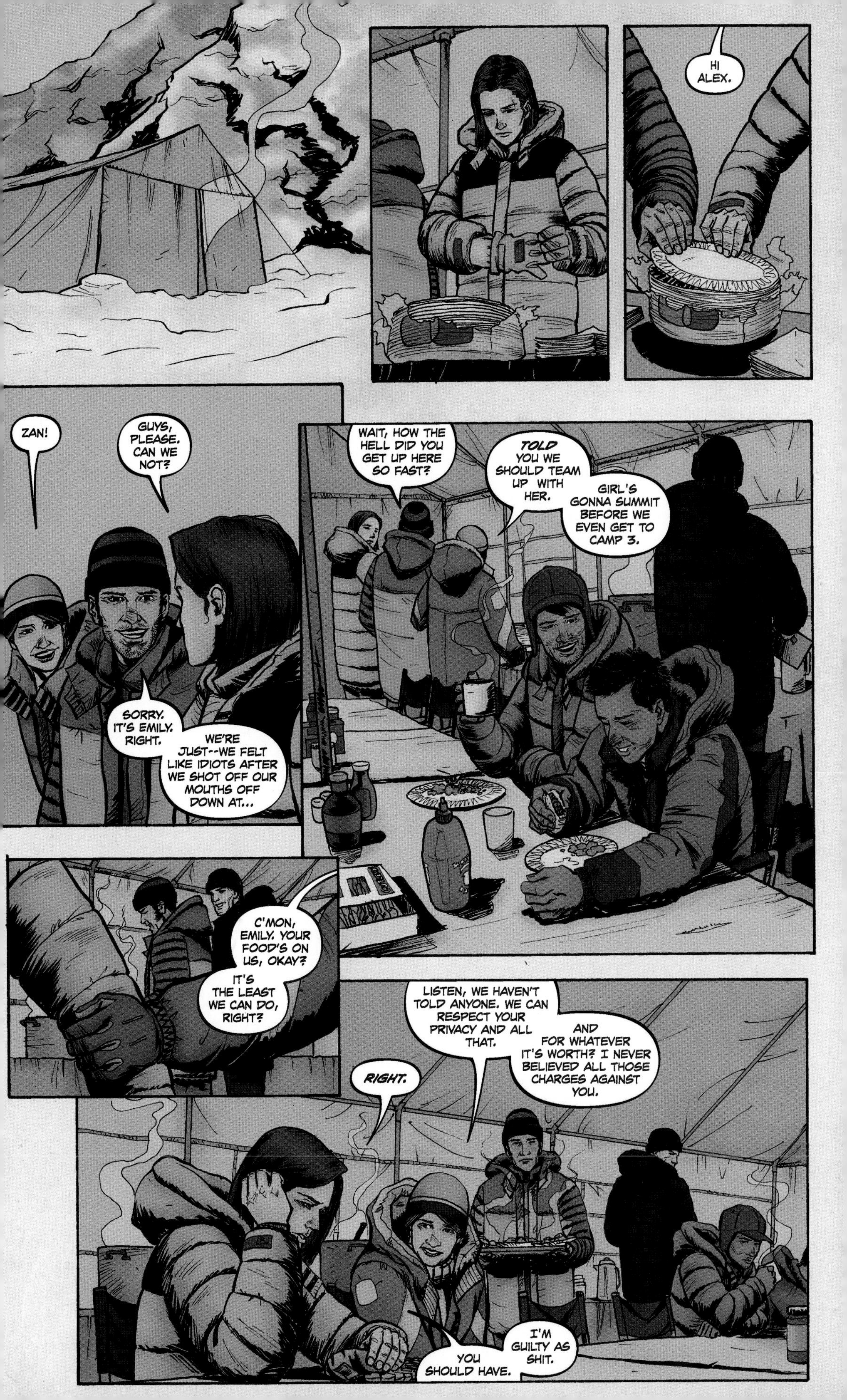
HI ALEX.
ZAN!
GUYS, PLEASE. CAN WE NOT?
SORRY. IT'S EMILY. RIGHT.
WE'RE JUST--WE FELT LIKE IDIOTS AFTER WE SHOT OFF OUR MOUTHS OFF DOWN AT...
WAIT, HOW THE HELL DID YOU GET UP HERE SO FAST?
TOLD YOU WE SHOULD TEAM UP WITH HER.
GIRL'S GONNA SUMMIT BEFORE WE EVEN GET TO CAMP 3.
C'MON, EMILY. YOUR FOOD'S ON US, OKAY?
IT'S THE LEAST WE CAN DO, RIGHT?
LISTEN, WE HAVEN'T TOLD ANYONE. WE CAN RESPECT YOUR PRIVACY AND ALL THAT.
AND FOR WHATEVER IT'S WORTH? I NEVER BELIEVED ALL THOSE CHARGES AGAINST YOU.
RIGHT.
YOU SHOULD HAVE.
I'M GUILTY AS SHIT.

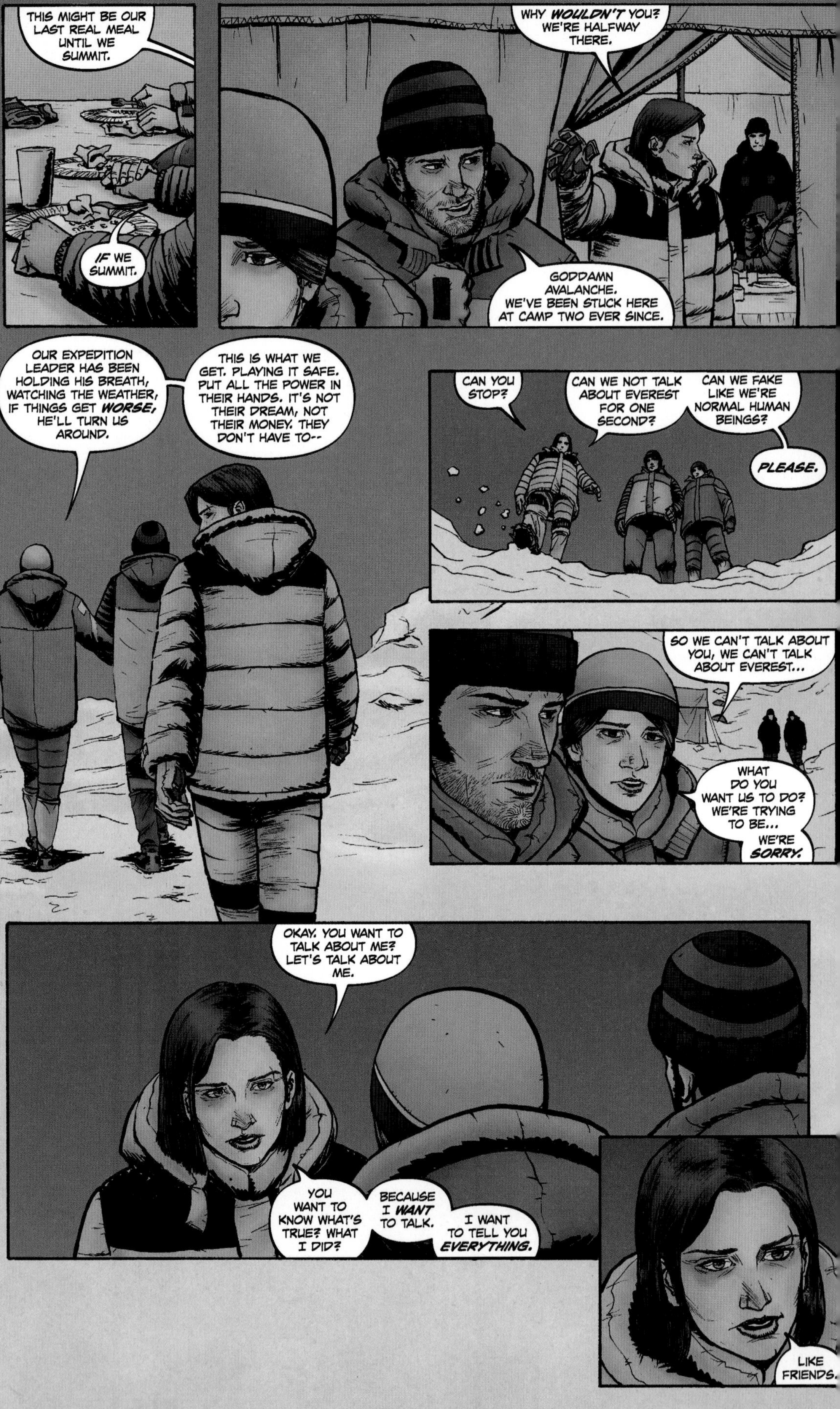
THIS MIGHT BE OUR LAST REAL MEAL UNTIL WE SUMMIT.
IF WE SUMMIT.
WHY WOULDN'T YOU? WE'RE HALFWAY THERE.
GODDAMN AVALANCHE. WE'VE BEEN STUCK HERE AT CAMP TWO EVER SINCE.
OUR EXPEDITION LEADER HAS BEEN HOLDING HIS BREATH, WATCHING THE WEATHER, IF THINGS GET WORSE, HE'LL TURN US AROUND.
THIS IS WHAT WE GET. PLAYING IT SAFE. PUT ALL THE POWER IN THEIR HANDS. IT'S NOT THEIR DREAM, NOT THEIR MONEY. THEY DON'T HAVE TO--
CAN YOU STOP?
CAN WE NOT TALK ABOUT EVEREST FOR ONE SECOND?
CAN WE FAKE LIKE WE'RE NORMAL HUMAN BEINGS?
PLEASE.
SO WE CAN'T TALK ABOUT YOU, WE CAN'T TALK ABOUT EVEREST...
WHAT DO YOU WANT US TO DO? WE'RE TRYING TO BE...
WE'RE SORRY.
OKAY. YOU WANT TO TALK ABOUT ME? LET'S TALK ABOUT ME.
YOU WANT TO KNOW WHAT'S TRUE? WHAT I DID?
BECAUSE I WANT TO TALK.
I WANT TO TELL YOU EVERYTHING.
LIKE FRIENDS.

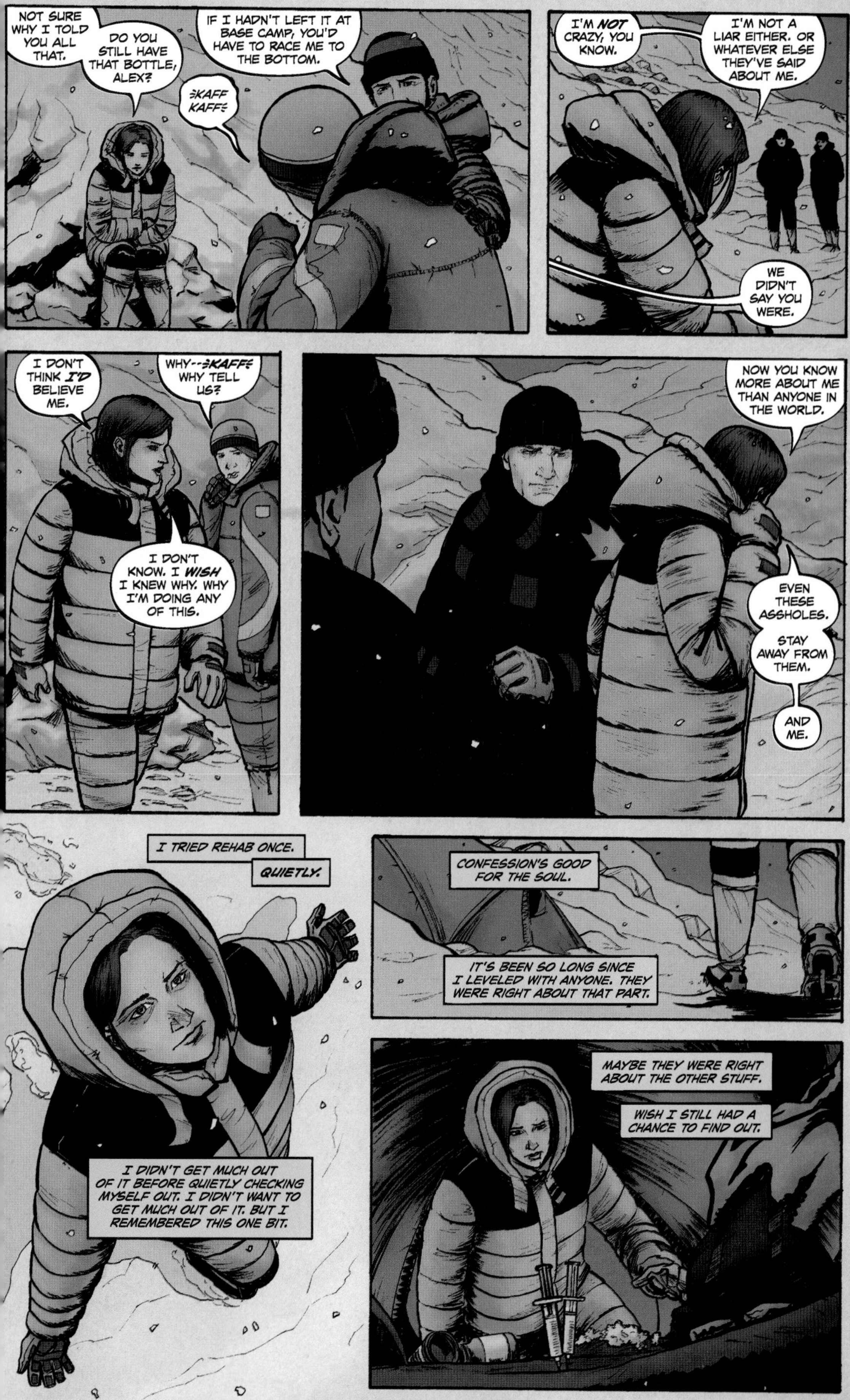
NOT SURE WHY I TOLD YOU ALL THAT.
DO YOU STILL HAVE THAT BOTTLE, ALEX?
IF I HADN'T LEFT IT AT BASE CAMP, YOU'D HAVE TO RACE ME TO THE BOTTOM.
=KAFF KAFF=
I'M NOT CRAZY, YOU KNOW.
I'M NOT A LIAR EITHER. OR WHATEVER ELSE THEY'VE SAID ABOUT ME.
WE DIDN'T SAY YOU WERE.
I DON'T THINK I'D BELIEVE ME.
WHY--=KAFF= WHY TELL US?
I DON'T KNOW. I WISH I KNEW WHY. WHY I'M DOING ANY OF THIS.
NOW YOU KNOW MORE ABOUT ME THAN ANYONE IN THE WORLD.
EVEN THESE ASSHOLES.
STAY AWAY FROM THEM.
AND ME.
I TRIED REHAB ONCE.
QUIETLY.
I DIDN'T GET MUCH OUT OF IT BEFORE QUIETLY CHECKING MYSELF OUT. I DIDN'T WANT TO GET MUCH OUT OF IT. BUT I REMEMBERED THIS ONE BIT.
CONFESSION'S GOOD FOR THE SOUL.
IT'S BEEN SO LONG SINCE I LEVELED WITH ANYONE. THEY WERE RIGHT ABOUT THAT PART.
MAYBE THEY WERE RIGHT ABOUT THE OTHER STUFF.
WISH I STILL HAD A CHANCE TO FIND OUT.

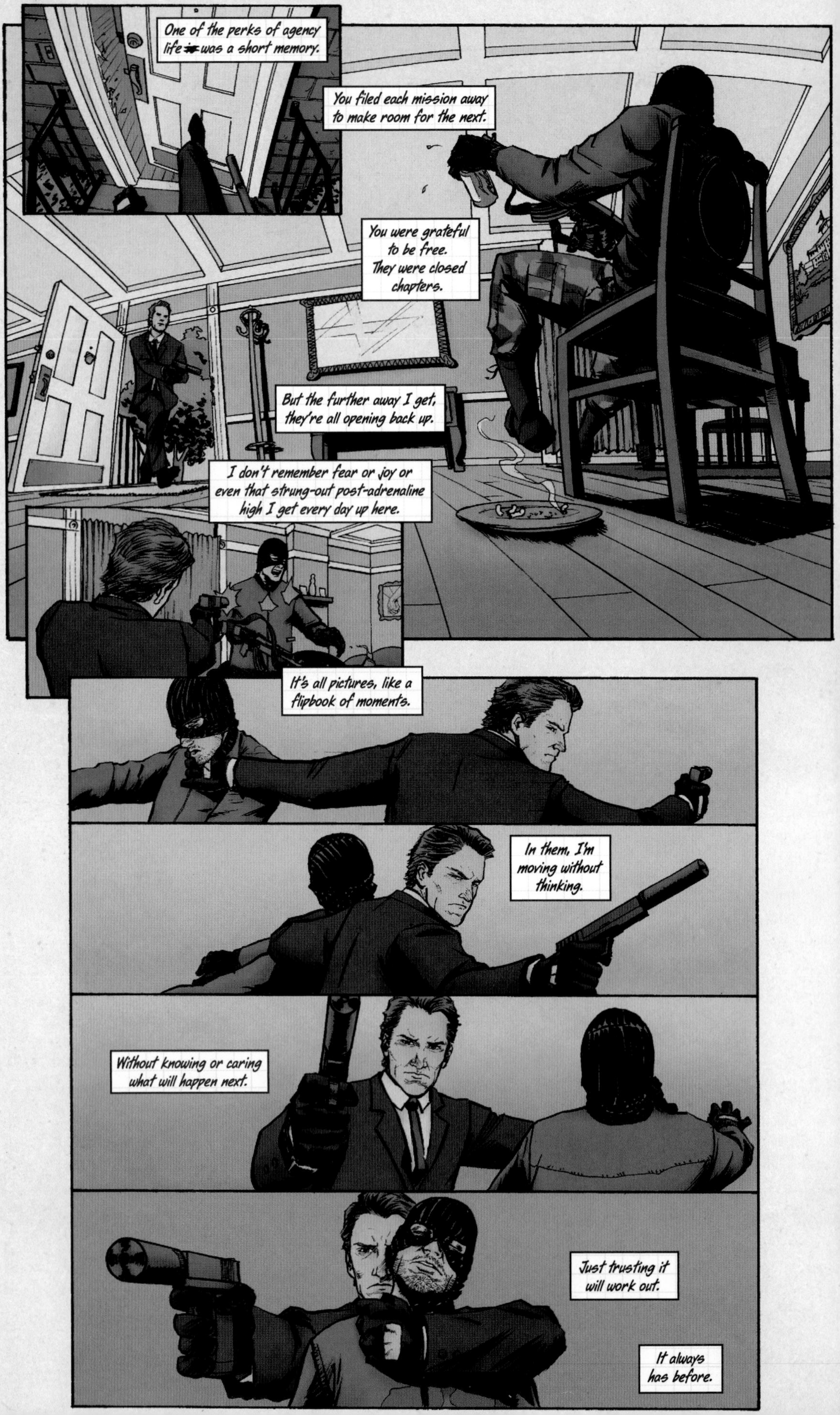
One of the perks of agency life was a short memory.
You filed each mission away to make room for the next.
You were grateful to be free. They were closed chapters.
But the further away I get, they're all opening back up.
I don't remember fear or joy or even that strung-out post-adrenaline high I get every day up here.
It's all pictures, like a flipbook of moments.
In them, I'm moving without thinking.
Without knowing or caring what will happen next.
Just trusting it will work out.
It always has before.

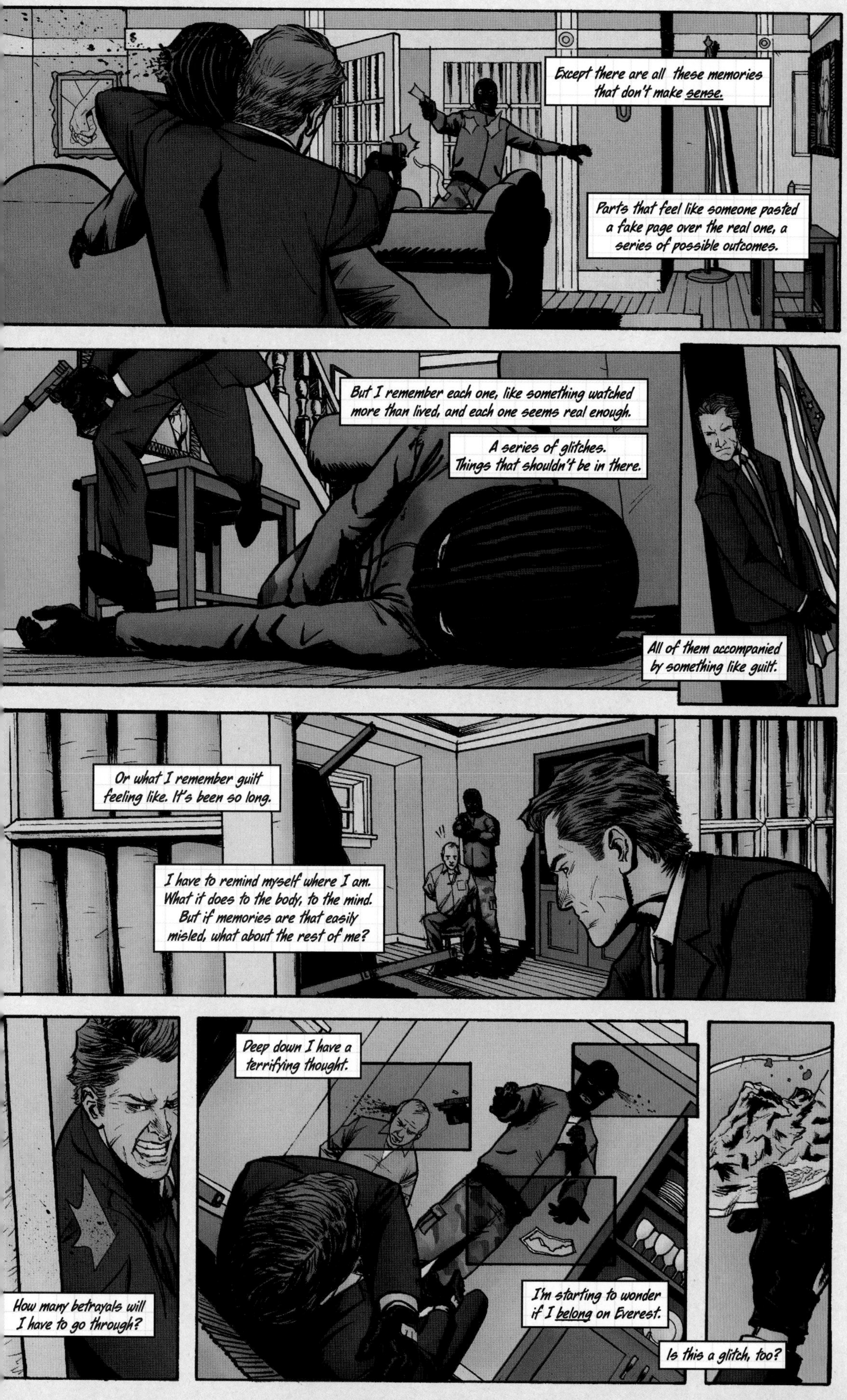
Except there are all these memories that don't make sense.
Parts that feel like someone pasted a fake page over the real one, a series of possible outcomes.
But I remember each one, like something watched more than lived, and each one seems real enough.
A series of glitches. Things that shouldn't be in there.
All of them accompanied by something like guilt.
Or what I remember guilt feeling like. It's been so long.
I have to remind myself where I am. What it does to the body, to the mind. But if memories are that easily misled, what about the rest of me?
How many betrayals will I have to go through?
Deep down I have a terrifying thought.
I'm starting to wonder if I belong on Everest.
Is this a glitch, too?

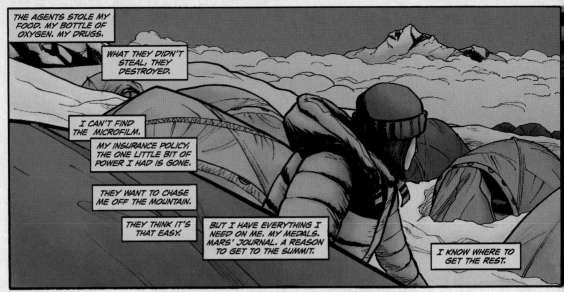

THE AGENTS STOLE MY FOOD. MY BOTTLE OF OXYGEN. MY DRUGS.

WHAT THEY DIDN'T STEAL, THEY DESTROYED.

I CAN'T FIND THE MICROFILM.

MY INSURANCE POLICY, THE ONE LITTLE BIT OF POWER I HAD IS GONE.

THEY WANT TO CHASE ME OFF THE MOUNTAIN.

THEY THINK IT'S THAT EASY.

BUT I HAVE EVERYTHING I NEED ON ME. MY MEDALS. MARS' JOURNAL. A REASON TO GET TO THE SUMMIT.

I KNOW WHERE TO GET THE REST.

DORJE? I KNOW YOU'RE MAD AT ME, BUT I NEED YOUR HELP.

OKAY, COMING IN.

DORJE, COME ON, WAKE UP.

GO AWAY, ZAN.

I DON'T THINK YOU'RE HEARING ME, I NEED--

THIS IS NOT ABOUT WHAT YOU NEED.

I'M HERE TO CLIMB MY MOUNTAIN.

NOT TO HELP YOU DO WHATEVER YOU'RE DOING.

AT LEAST NO MORE THAN YOU HAVE ALREADY FOOLED ME INTO DOING.

"DORJE, COME ON, I DON'T--"

"WE'LL TALK TOMORROW.

"ACTUALLY TALK."

"MAYBE FOR THE FIRST TIME EVER."

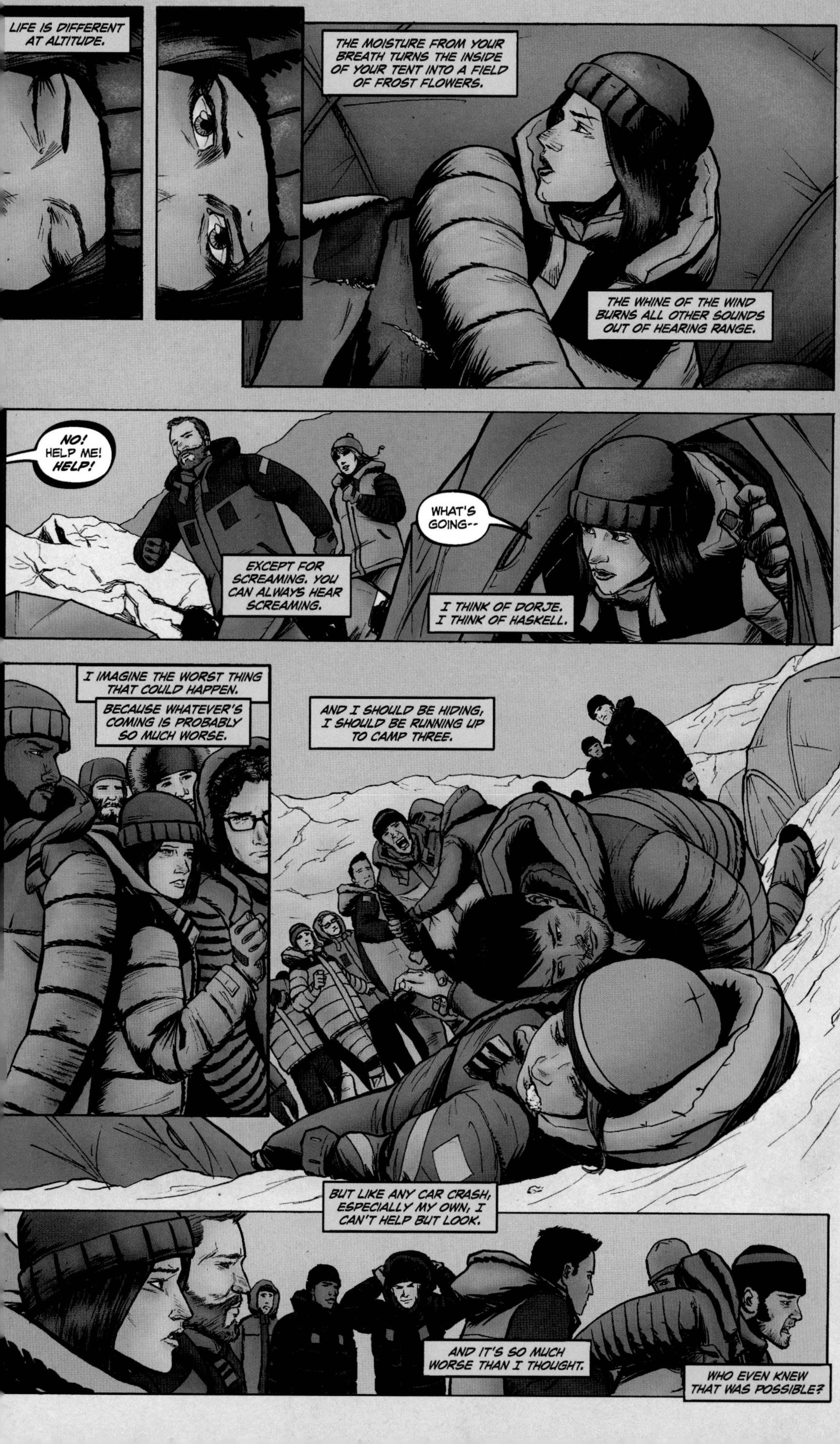
LIFE IS DIFFERENT AT ALTITUDE.
THE MOISTURE FROM YOUR BREATH TURNS THE INSIDE OF YOUR TENT INTO A FIELD OF FROST FLOWERS.
THE WHINE OF THE WIND BURNS ALL OTHER SOUNDS OUT OF HEARING RANGE.
NO! HELP ME! HELP!
EXCEPT FOR SCREAMING. YOU CAN ALWAYS HEAR SCREAMING.
WHAT'S GOING--
I THINK OF DORJE. I THINK OF HASKELL.
I IMAGINE THE WORST THING THAT COULD HAPPEN.
BECAUSE WHATEVER'S COMING IS PROBABLY SO MUCH WORSE.
AND I SHOULD BE HIDING, I SHOULD BE RUNNING UP TO CAMP THREE.
BUT LIKE ANY CAR CRASH, ESPECIALLY MY OWN, I CAN'T HELP BUT LOOK.
AND IT'S SO MUCH WORSE THAN I THOUGHT.
WHO EVEN KNEW THAT WAS POSSIBLE?

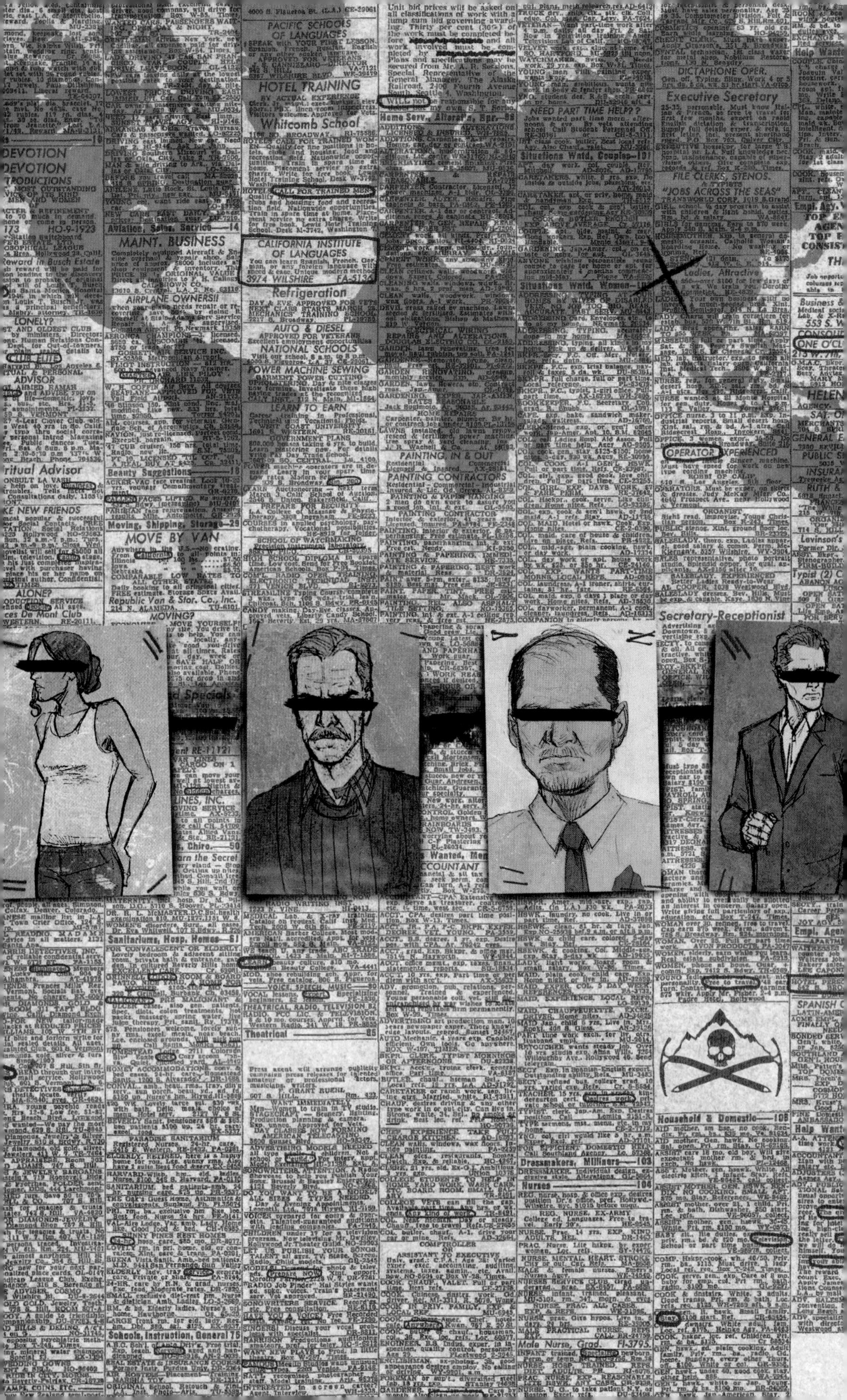
PACIFIC SCHOOLS OF LANGUAGES
HOTEL TRAINING
Whitcomb School
CALIFORNIA INSTITUTE OF LANGUAGES
3974 WILSHIRE
Refrigeration
AUTO & DIESEL
NATIONAL SCHOOLS
POWER MACHINE SEWING
LEARN TO EARN
DEVOTION
DEVOTION
LONELY?
ADVISOR
Spiritual Advisor
MAKE NEW FRIENDS
ALONE?
MAINT. BUSINESS
AIRPLANE OWNERS!!
MOVE BY VAN
Republic Van & Stor. Co., Inc.
MOVING?
PAINTING, IN & OUT
PAINTING CONTRACTORS
Situations Wntd, Couples
Situations Wntd, Women
NEED PART TIME HELP??
DICTAPHONE OPER.
Executive Secretary
FILE CLERKS, STENOS.
"JOBS ACROSS THE SEAS"
Ladies, Attractive
OPERATOR, EXPERIENCED
Secretary-Receptionist
ACCOUNTANT
Theatrical
COMPTROLLER
Dressmakers, Milliners
Nurses
Male Nurse, Grad.
Household & Domestic
Schools, Instruction, General
Sanitariums, Hosp, Homes
Aviation, Sales, Service
Beauty Suggestions
Moving, Shipping, Storage
Home Serv., Alteration, Rep.

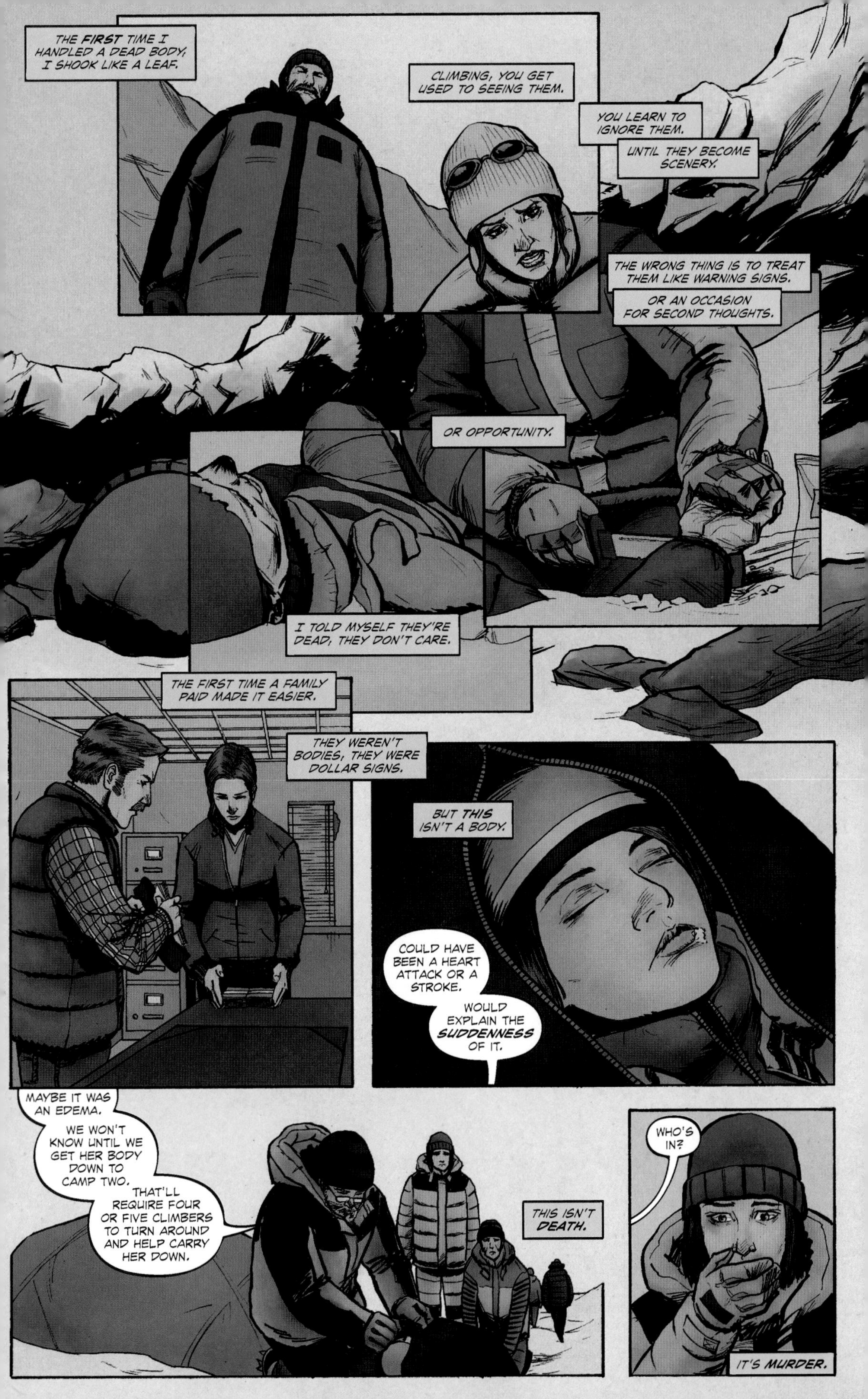
THE FIRST TIME I HANDLED A DEAD BODY, I SHOOK LIKE A LEAF.
CLIMBING, YOU GET USED TO SEEING THEM.
YOU LEARN TO IGNORE THEM.
UNTIL THEY BECOME SCENERY.
THE WRONG THING IS TO TREAT THEM LIKE WARNING SIGNS.
OR AN OCCASION FOR SECOND THOUGHTS.
OR OPPORTUNITY.
I TOLD MYSELF THEY'RE DEAD, THEY DON'T CARE.
THE FIRST TIME A FAMILY PAID MADE IT EASIER.
THEY WEREN'T BODIES, THEY WERE DOLLAR SIGNS.
BUT THIS ISN'T A BODY.
COULD HAVE BEEN A HEART ATTACK OR A STROKE.
WOULD EXPLAIN THE SUDDENNESS OF IT.
MAYBE IT WAS AN EDEMA.
WE WON'T KNOW UNTIL WE GET HER BODY DOWN TO CAMP TWO.
THAT'LL REQUIRE FOUR OR FIVE CLIMBERS TO TURN AROUND AND HELP CARRY HER DOWN.
THIS ISN'T DEATH.
WHO'S IN?
IT'S MURDER.

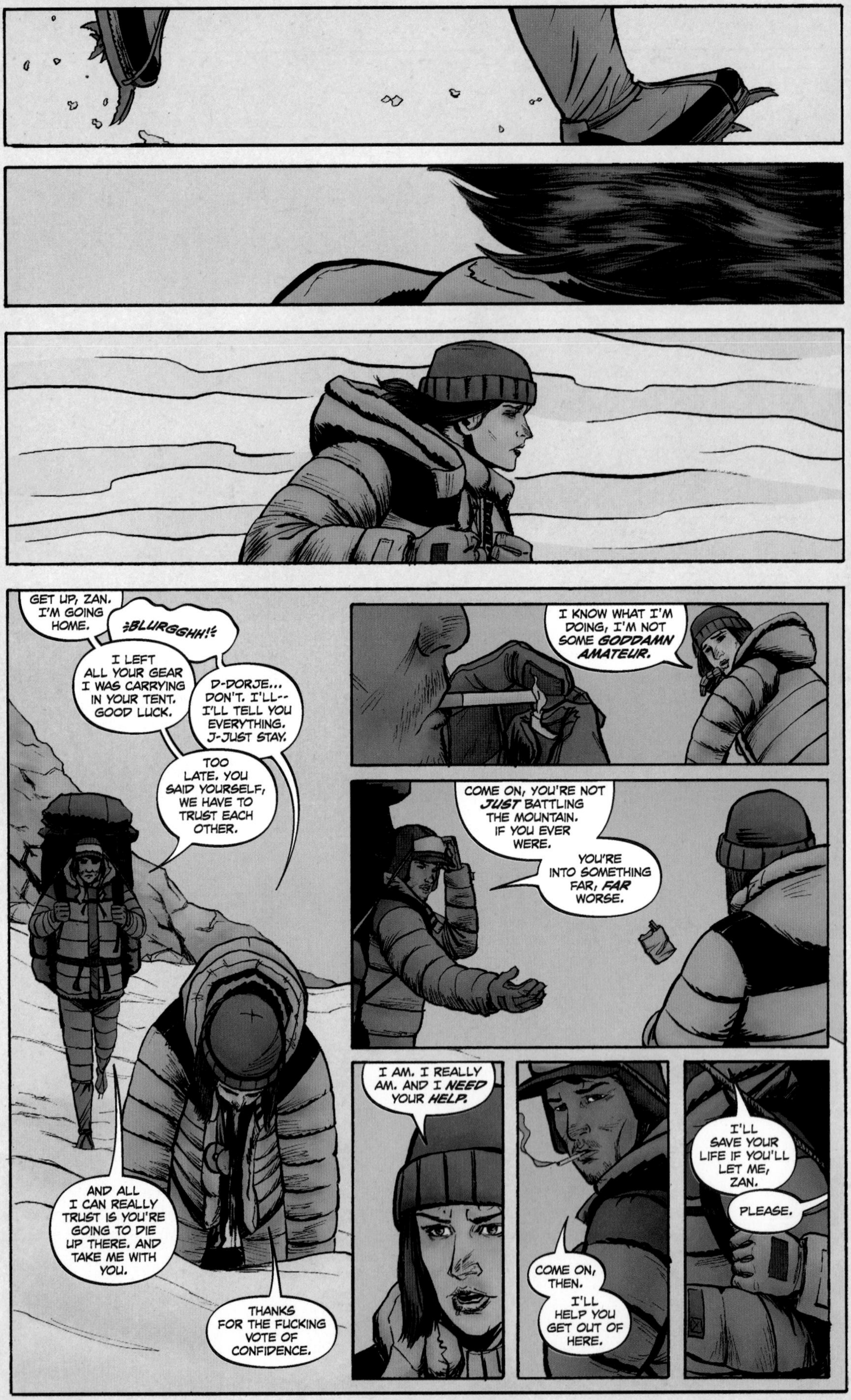
GET UP, ZAN. I'M GOING HOME.
BLURGGHH!
I LEFT ALL YOUR GEAR I WAS CARRYING IN YOUR TENT. GOOD LUCK.
D-DORJE... DON'T. I'LL-- I'LL TELL YOU EVERYTHING. J-JUST STAY.
TOO LATE. YOU SAID YOURSELF, WE HAVE TO TRUST EACH OTHER.
AND ALL I CAN REALLY TRUST IS YOU'RE GOING TO DIE UP THERE. AND TAKE ME WITH YOU.
THANKS FOR THE FUCKING VOTE OF CONFIDENCE.
I KNOW WHAT I'M DOING, I'M NOT SOME GODDAMN AMATEUR.
COME ON, YOU'RE NOT JUST BATTLING THE MOUNTAIN. IF YOU EVER WERE.
YOU'RE INTO SOMETHING FAR, FAR WORSE.
I AM. I REALLY AM. AND I NEED YOUR HELP.
COME ON, THEN.
I'LL HELP YOU GET OUT OF HERE.
I'LL SAVE YOUR LIFE IF YOU'LL LET ME, ZAN.
PLEASE.

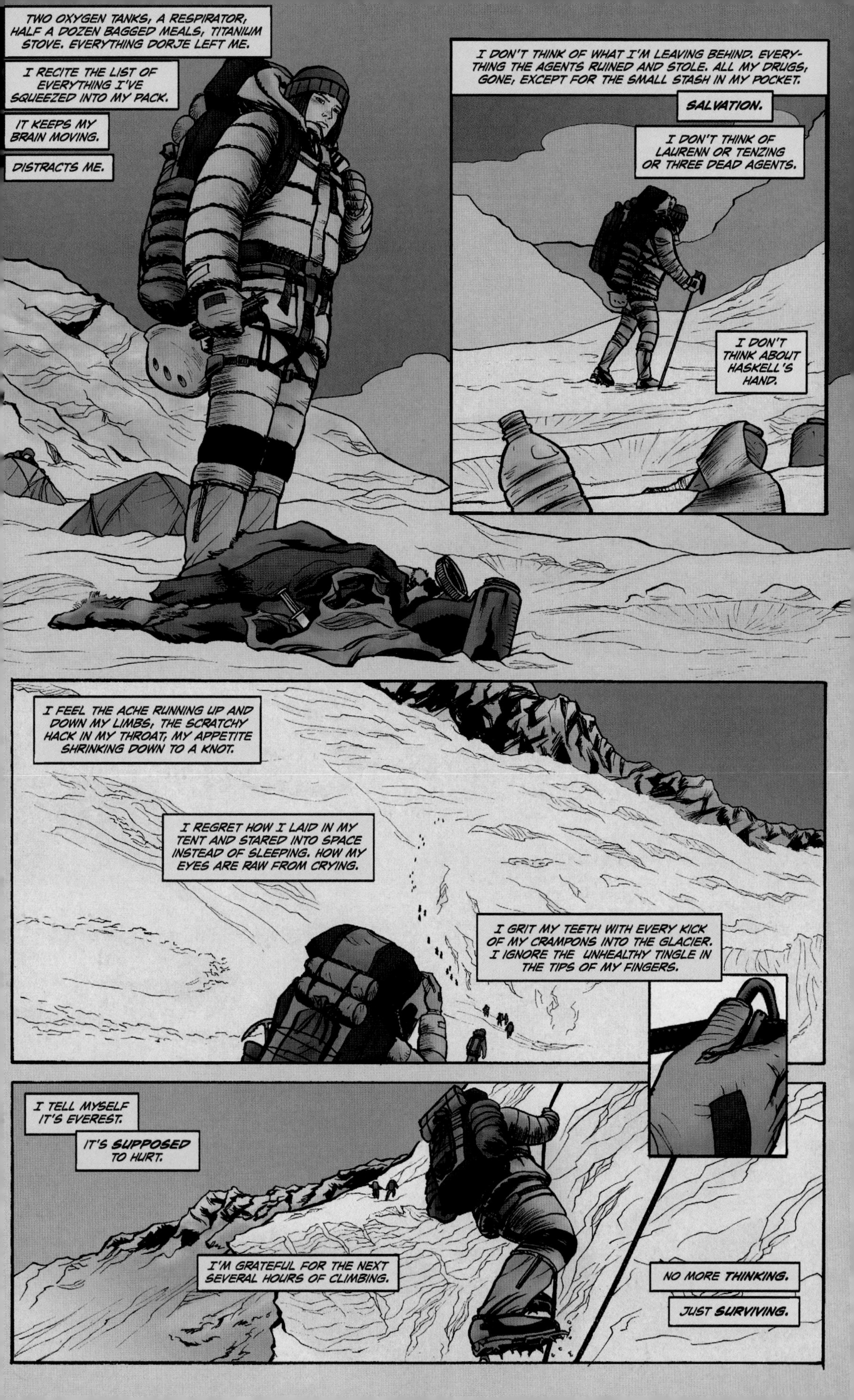
TWO OXYGEN TANKS, A RESPIRATOR, HALF A DOZEN BAGGED MEALS, TITANIUM STOVE. EVERYTHING DORJE LEFT ME.
I RECITE THE LIST OF EVERYTHING I'VE SQUEEZED INTO MY PACK.
IT KEEPS MY BRAIN MOVING.
DISTRACTS ME.
I DON'T THINK OF WHAT I'M LEAVING BEHIND. EVERY-THING THE AGENTS RUINED AND STOLE. ALL MY DRUGS, GONE, EXCEPT FOR THE SMALL STASH IN MY POCKET.
SALVATION.
I DON'T THINK OF LAURENN OR TENZING OR THREE DEAD AGENTS.
I DON'T THINK ABOUT HASKELL'S HAND.
I FEEL THE ACHE RUNNING UP AND DOWN MY LIMBS, THE SCRATCHY HACK IN MY THROAT, MY APPETITE SHRINKING DOWN TO A KNOT.
I REGRET HOW I LAID IN MY TENT AND STARED INTO SPACE INSTEAD OF SLEEPING. HOW MY EYES ARE RAW FROM CRYING.
I GRIT MY TEETH WITH EVERY KICK OF MY CRAMPONS INTO THE GLACIER. I IGNORE THE UNHEALTHY TINGLE IN THE TIPS OF MY FINGERS.
I TELL MYSELF IT'S EVEREST.
IT'S SUPPOSED TO HURT.
I'M GRATEFUL FOR THE NEXT SEVERAL HOURS OF CLIMBING.
NO MORE THINKING.
JUST SURVIVING.

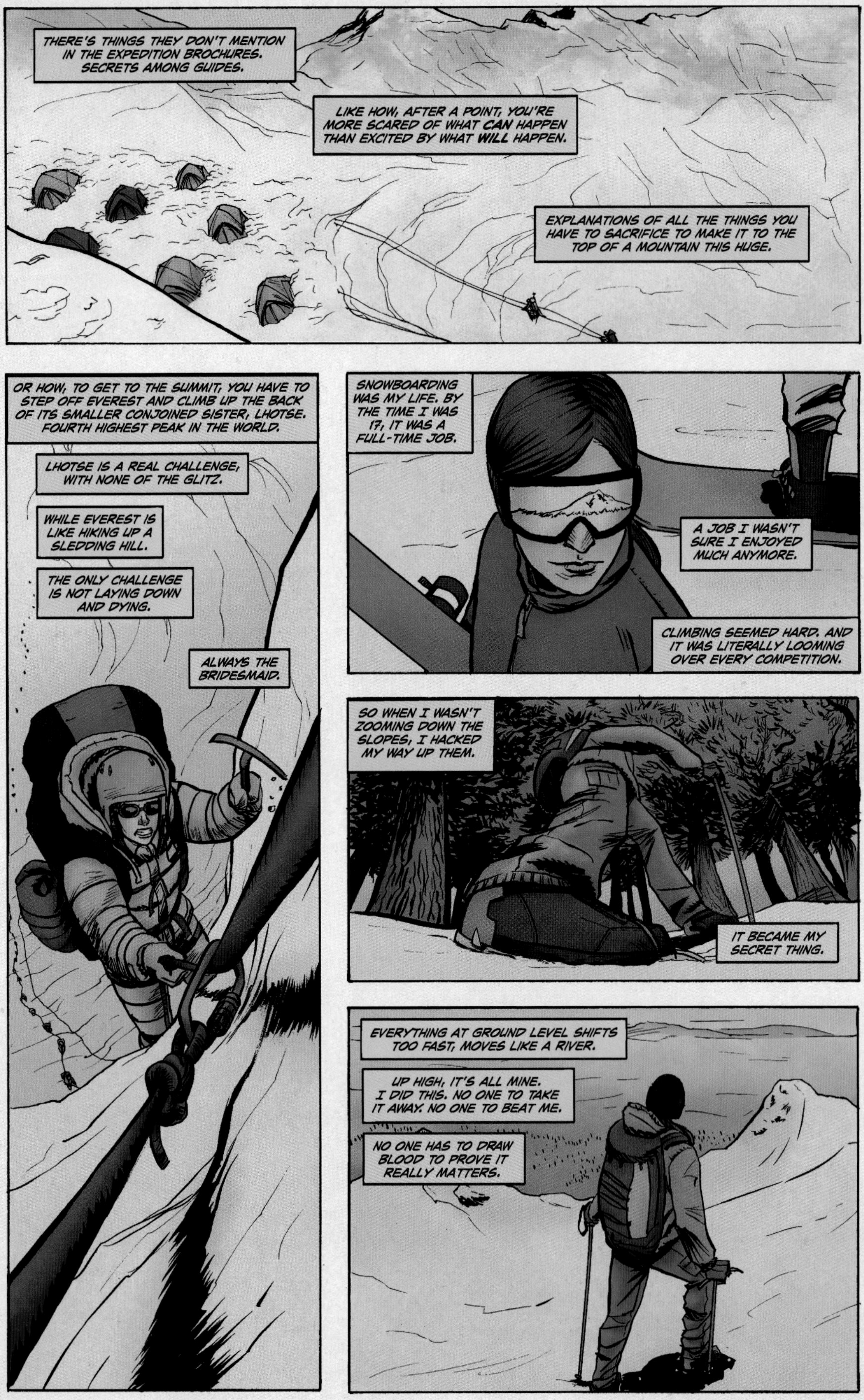
THERE'S THINGS THEY DON'T MENTION IN THE EXPEDITION BROCHURES. SECRETS AMONG GUIDES.
LIKE HOW, AFTER A POINT, YOU'RE MORE SCARED OF WHAT CAN HAPPEN THAN EXCITED BY WHAT WILL HAPPEN.
EXPLANATIONS OF ALL THE THINGS YOU HAVE TO SACRIFICE TO MAKE IT TO THE TOP OF A MOUNTAIN THIS HUGE.
OR HOW, TO GET TO THE SUMMIT, YOU HAVE TO STEP OFF EVEREST AND CLIMB UP THE BACK OF ITS SMALLER CONJOINED SISTER, LHOTSE. FOURTH HIGHEST PEAK IN THE WORLD.
LHOTSE IS A REAL CHALLENGE, WITH NONE OF THE GLITZ.
WHILE EVEREST IS LIKE HIKING UP A SLEDDING HILL.
THE ONLY CHALLENGE IS NOT LAYING DOWN AND DYING.
ALWAYS THE BRIDESMAID.
SNOWBOARDING WAS MY LIFE. BY THE TIME I WAS 17, IT WAS A FULL-TIME JOB.
A JOB I WASN'T SURE I ENJOYED MUCH ANYMORE.
CLIMBING SEEMED HARD. AND IT WAS LITERALLY LOOMING OVER EVERY COMPETITION.
SO WHEN I WASN'T ZOOMING DOWN THE SLOPES, I HACKED MY WAY UP THEM.
IT BECAME MY SECRET THING.
EVERYTHING AT GROUND LEVEL SHIFTS TOO FAST, MOVES LIKE A RIVER.
UP HIGH, IT'S ALL MINE. I DID THIS. NO ONE TO TAKE IT AWAY. NO ONE TO BEAT ME.
NO ONE HAS TO DRAW BLOOD TO PROVE IT REALLY MATTERS.

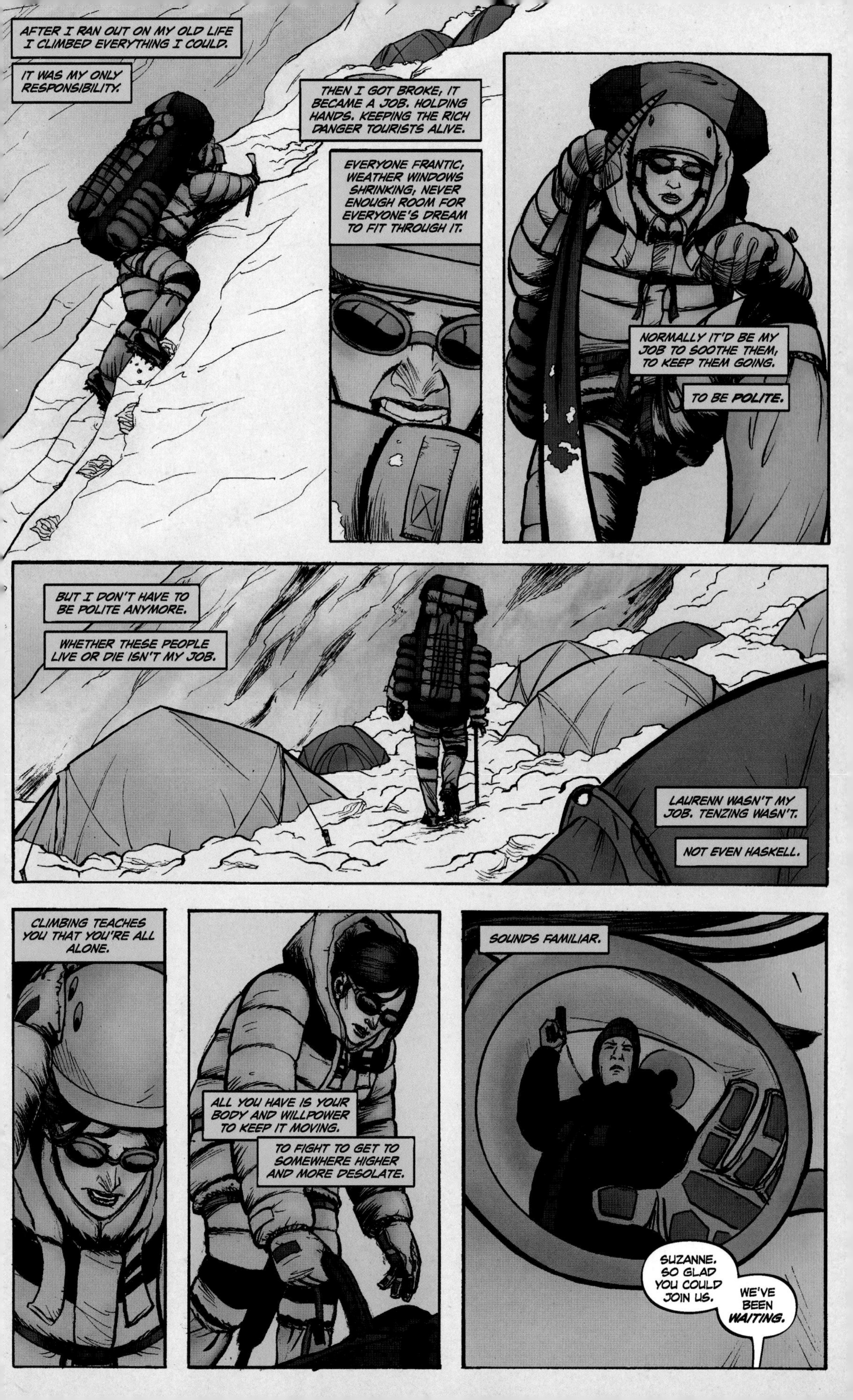
AFTER I RAN OUT ON MY OLD LIFE I CLIMBED EVERYTHING I COULD.
IT WAS MY ONLY RESPONSIBILITY.
THEN I GOT BROKE; IT BECAME A JOB. HOLDING HANDS. KEEPING THE RICH DANGER TOURISTS ALIVE.
EVERYONE FRANTIC, WEATHER WINDOWS SHRINKING, NEVER ENOUGH ROOM FOR EVERYONE'S DREAM TO FIT THROUGH IT.
NORMALLY IT'D BE MY JOB TO SOOTHE THEM, TO KEEP THEM GOING.
TO BE POLITE.
BUT I DON'T HAVE TO BE POLITE ANYMORE.
WHETHER THESE PEOPLE LIVE OR DIE ISN'T MY JOB.
LAURENN WASN'T MY JOB. TENZING WASN'T.
NOT EVEN HASKELL.
CLIMBING TEACHES YOU THAT YOU'RE ALL ALONE.
ALL YOU HAVE IS YOUR BODY AND WILLPOWER TO KEEP IT MOVING.
TO FIGHT TO GET TO SOMEWHERE HIGHER AND MORE DESOLATE.
SOUNDS FAMILIAR.
SUZANNE. SO GLAD YOU COULD JOIN US.
WE'VE BEEN WAITING.

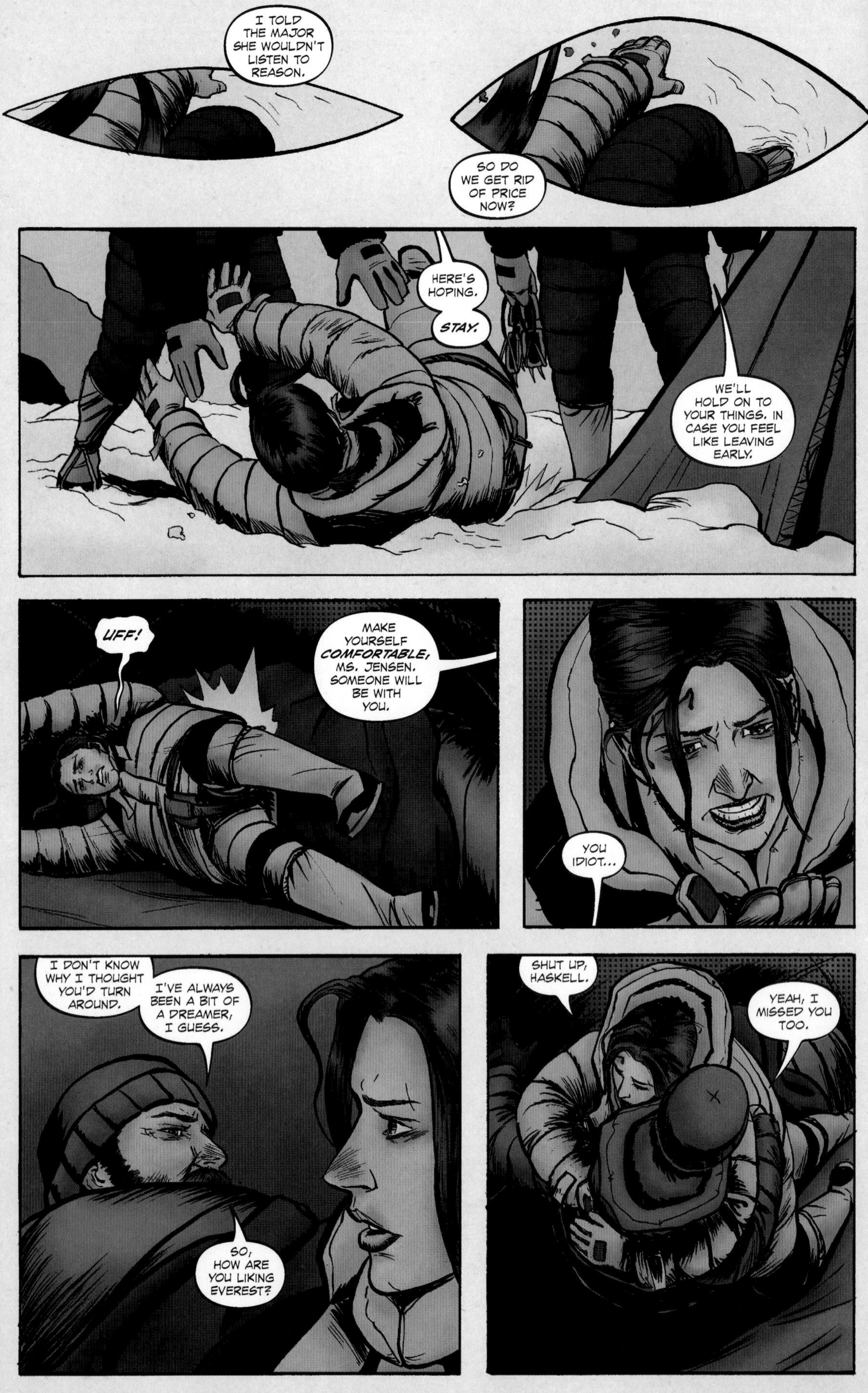
I TOLD THE MAJOR SHE WOULDN'T LISTEN TO REASON.
SO DO WE GET RID OF PRICE NOW?
HERE'S HOPING.
STAY.
WE'LL HOLD ON TO YOUR THINGS. IN CASE YOU FEEL LIKE LEAVING EARLY.
UFF!
MAKE YOURSELF COMFORTABLE, MS. JENSEN. SOMEONE WILL BE WITH YOU.
YOU IDIOT...
I DON'T KNOW WHY I THOUGHT YOU'D TURN AROUND.
I'VE ALWAYS BEEN A BIT OF A DREAMER, I GUESS.
SO, HOW ARE YOU LIKING EVEREST?
SHUT UP, HASKELL.
YEAH, I MISSED YOU TOO.

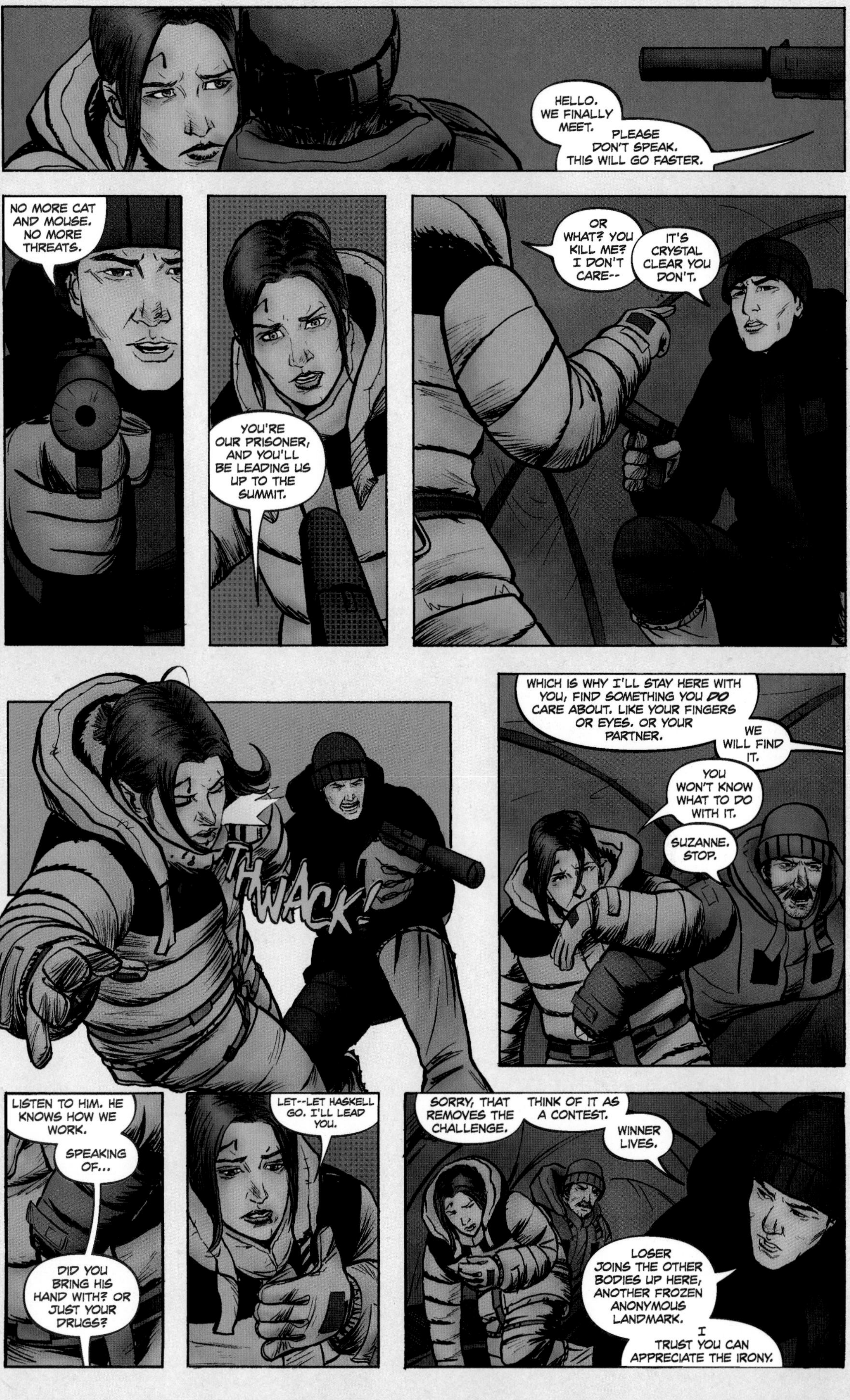
HELLO. WE FINALLY MEET.
PLEASE DON'T SPEAK. THIS WILL GO FASTER.
NO MORE CAT AND MOUSE. NO MORE THREATS.
YOU'RE OUR PRISONER, AND YOU'LL BE LEADING US UP TO THE SUMMIT.
OR WHAT? YOU KILL ME? I DON'T CARE--
IT'S CRYSTAL CLEAR YOU DON'T.
THWACK!
WHICH IS WHY I'LL STAY HERE WITH YOU, FIND SOMETHING YOU DO CARE ABOUT. LIKE YOUR FINGERS OR EYES. OR YOUR PARTNER.
WE WILL FIND IT.
YOU WON'T KNOW WHAT TO DO WITH IT.
SUZANNE. STOP.
LISTEN TO HIM. HE KNOWS HOW WE WORK.
SPEAKING OF...
DID YOU BRING HIS HAND WITH? OR JUST YOUR DRUGS?
LET--LET HASKELL GO. I'LL LEAD YOU.
SORRY, THAT REMOVES THE CHALLENGE.
THINK OF IT AS A CONTEST.
WINNER LIVES.
LOSER JOINS THE OTHER BODIES UP HERE, ANOTHER FROZEN ANONYMOUS LANDMARK.
I TRUST YOU CAN APPRECIATE THE IRONY.

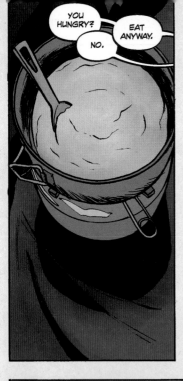

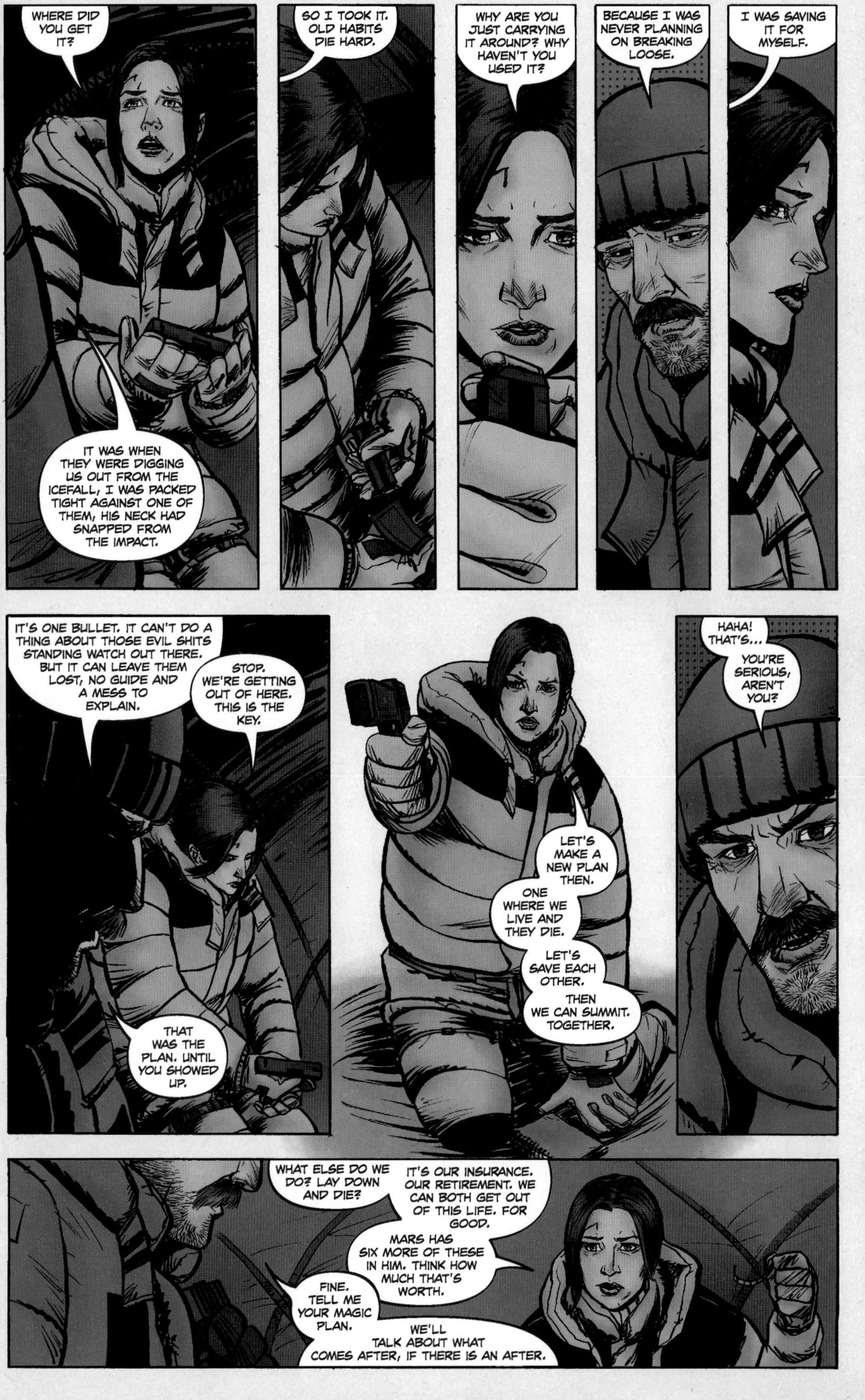

WHERE DID YOU GET IT?
IT WAS WHEN THEY WERE DIGGING US OUT FROM THE ICEFALL, I WAS PACKED TIGHT AGAINST ONE OF THEM, HIS NECK HAD SNAPPED FROM THE IMPACT.
SO I TOOK IT. OLD HABITS DIE HARD.
WHY ARE YOU JUST CARRYING IT AROUND? WHY HAVEN'T YOU USED IT?
BECAUSE I WAS NEVER PLANNING ON BREAKING LOOSE.
I WAS SAVING IT FOR MYSELF.
IT'S ONE BULLET. IT CAN'T DO A THING ABOUT THOSE EVIL SHITS STANDING WATCH OUT THERE. BUT IT CAN LEAVE THEM LOST, NO GUIDE AND A MESS TO EXPLAIN.
STOP. WE'RE GETTING OUT OF HERE. THIS IS THE KEY.
THAT WAS THE PLAN. UNTIL YOU SHOWED UP.
LET'S MAKE A NEW PLAN THEN.
ONE WHERE WE LIVE AND THEY DIE.
LET'S SAVE EACH OTHER.
THEN WE CAN SUMMIT. TOGETHER.
HAHA! THAT'S...
YOU'RE SERIOUS, AREN'T YOU?
WHAT ELSE DO WE DO? LAY DOWN AND DIE?
IT'S OUR INSURANCE. OUR RETIREMENT. WE CAN BOTH GET OUT OF THIS LIFE. FOR GOOD.
MARS HAS SIX MORE OF THESE IN HIM. THINK HOW MUCH THAT'S WORTH.
FINE. TELL ME YOUR MAGIC PLAN.
WE'LL TALK ABOUT WHAT COMES AFTER, IF THERE IS AN AFTER.

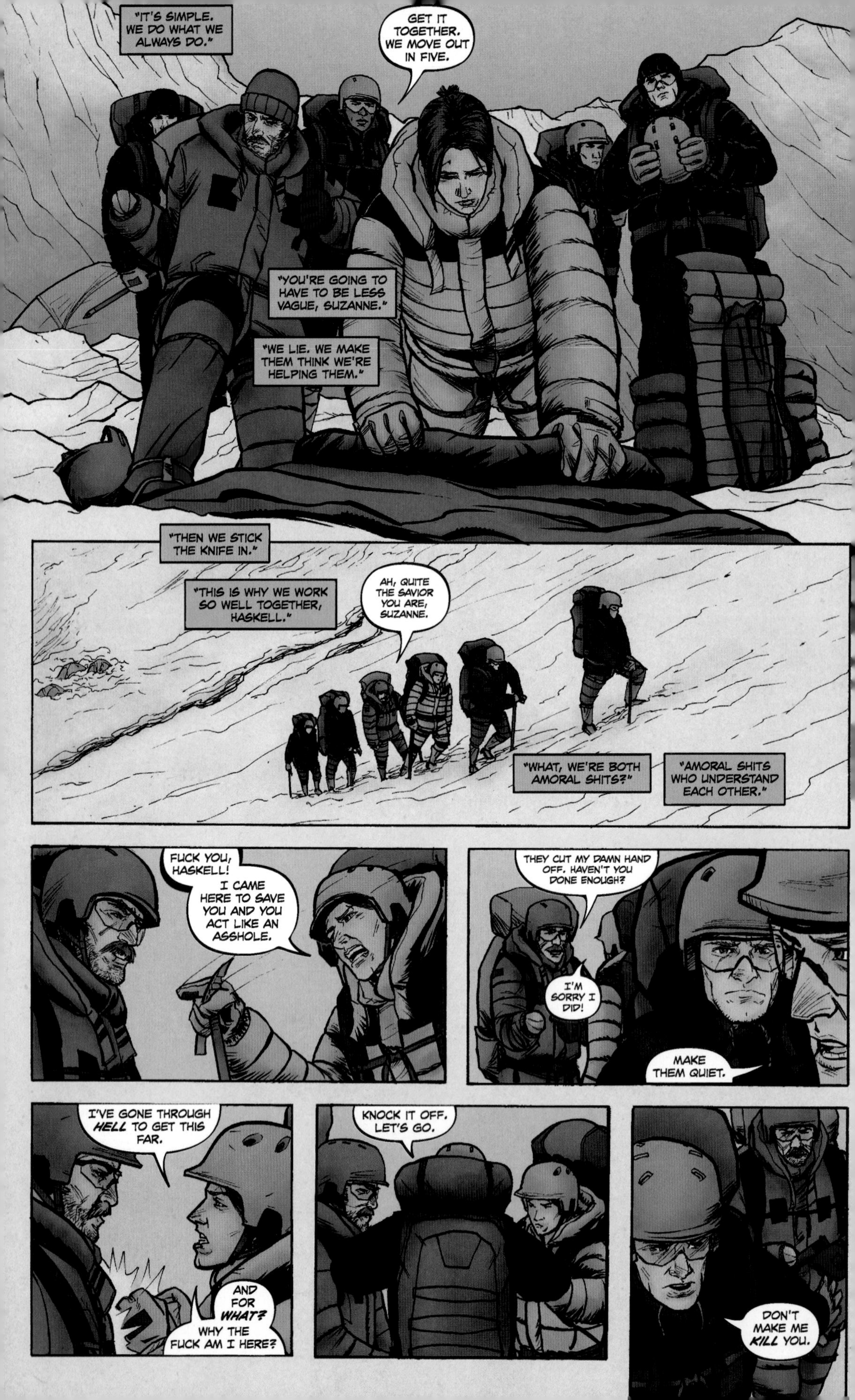
"IT'S SIMPLE. WE DO WHAT WE ALWAYS DO."
GET IT TOGETHER. WE MOVE OUT IN FIVE.
"YOU'RE GOING TO HAVE TO BE LESS VAGUE, SUZANNE."
"WE LIE. WE MAKE THEM THINK WE'RE HELPING THEM."
"THEN WE STICK THE KNIFE IN."
"THIS IS WHY WE WORK SO WELL TOGETHER, HASKELL."
AH, QUITE THE SAVIOR YOU ARE, SUZANNE.
"WHAT, WE'RE BOTH AMORAL SHITS?"
"AMORAL SHITS WHO UNDERSTAND EACH OTHER."
FUCK YOU, HASKELL!
I CAME HERE TO SAVE YOU AND YOU ACT LIKE AN ASSHOLE.
THEY CUT MY DAMN HAND OFF. HAVEN'T YOU DONE ENOUGH?
I'M SORRY I DID!
MAKE THEM QUIET.
I'VE GONE THROUGH HELL TO GET THIS FAR.
AND FOR WHAT?
WHY THE FUCK AM I HERE?
KNOCK IT OFF. LET'S GO.
DON'T MAKE ME KILL YOU.

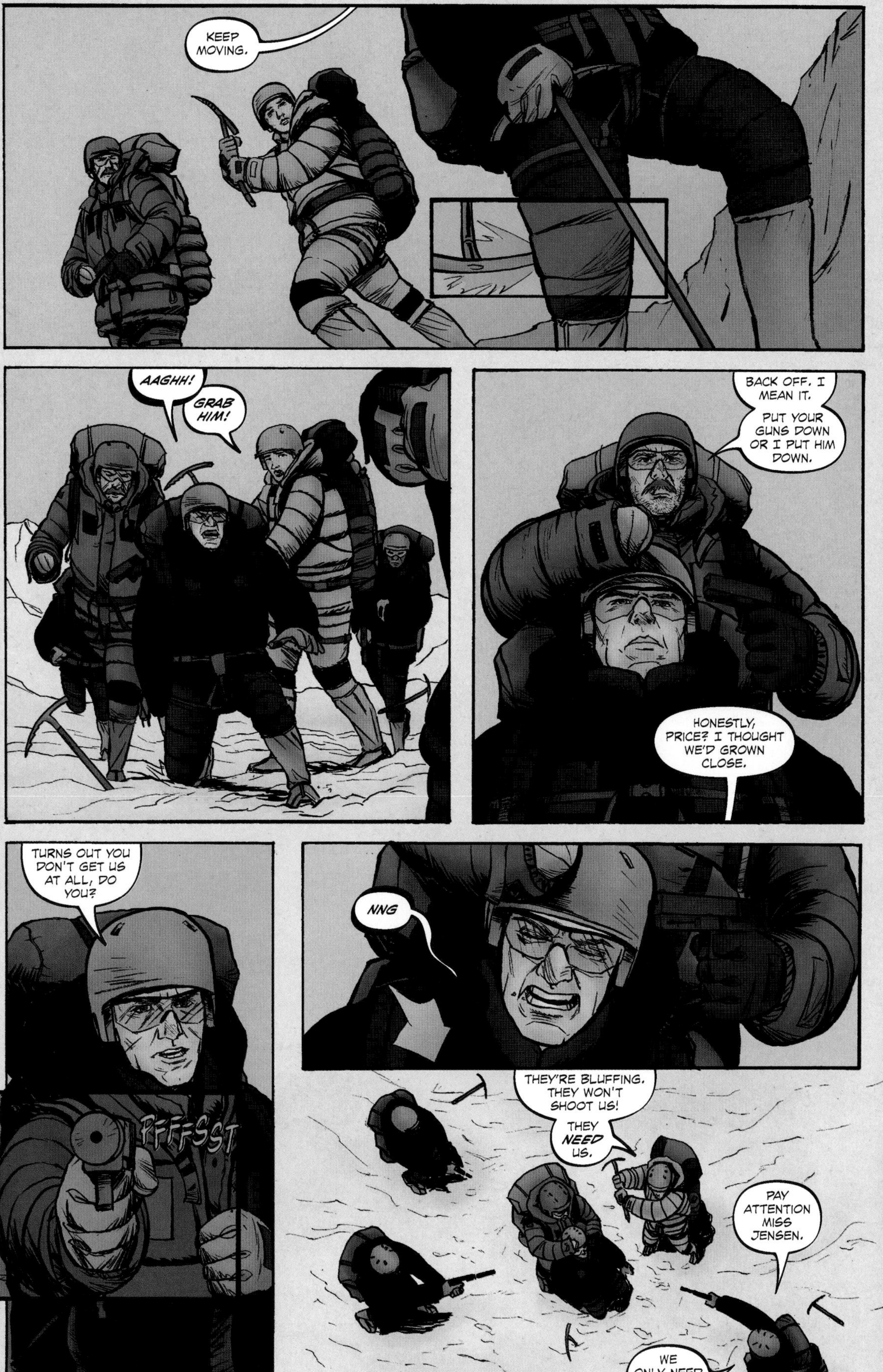
KEEP MOVING.
AAGHH!
GRAB HIM!
BACK OFF. I MEAN IT.
PUT YOUR GUNS DOWN OR I PUT HIM DOWN.
HONESTLY, PRICE? I THOUGHT WE'D GROWN CLOSE.
TURNS OUT YOU DON'T GET US AT ALL, DO YOU?
PFFFSST
NNG
THEY'RE BLUFFING. THEY WON'T SHOOT US!
THEY NEED US.
PAY ATTENTION MISS JENSEN.
WE ONLY NEED ONE OF YOU.

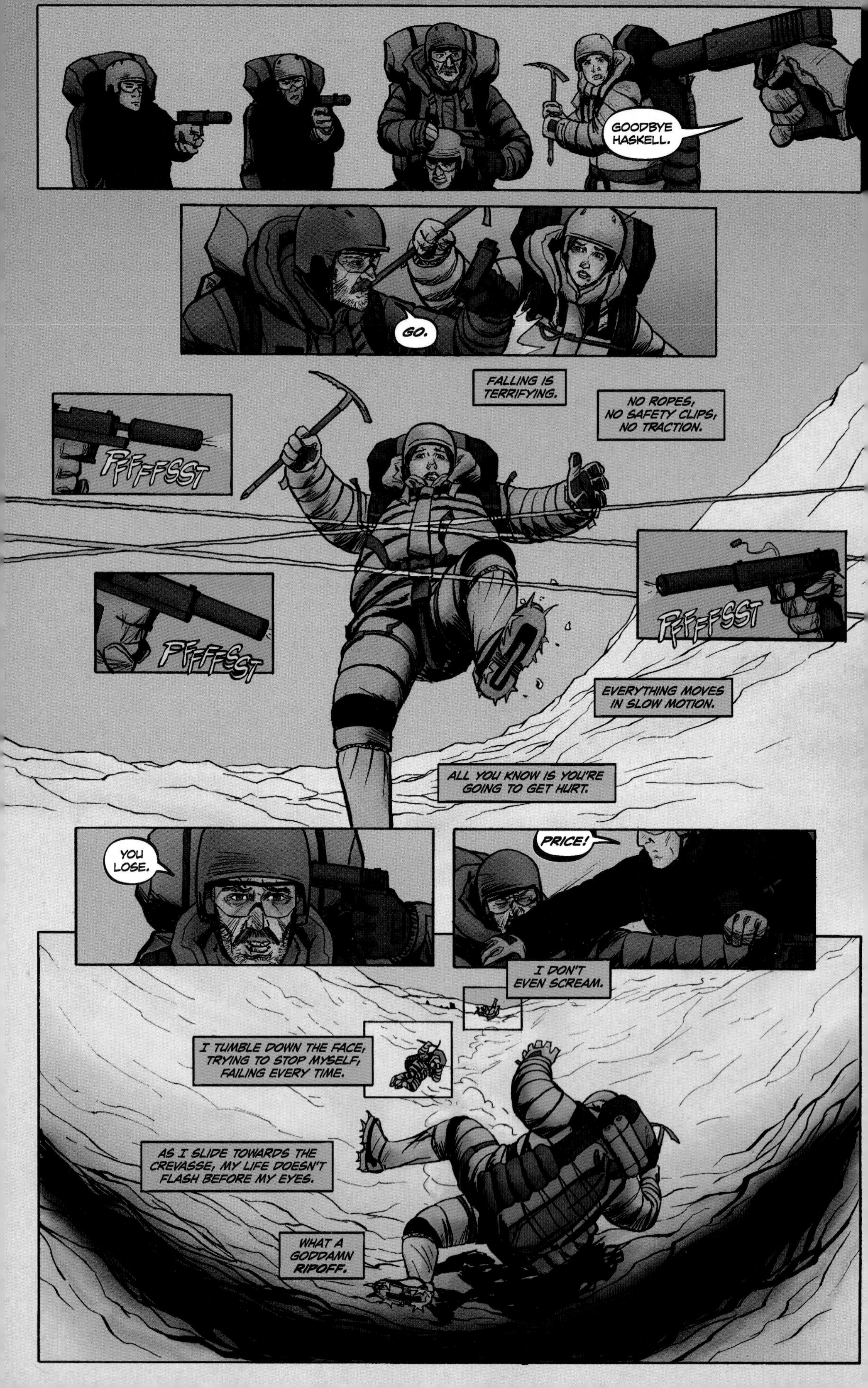
GOODBYE HASKELL.
GO.
FALLING IS TERRIFYING.
NO ROPES, NO SAFETY CLIPS, NO TRACTION.
PFFFFFSST
PFFFFSST
PFFFFSST
EVERYTHING MOVES IN SLOW MOTION.
ALL YOU KNOW IS YOU'RE GOING TO GET HURT.
YOU LOSE.
PRICE!
I DON'T EVEN SCREAM.
I TUMBLE DOWN THE FACE, TRYING TO STOP MYSELF, FAILING EVERY TIME.
AS I SLIDE TOWARDS THE CREVASSE, MY LIFE DOESN'T FLASH BEFORE MY EYES.
WHAT A GODDAMN RIPOFF.

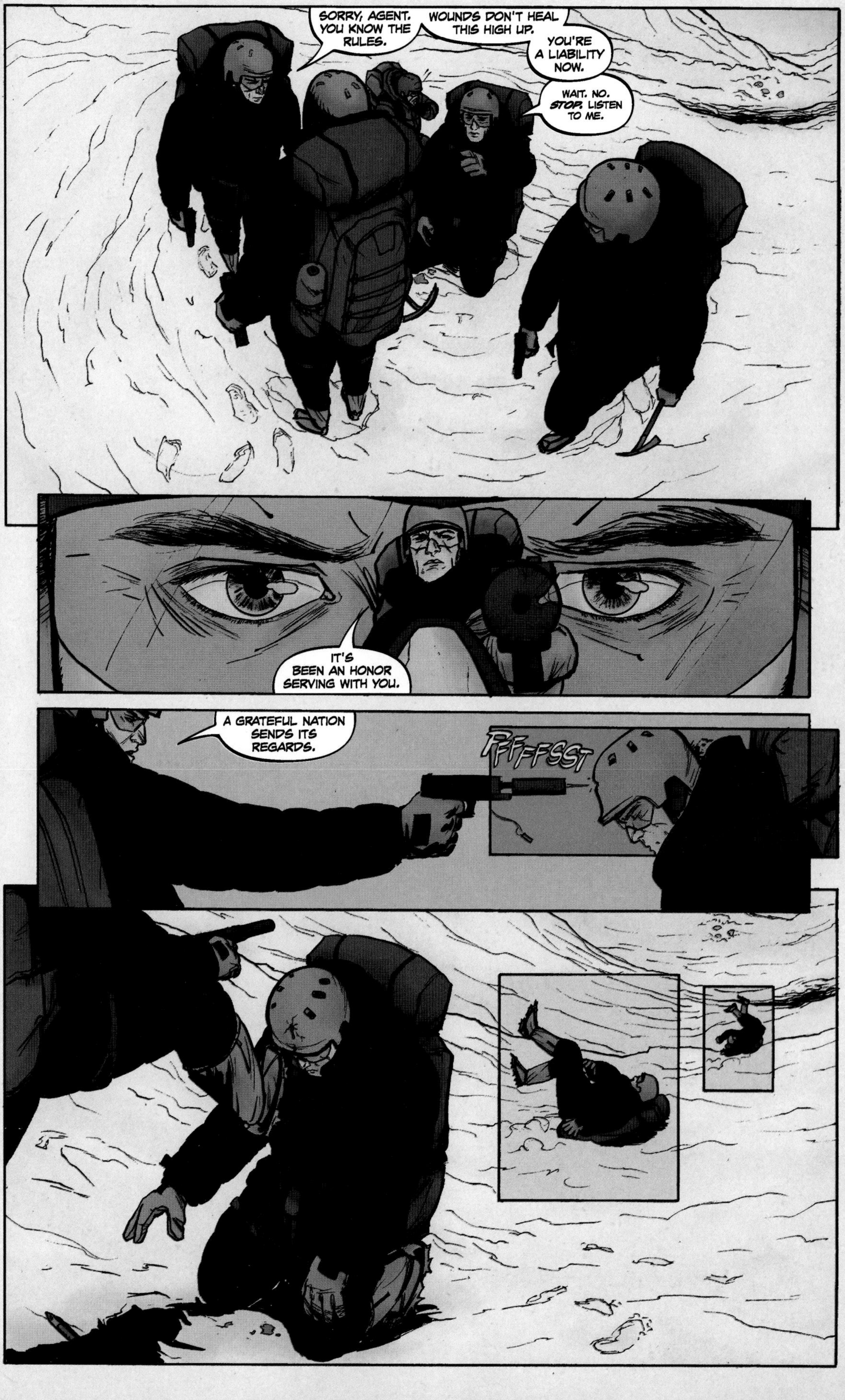
SORRY, AGENT. YOU KNOW THE RULES.
WOUNDS DON'T HEAL THIS HIGH UP.
YOU'RE A LIABILITY NOW.
WAIT. NO. STOP. LISTEN TO ME.
IT'S BEEN AN HONOR SERVING WITH YOU.
A GRATEFUL NATION SENDS ITS REGARDS.
PFFFFSST

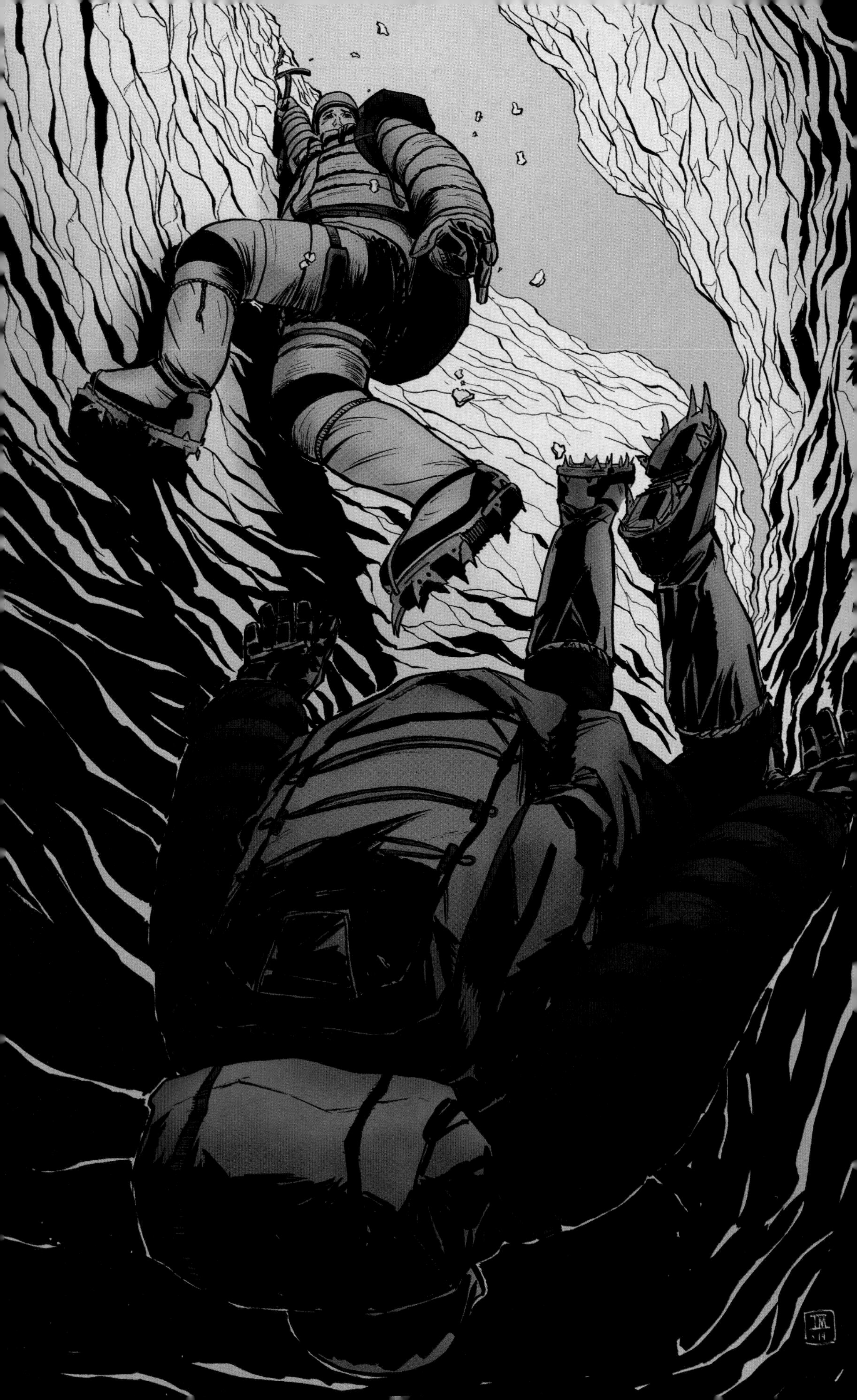

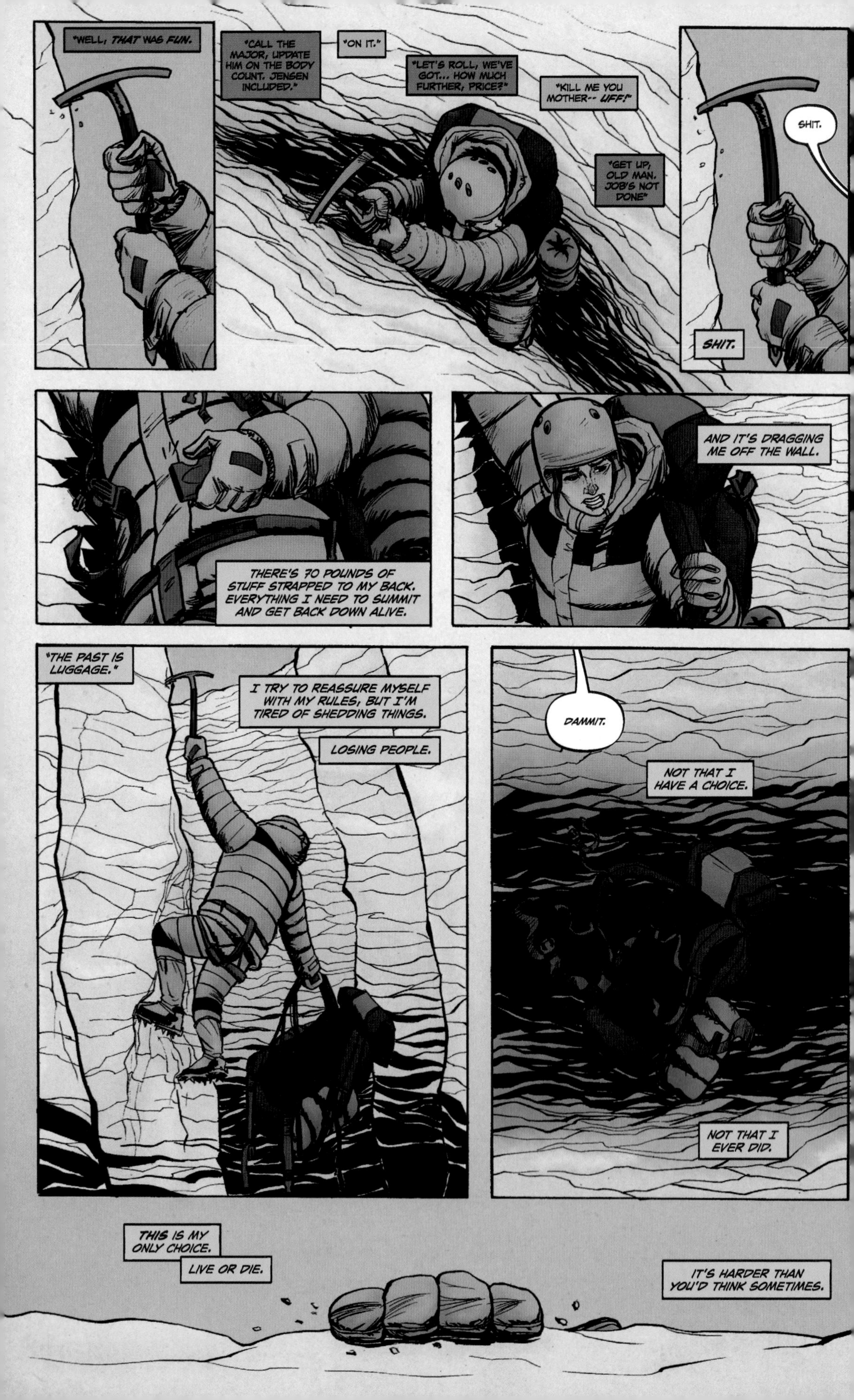
"WELL, THAT WAS FUN.
"CALL THE MAJOR, UPDATE HIM ON THE BODY COUNT. JENSEN INCLUDED."
"ON IT."
"LET'S ROLL, WE'VE GOT... HOW MUCH FURTHER, PRICE?"
"KILL ME YOU MOTHER-- UFF!"
"GET UP, OLD MAN. JOB'S NOT DONE"
SHIT.
SHIT.
THERE'S 70 POUNDS OF STUFF STRAPPED TO MY BACK. EVERYTHING I NEED TO SUMMIT AND GET BACK DOWN ALIVE.
AND IT'S DRAGGING ME OFF THE WALL.
"THE PAST IS LUGGAGE."
I TRY TO REASSURE MYSELF WITH MY RULES, BUT I'M TIRED OF SHEDDING THINGS.
LOSING PEOPLE.
DAMMIT.
NOT THAT I HAVE A CHOICE.
NOT THAT I EVER DID.
THIS IS MY ONLY CHOICE.
LIVE OR DIE.
IT'S HARDER THAN YOU'D THINK SOMETIMES.

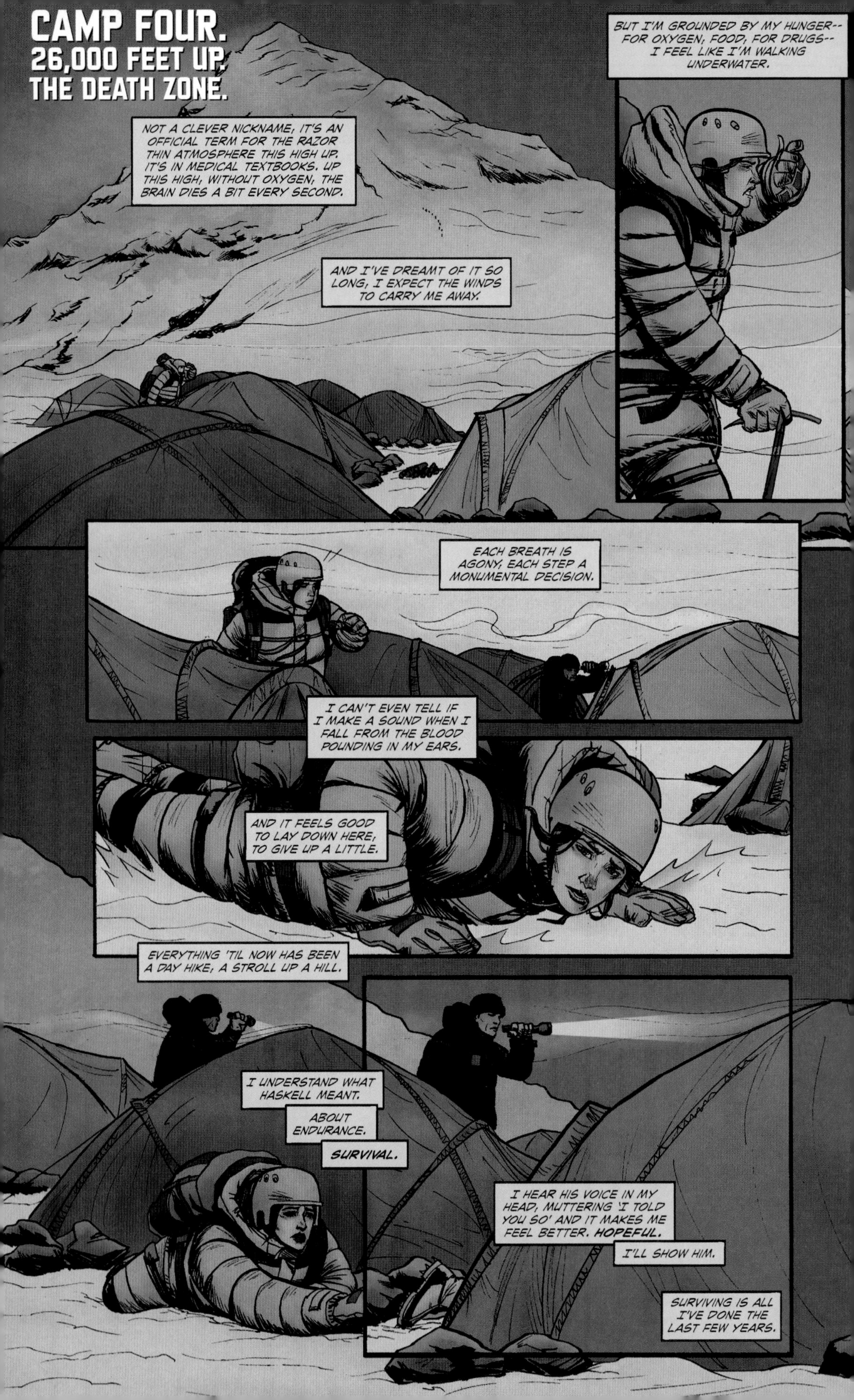

CAMP FOUR. 26,000 FEET UP. THE DEATH ZONE.
NOT A CLEVER NICKNAME; IT'S AN OFFICIAL TERM FOR THE RAZOR THIN ATMOSPHERE THIS HIGH UP. IT'S IN MEDICAL TEXTBOOKS. UP THIS HIGH, WITHOUT OXYGEN, THE BRAIN DIES A BIT EVERY SECOND.
AND I'VE DREAMT OF IT SO LONG, I EXPECT THE WINDS TO CARRY ME AWAY.
BUT I'M GROUNDED BY MY HUNGER--FOR OXYGEN, FOOD, FOR DRUGS--I FEEL LIKE I'M WALKING UNDERWATER.
EACH BREATH IS AGONY, EACH STEP A MONUMENTAL DECISION.
I CAN'T EVEN TELL IF I MAKE A SOUND WHEN I FALL FROM THE BLOOD POUNDING IN MY EARS.
AND IT FEELS GOOD TO LAY DOWN HERE, TO GIVE UP A LITTLE.
EVERYTHING 'TIL NOW HAS BEEN A DAY HIKE, A STROLL UP A HILL.
I UNDERSTAND WHAT HASKELL MEANT.
ABOUT ENDURANCE.
SURVIVAL.
I HEAR HIS VOICE IN MY HEAD, MUTTERING 'I TOLD YOU SO' AND IT MAKES ME FEEL BETTER. HOPEFUL.
I'LL SHOW HIM.
SURVIVING IS ALL I'VE DONE THE LAST FEW YEARS.

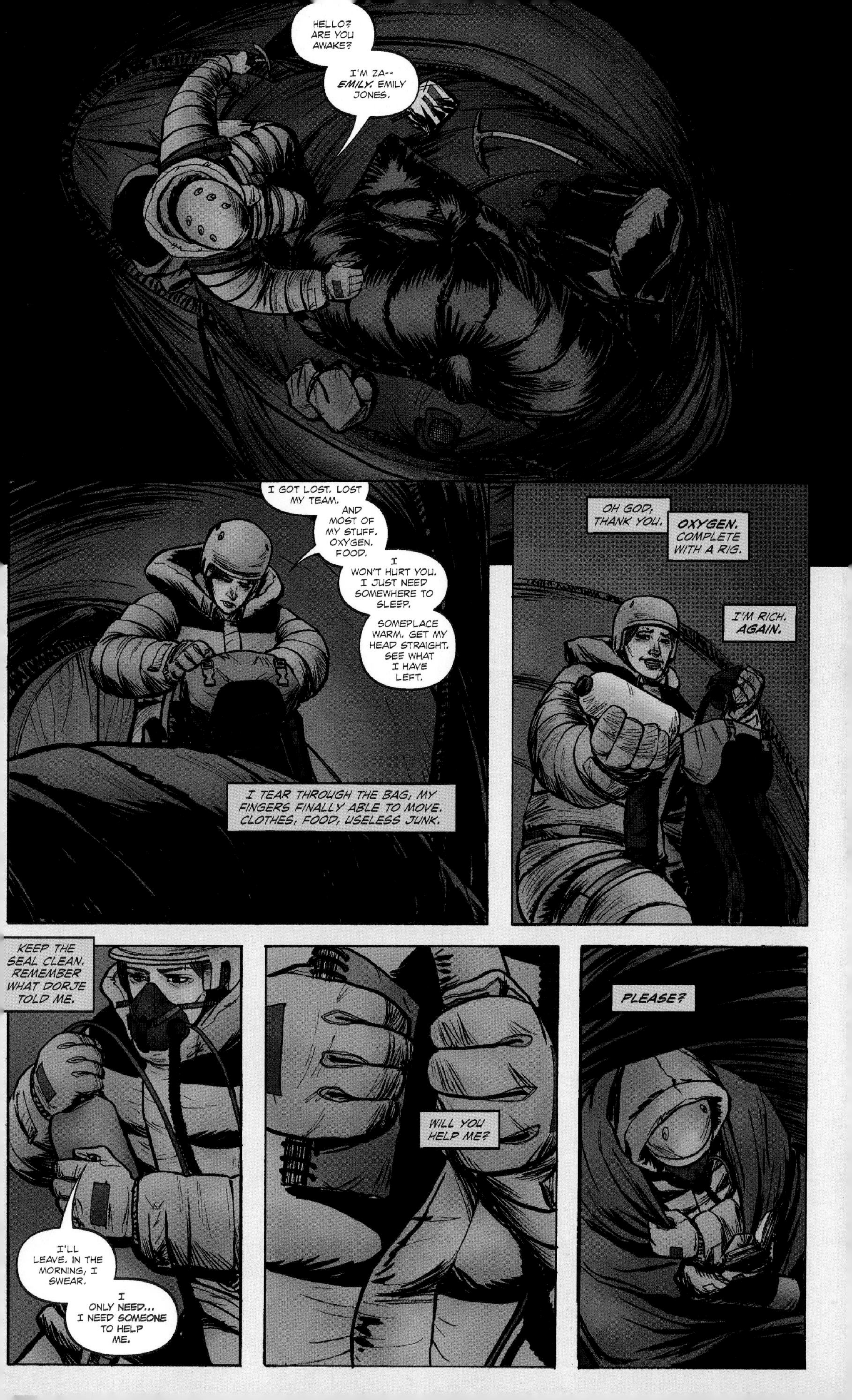
HELLO? ARE YOU AWAKE?
I'M ZA-- *EMILY.* EMILY JONES.
I GOT LOST. LOST MY TEAM.
AND MOST OF MY STUFF. OXYGEN. FOOD.
I WON'T HURT YOU. I JUST NEED SOMEWHERE TO SLEEP.
SOMEPLACE WARM. GET MY HEAD STRAIGHT. SEE WHAT I HAVE LEFT.
I TEAR THROUGH THE BAG, MY FINGERS FINALLY ABLE TO MOVE. CLOTHES, FOOD, USELESS JUNK.
OH GOD, THANK YOU.
OXYGEN. COMPLETE WITH A RIG.
I'M RICH. *AGAIN.*
KEEP THE SEAL CLEAN. REMEMBER WHAT DORJE TOLD ME.
I'LL LEAVE. IN THE MORNING, I SWEAR.
I ONLY NEED... I NEED *SOMEONE* TO HELP ME.
WILL YOU HELP ME?
PLEASE?

My father taught me to never beg for help. To stand on my own two feet and face what comes.

The war taught me nothing could harm me. That I could harm everything I set my eyes on.

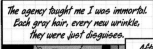

The agency taught me I was immortal. Each gray hair, every new wrinkle, they were just disguises.

After every mission we'd go into the room. Swallow our pills, let the program swallow us.

Come out clean on the other side. All we needed to know was that we'd done something important, meaningful.

Even if it wasn't *true.*

We were supposed to do our jobs and forget; the program was meant to keep us from being saddled with guilt and questions.

But I never had any of either. I was grateful for the job, almost eager for it. All I ever knew well was *killing.*

Here, tens of thousands of miles away it's still all I really know how to do.

No one ever taught me that. They just pointed me. Some away from it, most right towards it.

All I cared about was the quiet moments after, when all the noise went away.

All I can hear now is the wind screaming across Everest. It sounds familiar.

And I know what to do.

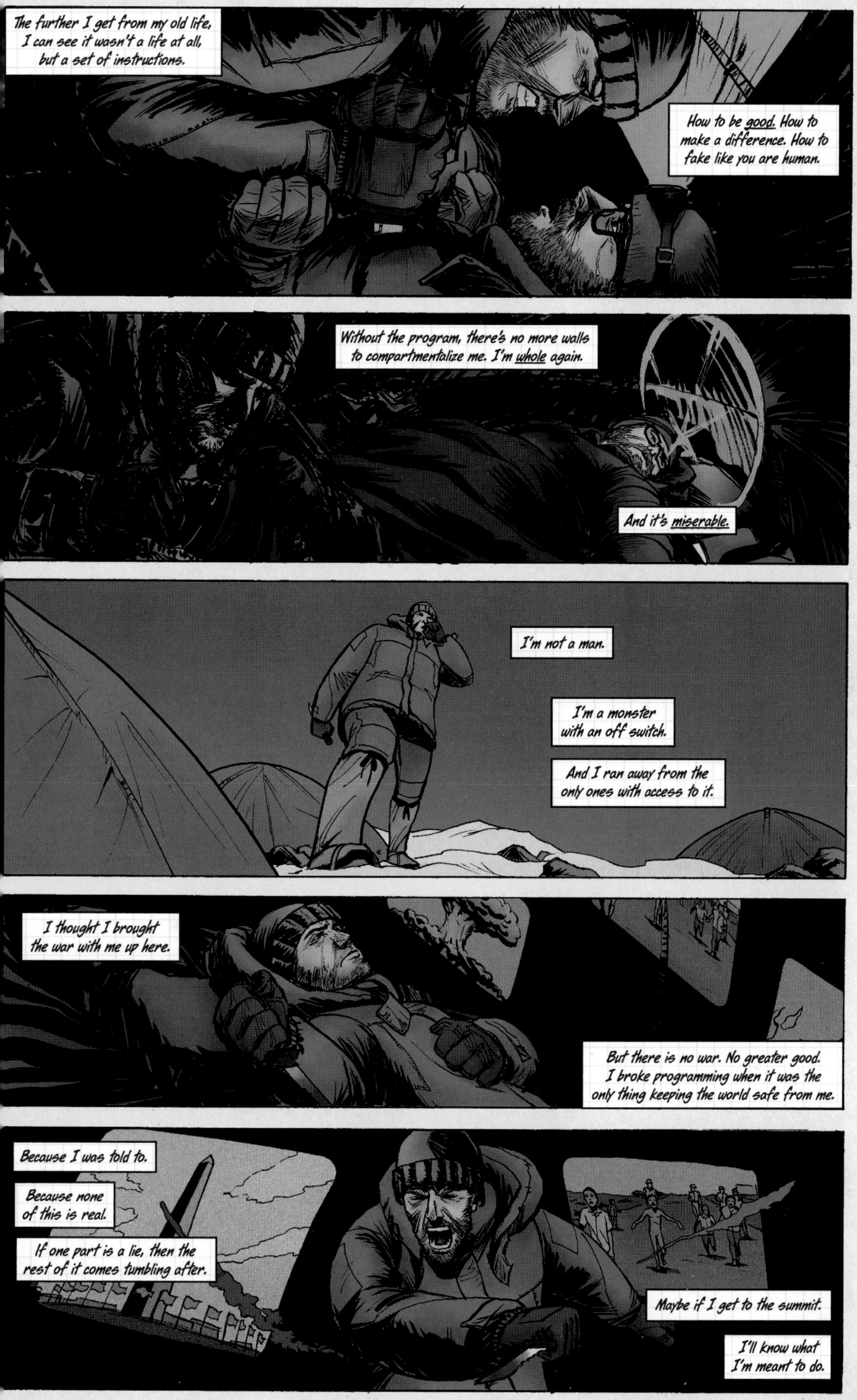
The further I get from my old life, I can see it wasn't a life at all, but a set of instructions.
How to be good. How to make a difference. How to fake like you are human.
Without the program, there's no more walls to compartmentalize me. I'm whole again.
And it's miserable.
I'm not a man.
I'm a monster with an off switch.
And I ran away from the only ones with access to it.
I thought I brought the war with me up here.
But there is no war. No greater good. I broke programming when it was the only thing keeping the world safe from me.
Because I was told to.
Because none of this is real.
If one part is a lie, then the rest of it comes tumbling after.
Maybe if I get to the summit.
I'll know what I'm meant to do.

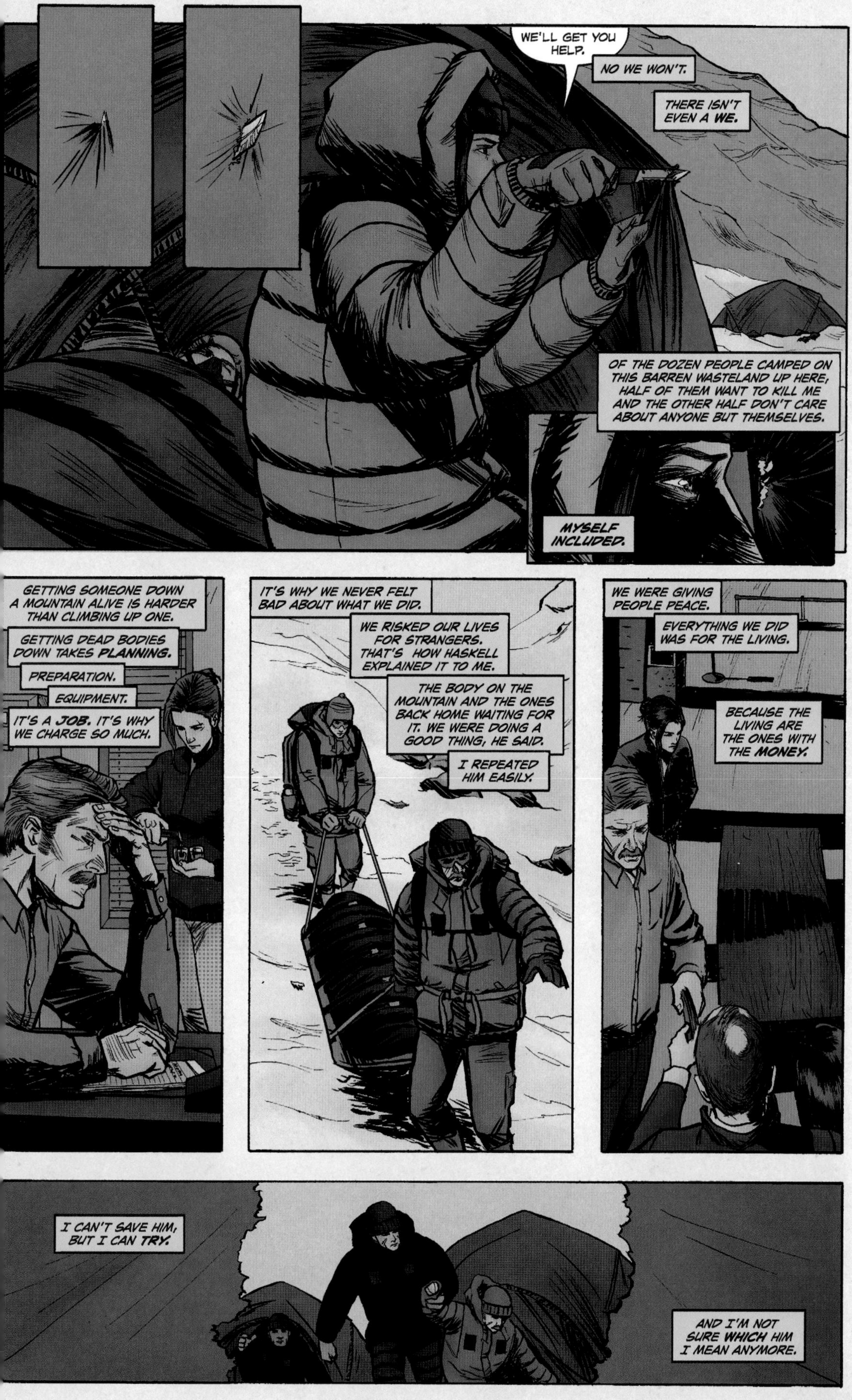

WE'LL GET YOU HELP.
NO WE WON'T.
THERE ISN'T EVEN A WE.
OF THE DOZEN PEOPLE CAMPED ON THIS BARREN WASTELAND UP HERE, HALF OF THEM WANT TO KILL ME AND THE OTHER HALF DON'T CARE ABOUT ANYONE BUT THEMSELVES.
MYSELF INCLUDED.
GETTING SOMEONE DOWN A MOUNTAIN ALIVE IS HARDER THAN CLIMBING UP ONE.
GETTING DEAD BODIES DOWN TAKES PLANNING.
PREPARATION.
EQUIPMENT.
IT'S A JOB. IT'S WHY WE CHARGE SO MUCH.
IT'S WHY WE NEVER FELT BAD ABOUT WHAT WE DID.
WE RISKED OUR LIVES FOR STRANGERS. THAT'S HOW HASKELL EXPLAINED IT TO ME.
THE BODY ON THE MOUNTAIN AND THE ONES BACK HOME WAITING FOR IT. WE WERE DOING A GOOD THING, HE SAID.
I REPEATED HIM EASILY.
WE WERE GIVING PEOPLE PEACE.
EVERYTHING WE DID WAS FOR THE LIVING.
BECAUSE THE LIVING ARE THE ONES WITH THE MONEY.
I CAN'T SAVE HIM, BUT I CAN TRY.
AND I'M NOT SURE WHICH HIM I MEAN ANYMORE.

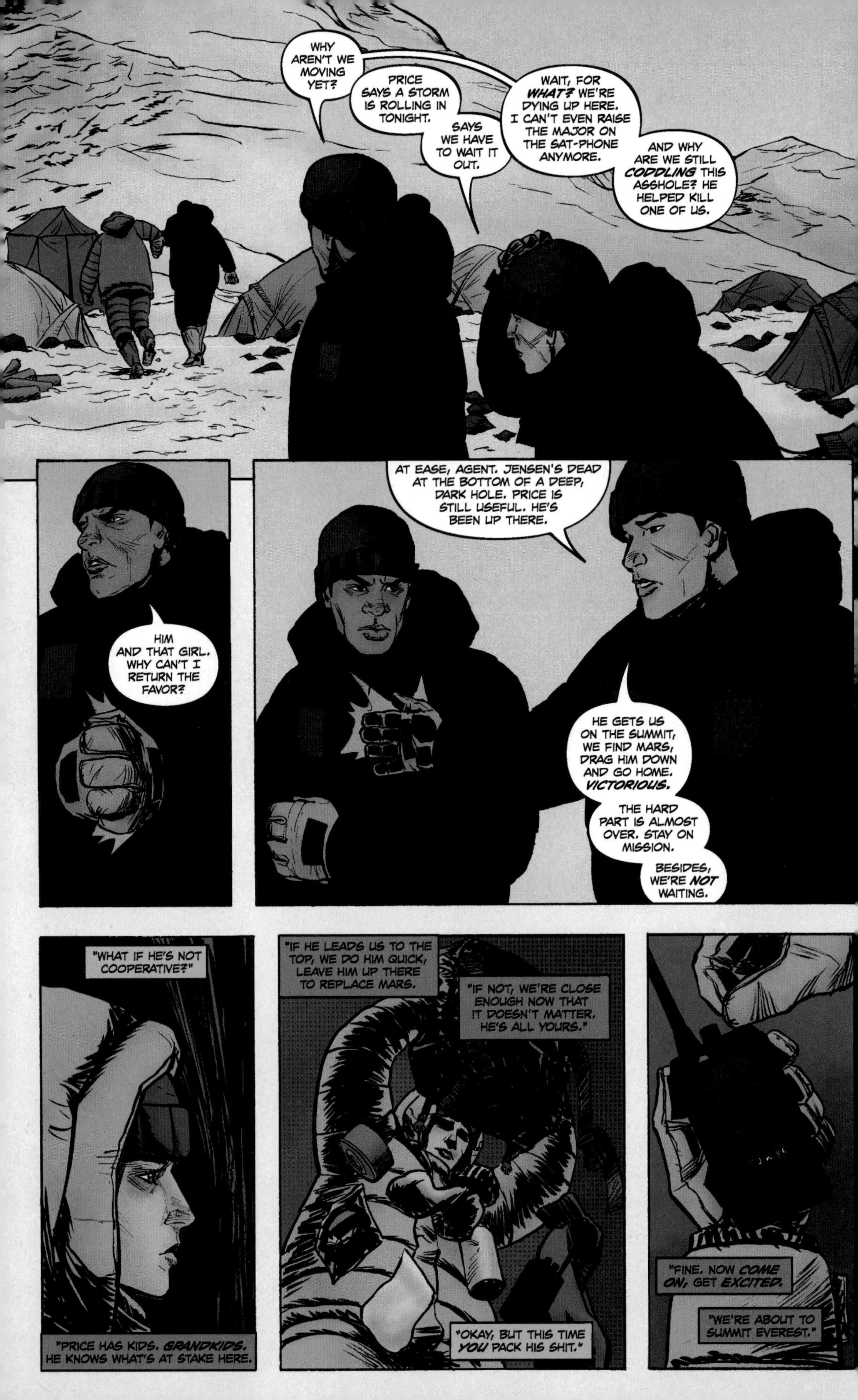
WHY AREN'T WE MOVING YET?
PRICE SAYS A STORM IS ROLLING IN TONIGHT.
SAYS WE HAVE TO WAIT IT OUT.
WAIT, FOR WHAT? WE'RE DYING UP HERE. I CAN'T EVEN RAISE THE MAJOR ON THE SAT-PHONE ANYMORE.
AND WHY ARE WE STILL CODDLING THIS ASSHOLE? HE HELPED KILL ONE OF US.
AT EASE, AGENT. JENSEN'S DEAD AT THE BOTTOM OF A DEEP, DARK HOLE. PRICE IS STILL USEFUL. HE'S BEEN UP THERE.
HIM AND THAT GIRL. WHY CAN'T I RETURN THE FAVOR?
HE GETS US ON THE SUMMIT, WE FIND MARS, DRAG HIM DOWN AND GO HOME. VICTORIOUS.
THE HARD PART IS ALMOST OVER. STAY ON MISSION.
BESIDES, WE'RE NOT WAITING.
"WHAT IF HE'S NOT COOPERATIVE?"
"PRICE HAS KIDS. GRANDKIDS. HE KNOWS WHAT'S AT STAKE HERE.
"IF HE LEADS US TO THE TOP, WE DO HIM QUICK, LEAVE HIM UP THERE TO REPLACE MARS.
"IF NOT, WE'RE CLOSE ENOUGH NOW THAT IT DOESN'T MATTER. HE'S ALL YOURS."
"OKAY, BUT THIS TIME YOU PACK HIS SHIT."
"FINE. NOW COME ON, GET EXCITED.
"WE'RE ABOUT TO SUMMIT EVEREST."

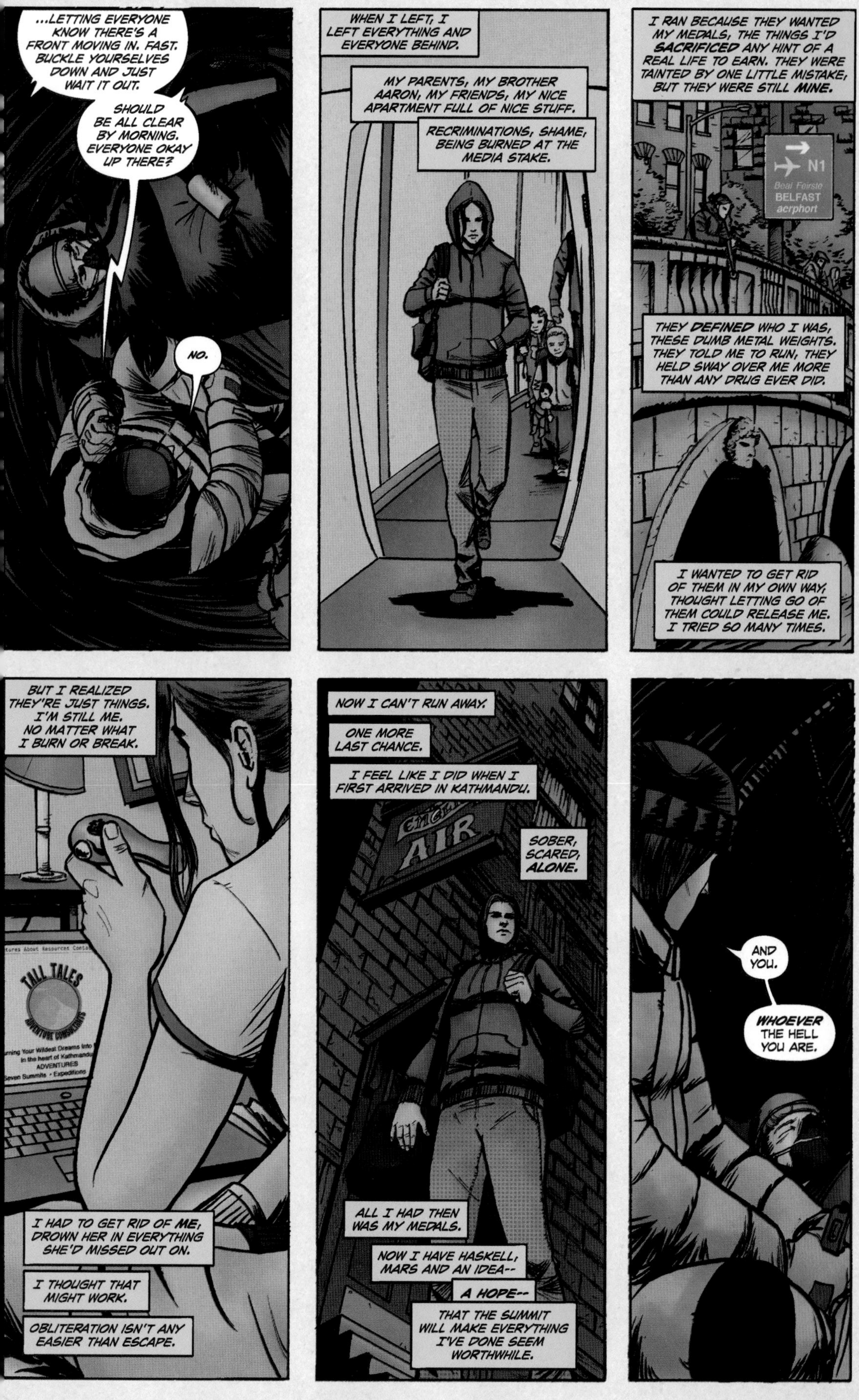
...LETTING EVERYONE KNOW THERE'S A FRONT MOVING IN. FAST. BUCKLE YOURSELVES DOWN AND JUST WAIT IT OUT.
SHOULD BE ALL CLEAR BY MORNING. EVERYONE OKAY UP THERE?
NO.
WHEN I LEFT, I LEFT EVERYTHING AND EVERYONE BEHIND.
MY PARENTS, MY BROTHER AARON, MY FRIENDS, MY NICE APARTMENT FULL OF NICE STUFF.
RECRIMINATIONS, SHAME; BEING BURNED AT THE MEDIA STAKE.
I RAN BECAUSE THEY WANTED MY MEDALS, THE THINGS I'D SACRIFICED ANY HINT OF A REAL LIFE TO EARN. THEY WERE TAINTED BY ONE LITTLE MISTAKE, BUT THEY WERE STILL MINE.
N1
Beal Feirste
BELFAST
acrphort
THEY DEFINED WHO I WAS, THESE DUMB METAL WEIGHTS. THEY TOLD ME TO RUN, THEY HELD SWAY OVER ME MORE THAN ANY DRUG EVER DID.
I WANTED TO GET RID OF THEM IN MY OWN WAY, THOUGHT LETTING GO OF THEM COULD RELEASE ME. I TRIED SO MANY TIMES.
BUT I REALIZED THEY'RE JUST THINGS. I'M STILL ME. NO MATTER WHAT I BURN OR BREAK.
tures About Resources Conta
TALL TALES
ADVENTURE CONSULTANTS
rning Your Wildest Dreams Into
In the heart of Kathmandu
ADVENTURES
Seven Summits • Expeditions
I HAD TO GET RID OF ME, DROWN HER IN EVERYTHING SHE'D MISSED OUT ON.
I THOUGHT THAT MIGHT WORK.
OBLITERATION ISN'T ANY EASIER THAN ESCAPE.
NOW I CAN'T RUN AWAY.
ONE MORE LAST CHANCE.
I FEEL LIKE I DID WHEN I FIRST ARRIVED IN KATHMANDU.
AIR
SOBER, SCARED, ALONE.
ALL I HAD THEN WAS MY MEDALS.
NOW I HAVE HASKELL, MARS AND AN IDEA--
A HOPE--
THAT THE SUMMIT WILL MAKE EVERYTHING I'VE DONE SEEM WORTHWHILE.
AND YOU.
WHOEVER THE HELL YOU ARE.

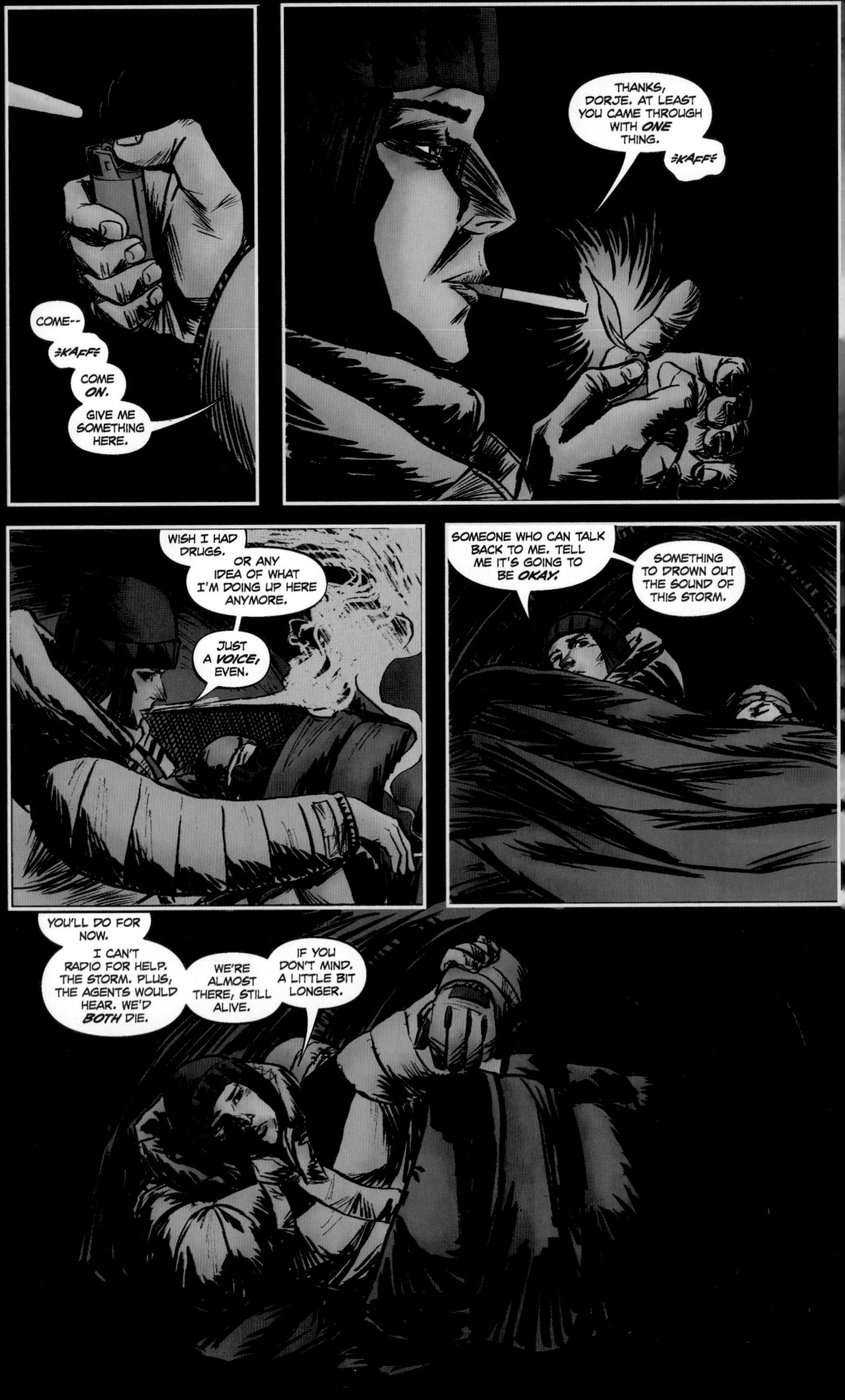
COME--
KAFF
COME ON.
GIVE ME SOMETHING HERE.
THANKS, DORJE. AT LEAST YOU CAME THROUGH WITH ONE THING.
KAFF
WISH I HAD DRUGS.
OR ANY IDEA OF WHAT I'M DOING UP HERE ANYMORE.
JUST A VOICE, EVEN.
SOMEONE WHO CAN TALK BACK TO ME. TELL ME IT'S GOING TO BE OKAY.
SOMETHING TO DROWN OUT THE SOUND OF THIS STORM.
YOU'LL DO FOR NOW.
I CAN'T RADIO FOR HELP. THE STORM. PLUS, THE AGENTS WOULD HEAR. WE'D BOTH DIE.
WE'RE ALMOST THERE, STILL ALIVE.
IF YOU DON'T MIND. A LITTLE BIT LONGER.

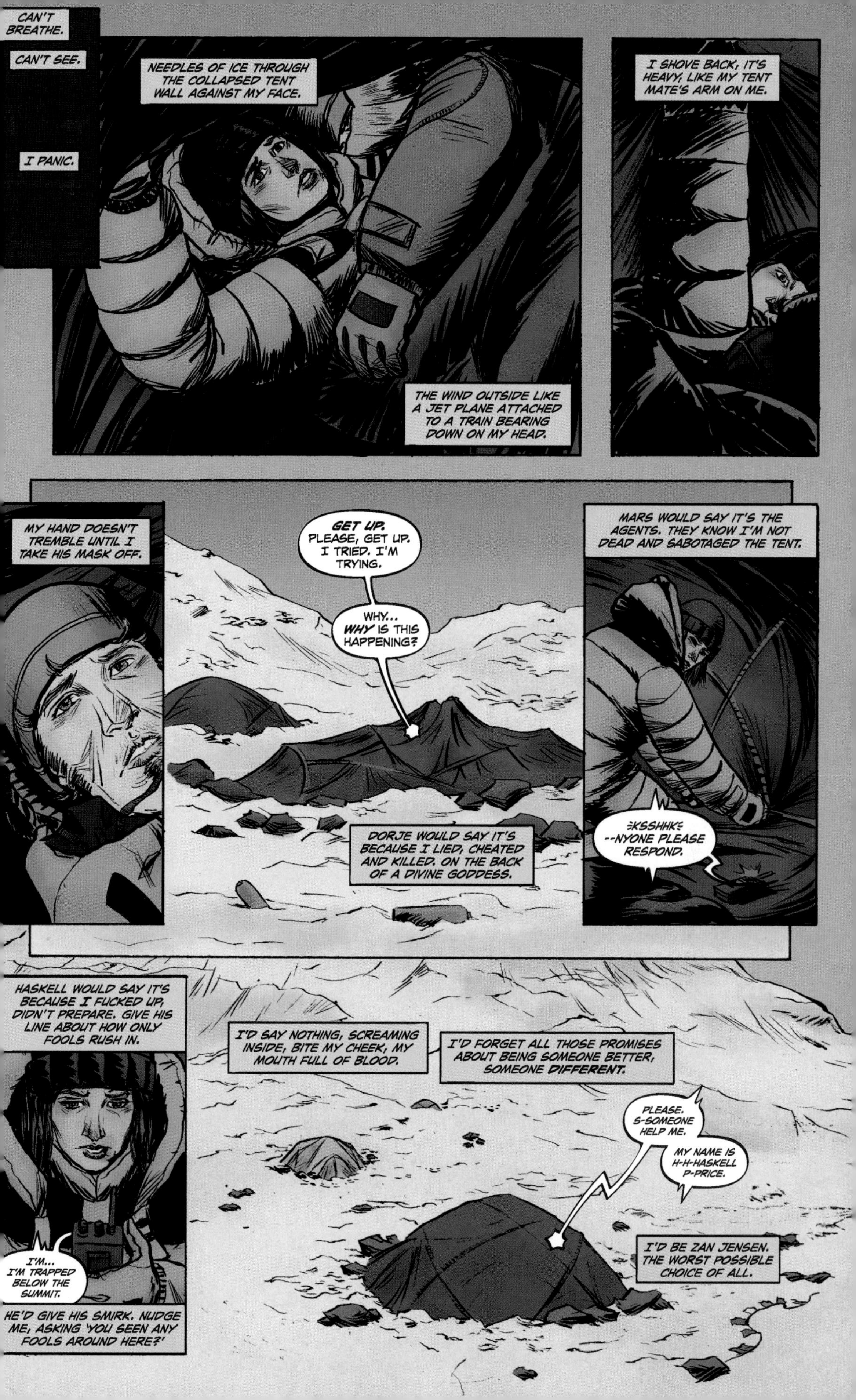
CAN'T BREATHE.
CAN'T SEE.
NEEDLES OF ICE THROUGH THE COLLAPSED TENT WALL AGAINST MY FACE.
I PANIC.
THE WIND OUTSIDE LIKE A JET PLANE ATTACHED TO A TRAIN BEARING DOWN ON MY HEAD.
I SHOVE BACK, IT'S HEAVY, LIKE MY TENT MATE'S ARM ON ME.
MY HAND DOESN'T TREMBLE UNTIL I TAKE HIS MASK OFF.
GET UP. PLEASE, GET UP. I TRIED. I'M TRYING.
WHY... WHY IS THIS HAPPENING?
MARS WOULD SAY IT'S THE AGENTS. THEY KNOW I'M NOT DEAD AND SABOTAGED THE TENT.
DORJE WOULD SAY IT'S BECAUSE I LIED, CHEATED AND KILLED. ON THE BACK OF A DIVINE GODDESS.
=KSSHHK= --NYONE PLEASE RESPOND.
HASKELL WOULD SAY IT'S BECAUSE I FUCKED UP, DIDN'T PREPARE. GIVE HIS LINE ABOUT HOW ONLY FOOLS RUSH IN.
I'M... I'M TRAPPED BELOW THE SUMMIT.
HE'D GIVE HIS SMIRK. NUDGE ME, ASKING 'YOU SEEN ANY FOOLS AROUND HERE?'
I'D SAY NOTHING, SCREAMING INSIDE, BITE MY CHEEK, MY MOUTH FULL OF BLOOD.
I'D FORGET ALL THOSE PROMISES ABOUT BEING SOMEONE BETTER, SOMEONE DIFFERENT.
PLEASE. S-SOMEONE HELP ME.
MY NAME IS H-H-HASKELL P-PRICE.
I'D BE ZAN JENSEN. THE WORST POSSIBLE CHOICE OF ALL.

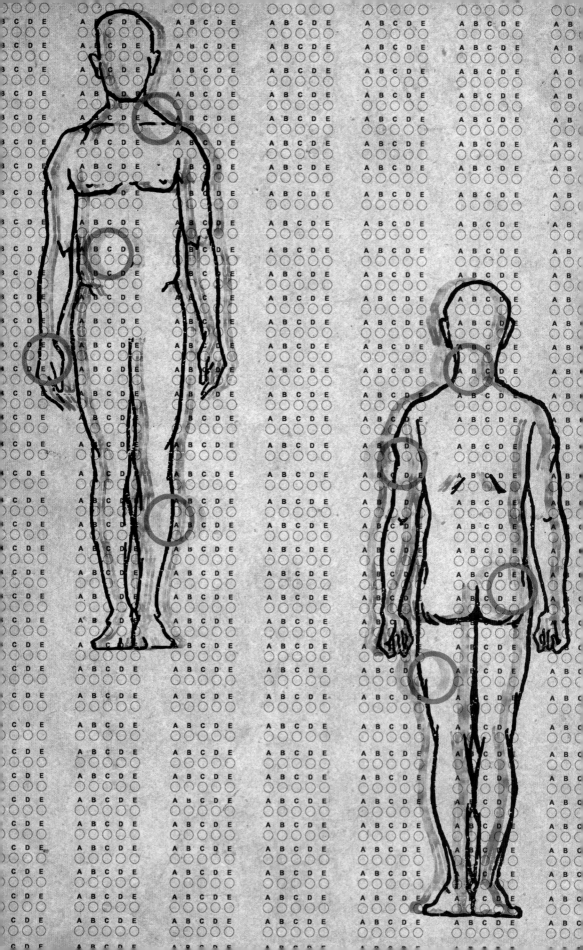

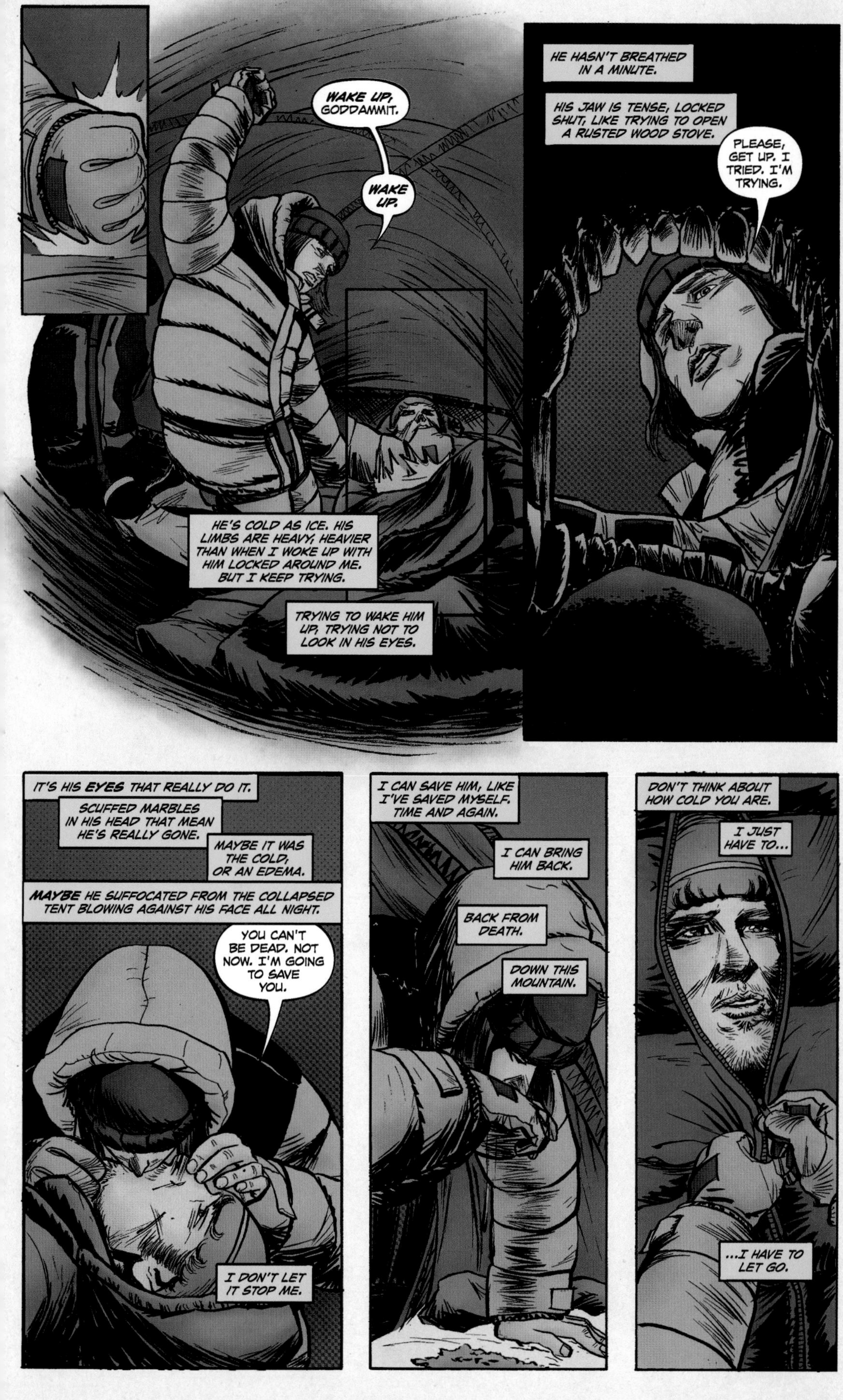
WAKE UP, GODDAMMIT.
WAKE UP.
HE'S COLD AS ICE. HIS LIMBS ARE HEAVY; HEAVIER THAN WHEN I WOKE UP WITH HIM LOCKED AROUND ME. BUT I KEEP TRYING.
TRYING TO WAKE HIM UP, TRYING NOT TO LOOK IN HIS EYES.
HE HASN'T BREATHED IN A MINUTE.
HIS JAW IS TENSE; LOCKED SHUT, LIKE TRYING TO OPEN A RUSTED WOOD STOVE.
PLEASE, GET UP. I TRIED. I'M TRYING.
IT'S HIS EYES THAT REALLY DO IT.
SCUFFED MARBLES IN HIS HEAD THAT MEAN HE'S REALLY GONE.
MAYBE IT WAS THE COLD, OR AN EDEMA.
MAYBE HE SUFFOCATED FROM THE COLLAPSED TENT BLOWING AGAINST HIS FACE ALL NIGHT.
YOU CAN'T BE DEAD. NOT NOW. I'M GOING TO SAVE YOU.
I DON'T LET IT STOP ME.
I CAN SAVE HIM, LIKE I'VE SAVED MYSELF. TIME AND AGAIN.
I CAN BRING HIM BACK.
BACK FROM DEATH.
DOWN THIS MOUNTAIN.
DON'T THINK ABOUT HOW COLD YOU ARE.
I JUST HAVE TO...
...I HAVE TO LET GO.

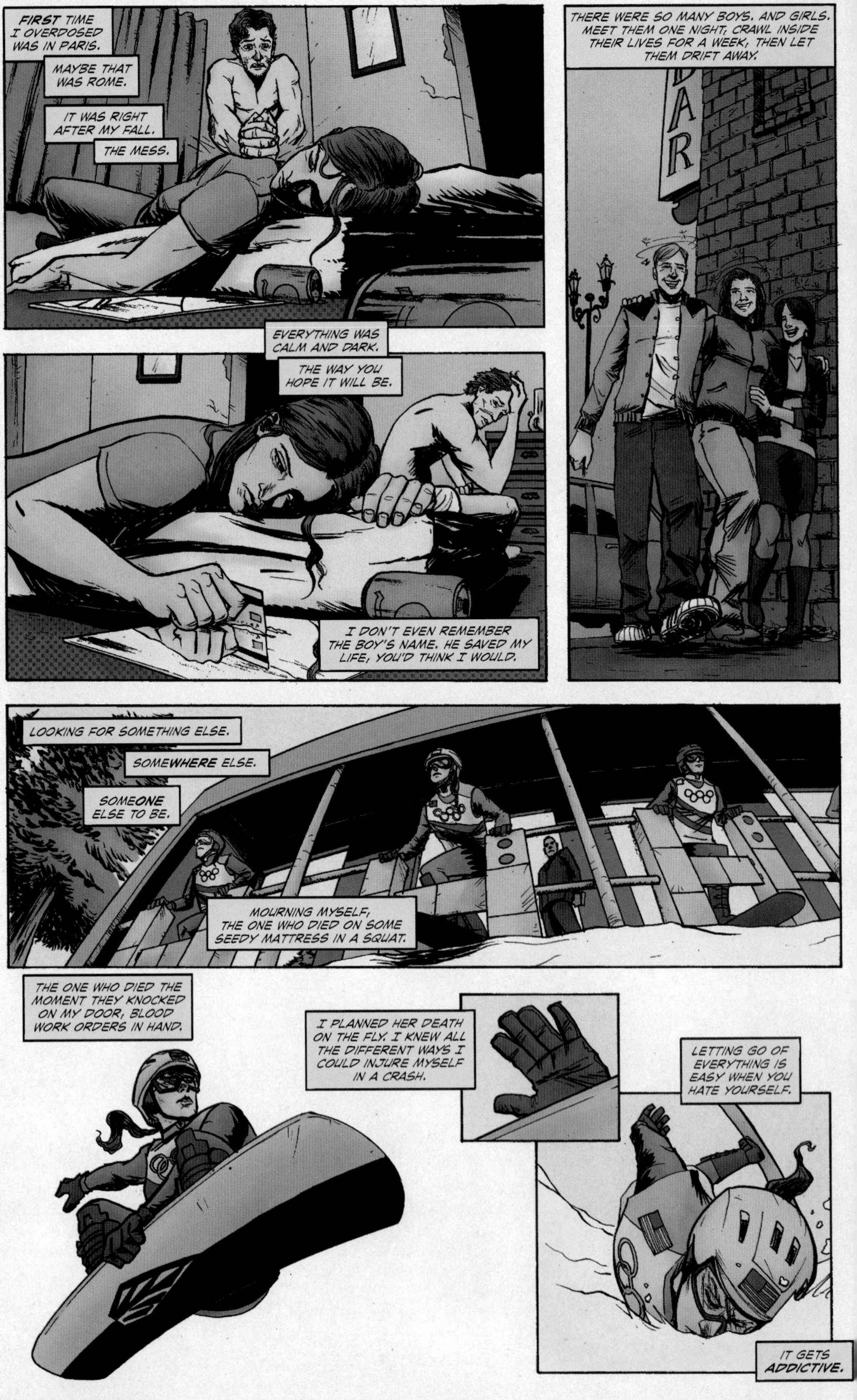

FIRST TIME I OVERDOSED WAS IN PARIS.
MAYBE THAT WAS ROME.
IT WAS RIGHT AFTER MY FALL.
THE MESS.
EVERYTHING WAS CALM AND DARK.
THE WAY YOU HOPE IT WILL BE.
I DON'T EVEN REMEMBER THE BOY'S NAME. HE SAVED MY LIFE, YOU'D THINK I WOULD.
THERE WERE SO MANY BOYS. AND GIRLS. MEET THEM ONE NIGHT, CRAWL INSIDE THEIR LIVES FOR A WEEK, THEN LET THEM DRIFT AWAY.
BAR
LOOKING FOR SOMETHING ELSE.
SOMEWHERE ELSE.
SOMEONE ELSE TO BE.
MOURNING MYSELF, THE ONE WHO DIED ON SOME SEEDY MATTRESS IN A SQUAT.
THE ONE WHO DIED THE MOMENT THEY KNOCKED ON MY DOOR, BLOOD WORK ORDERS IN HAND.
I PLANNED HER DEATH ON THE FLY. I KNEW ALL THE DIFFERENT WAYS I COULD INJURE MYSELF IN A CRASH.
LETTING GO OF EVERYTHING IS EASY WHEN YOU HATE YOURSELF.
IT GETS ADDICTIVE.

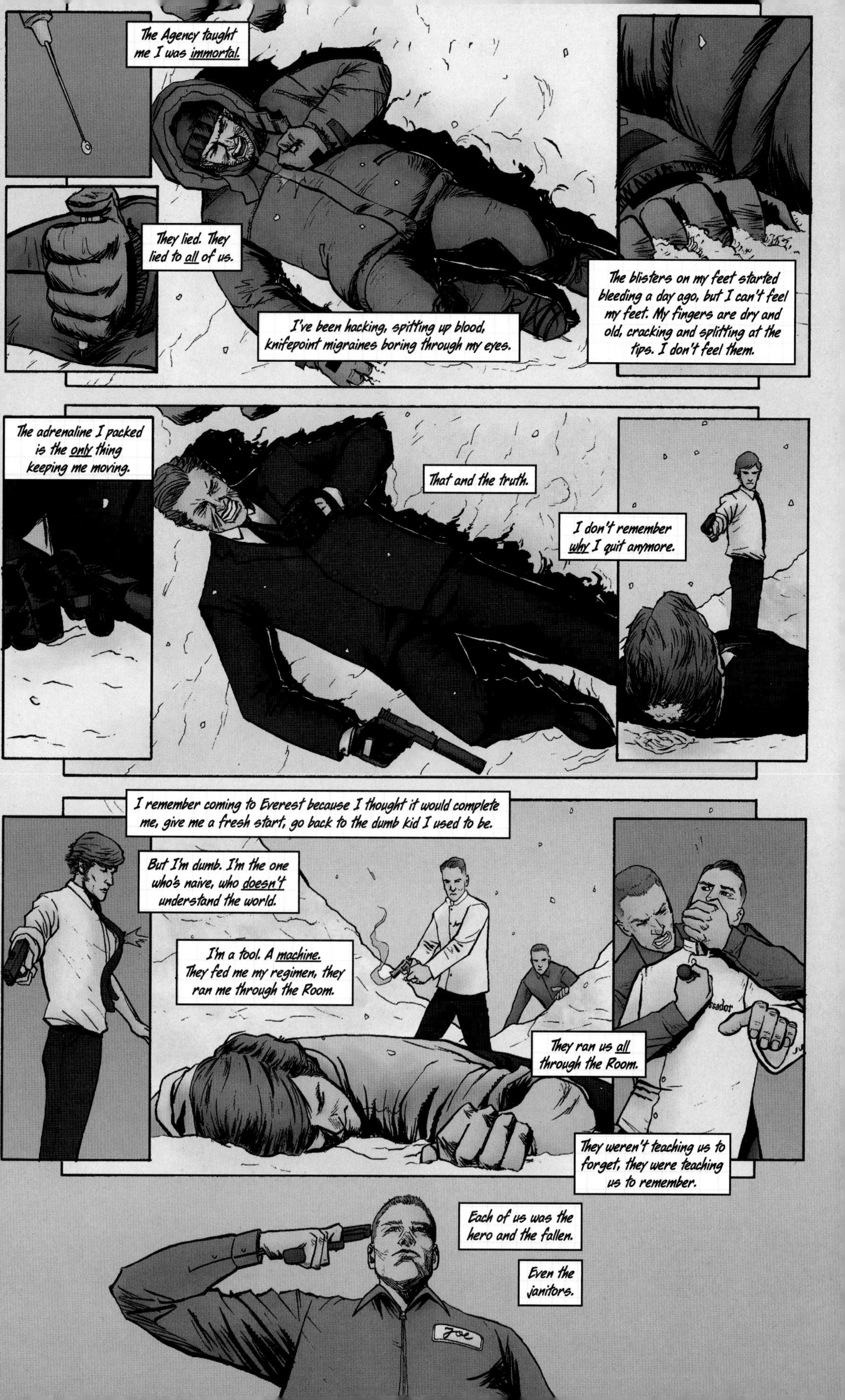

The Agency taught me I was immortal.
They lied. They lied to all of us.
I've been hacking, spitting up blood, knifepoint migraines boring through my eyes.
The blisters on my feet started bleeding a day ago, but I can't feel my feet. My fingers are dry and old, cracking and splitting at the tips. I don't feel them.
The adrenaline I packed is the only thing keeping me moving.
That and the truth.
I don't remember why I quit anymore.
I remember coming to Everest because I thought it would complete me, give me a fresh start, go back to the dumb kid I used to be.
But I'm dumb. I'm the one who's naive, who doesn't understand the world.
I'm a tool. A machine. They fed me my regimen, they ran me through the Room.
They ran us all through the Room.
They weren't teaching us to forget, they were teaching us to remember.
Each of us was the hero and the fallen.
Even the janitors.
Joe

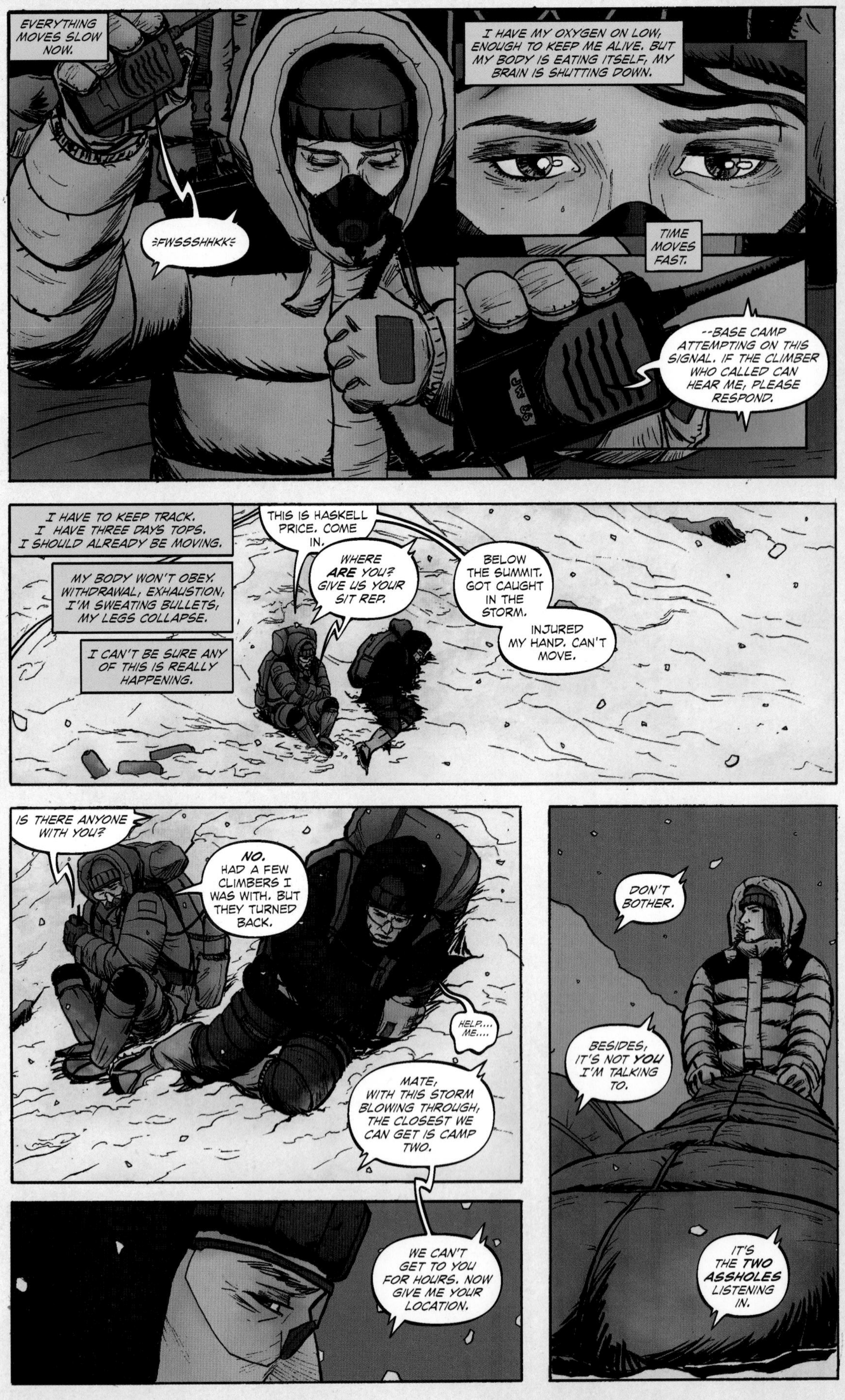
EVERYTHING MOVES SLOW NOW.
FWSSSHHKK
I HAVE MY OXYGEN ON LOW, ENOUGH TO KEEP ME ALIVE. BUT MY BODY IS EATING ITSELF, MY BRAIN IS SHUTTING DOWN.
TIME MOVES FAST.
--BASE CAMP ATTEMPTING ON THIS SIGNAL. IF THE CLIMBER WHO CALLED CAN HEAR ME, PLEASE RESPOND.
I HAVE TO KEEP TRACK. I HAVE THREE DAYS TOPS. I SHOULD ALREADY BE MOVING.
MY BODY WON'T OBEY. WITHDRAWAL, EXHAUSTION, I'M SWEATING BULLETS, MY LEGS COLLAPSE.
I CAN'T BE SURE ANY OF THIS IS REALLY HAPPENING.
THIS IS HASKELL PRICE. COME IN.
WHERE **ARE** YOU? GIVE US YOUR SIT REP.
BELOW THE SUMMIT. GOT CAUGHT IN THE STORM.
INJURED MY HAND. CAN'T MOVE.
IS THERE ANYONE WITH YOU?
NO. HAD A FEW CLIMBERS I WAS WITH. BUT THEY TURNED BACK.
HELP.... ME....
MATE, WITH THIS STORM BLOWING THROUGH, THE CLOSEST WE CAN GET IS CAMP TWO.
WE CAN'T GET TO YOU FOR HOURS. NOW GIVE ME YOUR LOCATION.
DON'T BOTHER.
BESIDES, IT'S NOT **YOU** I'M TALKING TO.
IT'S THE **TWO ASSHOLES** LISTENING IN.

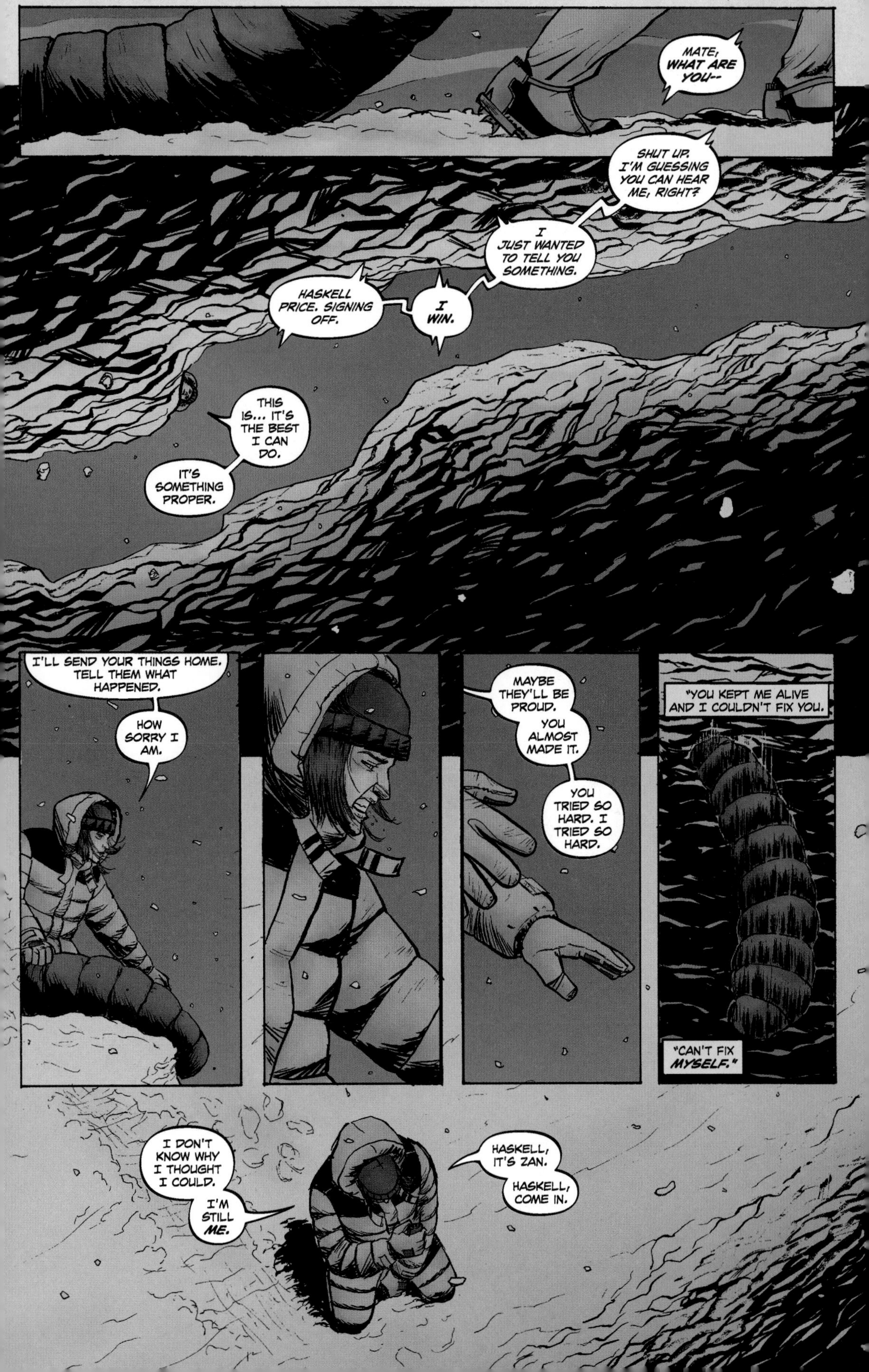
MATE, WHAT ARE YOU--
SHUT UP. I'M GUESSING YOU CAN HEAR ME, RIGHT?
I JUST WANTED TO TELL YOU SOMETHING.
I WIN.
HASKELL PRICE. SIGNING OFF.
THIS IS... IT'S THE BEST I CAN DO.
IT'S SOMETHING PROPER.
I'LL SEND YOUR THINGS HOME. TELL THEM WHAT HAPPENED.
HOW SORRY I AM.
MAYBE THEY'LL BE PROUD.
YOU ALMOST MADE IT.
YOU TRIED SO HARD. I TRIED SO HARD.
"YOU KEPT ME ALIVE AND I COULDN'T FIX YOU.
"CAN'T FIX MYSELF."
HASKELL, IT'S ZAN.
HASKELL, COME IN.
I DON'T KNOW WHY I THOUGHT I COULD.
I'M STILL ME.

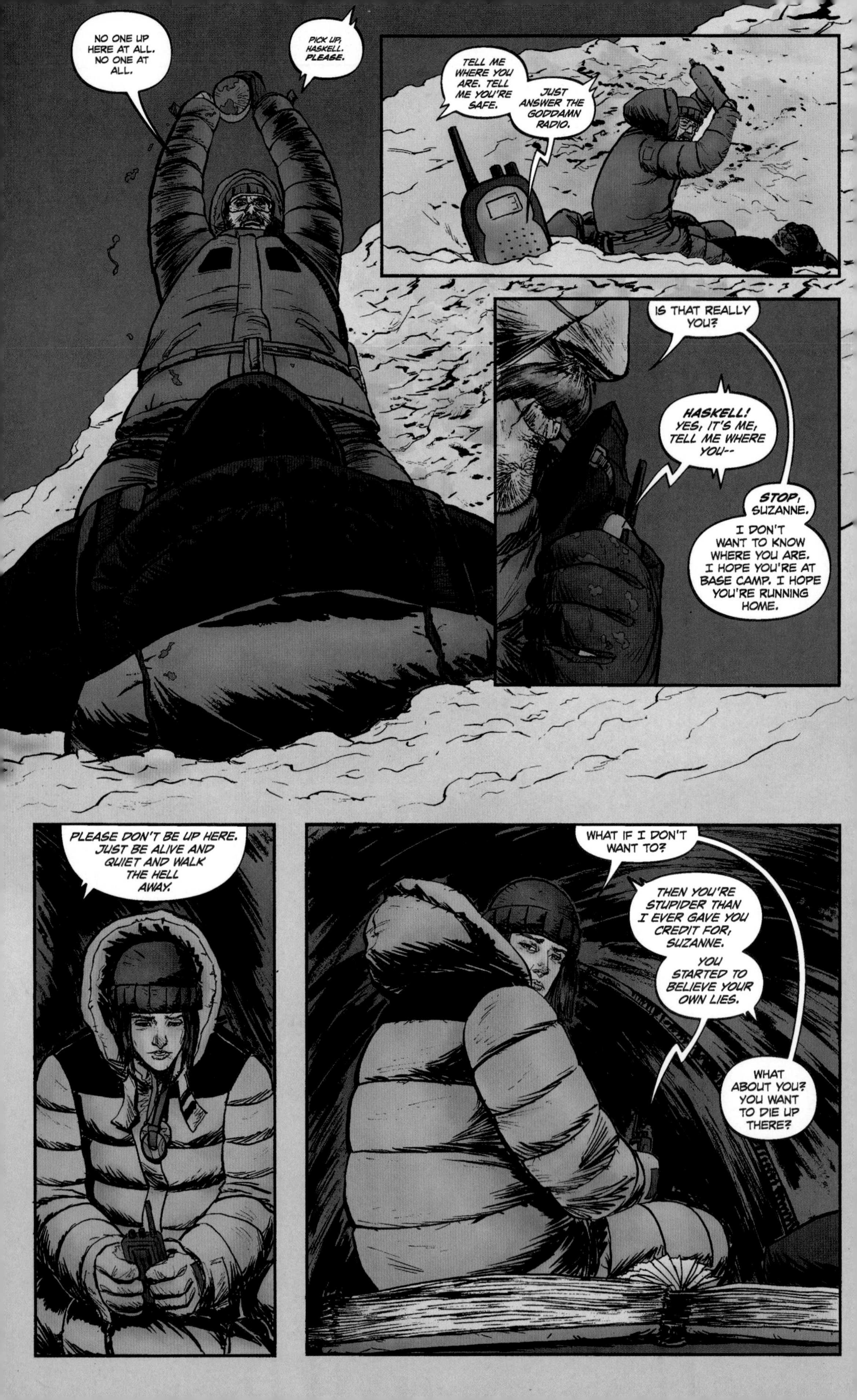
NO ONE UP HERE AT ALL. NO ONE AT ALL.
PICK UP, HASKELL. PLEASE.
TELL ME WHERE YOU ARE. TELL ME YOU'RE SAFE.
JUST ANSWER THE GODDAMN RADIO.
IS THAT REALLY YOU?
HASKELL! YES, IT'S ME, TELL ME WHERE YOU--
STOP, SUZANNE.
I DON'T WANT TO KNOW WHERE YOU ARE. I HOPE YOU'RE AT BASE CAMP. I HOPE YOU'RE RUNNING HOME.
PLEASE DON'T BE UP HERE. JUST BE ALIVE AND QUIET AND WALK THE HELL AWAY.
WHAT IF I DON'T WANT TO?
THEN YOU'RE STUPIDER THAN I EVER GAVE YOU CREDIT FOR, SUZANNE.
YOU STARTED TO BELIEVE YOUR OWN LIES.
WHAT ABOUT YOU? YOU WANT TO DIE UP THERE?

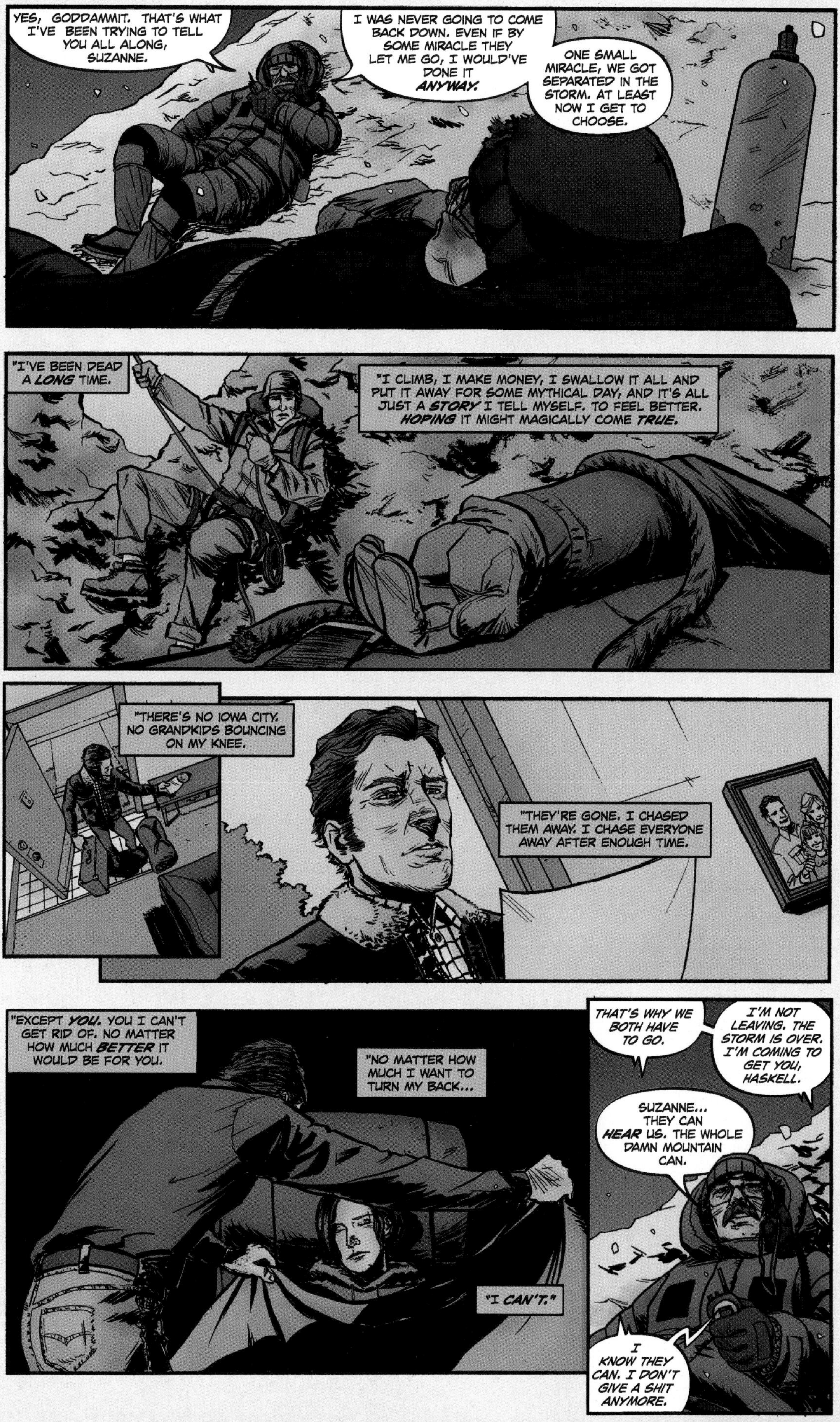
YES, GODDAMMIT. THAT'S WHAT I'VE BEEN TRYING TO TELL YOU ALL ALONG, SUZANNE.
I WAS NEVER GOING TO COME BACK DOWN. EVEN IF BY SOME MIRACLE THEY LET ME GO, I WOULD'VE DONE IT ANYWAY.
ONE SMALL MIRACLE, WE GOT SEPARATED IN THE STORM. AT LEAST NOW I GET TO CHOOSE.
"I'VE BEEN DEAD A LONG TIME.
"I CLIMB, I MAKE MONEY, I SWALLOW IT ALL AND PUT IT AWAY FOR SOME MYTHICAL DAY, AND IT'S ALL JUST A STORY I TELL MYSELF. TO FEEL BETTER. HOPING IT MIGHT MAGICALLY COME TRUE.
"THERE'S NO IOWA CITY. NO GRANDKIDS BOUNCING ON MY KNEE.
"THEY'RE GONE. I CHASED THEM AWAY. I CHASE EVERYONE AWAY AFTER ENOUGH TIME.
"EXCEPT YOU. YOU I CAN'T GET RID OF. NO MATTER HOW MUCH BETTER IT WOULD BE FOR YOU.
"NO MATTER HOW MUCH I WANT TO TURN MY BACK...
"I CAN'T."
THAT'S WHY WE BOTH HAVE TO GO.
I'M NOT LEAVING. THE STORM IS OVER. I'M COMING TO GET YOU, HASKELL.
SUZANNE... THEY CAN HEAR US. THE WHOLE DAMN MOUNTAIN CAN.
I KNOW THEY CAN. I DON'T GIVE A SHIT ANYMORE.

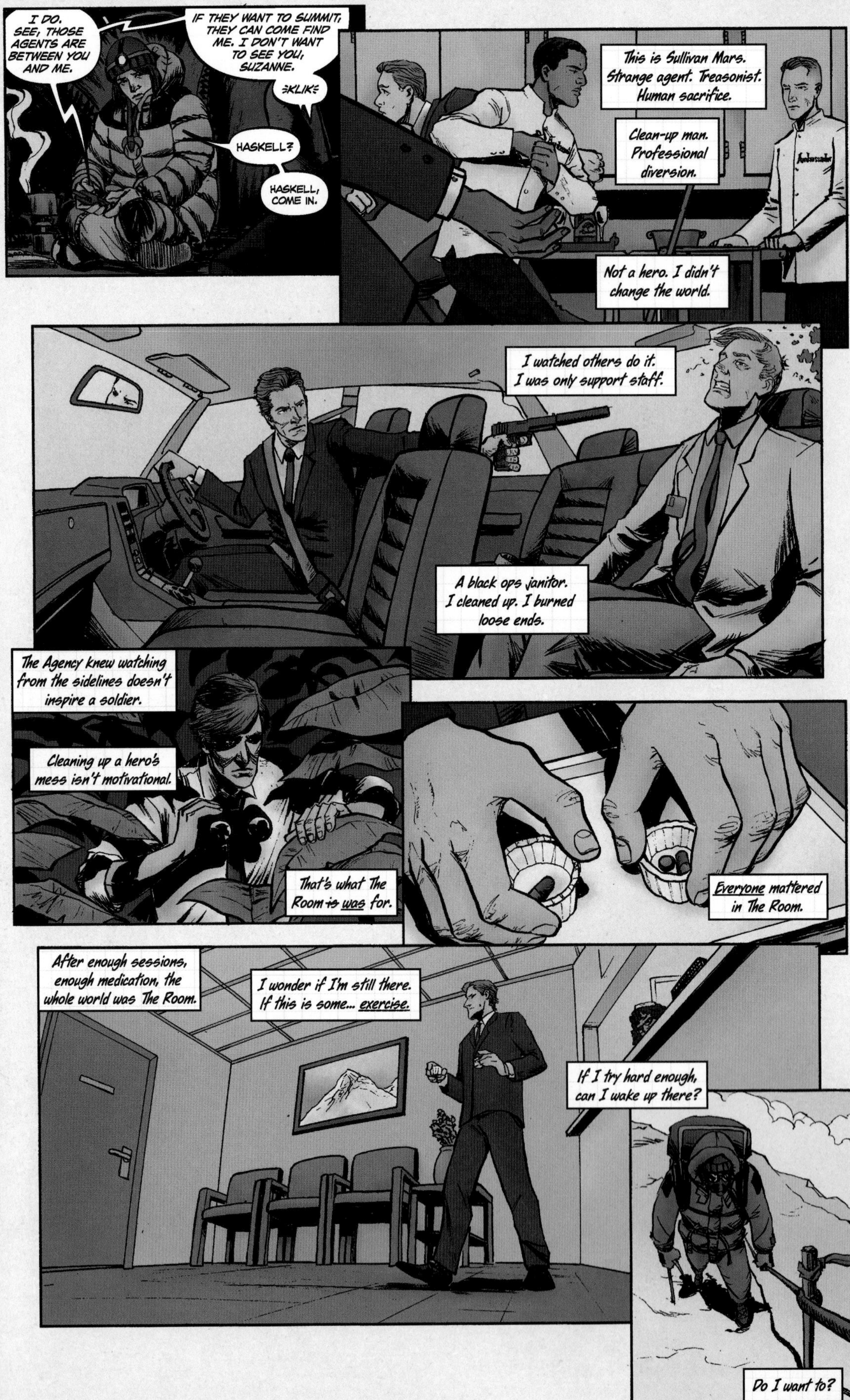
I DO. SEE, THOSE AGENTS ARE BETWEEN YOU AND ME.
IF THEY WANT TO SUMMIT, THEY CAN COME FIND ME. I DON'T WANT TO SEE YOU, SUZANNE.
KLIK
HASKELL?
HASKELL, COME IN.
This is Sullivan Mars. Strange agent. Treasonist. Human sacrifice.
Clean-up man. Professional diversion.
Not a hero. I didn't change the world.
I watched others do it. I was only support staff.
A black ops janitor. I cleaned up. I burned loose ends.
The Agency knew watching from the sidelines doesn't inspire a soldier.
Cleaning up a hero's mess isn't motivational.
That's what The Room ~~is~~ was for.
Everyone mattered in The Room.
After enough sessions, enough medication, the whole world was The Room.
I wonder if I'm still there. If this is some... exercise.
If I try hard enough, can I wake up there?
Do I want to?

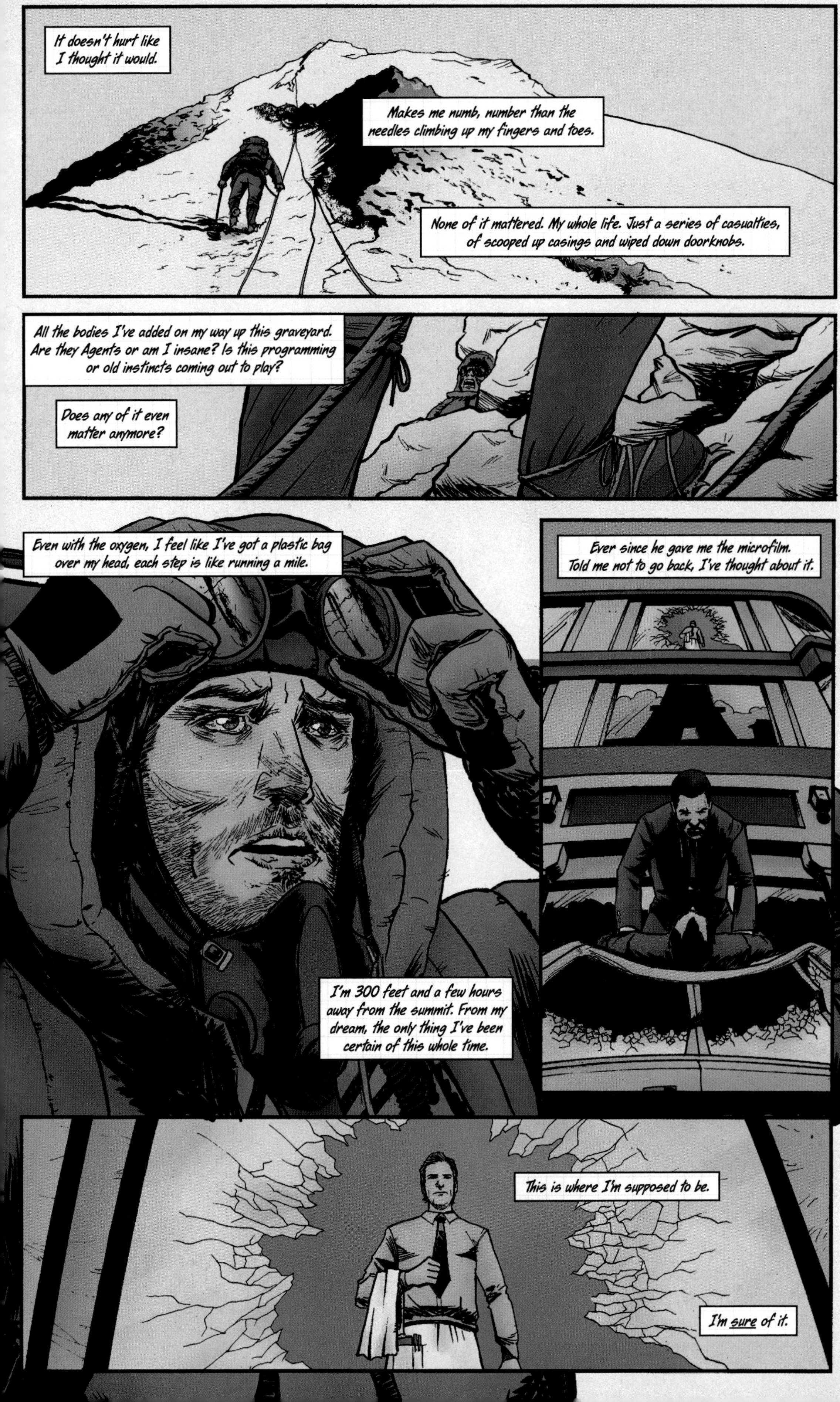
It doesn't hurt like I thought it would.
Makes me numb, number than the needles climbing up my fingers and toes.
None of it mattered. My whole life. Just a series of casualties, of scooped up casings and wiped down doorknobs.
All the bodies I've added on my way up this graveyard. Are they Agents or am I insane? Is this programming or old instincts coming out to play?
Does any of it even matter anymore?
Even with the oxygen, I feel like I've got a plastic bag over my head, each step is like running a mile.
Ever since he gave me the microfilm. Told me not to go back, I've thought about it.
I'm 300 feet and a few hours away from the summit. From my dream, the only thing I've been certain of this whole time.
This is where I'm supposed to be.
I'm sure of it.

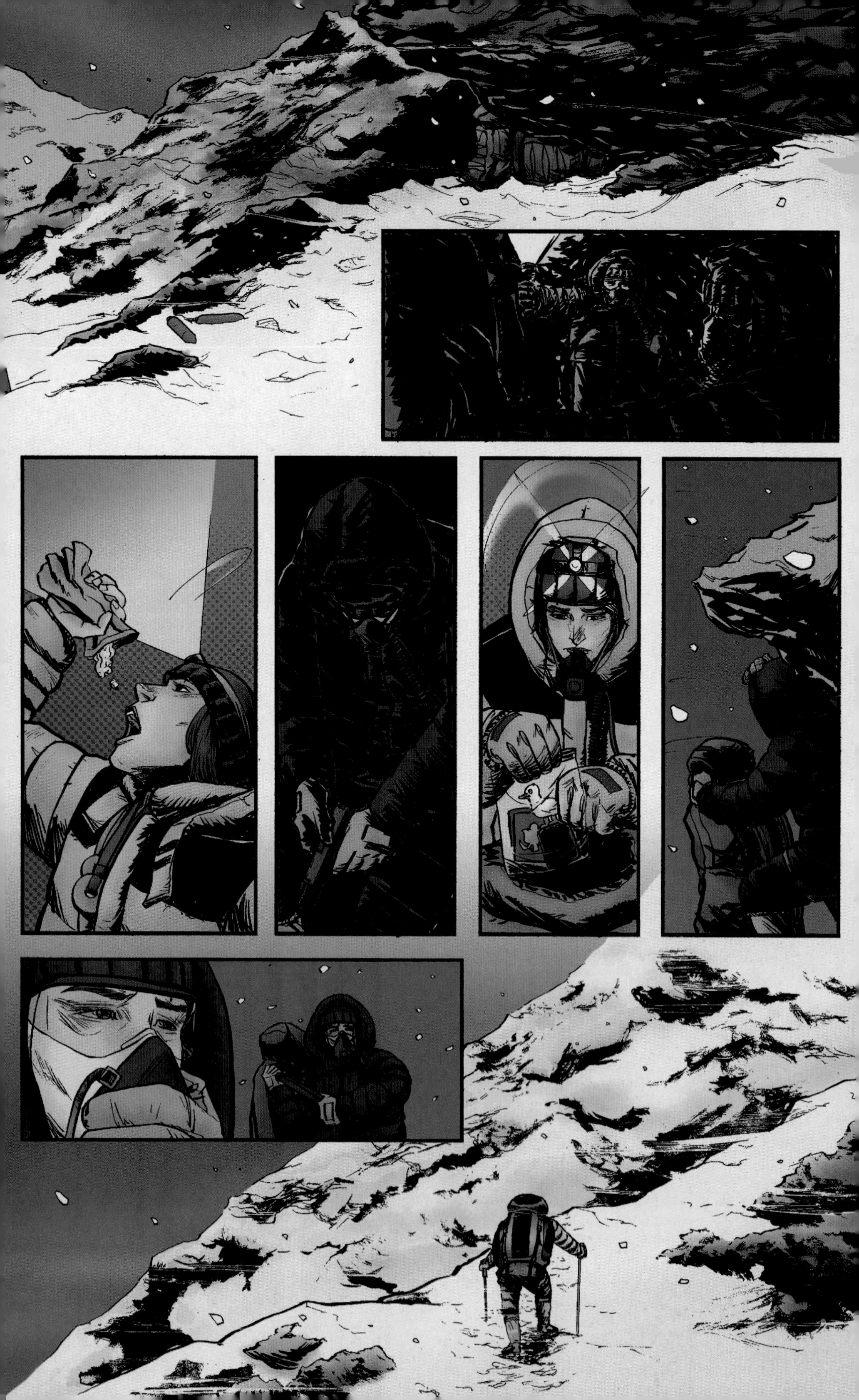

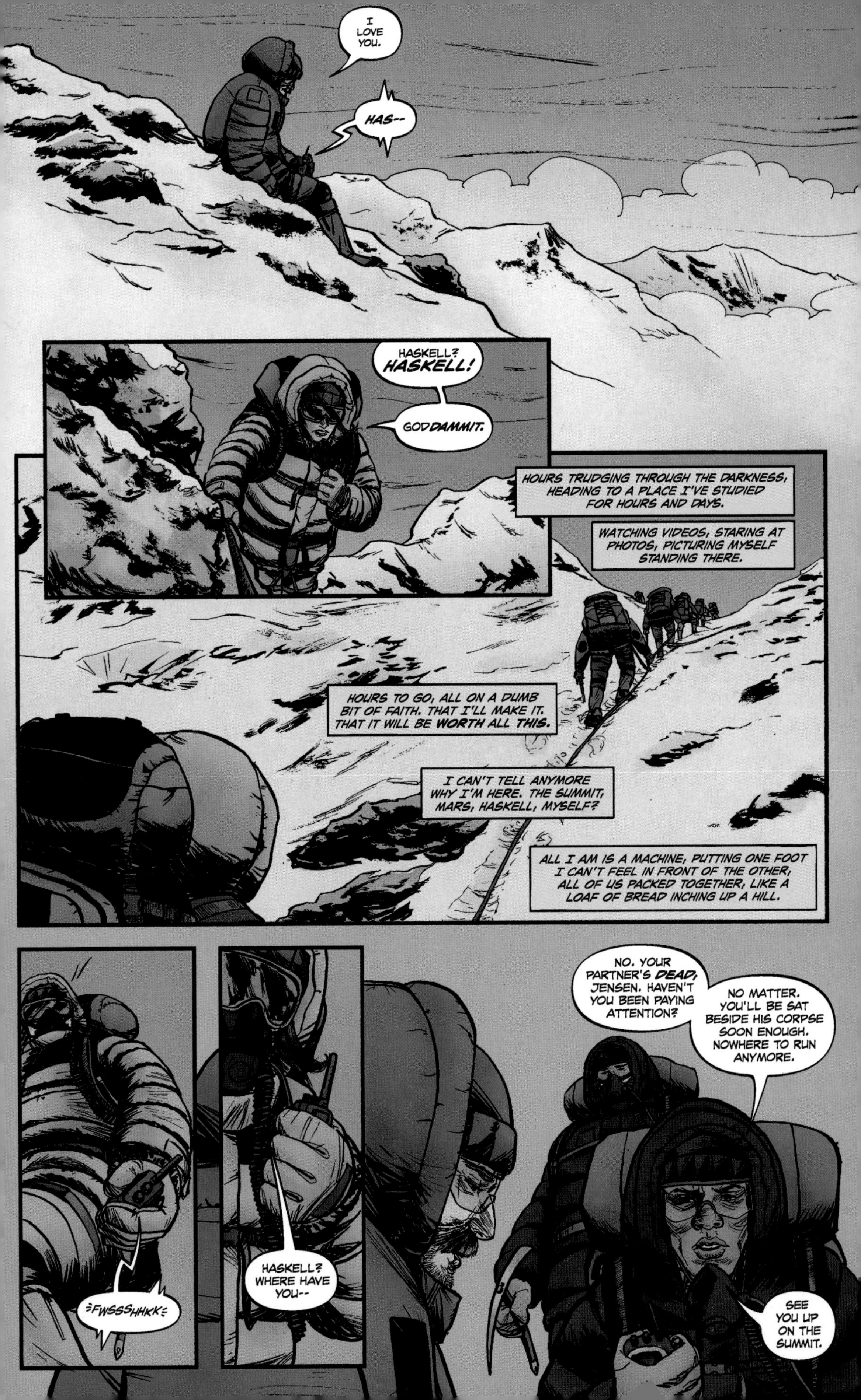
I LOVE YOU.
HAS--
HASKELL? HASKELL!
GODDAMMIT.
HOURS TRUDGING THROUGH THE DARKNESS, HEADING TO A PLACE I'VE STUDIED FOR HOURS AND DAYS.
WATCHING VIDEOS, STARING AT PHOTOS, PICTURING MYSELF STANDING THERE.
HOURS TO GO, ALL ON A DUMB BIT OF FAITH. THAT I'LL MAKE IT. THAT IT WILL BE WORTH ALL THIS.
I CAN'T TELL ANYMORE WHY I'M HERE. THE SUMMIT, MARS, HASKELL, MYSELF?
ALL I AM IS A MACHINE, PUTTING ONE FOOT I CAN'T FEEL IN FRONT OF THE OTHER, ALL OF US PACKED TOGETHER, LIKE A LOAF OF BREAD INCHING UP A HILL.
FWSSSHHKK
HASKELL? WHERE HAVE YOU--
NO. YOUR PARTNER'S DEAD, JENSEN. HAVEN'T YOU BEEN PAYING ATTENTION?
NO MATTER. YOU'LL BE SAT BESIDE HIS CORPSE SOON ENOUGH. NOWHERE TO RUN ANYMORE.
SEE YOU UP ON THE SUMMIT.

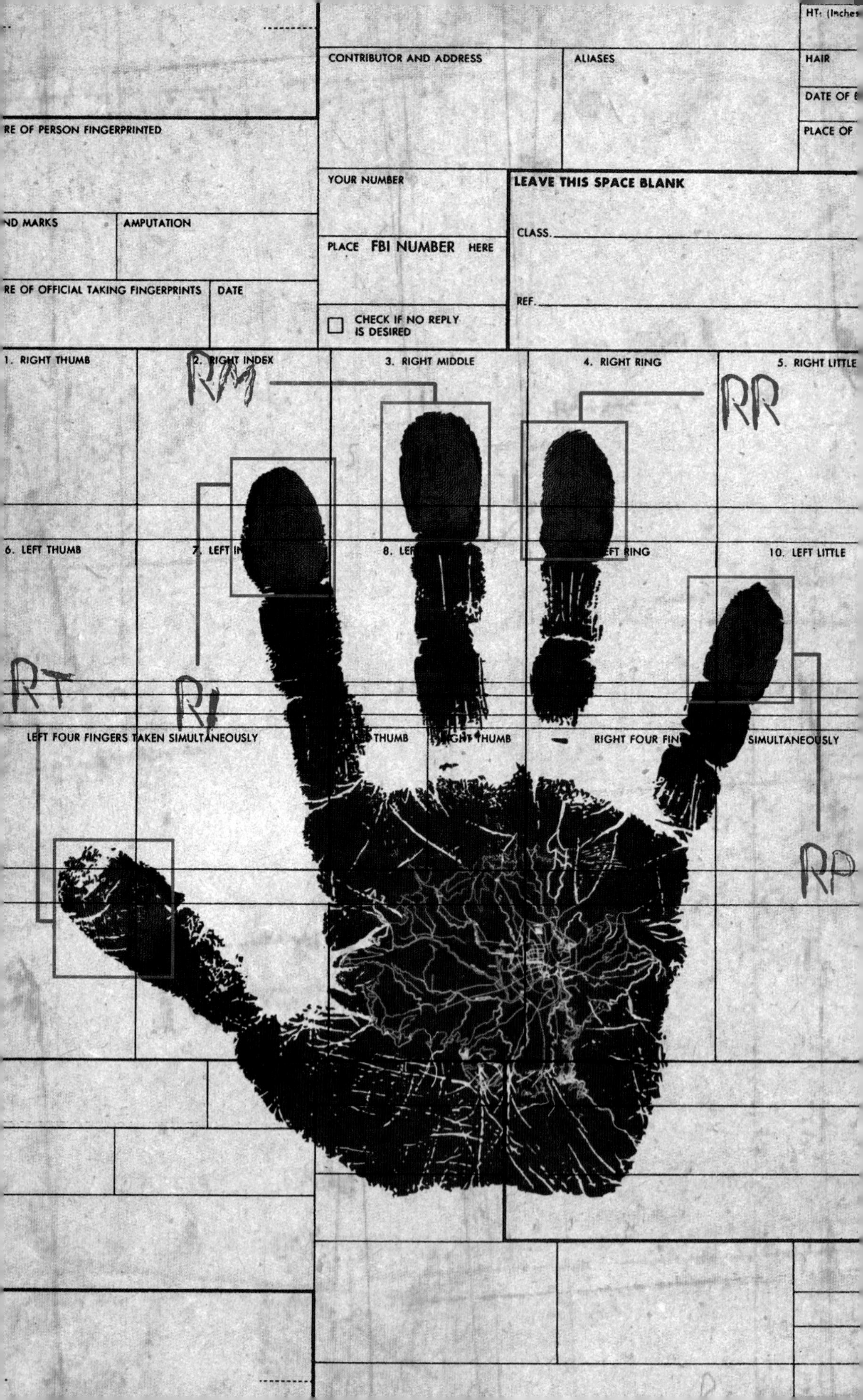

HT: (Inches
CONTRIBUTOR AND ADDRESS
ALIASES
HAIR
DATE OF B
RE OF PERSON FINGERPRINTED
PLACE OF
YOUR NUMBER
LEAVE THIS SPACE BLANK
ND MARKS
AMPUTATION
CLASS.
PLACE FBI NUMBER HERE
RE OF OFFICIAL TAKING FINGERPRINTS
DATE
REF.
CHECK IF NO REPLY IS DESIRED
1. RIGHT THUMB
2. RIGHT INDEX
3. RIGHT MIDDLE
4. RIGHT RING
5. RIGHT LITTLE
RM
RR
6. LEFT THUMB
10. LEFT LITTLE
RT
RI
LEFT FOUR FINGERS TAKEN SIMULTANEOUSLY
THUMB
RIGHT FOUR FIN
SIMULTANEOUSLY
RP

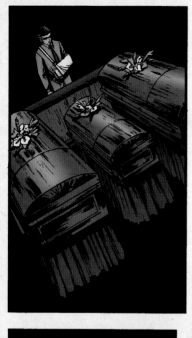

THAT'S WHAT I TELL MYSELF. THEY'D DO THE SAME.

ANYONE WOULD.

AN OLD EXCUSE. IT FEELS THREADBARE, SMOOTH, WORN OUT.

STILL, IT KEEPS ME MOVING FORWARD.

THAT AND MY STOLEN OXYGEN.

A FRESH TANK ON MEDIUM MAKES THINGS FEEL EFFORTLESS.

I'M WARMER, STRONGER, WIDE AWAKE.

FOR THE FIRST TIME IN DAYS, I'M NOT SICK.

I TRY NOT TO REMEMBER THAT ENOUGH OXYGEN CAN GET YOU HIGH.

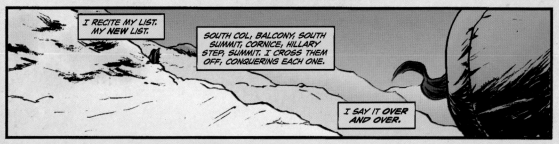

I RECITE MY LIST. MY NEW LIST.

SOUTH COL, BALCONY, SOUTH SUMMIT, CORNICE, HILLARY STEP, SUMMIT. I CROSS THEM OFF, CONQUERING EACH ONE.

I SAY IT OVER AND OVER.

IT'S STRANGE, BUT I FEEL GOOD.

IN A WAY I HAVEN'T IN FOREVER.

I SHOULD KNOW BETTER.

THERE'S NO SUCH THING AS MIRACLES.

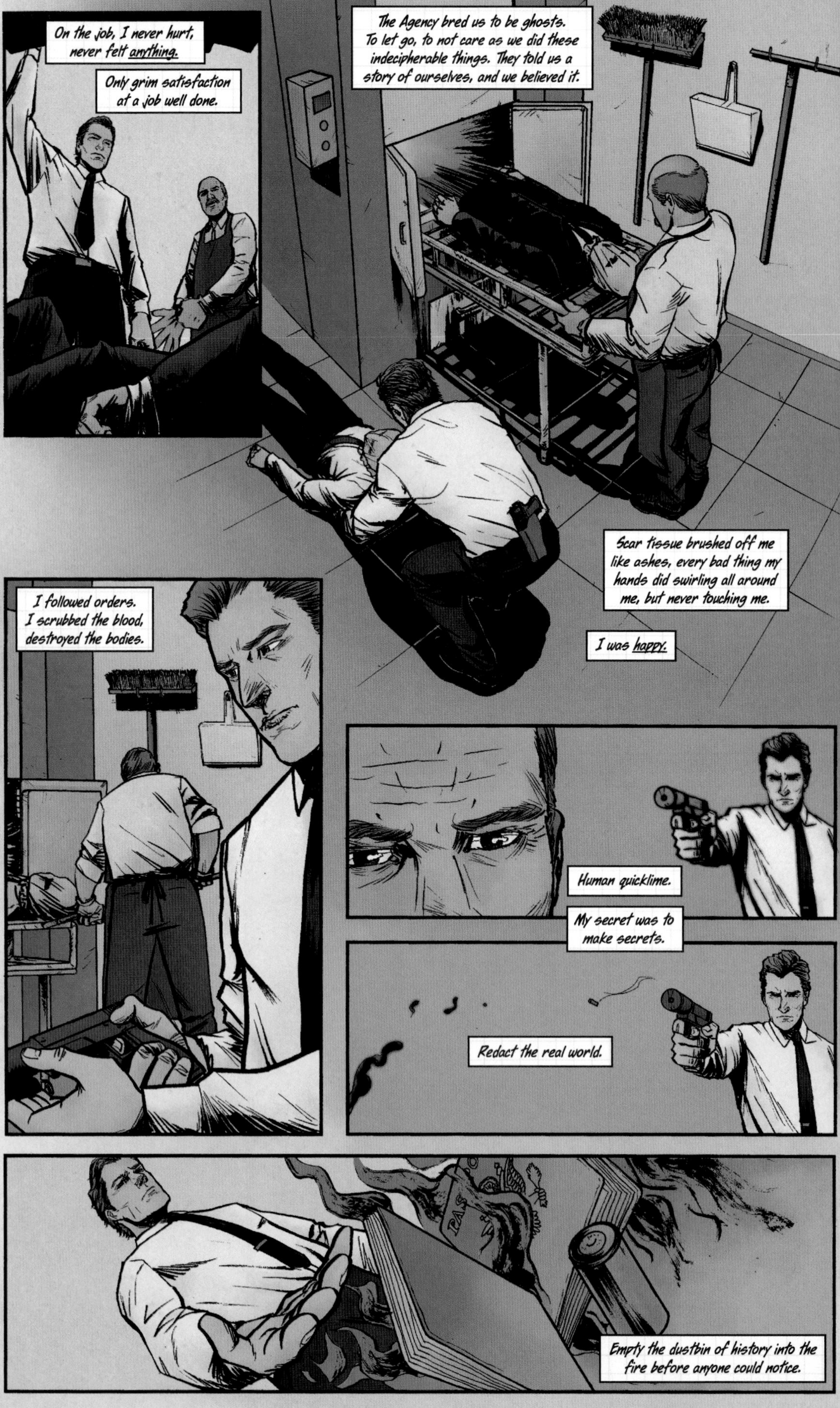
On the job, I never hurt, never felt anything.
Only grim satisfaction at a job well done.
The Agency bred us to be ghosts. To let go, to not care as we did these indecipherable things. They told us a story of ourselves, and we believed it.
Scar tissue brushed off me like ashes, every bad thing my hands did swirling all around me, but never touching me.
I was happy.
I followed orders. I scrubbed the blood, destroyed the bodies.
Human quicklime.
My secret was to make secrets.
Redact the real world.
Empty the dustbin of history into the fire before anyone could notice.

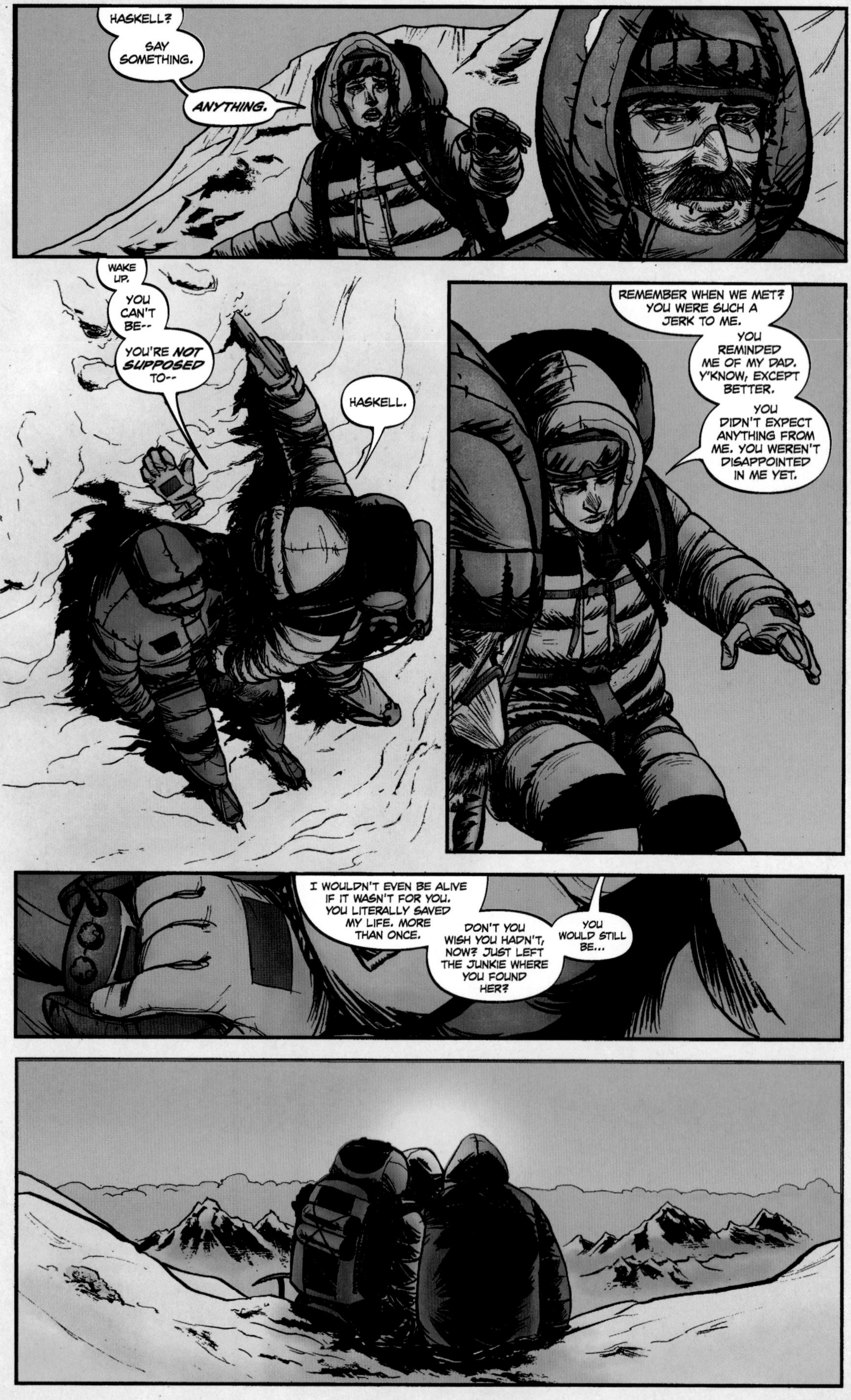
HASKELL?
SAY SOMETHING.
ANYTHING.
WAKE UP.
YOU CAN'T BE--
YOU'RE NOT SUPPOSED TO--
HASKELL.
REMEMBER WHEN WE MET? YOU WERE SUCH A JERK TO ME.
YOU REMINDED ME OF MY DAD. Y'KNOW, EXCEPT BETTER.
YOU DIDN'T EXPECT ANYTHING FROM ME. YOU WEREN'T DISAPPOINTED IN ME YET.
I WOULDN'T EVEN BE ALIVE IF IT WASN'T FOR YOU. YOU LITERALLY SAVED MY LIFE. MORE THAN ONCE.
DON'T YOU WISH YOU HADN'T, NOW? JUST LEFT THE JUNKIE WHERE YOU FOUND HER?
YOU WOULD STILL BE...

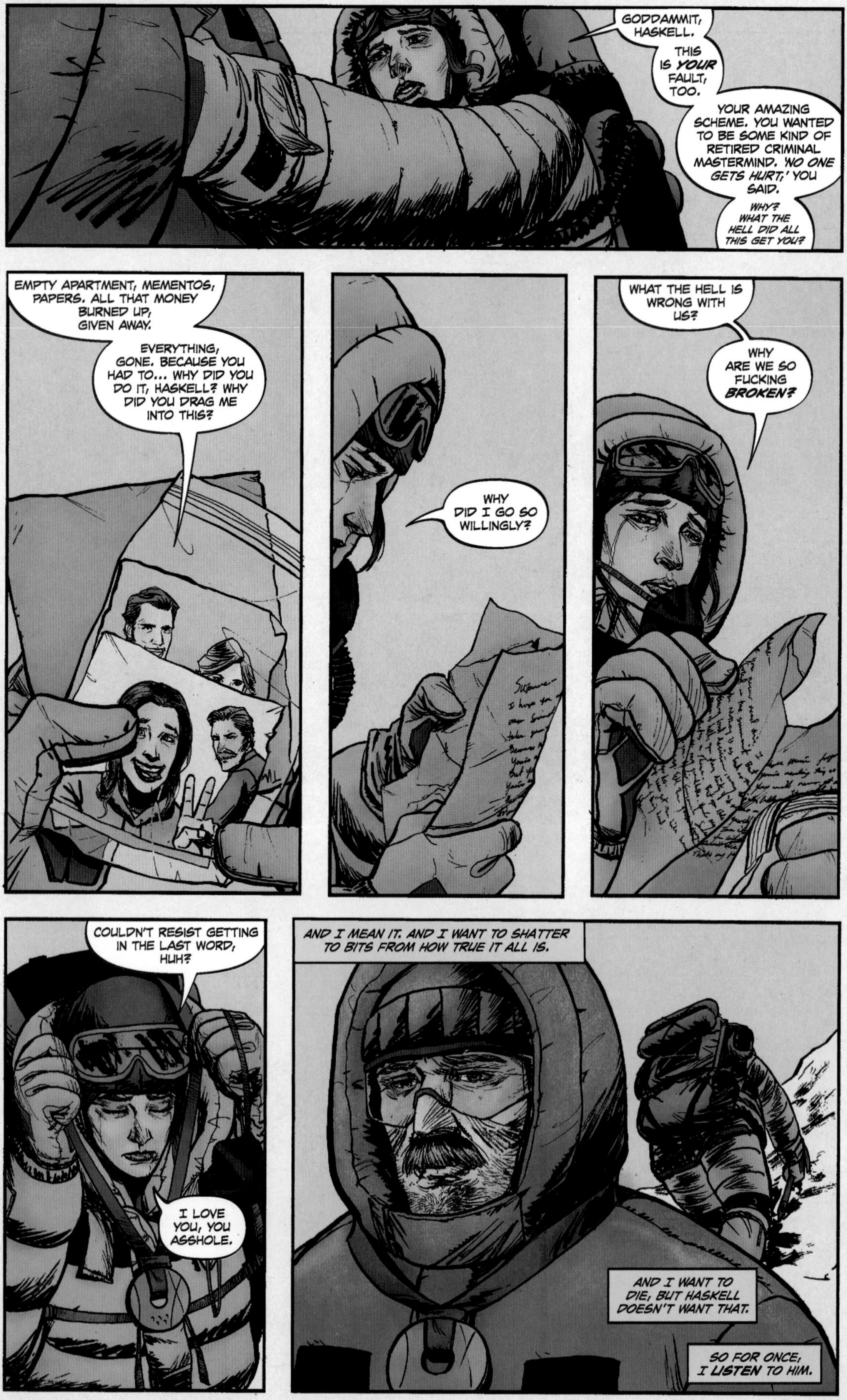
GODDAMMIT, HASKELL.
THIS IS YOUR FAULT, TOO.
YOUR AMAZING SCHEME. YOU WANTED TO BE SOME KIND OF RETIRED CRIMINAL MASTERMIND. 'NO ONE GETS HURT,' YOU SAID.
WHY? WHAT THE HELL DID ALL THIS GET YOU?
EMPTY APARTMENT, MEMENTOS, PAPERS. ALL THAT MONEY BURNED UP, GIVEN AWAY.
EVERYTHING, GONE. BECAUSE YOU HAD TO... WHY DID YOU DO IT, HASKELL? WHY DID YOU DRAG ME INTO THIS?
WHY DID I GO SO WILLINGLY?
WHAT THE HELL IS WRONG WITH US?
WHY ARE WE SO FUCKING BROKEN?
COULDN'T RESIST GETTING IN THE LAST WORD, HUH?
I LOVE YOU, YOU ASSHOLE.
AND I MEAN IT. AND I WANT TO SHATTER TO BITS FROM HOW TRUE IT ALL IS.
AND I WANT TO DIE, BUT HASKELL DOESN'T WANT THAT.
SO FOR ONCE, I LISTEN TO HIM.

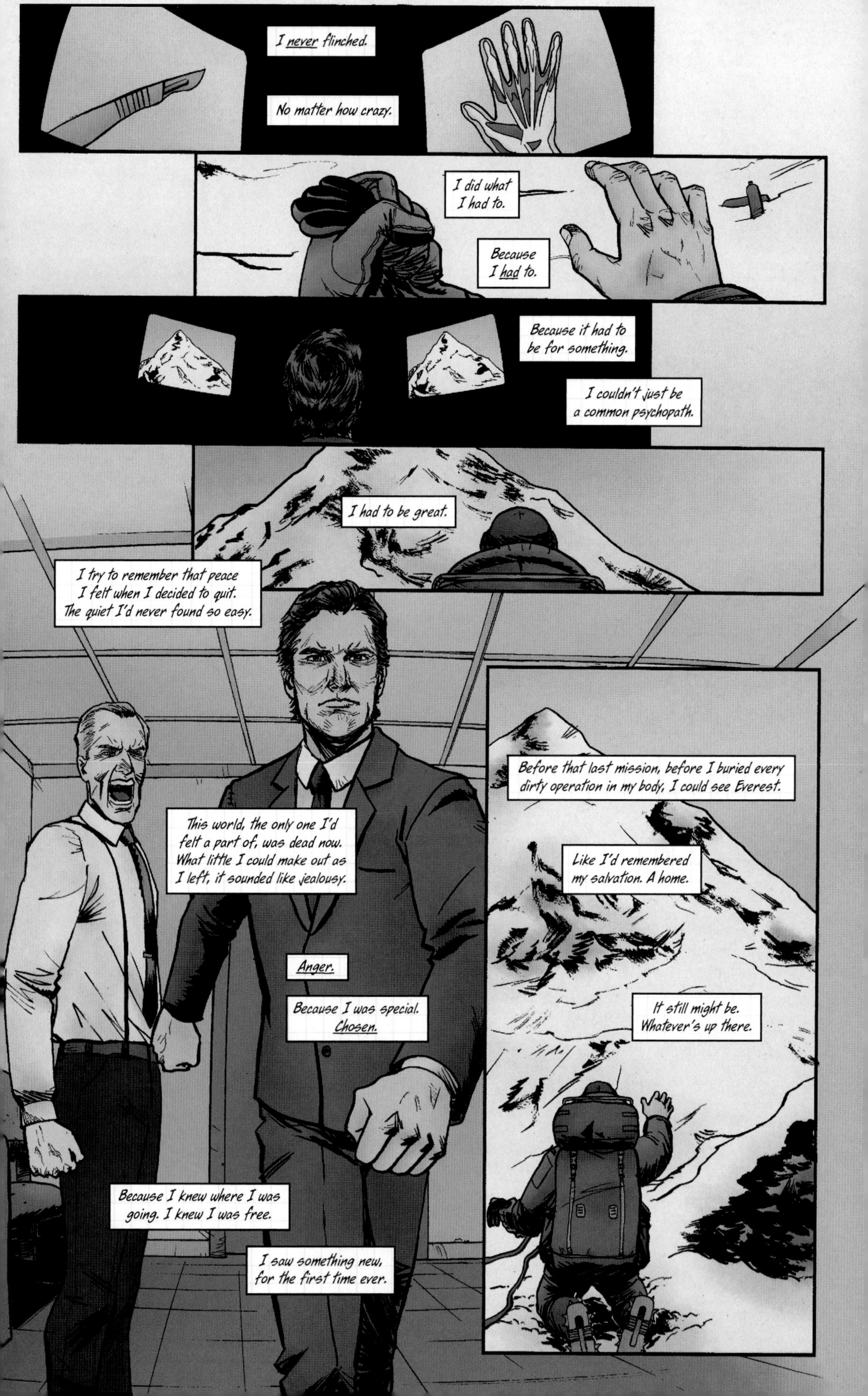
I never flinched.
No matter how crazy.
I did what I had to.
Because I had to.
Because it had to be for something.
I couldn't just be a common psychopath.
I had to be great.
I try to remember that peace I felt when I decided to quit. The quiet I'd never found so easy.
This world, the only one I'd felt a part of, was dead now. What little I could make out as I left, it sounded like jealousy.
Anger.
Because I was special. Chosen.
Because I knew where I was going. I knew I was free.
I saw something new, for the first time ever.
Before that last mission, before I buried every dirty operation in my body, I could see Everest.
Like I'd remembered my salvation. A home.
It still might be. Whatever's up there.

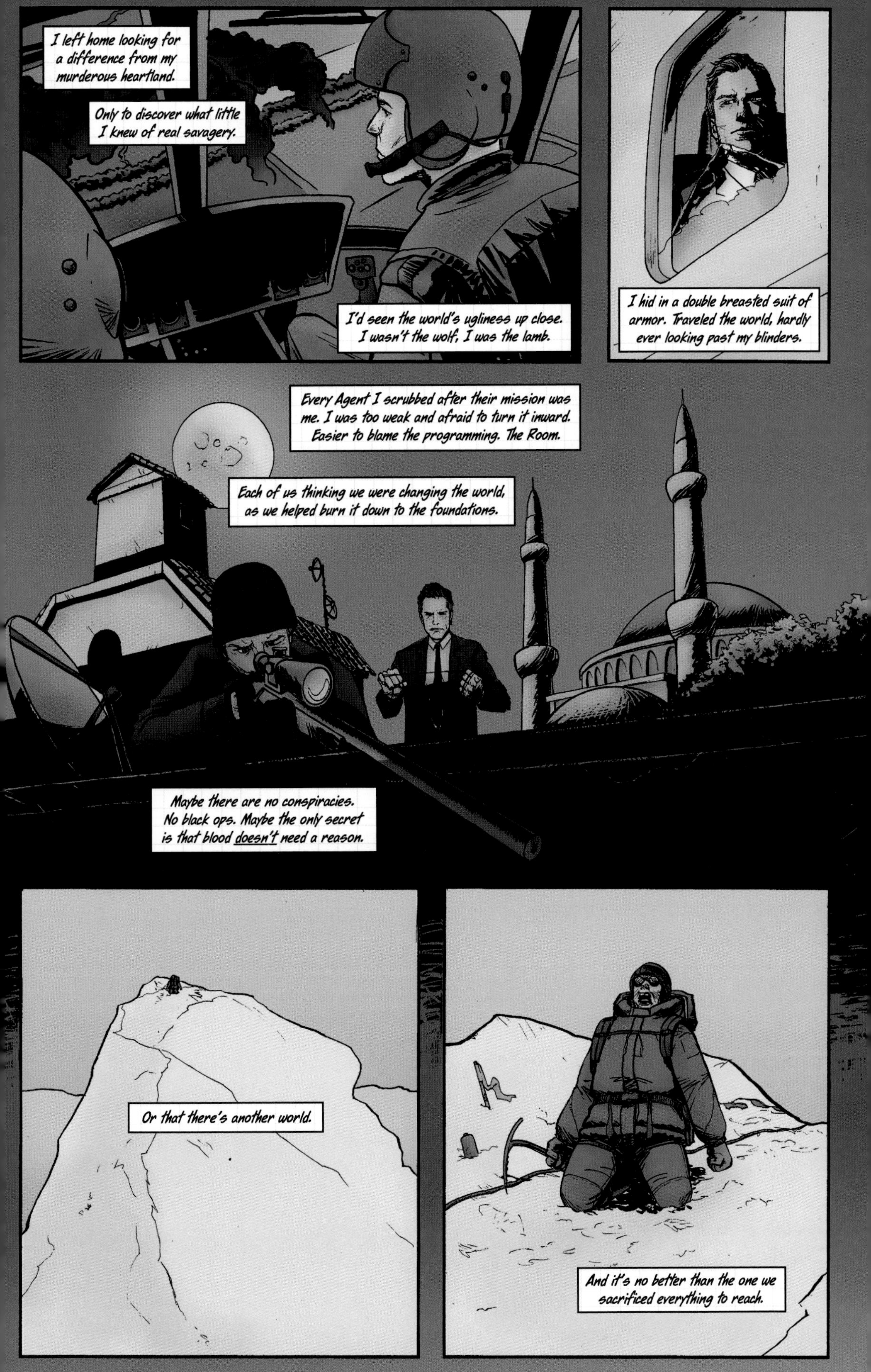
I left home looking for a difference from my murderous heartland.
Only to discover what little I knew of real savagery.
I'd seen the world's ugliness up close. I wasn't the wolf, I was the lamb.
I hid in a double breasted suit of armor. Traveled the world, hardly ever looking past my blinders.
Every Agent I scrubbed after their mission was me. I was too weak and afraid to turn it inward. Easier to blame the programming. The Room.
Each of us thinking we were changing the world, as we helped burn it down to the foundations.
Maybe there are no conspiracies. No black ops. Maybe the only secret is that blood doesn't need a reason.
Or that there's another world.
And it's no better than the one we sacrificed everything to reach.

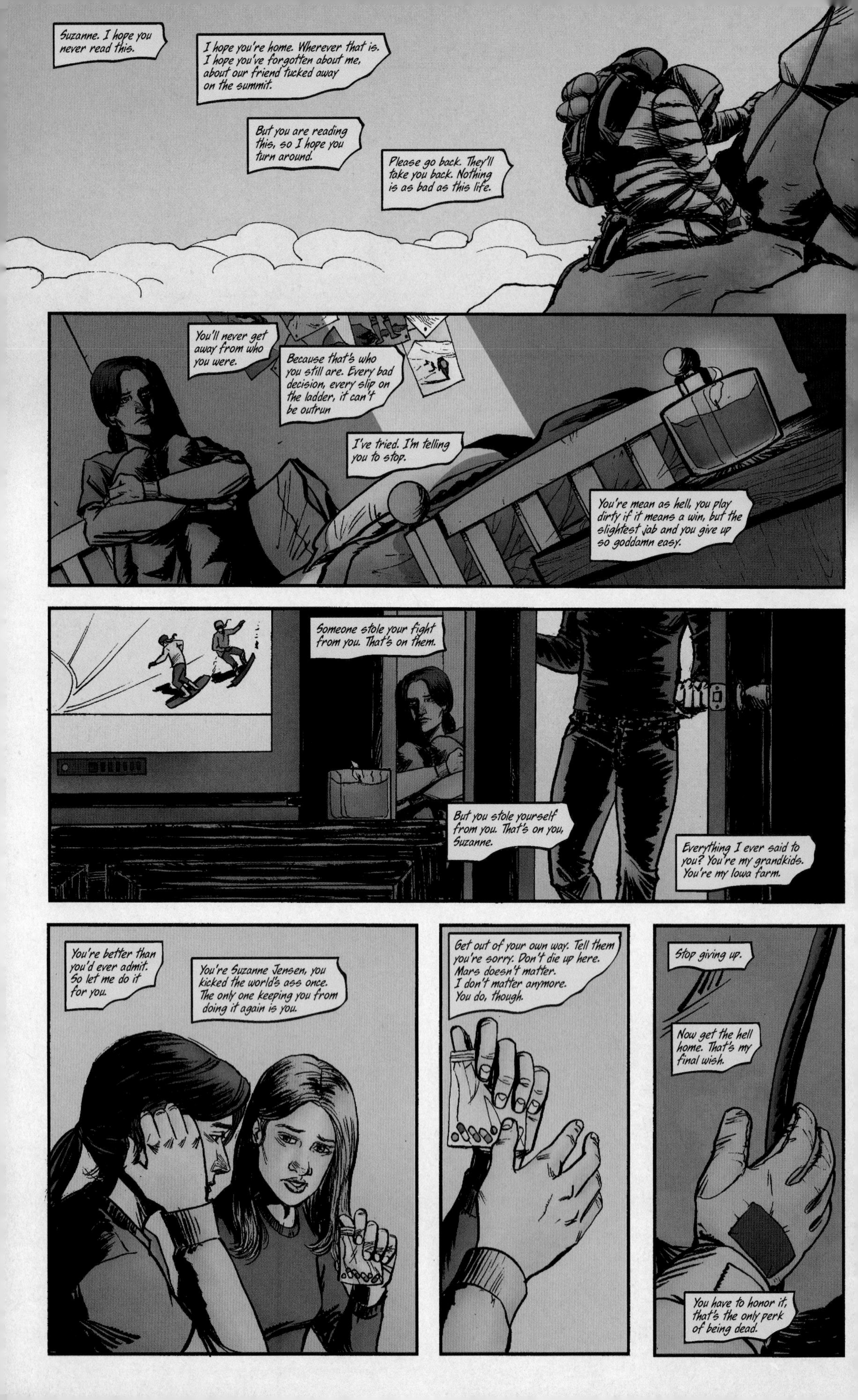
Suzanne. I hope you never read this.
I hope you're home. Wherever that is. I hope you've forgotten about me, about our friend tucked away on the summit.
But you are reading this, so I hope you turn around.
Please go back. They'll take you back. Nothing is as bad as this life.
You'll never get away from who you were.
Because that's who you still are. Every bad decision, every slip on the ladder, it can't be outrun
I've tried. I'm telling you to stop.
You're mean as hell, you play dirty if it means a win, but the slightest jab and you give up so goddamn easy.
Someone stole your fight from you. That's on them.
But you stole yourself from you. That's on you, Suzanne.
Everything I ever said to you? You're my grandkids. You're my Iowa farm.
You're better than you'd ever admit. So let me do it for you.
You're Suzanne Jensen, you kicked the world's ass once. The only one keeping you from doing it again is you.
Get out of your own way. Tell them you're sorry. Don't die up here. Mars doesn't matter. I don't matter anymore. You do, though.
Stop giving up.
Now get the hell home. That's my final wish.
You have to honor it, that's the only perk of being dead.

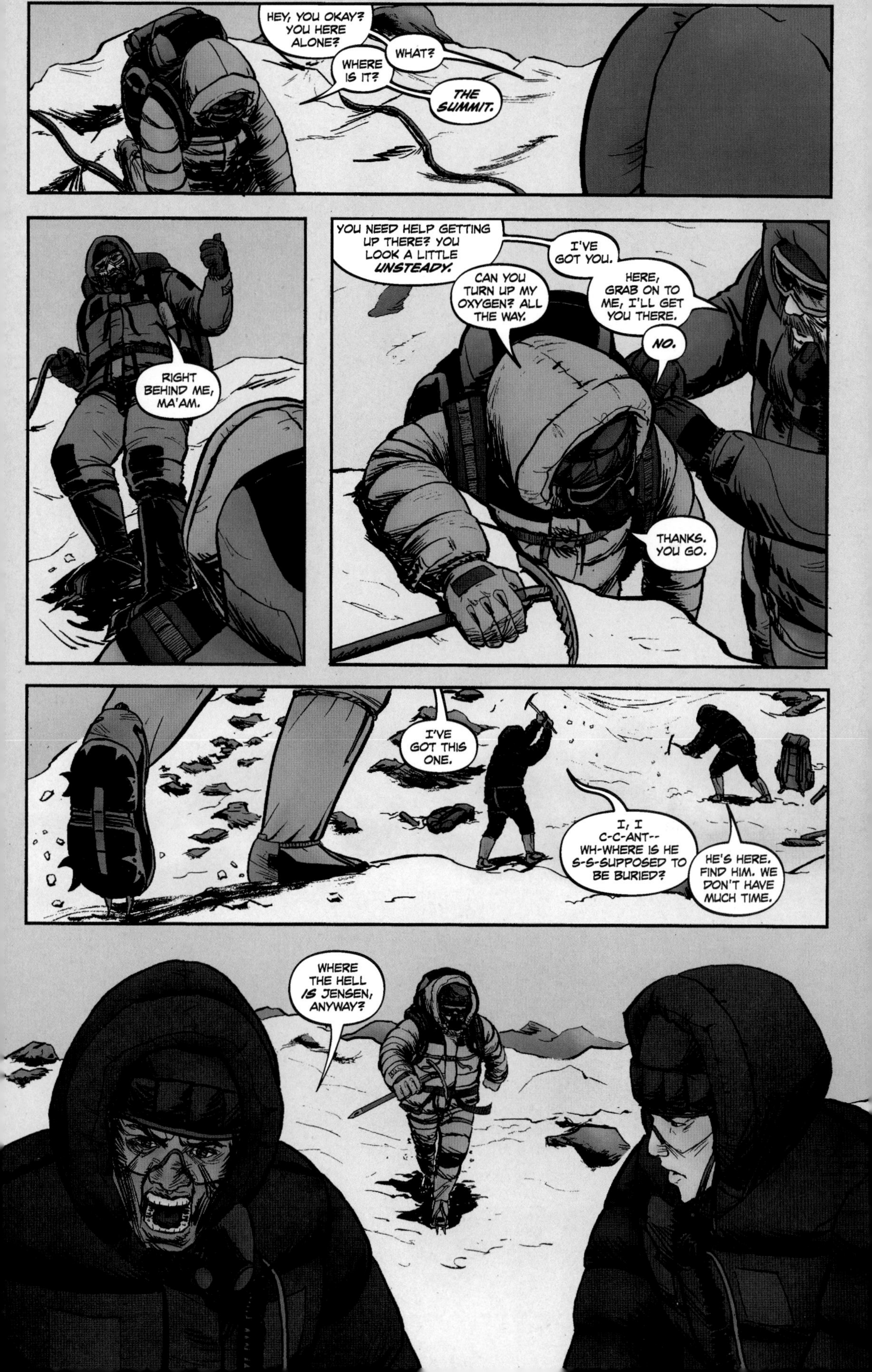
HEY, YOU OKAY? YOU HERE ALONE?
WHAT?
WHERE IS IT?
THE SUMMIT.
RIGHT BEHIND ME, MA'AM.
YOU NEED HELP GETTING UP THERE? YOU LOOK A LITTLE *UNSTEADY.*
I'VE GOT YOU.
CAN YOU TURN UP MY OXYGEN? ALL THE WAY.
HERE, GRAB ON TO ME, I'LL GET YOU THERE.
NO.
THANKS. YOU GO.
I'VE GOT THIS ONE.
I, I C-C-ANT-- WH-WHERE IS HE S-S-SUPPOSED TO BE BURIED?
HE'S HERE. FIND HIM. WE DON'T HAVE MUCH TIME.
WHERE THE HELL *IS* JENSEN, ANYWAY?

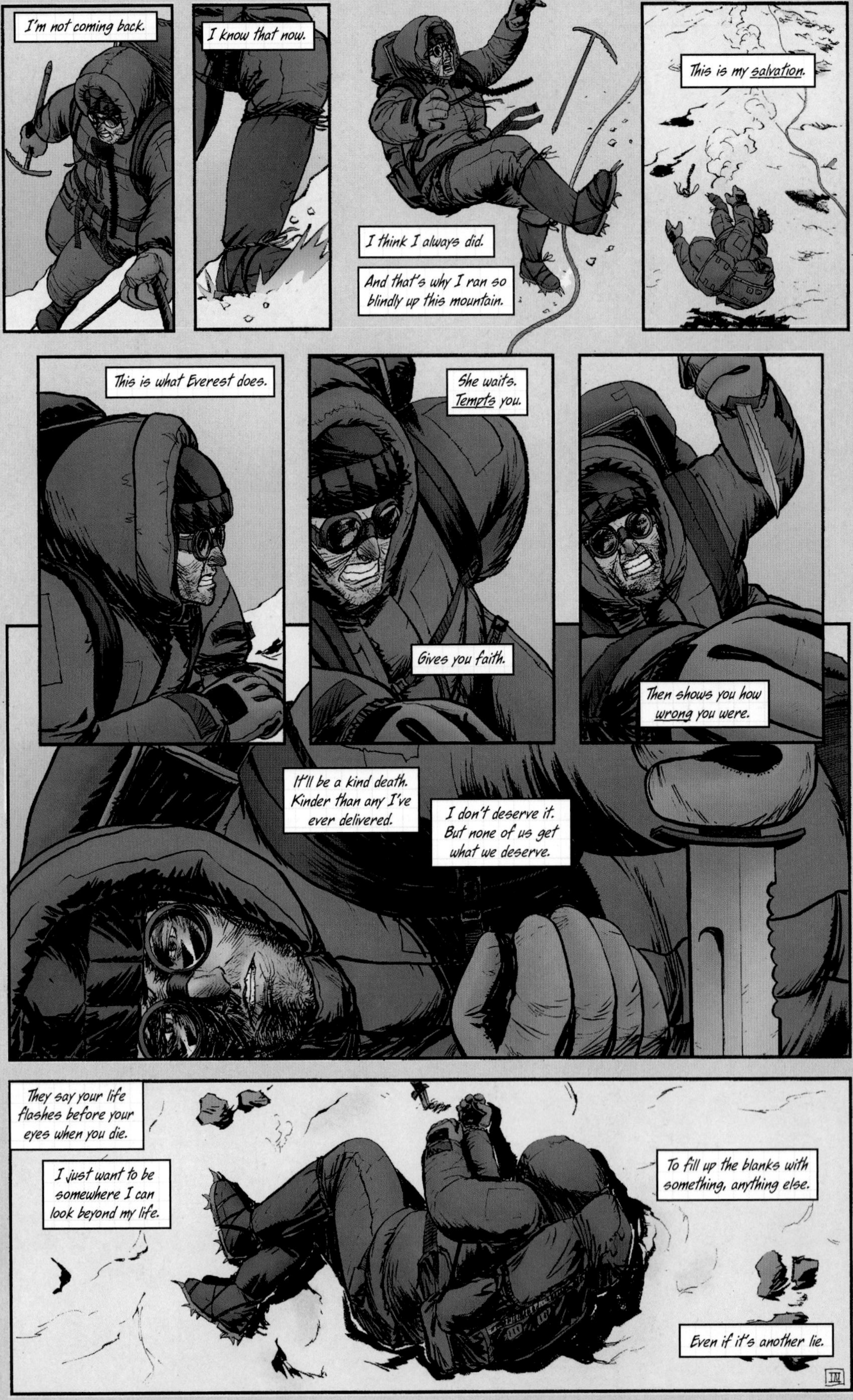
I'm not coming back.
I know that now.
I think I always did.
And that's why I ran so blindly up this mountain.
This is my salvation.
This is what Everest does.
She waits. Tempts you.
Gives you faith.
Then shows you how wrong you were.
It'll be a kind death. Kinder than any I've ever delivered.
I don't deserve it. But none of us get what we deserve.
They say your life flashes before your eyes when you die.
I just want to be somewhere I can look beyond my life.
To fill up the blanks with something, anything else.
Even if it's another lie.

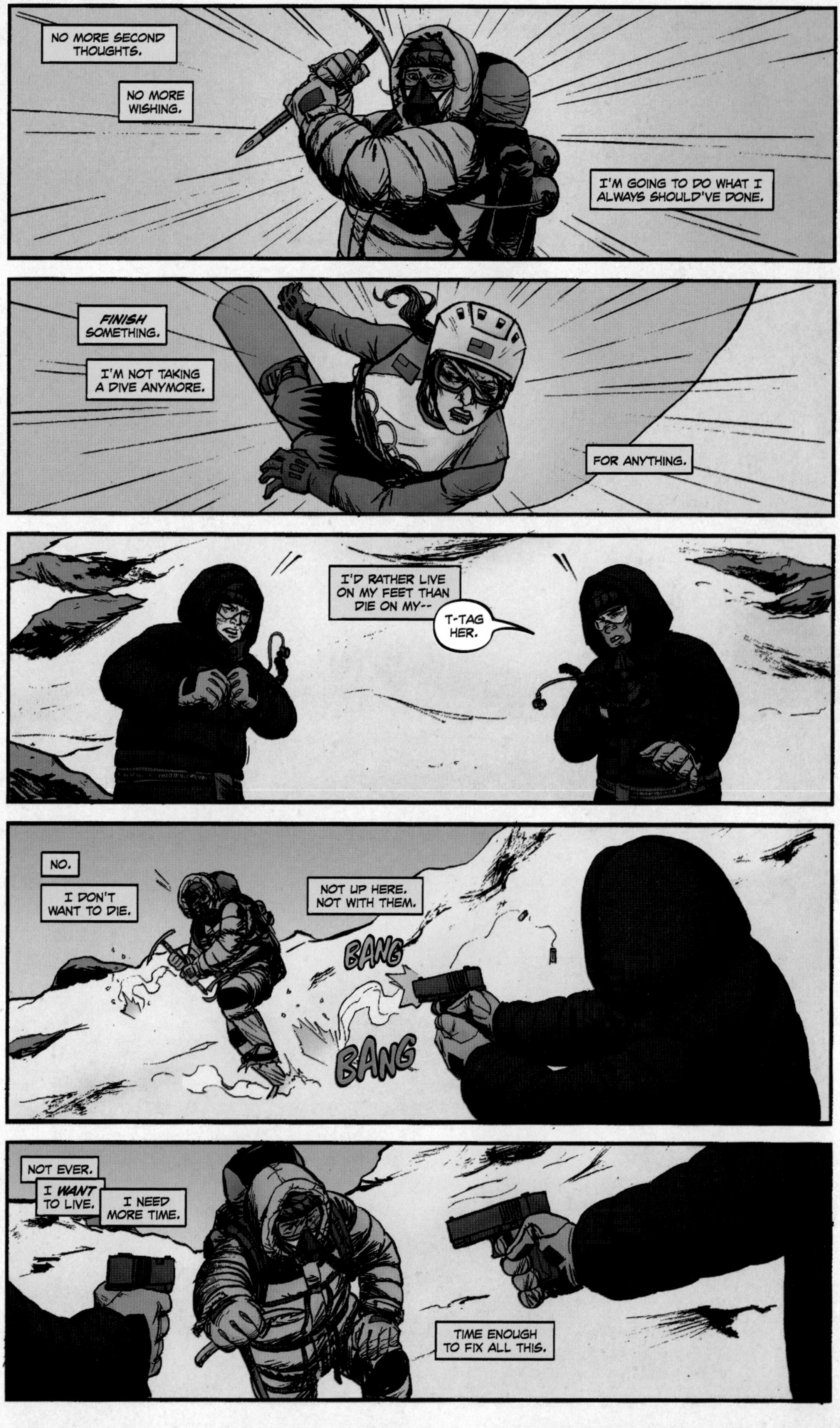

NO MORE SECOND THOUGHTS.
NO MORE WISHING.
I'M GOING TO DO WHAT I ALWAYS SHOULD'VE DONE.
FINISH SOMETHING.
I'M NOT TAKING A DIVE ANYMORE.
FOR ANYTHING.
I'D RATHER LIVE ON MY FEET THAN DIE ON MY--
T-TAG HER.
NO.
I DON'T WANT TO DIE.
NOT UP HERE. NOT WITH THEM.
BANG
BANG
NOT EVER.
I *WANT* TO LIVE.
I NEED MORE TIME.
TIME ENOUGH TO FIX ALL THIS.

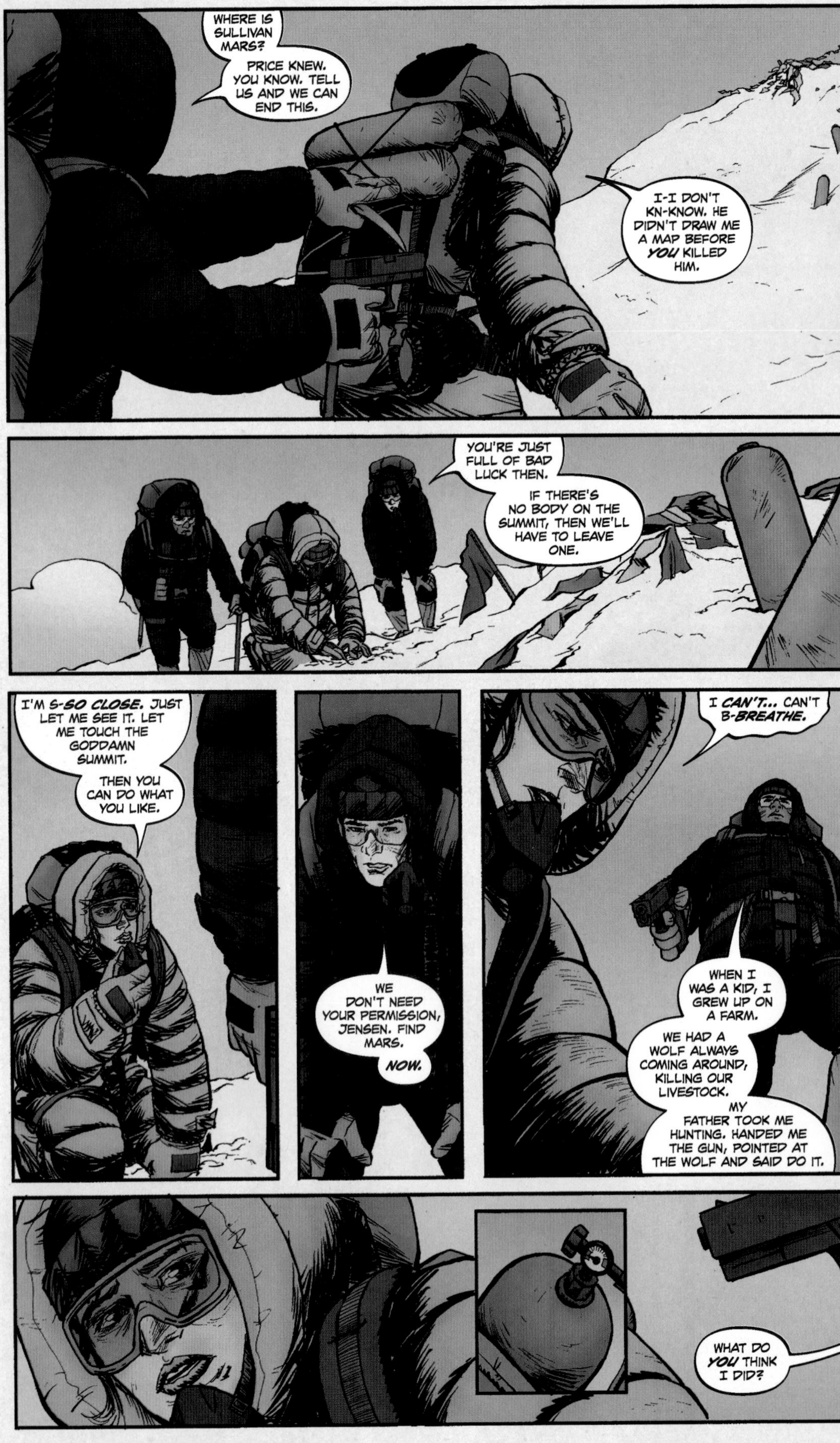
WHERE IS SULLIVAN MARS?
PRICE KNEW. YOU KNOW. TELL US AND WE CAN END THIS.
I-I DON'T KN-KNOW. HE DIDN'T DRAW ME A MAP BEFORE YOU KILLED HIM.
YOU'RE JUST FULL OF BAD LUCK THEN.
IF THERE'S NO BODY ON THE SUMMIT, THEN WE'LL HAVE TO LEAVE ONE.
I'M S-SO CLOSE. JUST LET ME SEE IT. LET ME TOUCH THE GODDAMN SUMMIT.
THEN YOU CAN DO WHAT YOU LIKE.
WE DON'T NEED YOUR PERMISSION, JENSEN. FIND MARS.
NOW.
I CAN'T... CAN'T B-BREATHE.
WHEN I WAS A KID, I GREW UP ON A FARM.
WE HAD A WOLF ALWAYS COMING AROUND, KILLING OUR LIVESTOCK.
MY FATHER TOOK ME HUNTING. HANDED ME THE GUN, POINTED AT THE WOLF AND SAID DO IT.
WHAT DO YOU THINK I DID?

FUNNY. I HAVE A STORY JUST LIKE THAT.

ONLY IT'S MY-- GOD DAMMIT. OXYGEN'S OUT.

CALL THE MAJOR.

BUT WE COULDN'T GET A SIGNAL LAST--

CALL HIM OR I'LL THROW YOU OFF THIS MOUNTAIN.

CALM DOWN, AGENT.

HE'S ON.

GIVE IT TO HER.

DECISION TIME, JENSEN. THIS ISN'T ONLY YOUR LIFE YOU'RE FLUSHING AWAY ANYMORE.

WE HAVE FILES ON YOUR FAMILY. EVERY FRIEND, FORMER FRIEND AND TEAMMATE YOU'VE EVER HAD. EVERYONE YOU'VE EVER SLEPT WITH.

WE'LL BURN YOUR LIFE TO THE GROUND, EVEN IF YOU'RE NOT LIVING IN IT ANYMORE.

I'LL STILL HAVE YOUR SECRETS.

SEND EVERYONE YOU WANT. THEY'LL NEVER FIND MARS EVEN IF THEY MANAGE TO GET UP HERE. OR BACK DOWN.

AND DO WHAT WITH THEM? TRY TO SELL THEM, MAIL COPIES TO JOURNALISTS? THIS ISN'T 20 YEARS AGO. WE HAVE OUR EYES ON EVERYTHING NOW.

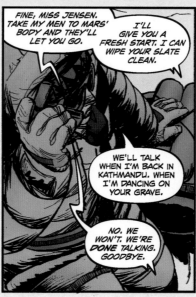

FINE, MISS JENSEN. TAKE MY MEN TO MARS' BODY AND THEY'LL LET YOU GO.

I'LL GIVE YOU A FRESH START. I CAN WIPE YOUR SLATE CLEAN.

WE'LL TALK WHEN I'M BACK IN KATHMANDU. WHEN I'M DANCING ON YOUR GRAVE.

NO. WE WON'T. WE'RE DONE TALKING. GOODBYE.

SOUNDS LIKE YOUR NEGOTIATIONS WENT BADLY.

YOU WON'T BE NEEDING THAT OXYGEN THEN.

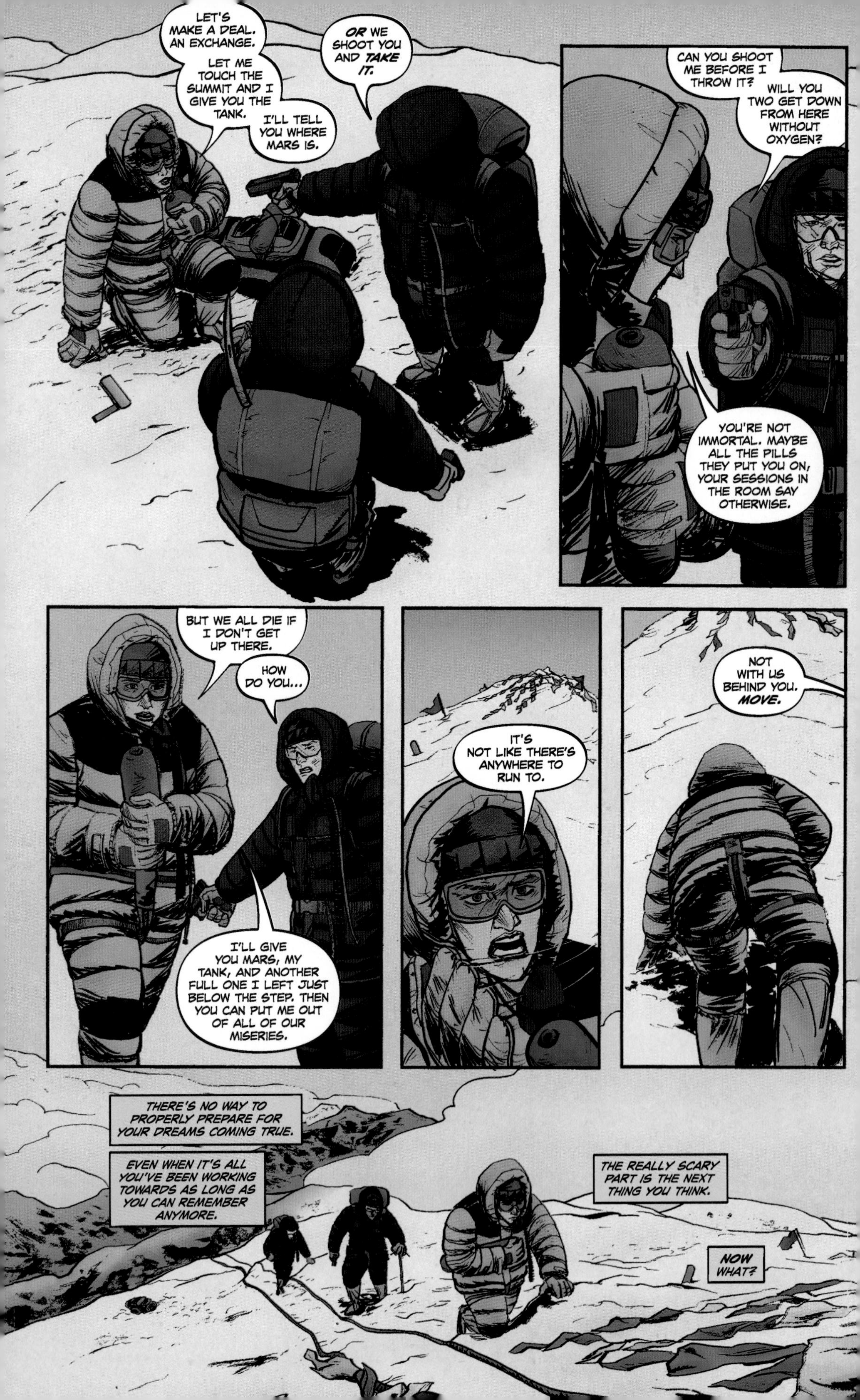
LET'S MAKE A DEAL. AN EXCHANGE.
LET ME TOUCH THE SUMMIT AND I GIVE YOU THE TANK.
OR WE SHOOT YOU AND TAKE IT.
I'LL TELL YOU WHERE MARS IS.
CAN YOU SHOOT ME BEFORE I THROW IT?
WILL YOU TWO GET DOWN FROM HERE WITHOUT OXYGEN?
YOU'RE NOT IMMORTAL. MAYBE ALL THE PILLS THEY PUT YOU ON, YOUR SESSIONS IN THE ROOM SAY OTHERWISE.
BUT WE ALL DIE IF I DON'T GET UP THERE.
HOW DO YOU...
I'LL GIVE YOU MARS, MY TANK, AND ANOTHER FULL ONE I LEFT JUST BELOW THE STEP. THEN YOU CAN PUT ME OUT OF ALL OF OUR MISERIES.
IT'S NOT LIKE THERE'S ANYWHERE TO RUN TO.
NOT WITH US BEHIND YOU. MOVE.
THERE'S NO WAY TO PROPERLY PREPARE FOR YOUR DREAMS COMING TRUE.
EVEN WHEN IT'S ALL YOU'VE BEEN WORKING TOWARDS AS LONG AS YOU CAN REMEMBER ANYMORE.
THE REALLY SCARY PART IS THE NEXT THING YOU THINK.
NOW WHAT?

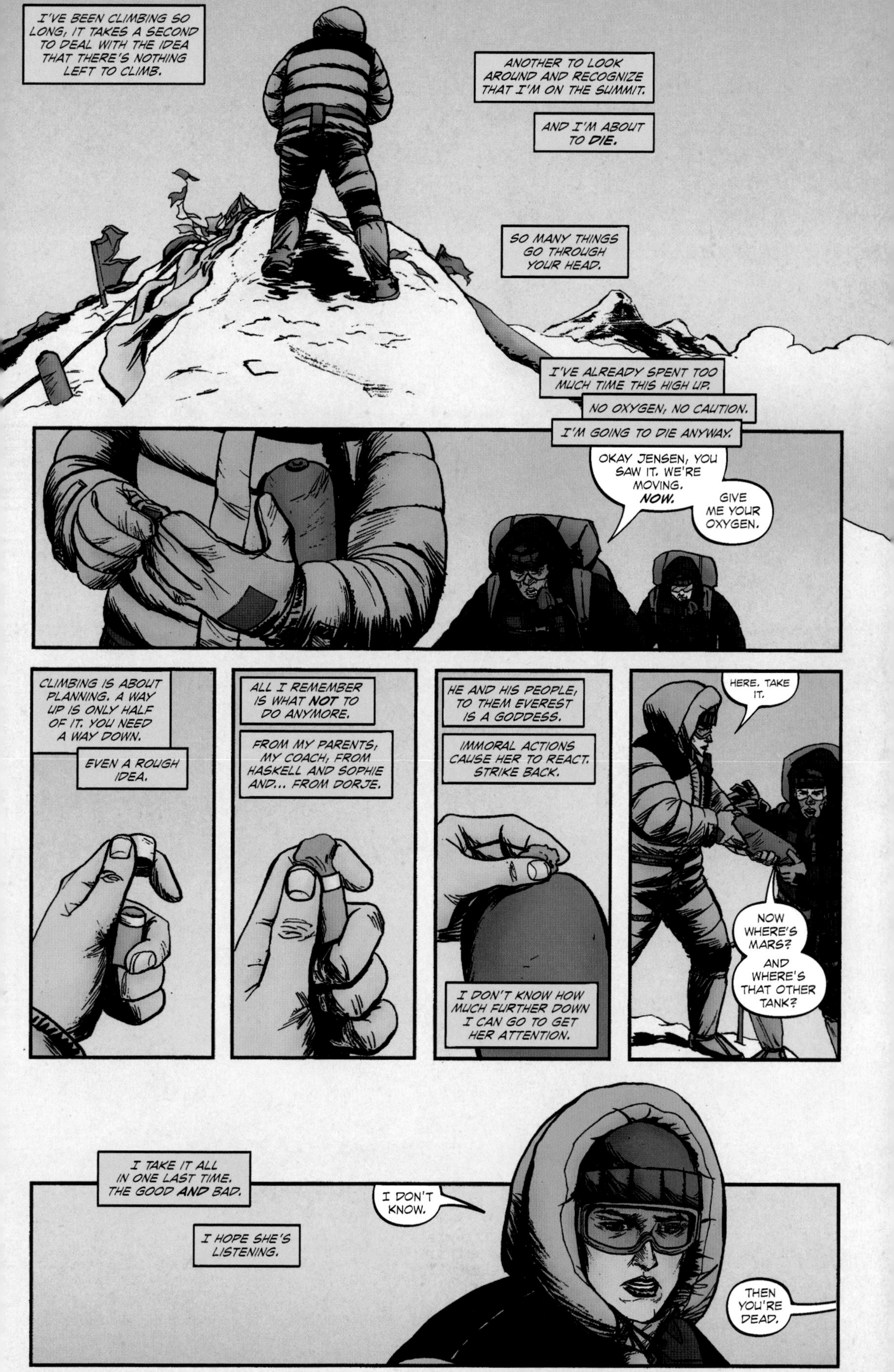
I'VE BEEN CLIMBING SO LONG, IT TAKES A SECOND TO DEAL WITH THE IDEA THAT THERE'S NOTHING LEFT TO CLIMB.
ANOTHER TO LOOK AROUND AND RECOGNIZE THAT I'M ON THE SUMMIT.
AND I'M ABOUT TO DIE.
SO MANY THINGS GO THROUGH YOUR HEAD.
I'VE ALREADY SPENT TOO MUCH TIME THIS HIGH UP.
NO OXYGEN; NO CAUTION.
I'M GOING TO DIE ANYWAY.
OKAY JENSEN, YOU SAW IT. WE'RE MOVING. NOW.
GIVE ME YOUR OXYGEN.
CLIMBING IS ABOUT PLANNING. A WAY UP IS ONLY HALF OF IT. YOU NEED A WAY DOWN.
EVEN A ROUGH IDEA.
ALL I REMEMBER IS WHAT NOT TO DO ANYMORE.
FROM MY PARENTS, MY COACH, FROM HASKELL AND SOPHIE AND... FROM DORJE.
HE AND HIS PEOPLE, TO THEM EVEREST IS A GODDESS.
IMMORAL ACTIONS CAUSE HER TO REACT. STRIKE BACK.
I DON'T KNOW HOW MUCH FURTHER DOWN I CAN GO TO GET HER ATTENTION.
HERE. TAKE IT.
NOW WHERE'S MARS?
AND WHERE'S THAT OTHER TANK?
I TAKE IT ALL IN ONE LAST TIME. THE GOOD AND BAD.
I HOPE SHE'S LISTENING.
I DON'T KNOW.
THEN YOU'RE DEAD.

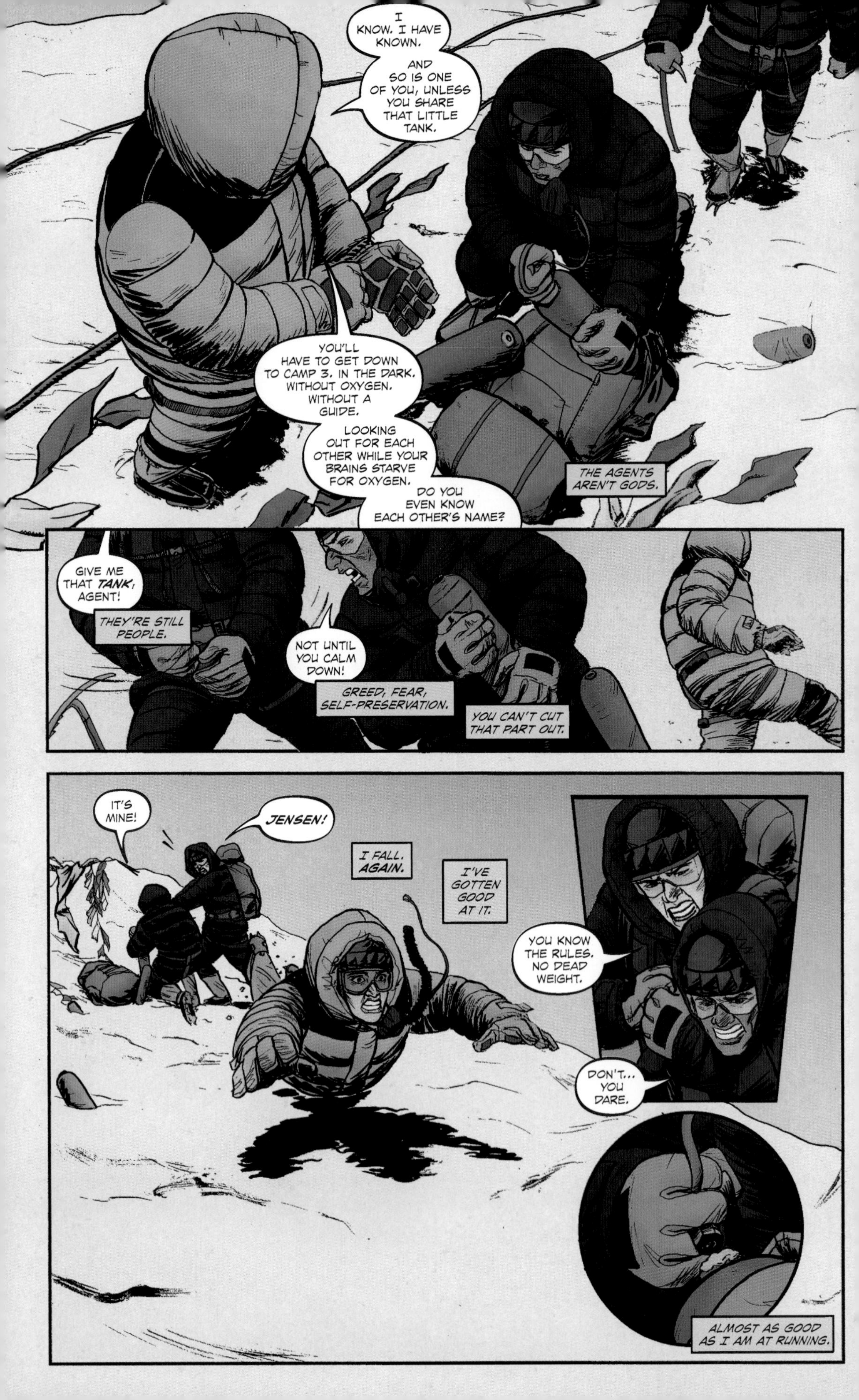
I KNOW. I HAVE KNOWN.
AND SO IS ONE OF YOU, UNLESS YOU SHARE THAT LITTLE TANK.
YOU'LL HAVE TO GET DOWN TO CAMP 3. IN THE DARK. WITHOUT OXYGEN. WITHOUT A GUIDE.
LOOKING OUT FOR EACH OTHER WHILE YOUR BRAINS STARVE FOR OXYGEN.
DO YOU EVEN KNOW EACH OTHER'S NAME?
THE AGENTS AREN'T GODS.
GIVE ME THAT TANK, AGENT!
THEY'RE STILL PEOPLE.
NOT UNTIL YOU CALM DOWN!
GREED, FEAR, SELF-PRESERVATION.
YOU CAN'T CUT THAT PART OUT.
IT'S MINE!
JENSEN!
I FALL. AGAIN.
I'VE GOTTEN GOOD AT IT.
YOU KNOW THE RULES. NO DEAD WEIGHT.
DON'T... YOU DARE.
ALMOST AS GOOD AS I AM AT RUNNING.

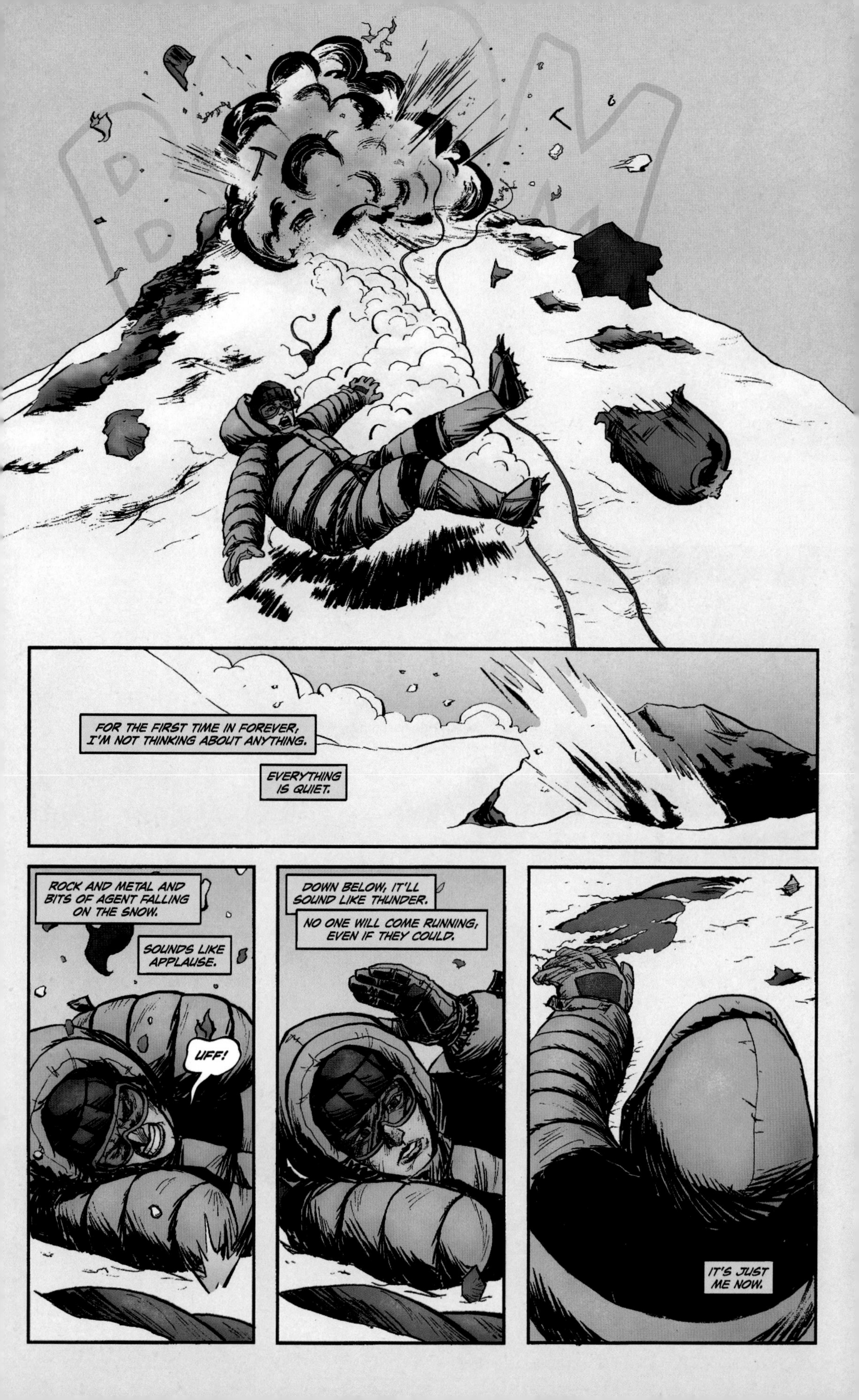

FOR THE FIRST TIME IN FOREVER, I'M NOT THINKING ABOUT ANYTHING.
EVERYTHING IS QUIET.
ROCK AND METAL AND BITS OF AGENT FALLING ON THE SNOW.
SOUNDS LIKE APPLAUSE.
UFF!
DOWN BELOW, IT'LL SOUND LIKE THUNDER.
NO ONE WILL COME RUNNING, EVEN IF THEY COULD.
IT'S JUST ME NOW.

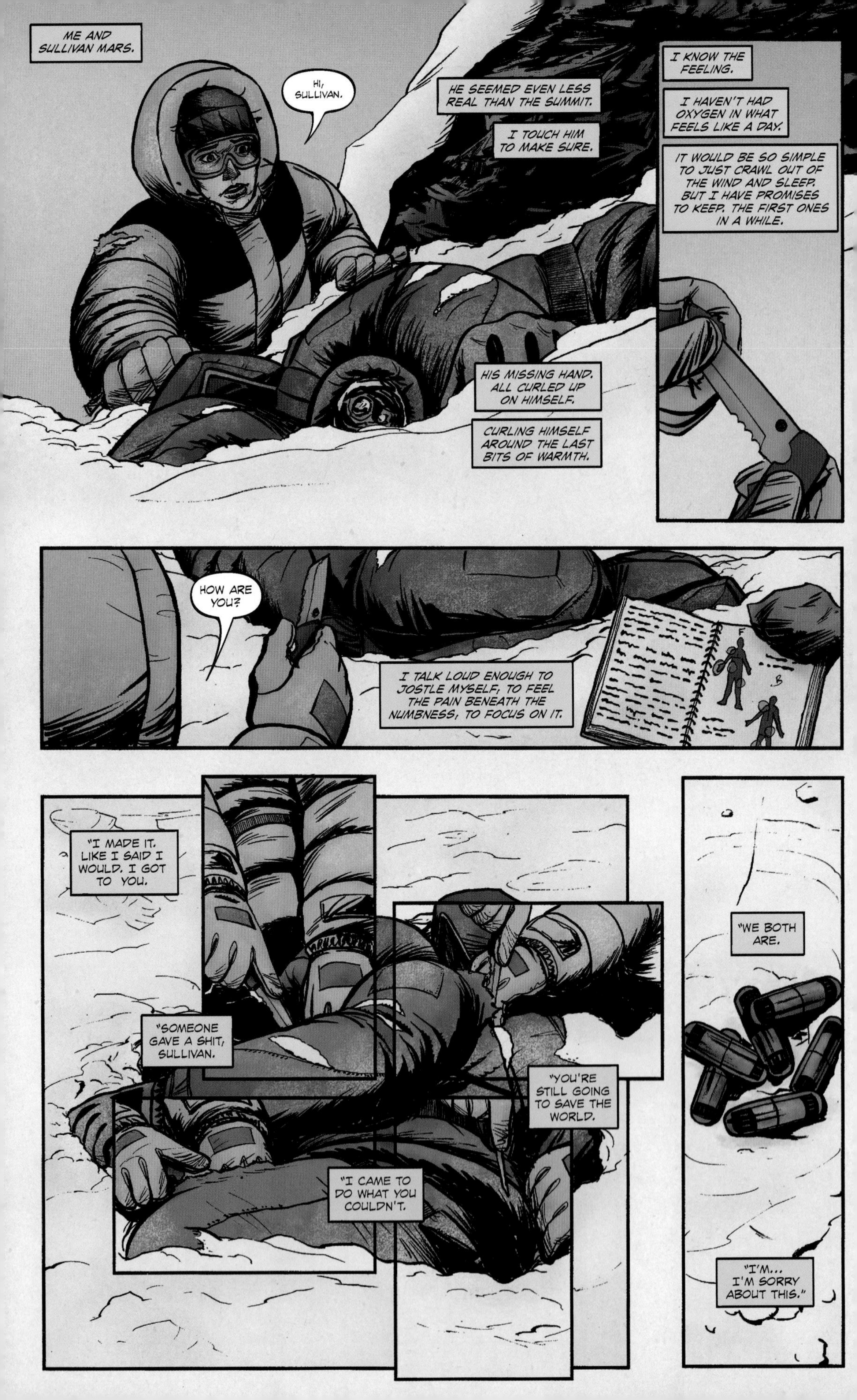

ME AND SULLIVAN MARS.
HI, SULLIVAN.
HE SEEMED EVEN LESS REAL THAN THE SUMMIT.
I TOUCH HIM TO MAKE SURE.
I KNOW THE FEELING.
I HAVEN'T HAD OXYGEN IN WHAT FEELS LIKE A DAY.
IT WOULD BE SO SIMPLE TO JUST CRAWL OUT OF THE WIND AND SLEEP. BUT I HAVE PROMISES TO KEEP. THE FIRST ONES IN A WHILE.
HIS MISSING HAND. ALL CURLED UP ON HIMSELF.
CURLING HIMSELF AROUND THE LAST BITS OF WARMTH.
HOW ARE YOU?
I TALK LOUD ENOUGH TO JOSTLE MYSELF, TO FEEL THE PAIN BENEATH THE NUMBNESS, TO FOCUS ON IT.
"I MADE IT. LIKE I SAID I WOULD. I GOT TO YOU.
"SOMEONE GAVE A SHIT, SULLIVAN.
"YOU'RE STILL GOING TO SAVE THE WORLD.
"I CAME TO DO WHAT YOU COULDN'T.
"WE BOTH ARE.
"I'M... I'M SORRY ABOUT THIS."

I REALIZED AFTER I FINISHED YOUR JOURNAL, THERE'S SO MUCH MISSING. PAGES GONE, TORN OUT.

YOU KEPT YOUR SECRETS SAFE. UP THROUGH THE END.

I'M TAKING THEM NOW, SULLIVAN.

GONNA BUY MYSELF A NEW LIFE WITH THEM.

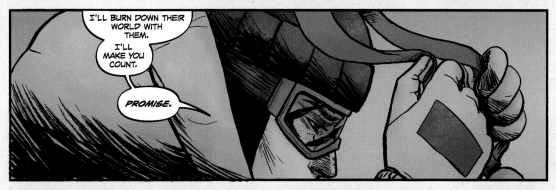

I'LL BURN DOWN THEIR WORLD WITH THEM.

I'LL MAKE YOU COUNT.

PROMISE.

I THINK IF YOU'D MADE IT BACK, YOU WOULD'VE BEEN CHANGED.

GONE ON TO LIVE SOME LIFE YOU COULD STAND TO REMEMBER.

GLORIOUSLY DULL AND NORMAL.

TELLING WAR STORIES, WHERE YOU'RE ALWAYS THE HERO.

YOU ARE. FOR ME, YOU ARE.

HOW FUCKED UP IS THAT?

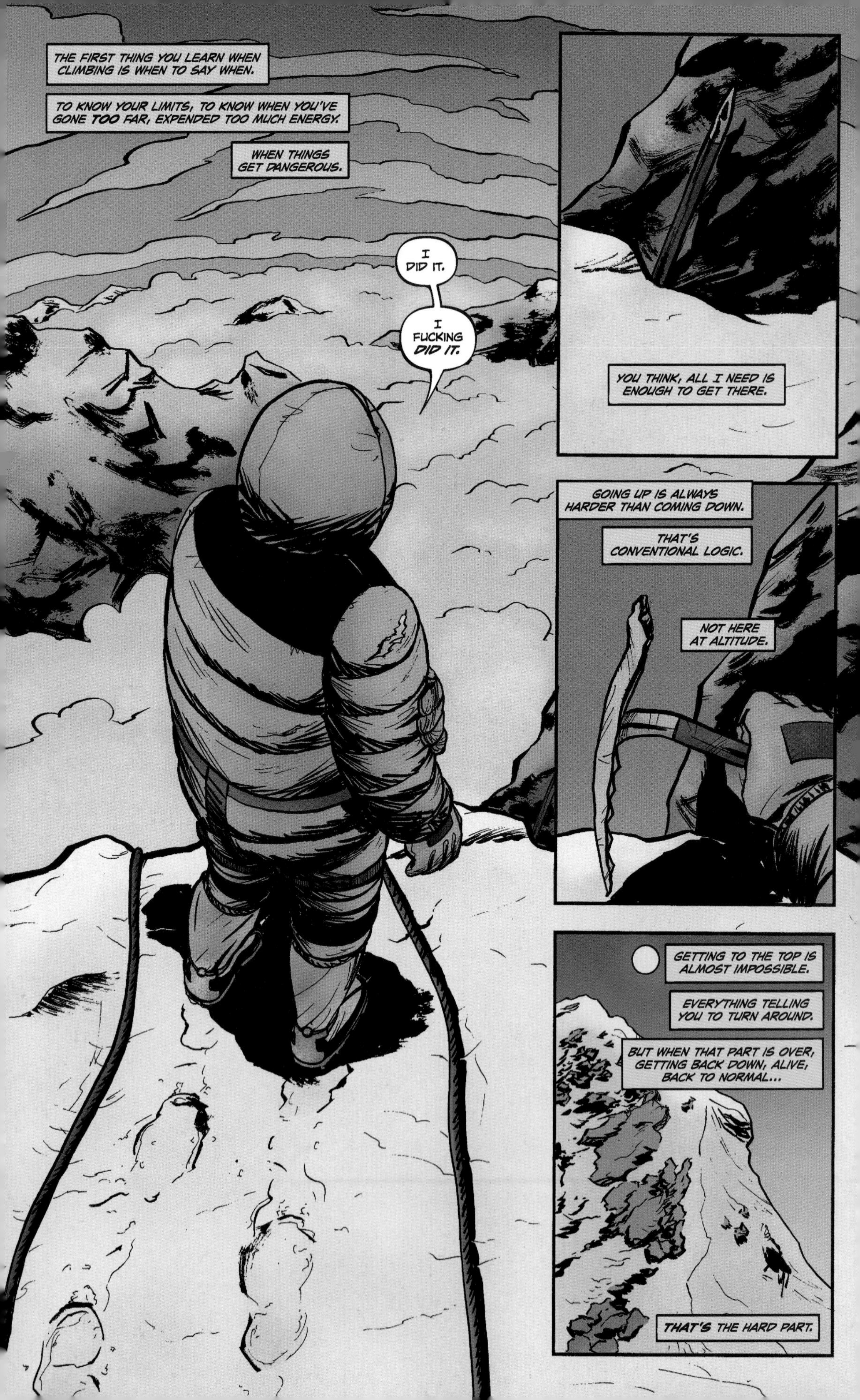
THE FIRST THING YOU LEARN WHEN CLIMBING IS WHEN TO SAY WHEN.
TO KNOW YOUR LIMITS, TO KNOW WHEN YOU'VE GONE TOO FAR, EXPENDED TOO MUCH ENERGY.
WHEN THINGS GET DANGEROUS.
I DID IT.
I FUCKING DID IT.
YOU THINK, ALL I NEED IS ENOUGH TO GET THERE.
GOING UP IS ALWAYS HARDER THAN COMING DOWN.
THAT'S CONVENTIONAL LOGIC.
NOT HERE AT ALTITUDE.
GETTING TO THE TOP IS ALMOST IMPOSSIBLE.
EVERYTHING TELLING YOU TO TURN AROUND.
BUT WHEN THAT PART IS OVER, GETTING BACK DOWN, ALIVE, BACK TO NORMAL...
THAT'S THE HARD PART.

4,712 feet above sea level

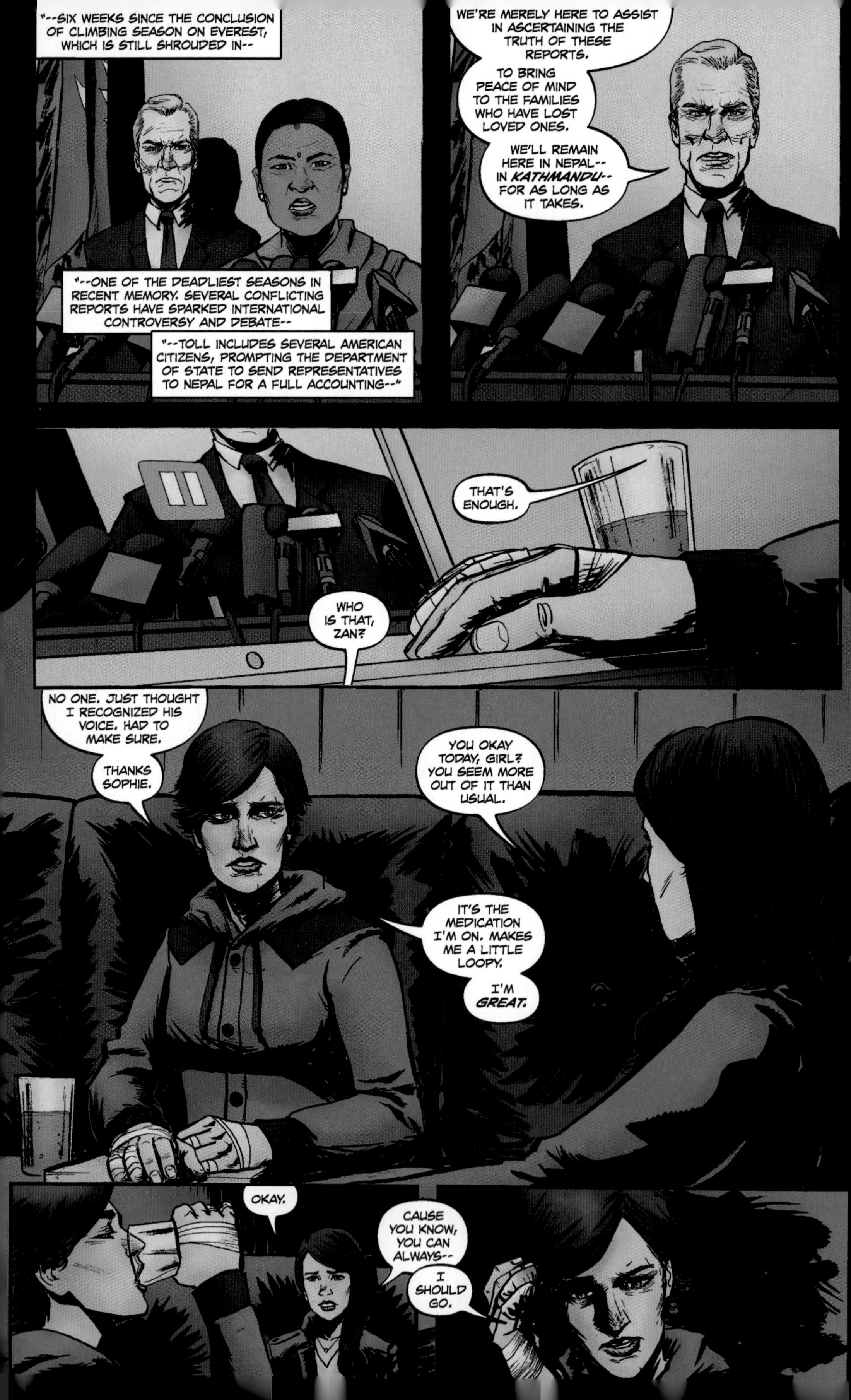
"--SIX WEEKS SINCE THE CONCLUSION OF CLIMBING SEASON ON EVEREST, WHICH IS STILL SHROUDED IN--
"--ONE OF THE DEADLIEST SEASONS IN RECENT MEMORY. SEVERAL CONFLICTING REPORTS HAVE SPARKED INTERNATIONAL CONTROVERSY AND DEBATE--
"--TOLL INCLUDES SEVERAL AMERICAN CITIZENS, PROMPTING THE DEPARTMENT OF STATE TO SEND REPRESENTATIVES TO NEPAL FOR A FULL ACCOUNTING--"
WE'RE MERELY HERE TO ASSIST IN ASCERTAINING THE TRUTH OF THESE REPORTS.
TO BRING PEACE OF MIND TO THE FAMILIES WHO HAVE LOST LOVED ONES.
WE'LL REMAIN HERE IN NEPAL-- IN *KATHMANDU*-- FOR AS LONG AS IT TAKES.
THAT'S ENOUGH.
WHO IS THAT, ZAN?
NO ONE. JUST THOUGHT I RECOGNIZED HIS VOICE. HAD TO MAKE SURE.
THANKS SOPHIE.
YOU OKAY TODAY, GIRL? YOU SEEM MORE OUT OF IT THAN USUAL.
IT'S THE MEDICATION I'M ON. MAKES ME A LITTLE LOOPY.
I'M *GREAT.*
OKAY.
CAUSE YOU KNOW, YOU CAN ALWAYS--
I SHOULD GO.

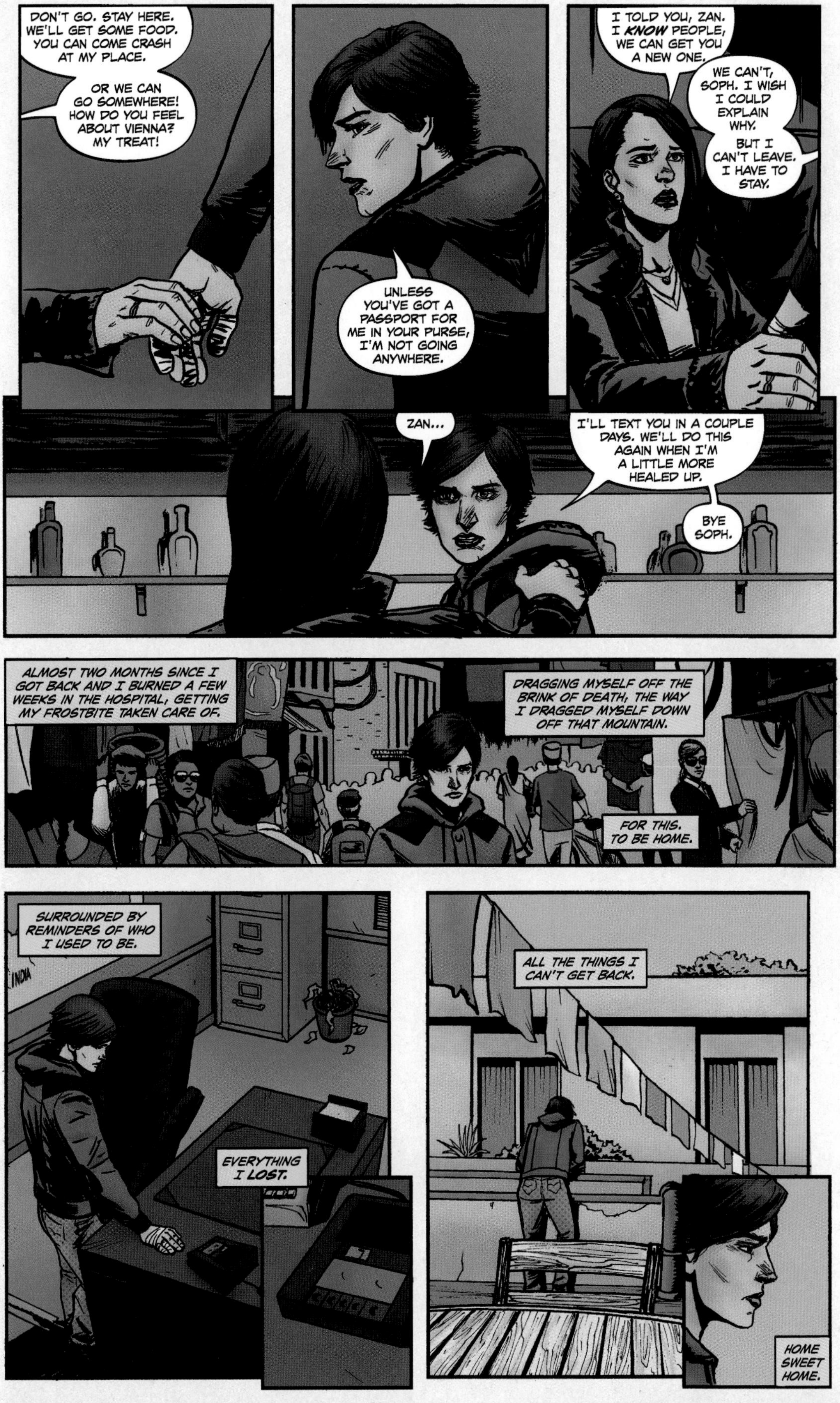
DON'T GO. STAY HERE. WE'LL GET SOME FOOD. YOU CAN COME CRASH AT MY PLACE.
OR WE CAN GO SOMEWHERE! HOW DO YOU FEEL ABOUT VIENNA? MY TREAT!
UNLESS YOU'VE GOT A PASSPORT FOR ME IN YOUR PURSE, I'M NOT GOING ANYWHERE.
I TOLD YOU, ZAN. I KNOW PEOPLE, WE CAN GET YOU A NEW ONE.
WE CAN'T, SOPH. I WISH I COULD EXPLAIN WHY.
BUT I CAN'T LEAVE. I HAVE TO STAY.
ZAN...
I'LL TEXT YOU IN A COUPLE DAYS. WE'LL DO THIS AGAIN WHEN I'M A LITTLE MORE HEALED UP.
BYE SOPH.
ALMOST TWO MONTHS SINCE I GOT BACK AND I BURNED A FEW WEEKS IN THE HOSPITAL, GETTING MY FROSTBITE TAKEN CARE OF.
DRAGGING MYSELF OFF THE BRINK OF DEATH, THE WAY I DRAGGED MYSELF DOWN OFF THAT MOUNTAIN.
FOR THIS. TO BE HOME.
SURROUNDED BY REMINDERS OF WHO I USED TO BE.
INDIA
EVERYTHING I LOST.
ALL THE THINGS I CAN'T GET BACK.
HOME SWEET HOME.

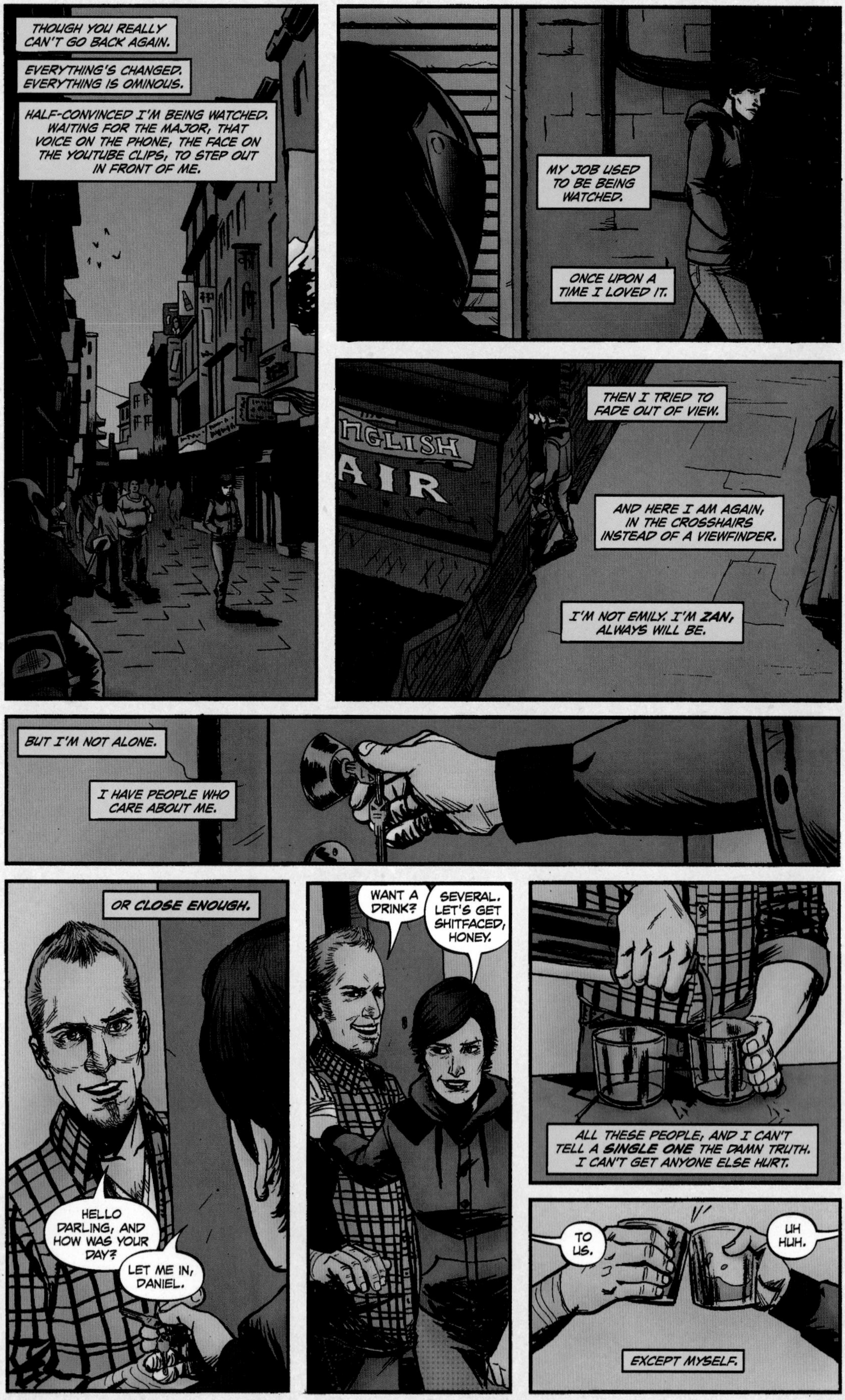
THOUGH YOU REALLY CAN'T GO BACK AGAIN.
EVERYTHING'S CHANGED. EVERYTHING IS OMINOUS.
HALF-CONVINCED I'M BEING WATCHED. WAITING FOR THE MAJOR, THAT VOICE ON THE PHONE, THE FACE ON THE YOUTUBE CLIPS, TO STEP OUT IN FRONT OF ME.
MY JOB USED TO BE BEING WATCHED.
ONCE UPON A TIME I LOVED IT.
NGLISH
AIR
THEN I TRIED TO FADE OUT OF VIEW.
AND HERE I AM AGAIN, IN THE CROSSHAIRS INSTEAD OF A VIEWFINDER.
I'M NOT EMILY. I'M ZAN, ALWAYS WILL BE.
BUT I'M NOT ALONE.
I HAVE PEOPLE WHO CARE ABOUT ME.
OR CLOSE ENOUGH.
HELLO DARLING, AND HOW WAS YOUR DAY?
LET ME IN, DANIEL.
WANT A DRINK?
SEVERAL. LET'S GET SHITFACED, HONEY.
ALL THESE PEOPLE, AND I CAN'T TELL A SINGLE ONE THE DAMN TRUTH. I CAN'T GET ANYONE ELSE HURT.
TO US.
UH HUH.
EXCEPT MYSELF.

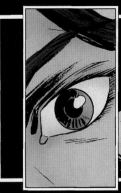

GODDAMMIT.

I HAVE THE DREAM EVERY OTHER NIGHT.

SOMETIMES EVERY NIGHT.

IT'S ALMOST A RELIEF TO WAKE UP TO MY LIFE.

EVERY TIME, EVERY NIGHT, I HAVE TO MAKE SURE THEY'RE STILL THERE.

THEY ALWAYS ARE.

SOME NIGHTS I HOPE THEY WON'T BE.

THAT THIS WAS JUST ANOTHER NIGHTMARE.

BUT NO.

I'M NOT THAT LUCKY.

MAYBE SOMEDAY I CAN DO SOMETHING WITH THEM.

IF I LAY LOW LONG ENOUGH, IF I LAST LONG ENOUGH.

THEY'RE ANOTHER SET OF MEDALS. TINY BURDENS OF A PAST LIFE I'D RATHER NOT RELIVE.

I REFUSE TO GIVE THEM UP.

I MADE A PROMISE.

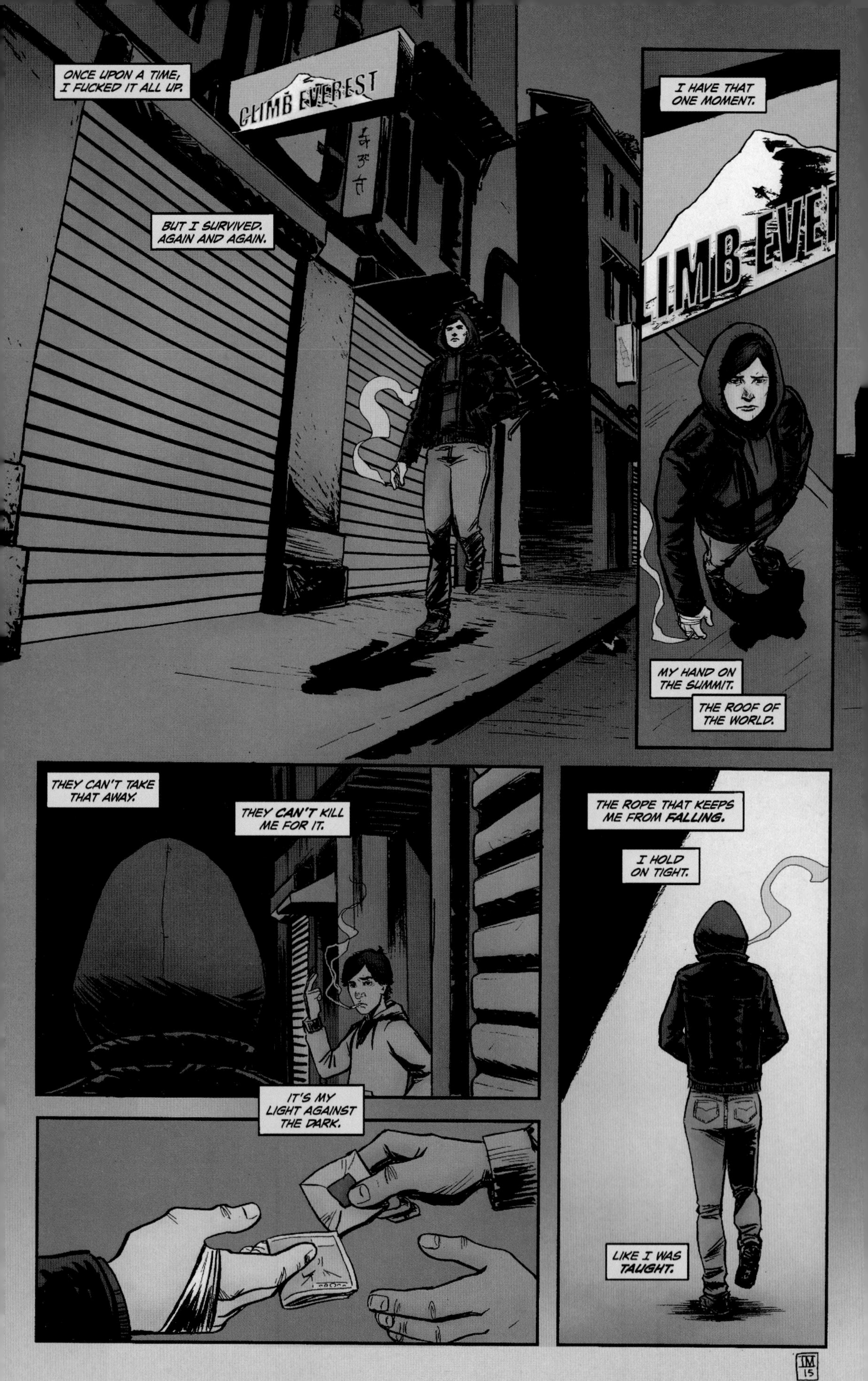
ONCE UPON A TIME, I FUCKED IT ALL UP.
CLIMB EVEREST
BUT I SURVIVED. AGAIN AND AGAIN.
I HAVE THAT ONE MOMENT.
LIMB EVE
MY HAND ON THE SUMMIT.
THE ROOF OF THE WORLD.
THEY CAN'T TAKE THAT AWAY.
THEY CAN'T KILL ME FOR IT.
IT'S MY LIGHT AGAINST THE DARK.
THE ROPE THAT KEEPS ME FROM FALLING.
I HOLD ON TIGHT.
LIKE I WAS TAUGHT.

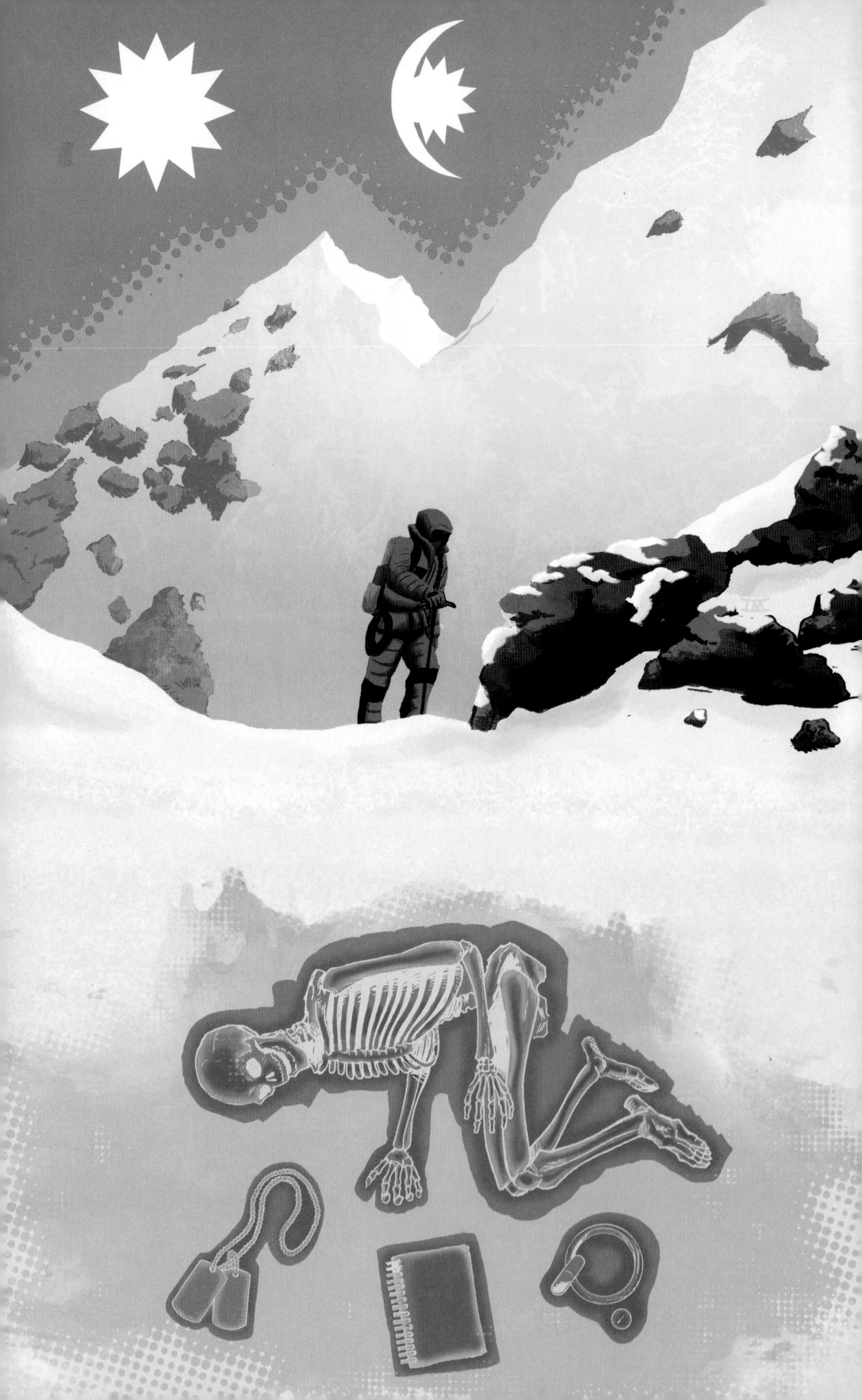

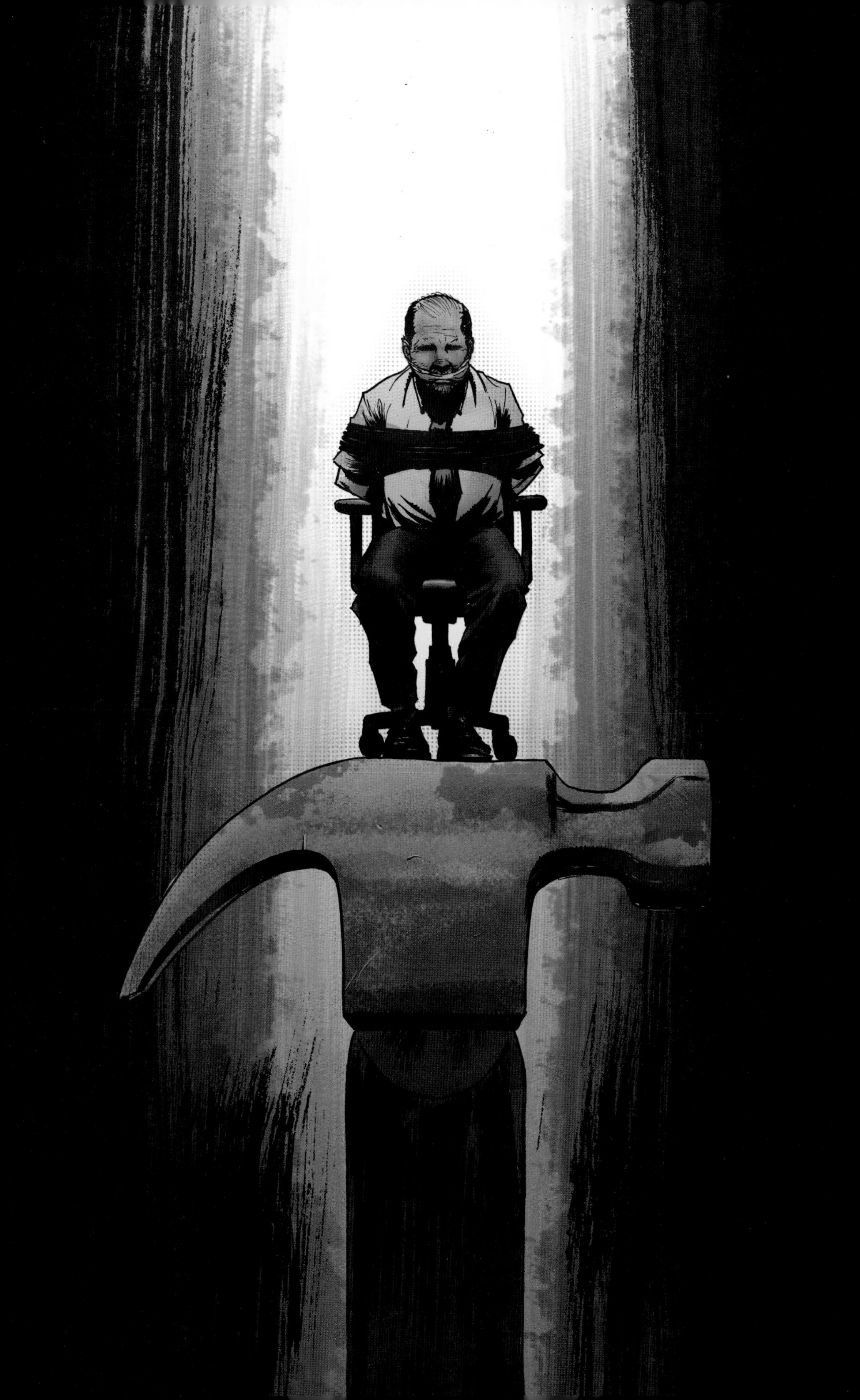

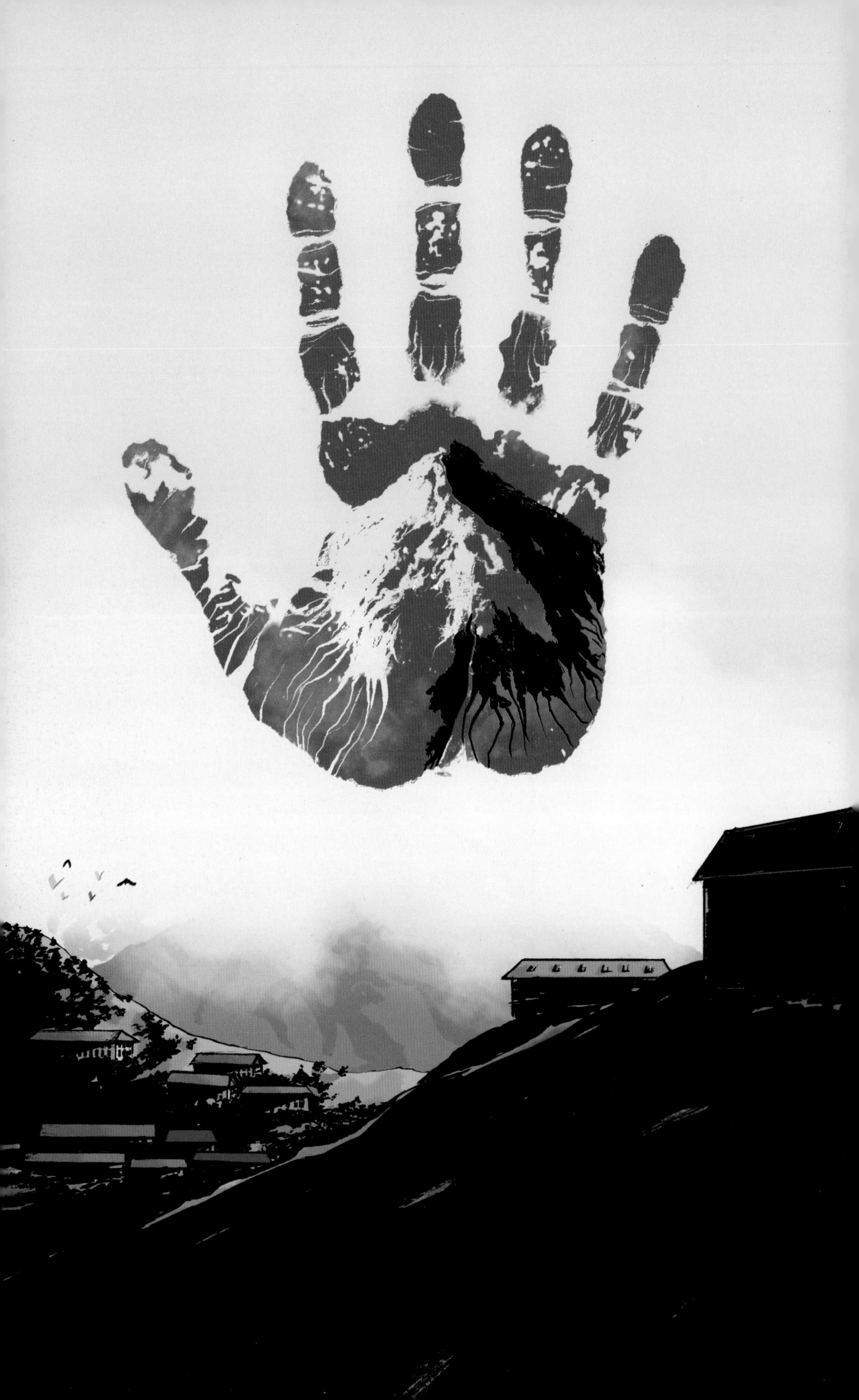

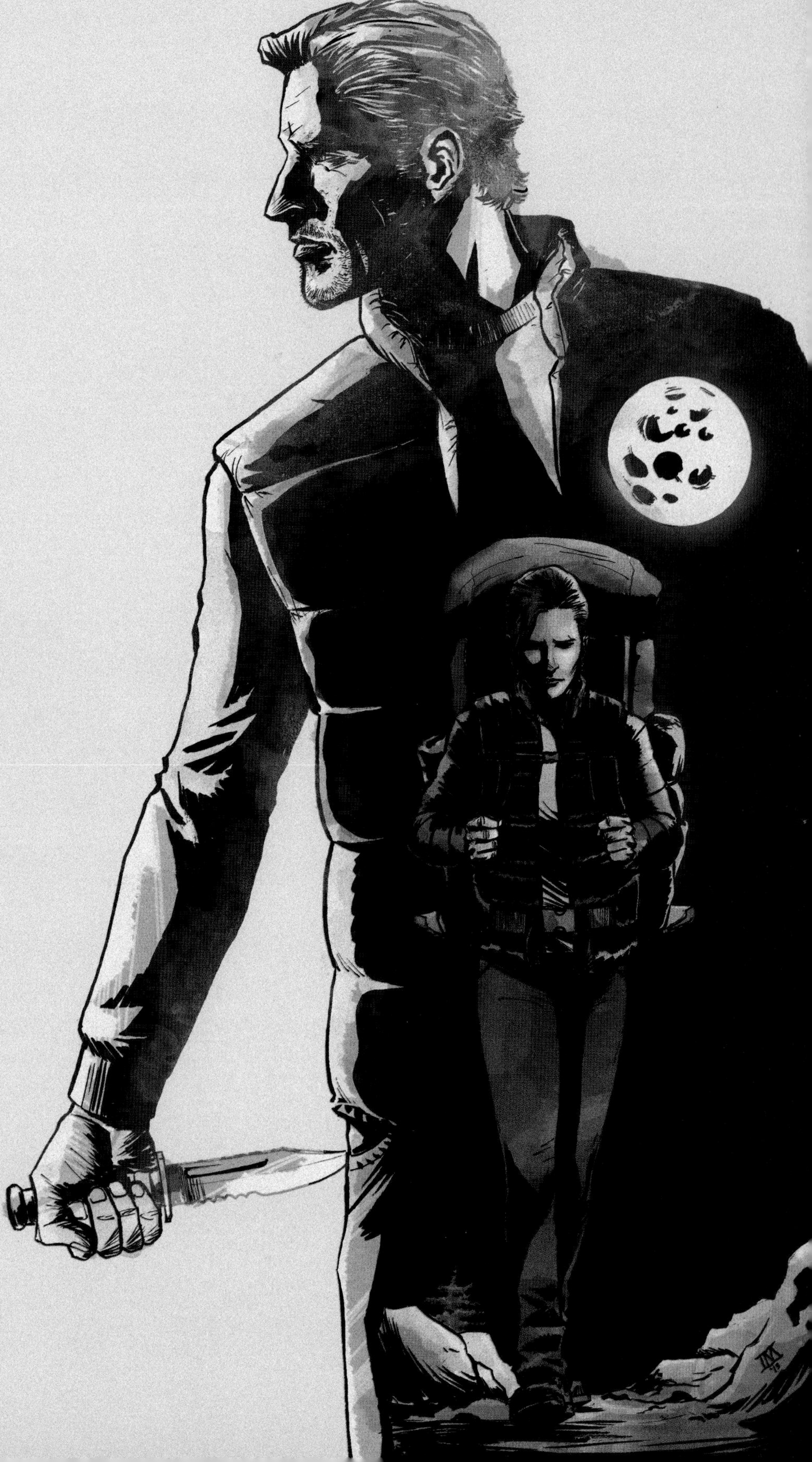

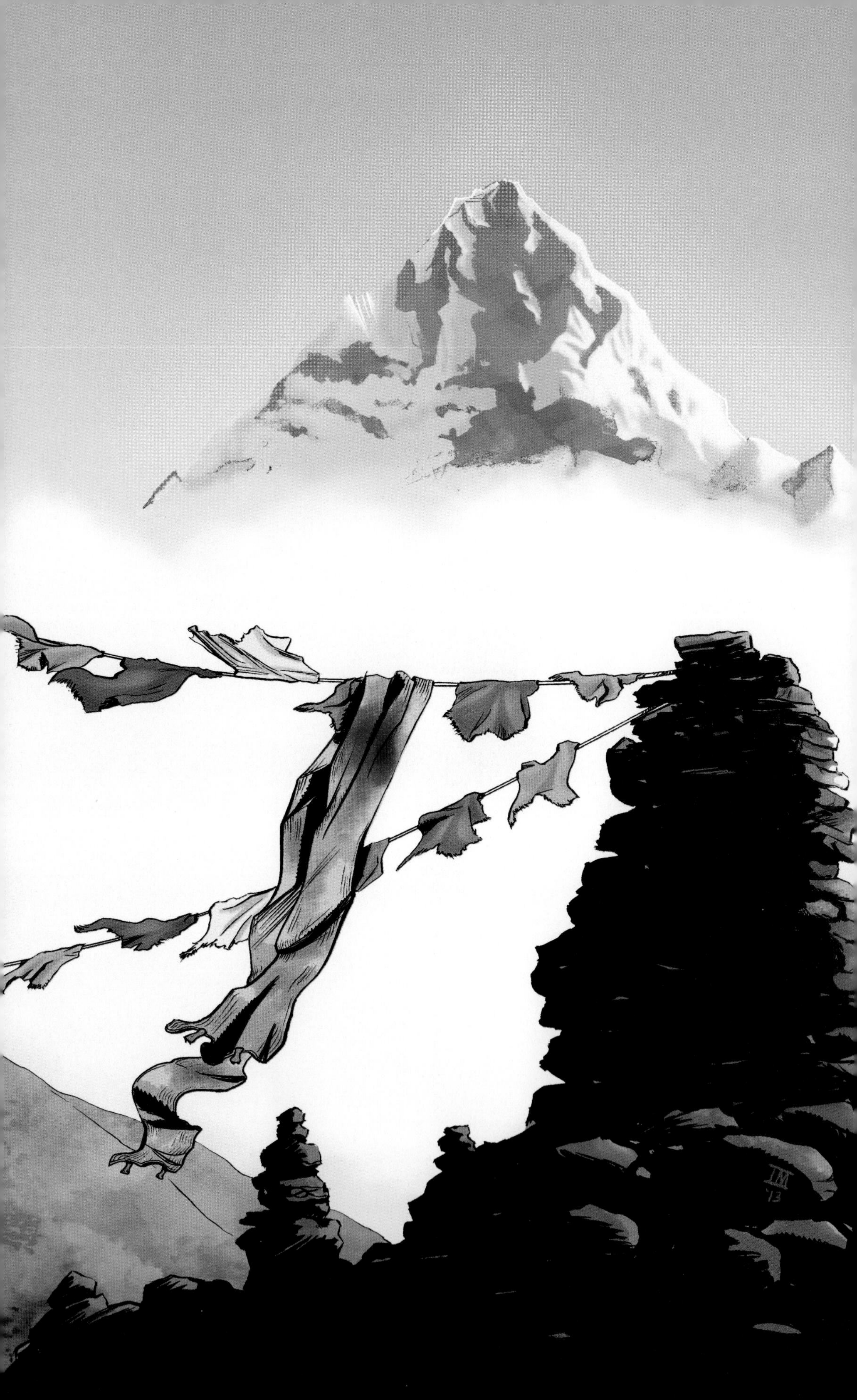

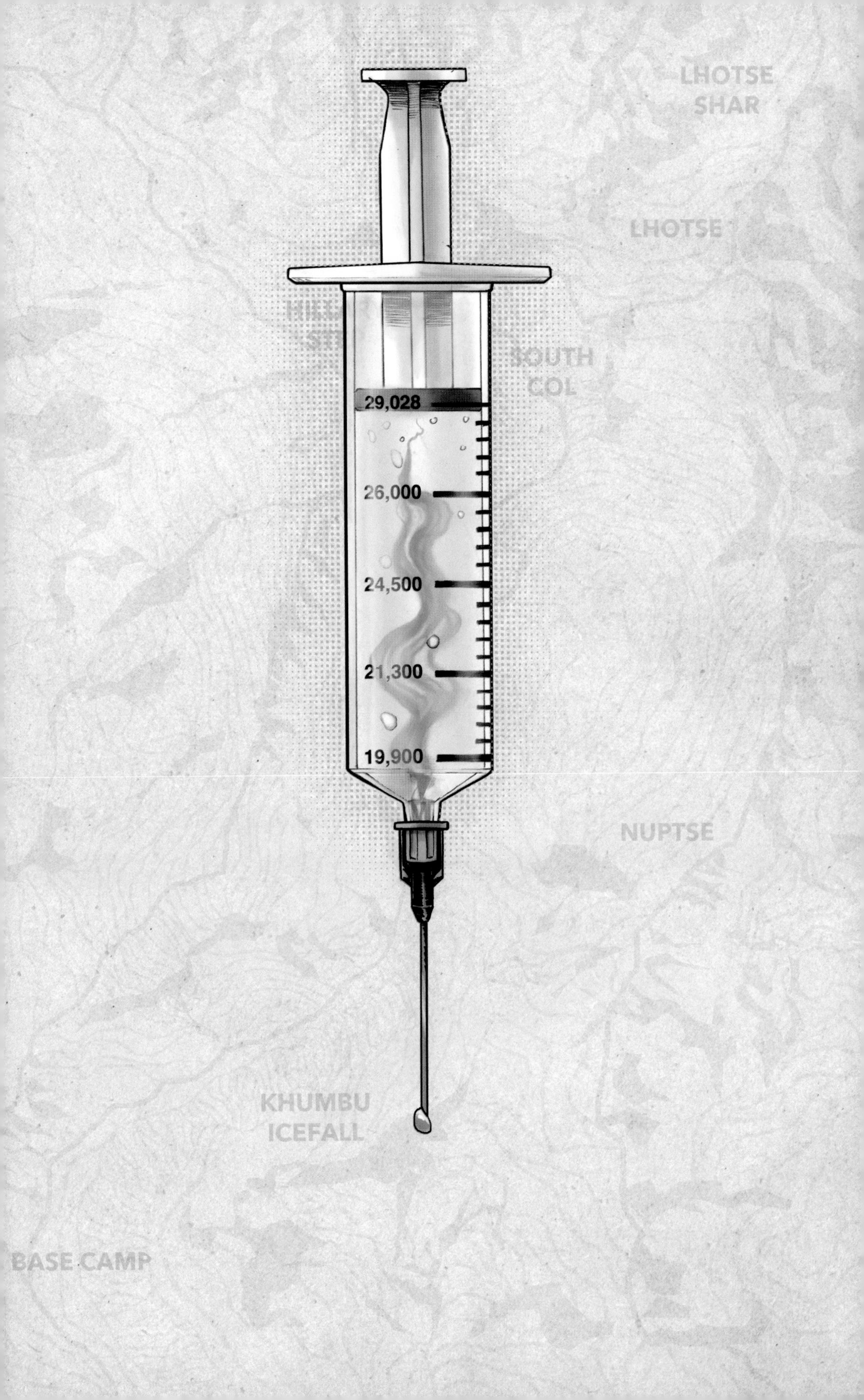
LHOTSE SHAR
LHOTSE
SOUTH COL
29,028
26,000
24,500
21,300
19,900
NUPTSE
KHUMBU ICEFALL
BASE CAMP

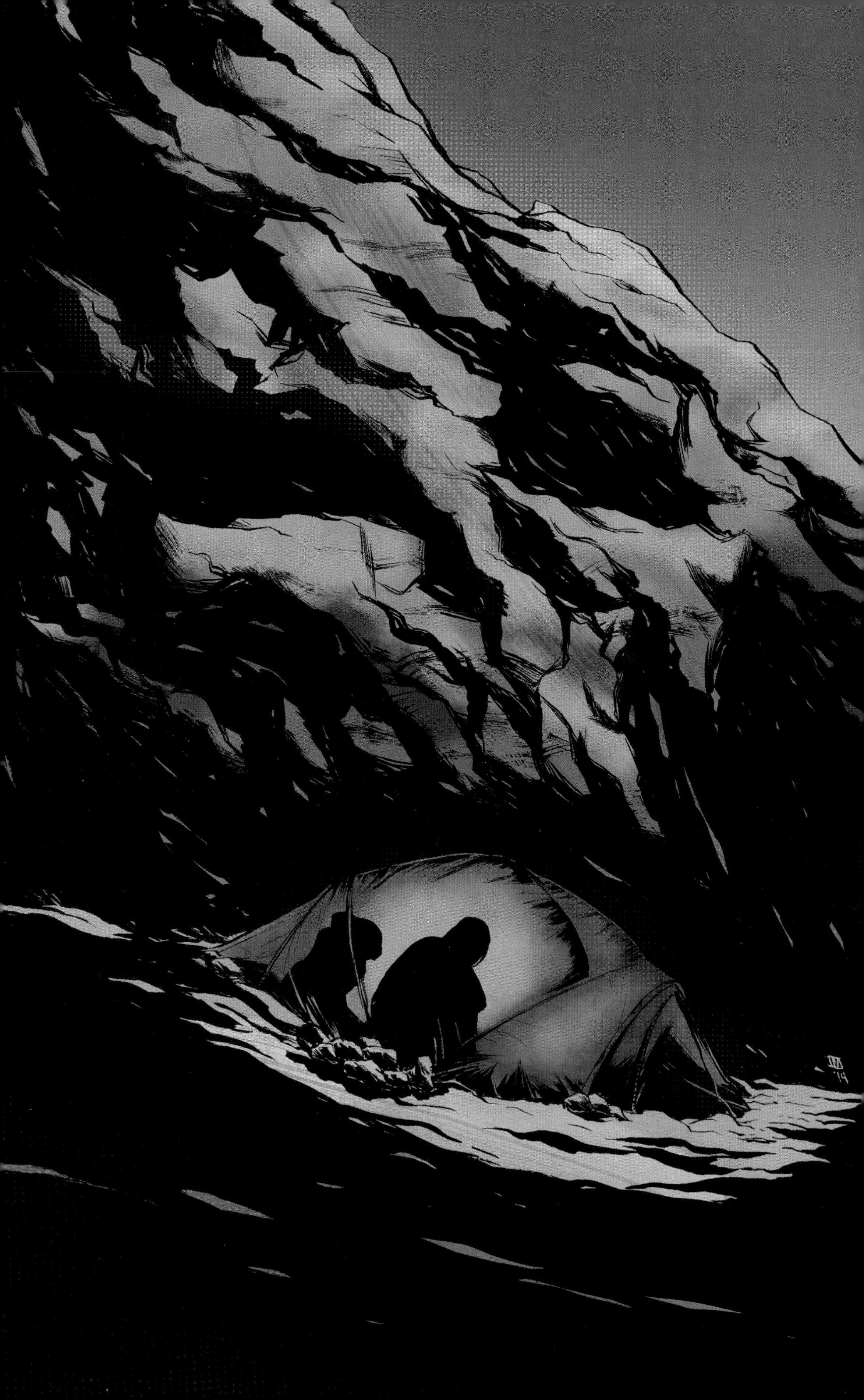

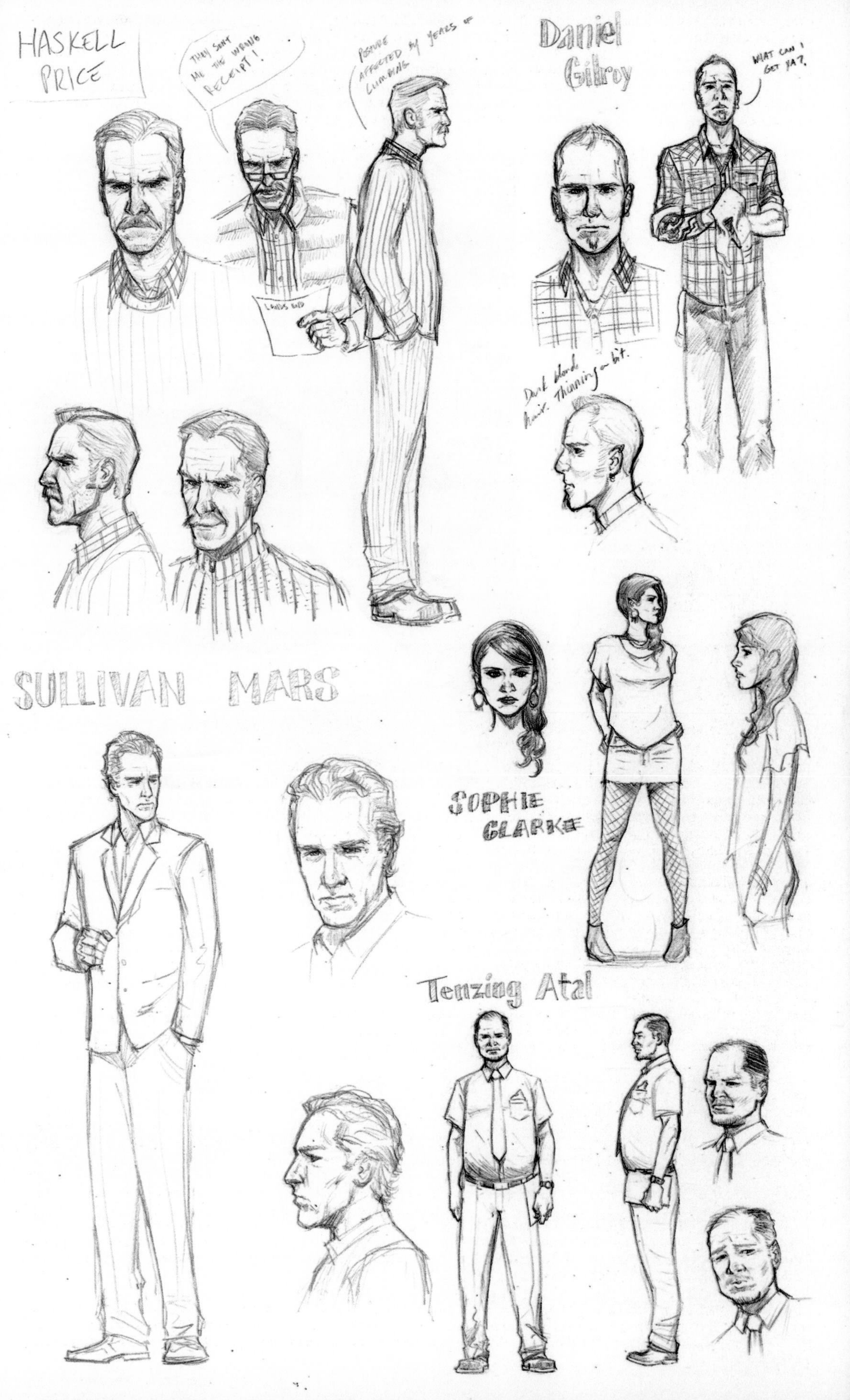
HASKELL PRICE
THEY SENT ME THE WRONG RECEIPT!
POSTURE AFFECTED BY YEARS OF CLIMBING
LANDS END
Daniel Gilroy
WHAT CAN I GET YA?
Dark blonde hair. Thinning a bit.
SULLIVAN MARS
SOPHIE CLARKE
Tenzing Atal

When Sir Edmund Hillary and Tenzing Norgay reached the summit of Everest, Hillary describes turning to his climbing partner to extend his hand for "a square Anglo-Saxon handshake." Norgay ignored the gesture and grabbed Hillary in a crushing bearhug. When they came down the mountain, they were global superstars, heroes of an era, achievers of the impossible. They were lauded, became synonymous with Everest, and eventually they went on with their lives.

Hillary continued climbing after his summit. He was part of the first party to reach the South Pole with motor vehicles. He led an expedition down the Ganges river and narrowly avoided dying in two airplane crashes through random luck, marrying the widowed wife of the guide who took his place on the second flight. He flew a twin engine plane with Neil Armstrong to the North Pole, becoming the first person to stand on both poles and the summit of Everest. He became a diplomat, an ambassador, was knighted and awarded the highest honors in the UK, New Zealand and Nepal, and was often called on to give his comments on the state of Everest. But most of all, Sir Ed founded the Himalayan Trust in 1960. The Trust has built dozens of schools in Sherpa villages, two hospitals, pipelines to bring water to villages and vaccines that saved thousands from smallpox. Ironically, they also built the airstrip in Lukla, making it easier for tourists to make their way to base camp from the Southeast. He died in 2008, his ashes scattered in Auckland, and a portion going to a Nepalese monastery near Everest. The plan to scatter these ashes on Everest was scrubbed by Sherpas due to Chomolungma's status as a Goddess Mother of the World.

Norgay received the UK, Nepal and India's highest civilian honors. He became the first Director of Field Training of the Himalayan Mountaineering Institute in Darjeeling, India. He married three times and had six children. Tenzing started Tenzing Norgay Adventures, which provided guided adventures in and around the Himalayas — but only as far as Everest base camp. He died in 1986, the year after Texas oilman Richard Bass became the first to summit Everest and achieve the Seven Summits, opening the door to inexperienced dreamers with money and professional expeditions to follow after. Sir Ed was among the thousands of local townspeople and hundreds of climbers who attended the cremation in Darjeeling, the place Norgay had come to love most.

Countless climbers have died on Everest. Even more have turned away, unable to summit, raise the funds or the momentum to try again. Others, after summiting, continue to climb, in pursuit of the next big challenge. Some never climb again. Some are haunted by it: the survivors of the 1996 disaster, Mark Inglis, the double amputee who came across David Sharp's body and sparked a worldwide controversy, the climbers of 2014 and 2015's tragic seasons.

The Sherpas continue to pack up and climb the mountain, doctor the icefall, and string the ropes. The adventure guides strategize how to get clients to the top. The obsessives sit in the comfort of their everyday lives and dream of it. Base Camp, The Death Zone, The Summit. Trying to understand what it's like to attempt Everest, to stand on the roof of the world. The rest of the world pays no attention to Everest until it's brought to their attention by tragedy.

Mount Everest is a place of stories. How the mountain went from an unconquerable mystery to a victim of commercialization. How climbers have gone from elite adventurers to the idle rich who want a new trophy for their wall. How Sherpas are always ignored — from Tenzing Norgay settling for a George Medal from Queen Elizabeth II instead of a knighting to the icefall doctors whose deaths become a footnote in the death of Westerners. How bodies have gone from morbid reminder to landmark to interesting anecdote. These stories are told in autobiographies, blog entries, and under shrinking newspaper headlines.

Us, we made up our story. It took us years. Even longer when you count how long the idea was there in my head, waiting to become a story, then a book.

It's kind of hard to believe, the way it must be hard to believe when you're at the summit of Everest. All this work, all this effort, and then you're there, this place you've dreamed of being for years.

Here, as I wrap the very last missing piece of High Crimes, the experience is bookended by two quotes. The first, from George Mallory — who had no idea he would die on Everest, whose summit is still disputed, whose body rests under a cairn of rocks 27,000 feet up the North face of the mountain — responding when asked why he'd even attempt such a thing as this, "Because it's there." The other is from Sir Edmund Hillary, who summed up his achievement as the first person to conquer Everest as unsentimentally as possible, with as much joy as a man who's been through the wringer could muster. As he and Tenzing Norgay descended from the summit, Sir Ed approached his lifelong friend and fellow expeditioner George Lowe, "Well, George, we knocked the bastard off."

Christopher Sebela
Portland, Oregon

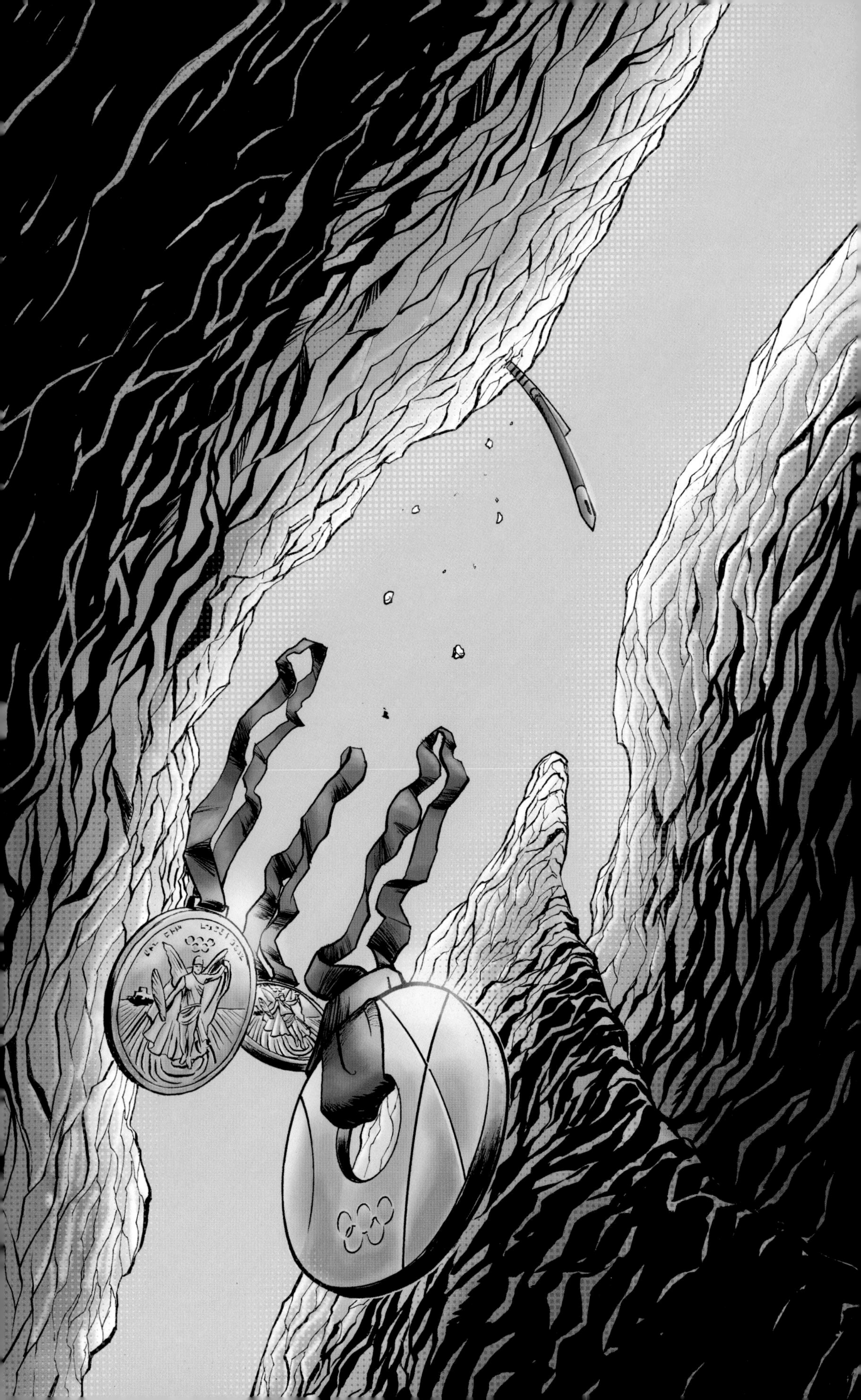

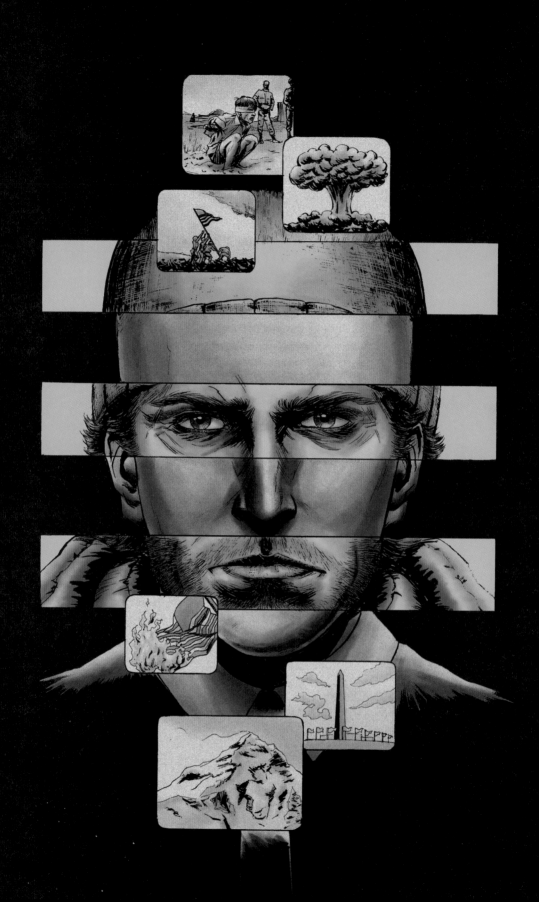

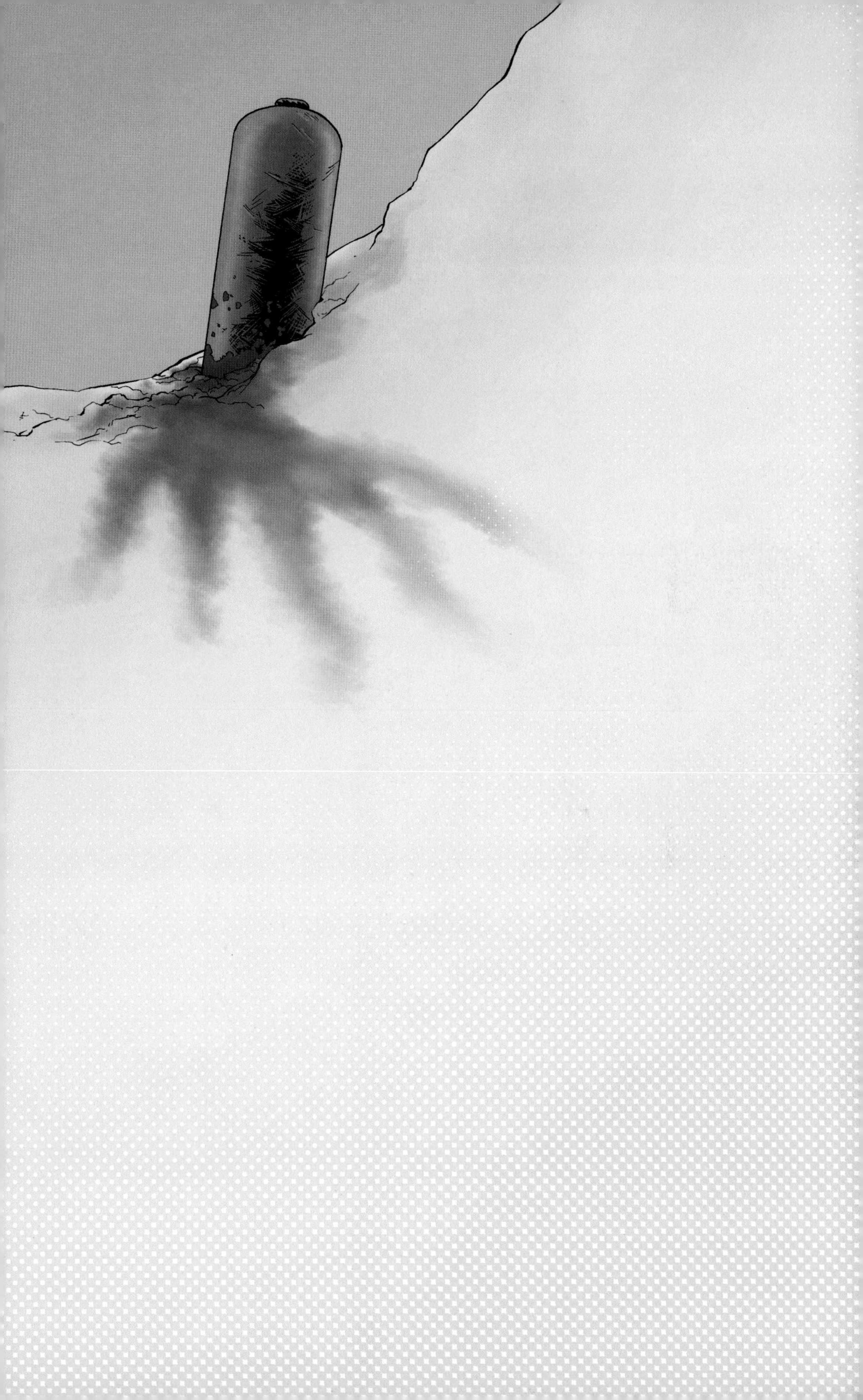

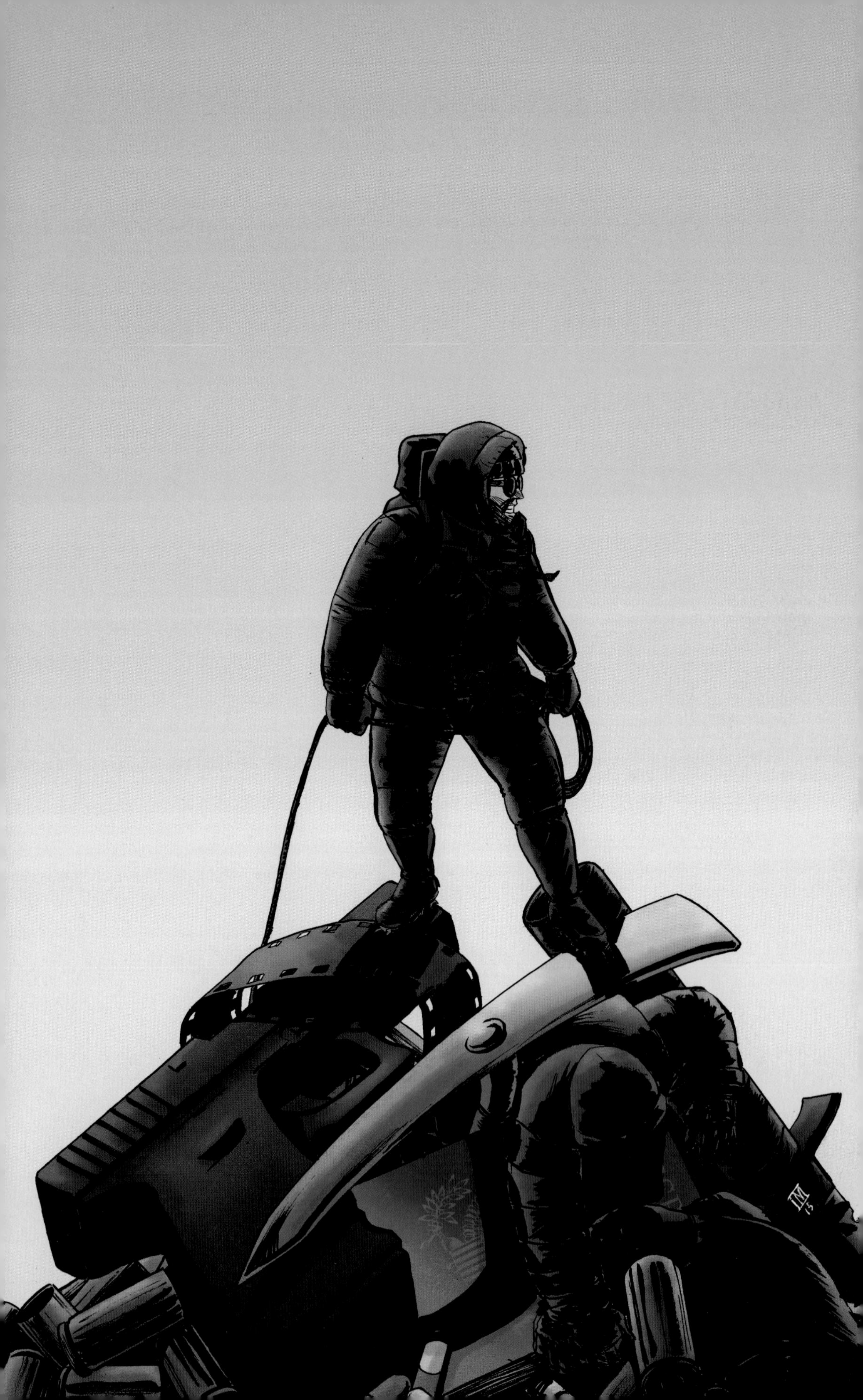

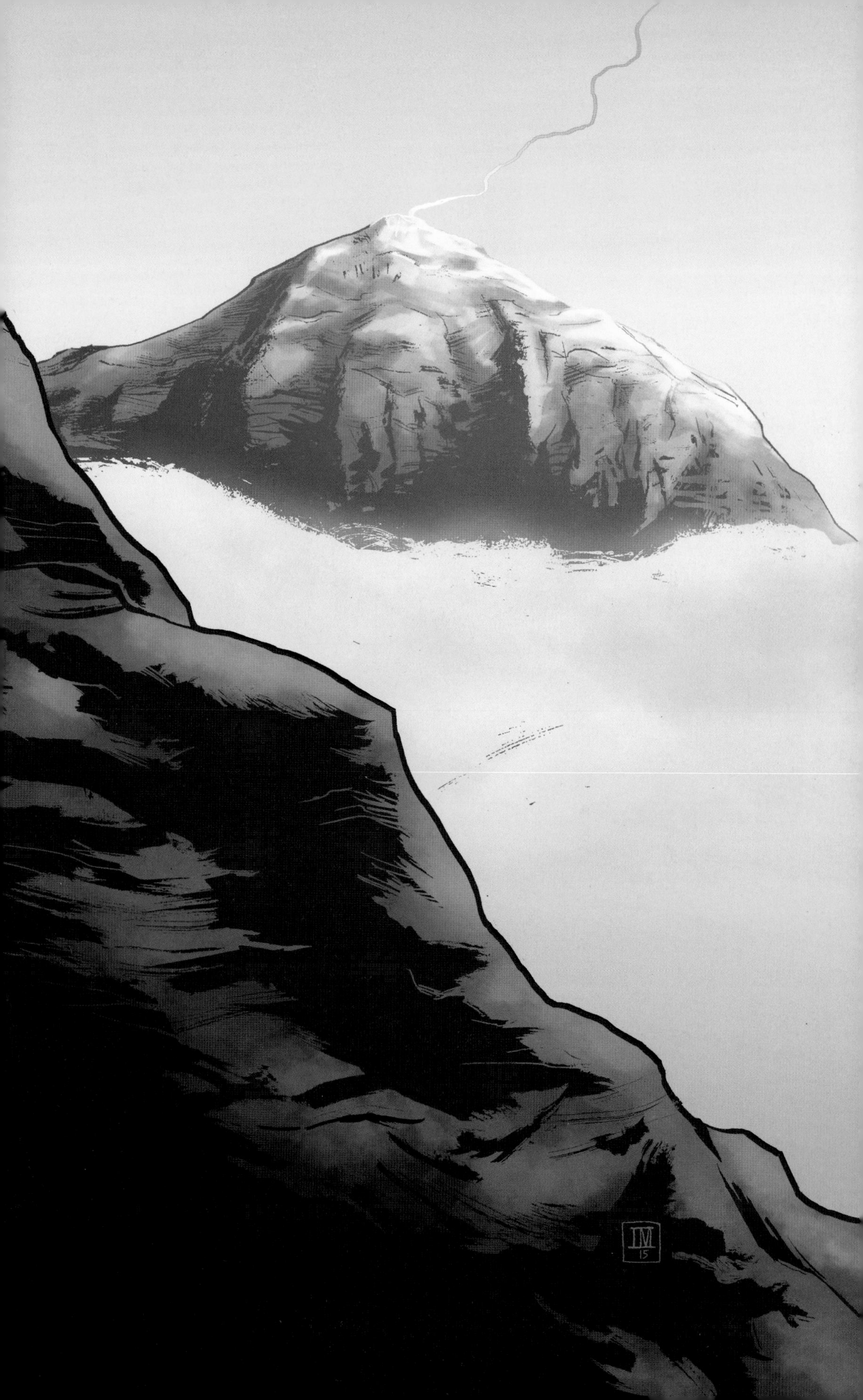

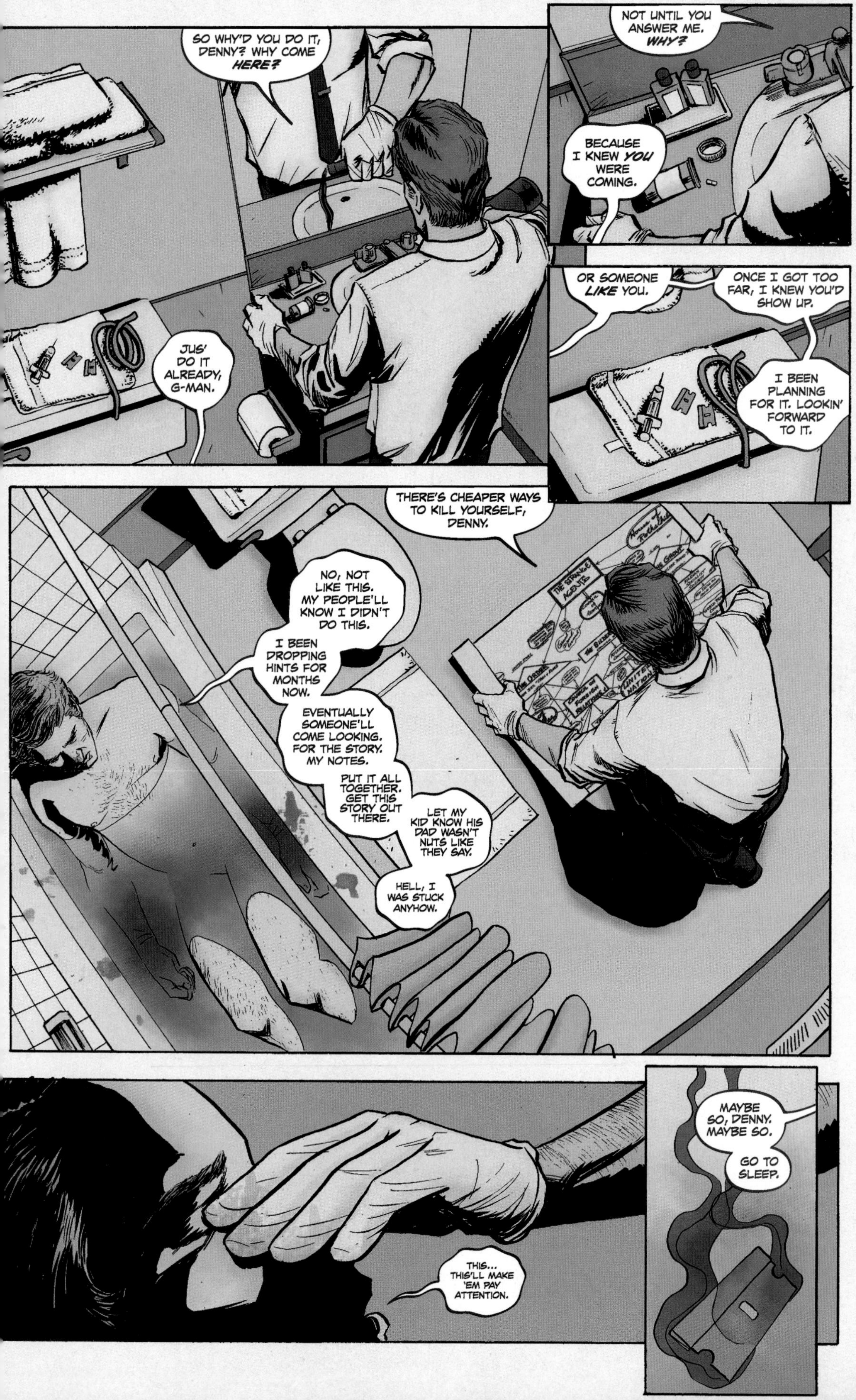
SO WHY'D YOU DO IT, DENNY? WHY COME *HERE?*
JUS' DO IT ALREADY, G-MAN.
NOT UNTIL YOU ANSWER ME. *WHY?*
BECAUSE I KNEW *YOU* WERE COMING.
OR SOMEONE *LIKE* YOU.
ONCE I GOT TOO FAR, I KNEW YOU'D SHOW UP.
I BEEN PLANNING FOR IT. LOOKIN' FORWARD TO IT.
THERE'S CHEAPER WAYS TO KILL YOURSELF, DENNY.
NO, NOT LIKE THIS. MY PEOPLE'LL KNOW I DIDN'T DO THIS.
I BEEN DROPPING HINTS FOR MONTHS NOW.
EVENTUALLY SOMEONE'LL COME LOOKING. FOR THE STORY. MY NOTES.
PUT IT ALL TOGETHER. GET THIS STORY OUT THERE.
LET MY KID KNOW HIS DAD WASN'T NUTS LIKE THEY SAY.
HELL, I WAS STUCK ANYHOW.
THIS... THIS'LL MAKE 'EM PAY ATTENTION.
MAYBE SO, DENNY. MAYBE SO.
GO TO SLEEP.

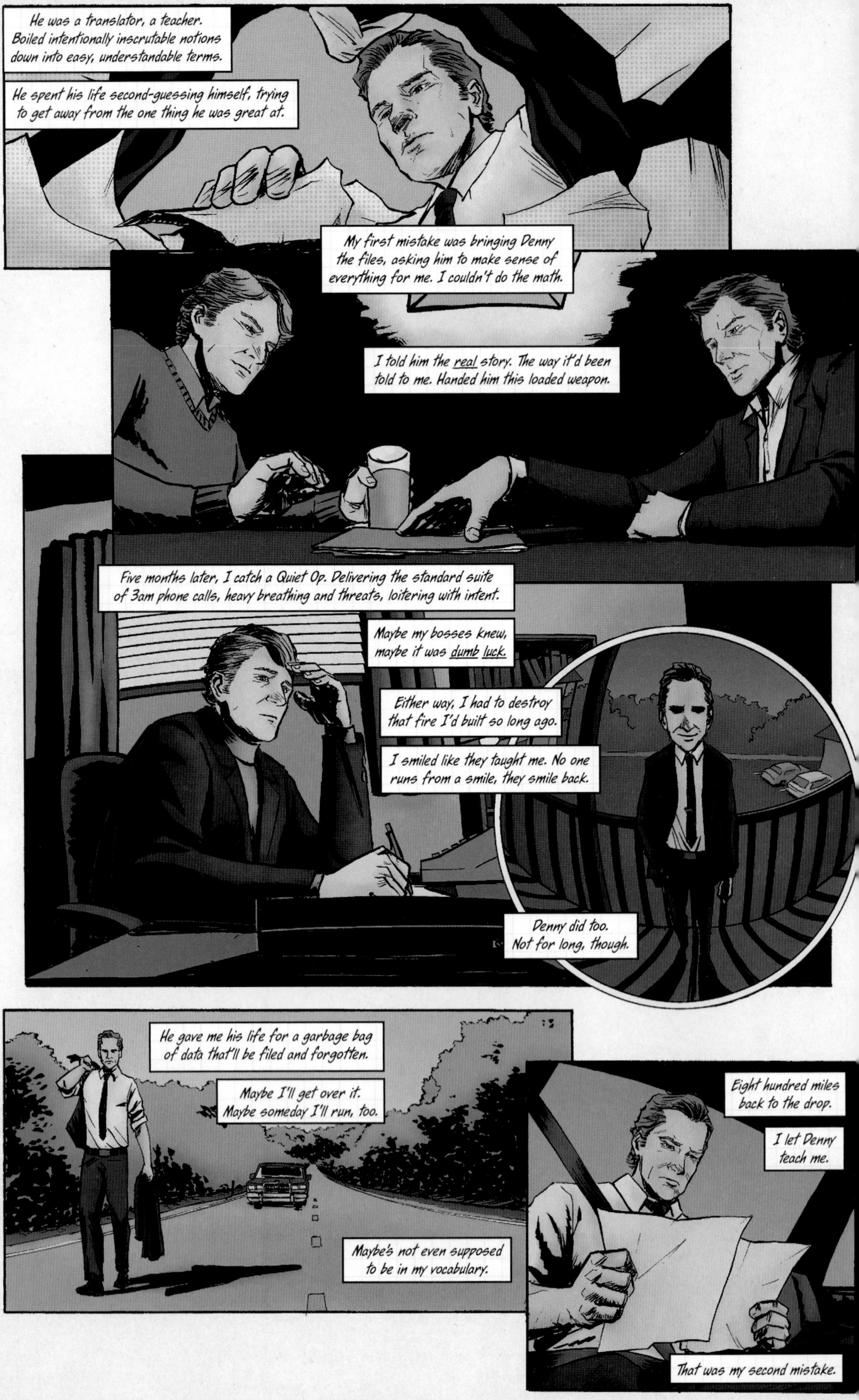
He was a translator, a teacher. Boiled intentionally inscrutable notions down into easy, understandable terms.
He spent his life second-guessing himself, trying to get away from the one thing he was great at.
My first mistake was bringing Denny the files, asking him to make sense of everything for me. I couldn't do the math.
I told him the real story. The way it'd been told to me. Handed him this loaded weapon.
Five months later, I catch a Quiet Op. Delivering the standard suite of 3am phone calls, heavy breathing and threats, loitering with intent.
Maybe my bosses knew, maybe it was dumb luck.
Either way, I had to destroy that fire I'd built so long ago.
I smiled like they taught me. No one runs from a smile, they smile back.
Denny did too. Not for long, though.
He gave me his life for a garbage bag of data that'll be filed and forgotten.
Maybe I'll get over it. Maybe someday I'll run, too.
Maybe's not even supposed to be in my vocabulary.
Eight hundred miles back to the drop.
I let Denny teach me.
That was my second mistake.

I begin with thumbnail sketches of each panel in the margins of the script page. Then, I begin a rough sketch of the page's composition, figuring out how to position the panels. Some are scrapped in favor of solutions that fit better with the other panels. The script page is then scanned into photoshop.

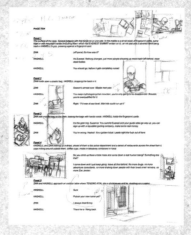

Once in photoshop, I open a template of the comic art board that I use for drawing, and I place the sketches from the script page into the desired format. I change the color of the sketches from their original graphite color to a non-photo blue (a specific color of blue that does not show up when scanned in a black and white setting), and I print the layout onto a piece of comic art board.

Now the penciled images are drawn over the faint non-photo blue layouts. Typically I may pencil a bit more loosely than this, leaving a lot of the heavy lifting for the inking stage, but for the first chapter, I wanted Chris to be able to see what I was doing, as this was the first time we'd ever worked together. As you can see in the image below, there is a lot of fine tuning and altering from the layout stage to the pencil stage.

In this stage, the penciled art is embellished with ink applied with a brush, and various pens. This is probably my favorite part of the process.

Chris and I tag-team the coloring stage. He makes the separations, filling each object on the page with an arbitrary color. Then I choose which colors to apply, and I render them further from there.

Ibrahim Moustafa

When Ibrahim and I first started discussing High Crimes, I sent him a list of characters, each one followed by a sometimes long stream of consciousness describing them. My descriptions are almost always more about a character's history, their mental state, fun facts and trivia. I figure the artist knows way more about this stuff than I do, and half the fun of the job is making stuff up from scratch, so I steered clear of too much description (and the descriptions I did get into, thankfully, got tossed. So here are Ibrahim's designs of Zan and my rambling description sent via email many years ago now.

27. White. Tall and lanky (but sporting a little bit of a belly these days) with long hair she usually keeps tucked up under her hat or messily stacked on her head, with no thought towards glamour or fashion. Chipped front tooth, pierced ears, tattoos, she has worked the last couple years to completely remake herself into the opposite of the fresh face that grinned out from sponsorship ads for sports drinks and snow gear. With that much visibility behind her, she's had to work hard to break herself down and rebuild from the ground up.

Even though she's still young, Zan looks worn out, exhausted and abused. She's covered in old scars and bruises, both from her decade plus of snowboarding and her last few years of mountain climbing. Lots of encounters with high-altitude temperatures and wind sheer and sleeping rough on rocky outcroppings. As a kid just getting into snowboarding, her parents signed her up with a trainer, sent her to schools devoted to it, she spent most of her life on a carefully-regimented diet and a harsh schedule of physical training. When she started doping with growth hormones and other designer drugs, she sculpted herself into an almost superhuman form. But ever since she got caught and bounced out of the life, she's been living on her own terms, no longer concerned with being the ultimate, but now is all about being just a regular human, as she sees it, Zan has been filling out to look a bit more human and less like a superhuman athlete.

When she was a hot-shit snowboarding god and Olympian, she dressed to impress, lots of flash and glitz, bright colors and flair. Nowadays she dresses for anonymity, not wanting to be recognized for her old glory, so she's really low-key, generic. Lots of plaids and hoodies and jeans and hats and casual cold weather gear, big boots, forever looks like she's ready to go bounding up a mountain if she should have to leg it out of Kathmandu. Basically making herself look like a Lonely Planet-type backpacker.

Zan is also a fairly regular drug user, which makes her eyes a bit hollow, her skin a bit sallow, none of which is helped by her general lack of self-maintenance. She eats when she remembers to, drinks more than she should, lurks in Nepalese opium dens and stays up all night, unable to sleep. She doesn't go out in the fresh air, she lives in a crappy apartment that is barely decorated, god only knows what she does with the money she earns both from guiding and the graverobbing sideline.

She's basically a nervous wreck packed into a calendar girl, sort of the harbinger of just how wrong things can go given enough time, self-loathing, scandal and aimless energy. She's not a lost cause, not yet, and she clings to the notion that she can still turn everything around.